Logan's Storm

Logan's Storm

A NOVEL

Ken Wells

Random House / New York

Copyright © 2002 by Ken Wells

All rights reserved under International and Pan-American Copyright Conventions. Published in the United States by Random House, Inc., New York, and simultaneously in Canada by Random House of Canada Limited, Toronto.

RANDOM HOUSE and colophon are registered trademarks of Random House, Inc.

Library of Congress Cataloging-in-Publication Data
Wells, Ken.
Logan's storm: a novel / Ken Wells.
p. cm.
ISBN 0-375-50525-3
1. Fathers and sons—Fiction.   2. Fugitives from justice—Fiction.
3. Teenage boys—Fiction.   4. Hurricanes—Fiction.   5. Louisiana—
Fiction.   6. Mississippi—Fiction.   7. Cajuns—Fiction.   I. Title.
PS3573.E4923 L64 2002
813'.54—dc21   2002024869

Printed in the United States of America on acid-free paper
Random House website address: www.randomhouse.com

24689753

First Edition

BOOK DESIGN BY JENNIFER ANN DADDIO

To the Wells Brothers—

BILL, PERSHING, CHRIS, AND BOBBY—

gifted swamp rats every one of 'em

Acknowledgments

A writer in debt to the usual suspects is a lucky writer indeed. First and foremost, to Lee Boudreaux, my ultra-smart, patient, and tireless editor at Random House; she makes my books better; she rocks. To Joe Regal, now of Regal Literary, and Timothy Seldes of Russell and Volkening, agents extraordinaire; to my *Wall Street Journal* colleague Elizabeth Seay, a faithful, keen, helpful, and blessedly nitpicky reader of this and past manuscripts; to Honi Werner, for her series of beautiful book jackets; to all my Louisiana podnahs, notably Jerry and Shannon Hermann in Houma, who throw a fine party; Al Delahaye in Thibodaux, my friend, mentor, and unflagging supporter; and Del and Anita Leggett out in Youngsville. Their gift of friendship, and a couple of pastoral days in the Cajun Shack overlooking their crawfish pond, provided this writer with some post–September 11 serenity necessary to finish this book. I'd also like to thank Leslie Donahue Schilling at the University of Louisiana–Lafayette, for her last-minute assist with Cajun etymology; the Friends of the Library and the Terrebonne Parish Council on Arts in Houma for their ongoing support; and Cynthia and Dickie Breaux in Breaux Bridge for their hospitality at Café Des Amis.

And, of course, to the family, Lisa, Becca, and Sara, the rock of all things.

PART ONE

The Swamp

1.

I see the snake slip out from behind a tangle of cypress knees and come side-windin' toward me, head arched up like a softshell turtle's, tongue tastin' the air.

It's just my luck that he's a cottonmouth. They come out of winter full of poison and cranky as a drunk man's dog.

He's a big boy, fat as a softball at the middle and close to six foot, which is about as big as they get around here. A spring moccasin that big could kill you quick, though not so quick you wouldn't know you was dyin'.

Once again, I ain't in a good place, which might not surprise the people who know me. It's not enough that I'm runnin' from the law or that I've left my boy, Meely, with a broke leg on the roadside to deal with the police. I'm also neck-deep in water, my feet tangled in ooze and a thicket of sunk willow branches.

Runnin's not an option.

Swimmin' ain't either. Stuck up in a low-hangin' hackberry branch above me is a wasp nest, 'bout as big around as a bushel basket, covered in them big ole red swamp wasps. A man could count to a thousand, maybe two thousand, and not count 'em all, I figger.

You don't wanna get them things after you. You tangle with 'em out here in a slow, open boat like this one, with no place to run, and you might as well shoot yourself with buckshot.

At least with buckshot it'd be over quick.

See, I had me a clever idea. Me and Chilly had been makin' pretty good time after we slipped off in the pirogue. Francis Hebert saw our wreck and promised to call the law and get help for Meely and them police that were busted up in that car that was chasin' us. Francis thinks us LaBauves are made for trouble, so that's about the one thing—callin' the law—he might be happy to do for me. I bet he done it cat quick.

For Meely's sake, I hope he did.

I ain't heard no boats or sirens but that don't mean they ain't comin'.

So me and Chilly paddled away hard till we come upon the entrance of this slough we're in now. This cut is a secret to most people, the entrance covered by a thicket of swamp maple, gum, and scrub willow. Papa John Prosperie, a trapper I knew way back when, used to trap muskrats back in these waters, before them muskrats got trapped out and them nootras started to take over. He showed it to me one time maybe a dozen years ago. It zigs and zags in a diagonal clear through the heart of the Great Catahoula and I figgered if we could find it and push on through, we'd be hard to spot and save ourselves twenty, thirty miles to where I hope we're goin'.

I've got a particular place in mind, though anywhere outta Catahoula Parish will do.

We were doin' okay, maybe had put two or three hard miles behind us, when we come upon this wasp nest. The slough's narrow here and the swamp tangled as a blackberry thicket. That wasp nest ain't but about three foot off the water and wadn't no way around it, so I said Logan, just go under it.

I got Chilly to lie down in the pirogue and I covered him up good with a coupla muddy, half-wet gunnysacks and said now, podnah, don't move till I tell you.

Chilly said Mr. LaBauve, what died in these sacks?

I said frogs, I guess. Crawfish, too. But that's the only cover I got.

I shucked my huntin' vest and shirt and boots and socks and slipped out of the pirogue and into the water. It's as warm and black as tea and smells old as the world. My feet hit oozy bottom and big swamp gas bubbles rose up 'tween my toes. My boy, Meely, calls them ghost bubbles, and

I can see why. I've took city people to the swamp and they've been spooked by them bubbles. Sometimes they just come boilin' up from the bottom for no reason.

Well, sometimes there's a reason. Sometimes there's an ole alligator snappin' turtle down there, big as a wheelbarrow, sneakin' along the bottom, blowin' bubbles. Them things got the spiky shells of a dinosaur and could bite a man's arm off.

You wouldn't wanna step on one barefooted.

This slough ain't but four or five foot deep. My idea was to slip down with just my head above the water, like them gators do, and push the pirogue in front of me real slow till we cleared that nest. Wasps are mean but they ain't clever.

It was a fine plan till that cottonmouth showed its wedgy head.

I whisper to Chilly, I gotta stop for a second. You just keep holdin' still.

He says you okay, Mr. LaBauve?

I say I am but I cain't talk about it now. Just don't move, okay?

He says don't worry, I ain't movin'. I wouldn't move for nuttin' in the world.

That snake's about ten foot from me now and comin' on slow. I freeze and it's clear he don't see me. A moccasin generally won't attack 'less you step on him or corner him.

A man who's still is invisible to a snake.

I hold my breath and hope he'll go 'round the front of the pirogue. And not climb into the boat with poor Chilly.

The cottonmouth slows and raises his head some and then stops, his tongue flickin' the air again.

I don't like my position. I got a mosquito on my forehead and an itch in my ear and a crick in my neck and sweat runnin' down my nose. I'm steppin' on a branch that's diggin' hard into the bottom of my right foot, and I wonder how long I can stay still. But it's too late to retreat.

The moccasin lifts his cussed head up higher then puts it down. Then he waggles that big tail of his and heads in my direction.

That's when a frog comes kickin' right by me, about a foot in front of my eyes. He's a young marsh frog, about half the size of my hand.

That snake sees the commotion and freezes.

That frog slows down then stops, like maybe he senses somethin'.

The frog just sits there.

The snake just lays there.

I'm wonderin' how I come up with this plan in the first place. I cain't just sit here forever.

I suddenly got another plan.

I reach down underwater with my right hand and then bring it up real slow and I poke that frog on the belly.

He jumps high, trailin' water, right toward the snake.

On his second jump, the cottonmouth practically lifts hisself out of the water and hits that frog in midair. Lightnin' don't strike quicker.

The snake lands with a splash about three feet from me.

Pretty soon we're eye to eye.

I know why people think snakes belong to the devil.

Them eyes are empty and dead to anything we feel.

I try not to blink.

He's got a mouthful of frog and I feel for that poor frog. His hind legs are stickin' out of the snake's mouth, shakin' like a man with palsy.

I know what this snake wants to do—crawl up on a log someplace and enjoy its breakfast. It comes right at me, thinkin' maybe I'm the log he's lookin' for.

He brushes up against my cheek and smells sour as the swamp.

This won't do.

I snatch at him hard and get him behind the head and I drag his big ole self down under the water and then I go with him.

I got no choice, if I don't wanna be swattin' wasps too.

He's thrashin' like a fire hose I once saw get loose. I wonder if I can hold on and I squeeze hard as I can and then I know I've made a bad mistake and grabbed him too low.

I feel him turn and somethin' smashes at my wrist.

I feel the hackles rise on my neck and wait for the burn. When it don't come I suddenly know he ain't got me—that his fangs are still buried in that poor frog. I come up quick with my other hand and grab higher, and by the way he whips and shudders I know I've got him right behind the head this time.

I start to feel the fire in my lungs and I kick hard, swimmin' under-water, freein' up my left hand and searchin' desperate for the boat. When I feel wood, I bring the snake up and rap his head hard three times against the bottom of the pirogue.

He goes limp, though he's still heavy as God.

Poor Chilly. I can only imagine what he's thinkin'.

I'm about to turn blue but I ain't forgot about them wasps. I ease my-self along the bottom of the boat and come up slow as I can, my face toward the light.

I hit the surface soft, but blowin' about like one of them whales I've seen at the movie show.

I hear Chilly say Mr. LaBauve, what the hell is goin' on? What was that splashin' and thumpin' all about?

I takes me a while to catch my breath.

Chilly, I know, don't like snakes one bit.

I say oh, nuttin' much, Chilly. I just had me a bit of a problem. I got tangled up in some vines down there is all.

For the first time, I look at that snake. I've broke his neck good. I don't mind snakes much, actually, and usually give 'em plenty of room. I feel bad he didn't get to enjoy his frog breakfast—that was a doggone good catch.

I hold that ole boy out far as I can from me and let him go. He sinks down into the tea-dark water and disappears.

I reach underwater and wipe my snake hand against my britches and then scratch my cheek where that mosquito bit me. I say, soft, okay, hold on, Chilly. We're movin'.

He says, quiet, too, I'm holdin' on.

I duck under again and get to the back of the boat, then push the pirogue ahead. I slow-walk us past that wasp nest, my feet strokin' the muddy bottom easy as I can.

I find a big fallen-over cypress log about twenty yards down the slough and pull myself up on it.

I notice I've got a coupla nice-sized leeches on me, one on my arm, one on my belly, but I could be worse off. They don't hurt and I'm anxious to get goin'. When we stop for the night, I'll get 'em off with fire.

I say we're okay, Chilly. We're through.

Chilly rises from under the gunnysacks and looks back.

He says I hope we've seen the last of them wasp nests.

I say well, keep a look out. We don't wanna run into one by accident. I banged into one them things in a palmetto thicket and lost a good Catahoula Cur that day. Them wasps stung him till he swole up like a balloon. Mighta got me, too, had I not made the slough.

He says are you serious, Mr. LaBauve?

I say I'd actually like it better if you'd call me Logan. And, yes, I'm serious.

Chilly says well, maybe we should go 'round this swamp stedda through it. I don't think it's a good idea for you to get in that water. All the money in the world wouldn't get me in that water. There's snakes in there. We've already seen two. Could be gators. Them big yellow and black swamp spiders are the size of hummin'birds, and for all I know them things can swim. Hell, maybe they fly. They give me the willies.

I say they call 'em banana spiders and I know they don't make a man feel better lookin' at 'em. I got one in my hair squirrel huntin' one mornin' and liked to beat my very own brains out gettin' it off. Anyway, I ain't seen none around here. As for them *cocodries,* I've hunted gators hard back here and they're all but gone. If we try to go around the swamp, we'll have to run out in the open, plus it could add lots of miles to our trip.

Chilly says well, if you get killed on me, I'm cooked as a crawfish. I don't know my left from my right in this swamp. If you want me to fight ten gangs of bullies, bring 'em on. But don't leave me stuck out here by myself, no sir.

I smile. I say don't worry about it, Chilly. We're a team. I'll let you handle the bad guys and I'll get us across the Great Catahoula. Now hold on, I'm comin' back in the boat.

I settle in and off we go, paddlin' away from Catahoula Parish. I know I've seen the last of that place, and my boy Meely, for a while.

2.

We paddle on through the day, hungry and thirsty, and beat as cane-haulin' mules on Sunday.

I'm plannin' to push ahead till I feel we've put plenty of miles 'tween us and any of them law doggies that might be on our tails. The goin' is slow. I've got out the pirogue three more times to pull us around fallen logs, or get us through some long stretches of shallows where the slough has silted in.

Swamp walkin's dirty, hard work. Sometimes this slough closes up altogether and I've got to pick my way out between cypresses and gum trees to find where it starts up again. Good thing I've got my compass 'cause it would be easy to get turned around out here. I could paddle us right back into the arms of the law.

The day's got hot, though not as hot as it would be if we were runnin' out in the open in the sun. But the air's heavy and wet as this swamp.

It's a day when a Cajun makes plans to sweat.

Back when I left Meely on the roadside, runnin' off into the swamps seemed like the only thing to do.

I ain't changed my mind necessarily.

But I ain't a man to fool himself about certain kinds of things—like crossin' the Great Catahoula with not much more than this boat, a compass, and some guns, one a li'l .22 peashooter. Plus, Chilly Cox is a big, strong kid and he paddles this pirogue pretty good for an amateur. But he ain't spent hardly a day in the swamp, or ever roughed it in the woods.

We ain't got no food, and even if we shoot some we ain't got no easy way to cook it. Shootin' or makin' a fire, for a while, ain't a particularly good idea anyway—if the law's chasin' hard, we might as well put up a sign where we are. We ain't got but one small canteen of water. I've had to ration it 'cause I don't know when we'll find more. We'll drink swamp water if we have to. But I once drunk raw swamp water in desperation and spent two days doubled up in the hollow of a giant cypress way back on the *Mauvais Bois,* my stomach boilin' like a pot of gumbo and drunk with fever. We got enough problems without gettin' sick. To be safe, we'd have to boil water in my canteen. But my canteen's like a lotta things I own— old and dented and made of cheap tin. It might not stand the fire, and then we'd be in a fix.

By my reckonin', we've got at least two or three days of hard sloggin'. The Great Catahoula is close to a hunderd miles across, and that's in a straight line. It's got more meanders than horseflies on a summer salt marsh cow and it's swallowed up men better than me, I s'pect. If the bugs or snakes or heat don't get you, spring lightnin' could—it kills one or two fellas just about every year, usually jug fishermen caught out in the middle of a lake someplace.

I hunt and fish for a livin' and I like it out here—in fact, I guess I love it. But that don't mean it ain't sometimes a hard place.

But what choice did I have but to run?

Us LaBauves ain't made for jail—I know that from personal experience. Plus, we're only in this mess 'cause of them good-for-nuttin', lyin' Guidrys—that big galoot Junior, who's been on Meely since Meely was a li'l podnah, and his butt-ugly uncle. Uncle's possum thick and mean as a broke-back water moccasin, and the fact that a man like him can get to be on the police should make everybody think poorly of the law. Meely stood up to Junior on the school grounds and when Junior tried to come after him, he got hisself pitched out of school. Him and his gang then tried to bushwhack Meely but, lucky for Meely, Chilly Cox come to the rescue.

It wadn't lucky for poor Chilly, though. Junior lied and said Chilly and Meely had ambushed *him.* He got Uncle to come down from town in his police getup and they caught Chilly walkin' the road and beat on him good. Called him a nigger. They had him tied up to a post on the ole cypress garage at our place when Meely stumbled in, and they started to beat on him, too. Me and Meely had been out gator huntin' all night—got us a monster gator, we did, and a good mess of frogs, too—and it was only 'cause we'd had a flat, and our ole spare was flat, that they didn't get me. I'd sent Meely ahead to fetch another spare out of the garage. When he didn't come back quick, I somehow had a bad feelin' about things and I slipped with my gun up through the sugarcane fields.

Junior turned into a crybaby pretty quick like a lotta bullies do when the tables are turned. I come this close to killin' Uncle and I did, I guess, murder his police car—shot it up good with my double-barrel 12-gauge. Enjoyed every second of it, I have to say, though I realize it has give the law another thing to hold against me.

We tied Junior and Uncle up to the same post they'd hog-tied Meely and Chilly to. Our plan was to drive someplace outside Loosiana—Texas was closest—'cause even Meely said we wouldn't get a fair shake if we called the law. Uncle and Junior would just spin more lies, and I can tell you for a fack that the law ain't tripped over itself believin' the LaBauves. But we didn't get too far. Somehow, a police car from town come up to chase us and we all went slip-slidin' on that squirrelly gravel road. I rolled the truck, and that's how Meely broke his leg. Lucky we wasn't all killed. But them ole boys in the police car got the worst of it. Our big gator got flung from the truck bed and speared that police car like God's own arrow.

'Course, the hide money from that gator woulda kept us in groceries for a month. It just gives me another reason to hate the law.

I do remember one more thing before we left the yard. Chilly Cox scooped up a big ole pile of red aints and put 'em down the front of Junior's and Uncle's pants.

I actually don't know Chilly so well but I gotta say I'm only sorry I hadn't thought of it myself.

Anyway, there we were, our truck wrecked and them police knocked silly by that flyin' gator, and Francis Hebert lookin' the whole deal over, cluckin' like Francis does.

Francis is a cane farmer richer than Rockefeller—acts like it, too.

Anyway, he drove off to fetch help. I wanted Meely to come with us but he said Daddy, I understand why you cain't stay, but my broke leg will just slow you down. You take Chilly and go 'cause you know what they'll do to him now.

I said they might do the same to you.

He said no, they won't. I doubt the police have got so low yet that they'd beat up a boy with a broke leg.

I wonder if Meely really believed that—I think he actually mighta been scared. But I appreciate the way he said it like he wadn't. He's only fifteen but he's already a better man than me.

Me and Chilly took off in the pirogue we'd been totin' in our truck. And here we are.

Them law doggies could be right behind. But I wouldn't put it past Meely to have told 'em we run off into the woods, in which case they've prob'ly got men and dogs runnin' all up and down Catahoula Bayou ridge lookin' for us.

I kinda hope they are. I hope they're sweatin' as much as I am.

I might care more about the law if I thought the law was the same for everybody.

Since my wife died, I've not spent a lot of times thinkin' things out but I'm thinkin' pretty hard right now.

Chilly tells me he has kin way up in Tupelo, Mississippi, and that's where he wants to go. There's lots of swamp and road and who knows how many law doggies 'tween here and there but I feel responsible for gettin' Chilly as close to Tupelo as I can.

I ain't even been to Tupelo, or actually outside of Loosiana, and I ain't got but fifteen dollars to my name and Chilly ain't got even that much. We'll have to find some more money someplace 'cause sooner or later we've got to quit the woods and start buyin' our food stedda shootin' it. Or stealin' it, if it comes to that.

But no use worryin' about that now. The first thing I wanna do is get us to a place called Samanie's Landin'. It's a run-down trapper's outpost on the north side of the swamp—I drove clear up there one time in the winter to go *sac-à-lait* fishin'. For one thing, it has the benefit of bein' outside of Catahoula Parish. For another, it has a bumpy blacktop road snakin' north that, as I recall, has got woods on one side and canefields on the other. I figger it's just the kinda road that a white man and a colored boy travelin' together through the country oughta take—there's lots of cover on both sides. If I remember my map right, that road comes out at a place called Braudville and meets up with a coupla highways, one joggin' east and the other northeast. Both will carry you all the way up into Mississippi and farther, if you want to go.

Gettin' to them highways is about as far as I can think for now.

I do wish I had some bug dope.

It's late afternoon now and in a few places them swamp gnats have got after us and there wadn't nuttin' I could do but paddle on through 'em. Not that bug dope stops 'em, anyway. It mostly liquors 'em up and slows 'em down some. Them gnats are worse than the *cousins,* if you want my opinion. Still, I don't even wanna think what them mosquitoes are gonna do to us when the sun goes down.

Chilly ain't said much since that wasp nest. His lip and face are still a bit puffy where Junior and Uncle beat on him. After the kind of night he had, I cain't blame him for bein' tuckered out. One time he almost keeled over out the boat, and nearly tipped us over doin' it.

Chilly says the only thing he hates about runnin' is that his momma and daddy will be worried sick about what's become of him. He wants to call 'em soon as we get close to a phone.

I haven't had the heart yet to tell him that this is big swamp, and that he'll have to hold on to his nickel for a few days.

We push on and on and on, one paddle stroke after another, drowsy and sore and tired, the heat wrappin' around us like a king snake.

About an hour before dark it starts to cool off. We hit an openin' of sorts and a stretch of that clear black water you find comin' off virgin marsh and I stop long enough to splash some on my face. Chilly does the same.

We flush a coupla wood ducks from a nest and they go wheelin' through the cypress tops. Bats come out and flutter through the trees. Swallows come click-clickin' low over the water, chasin' bugs. Them bugs make a low noise, like an electric wire hummin' in the rain. I hear a big ole bullfrog croakin' back deep in the swamp. Another one answers.

The Cajun name for them things is *ouaouaron*—'cause that's the sound they make when they bark out across the water.

I wish we had that sack of frogs me and Meely caught last night on our gator hunt 'cause my stomach's startin' to think about supper, havin' skipped breakfast and dinner. I'm shore poor Chilly is starved. Them bullfrogs ain't come out yet, though we can hear 'em. They like the night but the night won't do us any good as the battry to my headlantern—what we call a bulleye—is shot and I won't be able to shine any.

About that time I spy a possum lazin' up the side of a small cypress. I'd prefer a coon, better yet a rabbit or a squirrel. But this possum will have to do.

I've got Meely's single-shot .22, and even though it's a peashooter, I kinda hate to fire it. But its crack ain't nearly as loud as a shotgun's. And I guess I'm feelin' a bit better about things. I've stopped a few times in cover and listened good, and we ain't heard boat nor plane, nor heard nor seen another soul.

I point out the possum to Chilly and say I'm gonna get us a bit closer, then I'm gonna shoot him out the tree. You ever eat possum, Chilly?

He says no, I haven't, but right now I'm ready to eat anything that don't eat me first.

I say well, honest, a dog or a cat would prob'ly taste better than a possum, but he's big enough to fill up our bellies.

I get close and square up the possum in my sites and put a hollow-point in his ear. He crumples dead out the tree and falls with a splash in the water. He ain't knowed what's hit him, which is how I like to take critters. I pretty well live off animals. I eat 'em and sell their pelts, but I don't care to see any critter suffer. Sometimes I feel bad for them gators I shoot when I don't hit 'em proper. They're just like them ole snappin' turtles. They're hard critters and they don't die easy.

I dressed an alligator snapper one time and threw its heart in a bucket with the rest of the guts.

That heart kept beatin' for three hours.

I paddle hard to get to that possum before it sinks. I drag it wet between me and Chilly.

Chilly says damn, them things are seriously ugly, ain't they?

Yeah, I say. And they taste pretty much like they look.

He laughs at that, though he prob'ly won't once I've got it cooked.

We paddle on in the dyin' light and I've started to get antsy about findin' some high ground. If we're stuck in this boat tonight, it'll be a miserable night. It might not be much better on the ground but at least we can build a fire and stretch out. I'd have to be starvin' to death before I'd eat a possum raw. And you don't wanna be paddlin' around in the dark if you can help it. You tip over the pirogue at night out here and nuttin' good can come of it.

We come around a bend and I spy what I've been lookin' for, a clump of dwarf oaks. Them oaks always mark a *chenier,* which is but a low island risin' out of the swamp. Some of them *cheniers* ain't more than half an acre and some ain't but a foot or two above the swamp but they *are* dry ground in a place without much dry ground.

I find a small clearin' and steer the boat till the bow bumps soft against the bank. Chilly grabs on to both sides of the pirogue and steps out, totin' the shotgun we took from Uncle. It's a fine gun. Maybe we shouldn't took it, but we did. I figgered it might come in handy. I hand Chilly the .22 and my double-barrel, then grab the possum and walk forward, the boat wobblin', and step out, too.

We ain't there but a few seconds when the mosquitoes come out of the thickets in such a swarm that you could swing a quart bucket and catch a half a gallon.

Chilly drops his gun and starts swattin' and says man, I don't know about this place, Logan.

I'm swattin', too, and say let's hurry over there toward them trees. It's about dark and if we can hold out till it's dark, I'll build us a nice smoky fire. That'll drive 'em away, and the law won't be able to see our smoke.

Chilly looks at me like he'd rather be anywhere but here.

By the time we make the first thicket of oaks, I realize both my arms are black—covered solid in mosquitoes.

Chilly is swattin' hard everyplace with his ball cap.

I say Chilly, you just keep movin' and you just keep swattin'.

I realize I cain't wait till dark to start our fire. We'll be eat alive before then.

I slap at my face and splatter six or seven *cousins.*

I say I think we'll just have to take our chances with a fire now. But odds are we've got this big ole swamp to ourselves tonight.

I find a splintered oak branch on the ground and break it apart best as I can. I scrape up some dead leaves from the ground, then look around for what I really want—some of that dead Spanish moss. That stuff burns fast and hot and is the best kindlin' there is. I spy some hangin' black and scraggly from a nearby branch and grab a big double handful and run over and dump it on my pile.

I feel for my matches, which I keep in a dry-safe in my huntin' vest. I find 'em, and strike one on the side of my boot-heel, then kneel down and touch the flame to the moss.

The fire roars to life and I ain't never been happier to see a fire, not even a few I've made in the woods in the bitter, wet winter. I reach down at the bottom of my kindlin' pile and grab out some sticks and stoke the flames till I got it goin' good and hot. Then I yell at Chilly to look around and bring me whatever he thinks will burn and I go scroungin' for more wood myself.

We've soon got a big ole fire burnin'. I have Chilly stand as close to it as he can and I grab an armload of Spanish moss and go hustlin' back to the slough to wet it. I run back and start layin' the wet moss on the fire. Pretty soon, smoke's boilin' up black as a tornado. We'll be breathin' smoke all night and we'll prob'ly sweat like roughnecks on an oil rig in August. But at least we won't be eat up.

I say Chilly, you stay here. I'm gonna go cut us some palmetto fronds and gather up some more moss. We'll make a kind of lean-to on the edge of our smoke and crawl in there after supper. We should be okay.

He says you goin' back out in them mosquitoes?

I say well, I hope it won't be for too long.

I go bargin' out, my pocketknife ready. We've got about fifteen minutes of light left, I figger. I make right for a stand of palmettos and slash down about ten of them things fast as I can. I leave enough stem so I can sharpen 'em like stakes and drive 'em into the spongy ground. Pretty soon, I've scrabbled together a rickety shelter, by leanin' the tops of the palmetto fronds together tentlike. I've noticed there's a puff of breeze in these woods and I've built the lean-to downwind. I lay a bed of moss for Chilly and try to close up the openin's with more palmettos and moss.

I've also decided that thing's too small for both of us. I'll sleep just downwind covered in moss, my back against a tree.

When I'm done I turn to Chilly and I say well, there's the bedroom. After supper you'll crawl in there and I think you'll be okay.

I tell him where I'm sleepin' and he says you shore?

I say yep, that's how I've slept in the woods many a night.

Chilly says well, after tonight, I hope I've slept my last in the woods. He tries to grin when he says it but I can tell it ain't a real grin.

I say this is a big swamp. It's hard to say how long it'll take to get across it. Now, how 'bout some roasted possum, Chilly? I wish I could add smothered potatoes and poke salad.

Chilly looks at the possum and says man, I wish you could, too.

With my back to the smoke, I lay our possum out on the ground on his back and gut him, then run the guts over to the edge of the slough, where I throw 'em in. The turtles or *choupique* will get 'em, unless a gator does first.

I wash my hands, then rake mosquitoes off my arms, face, and neck and hustle back to our fire. There's hardly a place on me that don't itch. I take my knife and run it clear up the belly of that possum, then ring the snout and feet like I would a coon's, peelin' down the head fur clear to his neck. Then I rustle around in my huntin' vest till I come up with a three-foot length of twine. I make a loop and tie it around the possum's neck, then find a branch I can hang the possum from. Pretty soon I got it licked. I cut off the head and tail, then quarter the carcass. I find me a stout oak stick, about three foot long, and sharpen one end. I jab that end through the possum haunches and carve out a spot in the fire where it's not too smoky.

I fetch the bottle of Tabasco sauce I carry with me in my huntin' vest. I sprinkle them two haunches and put 'em to the fire like I was roastin' a weenie.

Possum is strong meat but I have to say it don't smell all that bad.

When the haunches are done, I've got to let them cool off a bit, 'cause we ain't exactly got plates.

Then I hand one of the haunches to Chilly and he takes a bite.

He says hhm, my compliments to the chef. This tastes like a baseball with Tabasco. 'Bout as tender, too.

I say it obviously turned out a li'l better than I thought it would.

While Chilly eats, I roast the forequarters.

We eat and eat till that possum's gnawed down to clean bones, then throw the bones into the fire. They'll stink—I'm hopin' the mosquitoes will think so, too.

I say Chilly, feel free to sack out any time you want to.

He says well, I'm beat.

I say okay, just crawl in there.

He says I'm takin' this here gun in. Case the cavalry comes.

I say if they come, we might as well shoot. It'll be about the same, whether we do or don't, 'cept we might take a couple of 'em with us.

Chilly looks at me in the fire's glow.

He says Logan, you ever killed a man?

I say no.

He says you really think you could?

I say yes. I almost did today with Uncle. Boy, he burned me up.

He nods, then slaps a mosquito on his chin.

He says I'm not shore I could but maybe I could.

I say don't worry about it, Chilly. I s'pect we'll live to see another day.

He says well, I wonder how that moron Junior is feelin' with them red aints I put down his pants? Uncle, too.

I haw-haw. I say tell you what, I've had them fire aints crawl up my britches and you can bet I shucked my britches faster than a mink takes a chicken. I'd say there's a chance ole Junior and Uncle ain't gonna be in the love business for a while.

Chilly busts out laughin' at that.

He says that just means the cows on Catahoula Bayou are safe for a coupla nights. Okay, Logan, if you don't mind, I'm gonna climb in this contraption you've made.

I say sleep tight.

Chilly crawls into my lean-to like a bear wigglin' into a small cave. After he's snuggled in, I heap more moss on the entrance to try to close it off best as I can. I hear him slappin' but sooner than I expect I hear him snorin'. Then I hear him say oh, Cassie. Oh, Cassie, girl.

Meely told me Cassie's Chilly's girlfriend. I feel bad about Chilly but it's right that he's come with me. Otherwise, he'd be sleepin' in a worse place than this.

I prop myself up against the oak and pull a pile of moss over me and grip my double-barrel and listen to them mosquitoes drone all around me. Then I remember them leeches.

I kick off the moss and strip off my vest and shirt and scrounge at the edge of the fire for a nice hot stick. I find one I can handle and touch the embers to them leeches and they let go and roll up into a ball and fall to the ground.

Them boys ate a lot better than I did tonight.

I put back on my shirt and vest and settle back up against the tree, pullin' up moss as best as I can. I can hear the buzz of them mosquitoes just out of the smoke line. They're hummin' like a bad church choir.

I'd love a cold drink of water.

This fire helps with the *cousins* but it's not ideal and I'll have to get myself up a coupla times tonight to stoke it. But I'm tired out as an ole tractor and I find myself driftin' off.

Things scrabble out in the dark woods, and once I start up, my double-barrel at the ready, thinkin' I've heard footsteps.

But the woods go quiet again, 'cept for the drone of the *cousins,* and I drift off, way, way off to some place where even the mosquitoes cain't get me.

3.

I wake up stiff with the moon shinin' through the trees and hear Chilly still snorin' away. That's good.

Our fire's burned down low but it's still smokin' pretty good.

It's even cooled off some, and somethin' else is differnt. It takes me a while to notice there ain't no mosquitoes hummin' in my ear. They seem to have flown off with the risin' moon.

I settle down, deeper into my mossy bed, and realize I've been dreamin' about my boy. Runnin' off this mornin' and leavin' him hurt on the side of the road feels about as bad as anything I've ever done. And that's in a life that's had a fair number of bad days.

Don't get me wrong. I believe a man makes a lot of his own luck, and I've made myself lots of the wrong kind.

I been a drinkin' man and a sinner, and the two of them things come close to bein' the same sometimes. I think I one day could be through with drinkin', though prob'ly not with sinnin'.

A man has a hard time givin' up everything at once, even if he wants to. I've not yet learned how to live without the pleasures a woman can provide, though I seem to have give up on love.

I had my love and I lost her, and though I feel the need to sometimes lie with women, I no longer care to love them. Maybe I've not tried very hard. Maybe you just don't try very hard when the women you lie with are the kind you pay. But I find them kind of women are easier on a man like me.

It's hard to explain how it was with Elizabeth and me. You don't know how she and me fit together. You'd think a man could quit his sorrow after all these years—eight so far—but my sorrow hangs on to me like the deep part of August. I know I could be a better man if I just give it up, but maybe I'm not ready yet.

Maybe I never will be.

When Elizabeth died, I fell, like the moon yanked from the sky and thrown down into a dark, dark field. I couldn't even comfort my boy. Losin' his momma broke his heart, and how could I explain that it broke my heart more?

You see, Elizabeth loved me and she civilized me and I was a man who didn't particularly think he needed to be loved or cared to be civilized. And I loved her with everything I had, not one thing held back.

And maybe that's the problem. Wadn't no fence 'tween me and the sadness when it come.

I grew up rough myself.

My own daddy died early of drink. I was but six or seven and don't remember him all that well, 'cept that he laughed big and drank hard and was gone a lot. He was a shrimper, and a poor one, I guess. He left me and Momma poor as oysters in fresh water.

Momma was a pretty woman but life wasn't pretty to her. We lived down in the salt marsh below a place called Bayou Go-to-Hell. It was the end of a dusty, broke-up oyster-shell road that began way up at Ville Canard, and it was mostly poor Injun folk and poor Cajuns—Daddy was a mix of both—tryin' to make a livin' off the water and not doin' very well at it.

If the hurricanes and mosquitoes didn't get us in the summer, the *coup nord* blew cold through them leaky, shotgun shacks in the winter. Every year, some people come down with polio, even malaria. A lot of the men-folk drunk too much and run what rickety cars they had in the bayou and kilt themselves early.

After Daddy passed, there were times when I thought we might starve. The church up the bayou would bring us money out of the poor box now and then and food sometimes. But it wadn't much money or food, and there was lots of poor people to give it to. Momma got work in a shrimp-peelin' factory, which was work only as long as the shrimp were runnin'. She'd peel shrimp for twelve hours a day and come home half-dead with her hands bloody and swole up. She got paid a nickel an hour. Sometimes they'd just pay the people in shrimp. One spring and summer, I ate so many shrimp that to this day I won't eat another.

I'da peeled shrimp, too, if they'da let me, but I wadn't old enough.

One day a man come down to Bayou Go-to-Hell to buy shrimp. He was a rich man of the kind I've known once or twice. He had a nice fancy car—a Packard, I remember, as I was fond of cars and had memorized every kind I saw. He didn't wanna buy his shrimp from the market. He wanted to come down to where the shrimp was caught and buy 'em right out the trawl.

He come down to the factory Momma was workin' in one day and bought a big load of shrimp. He saw Momma on the peelin' line and, though I never quite got the whole story, he come back a few times and they got to talkin'. One time, he come sat in the parlor of our sad house on the bayouside. Finally, he offered Momma a job. Maybe he was sweet on her. Like I said, back then she was a pretty woman. The job was lookin' after his children and included a small house for us on their big property.

Anything would beat peelin' shrimp and bein' broke and widowed on Bayou Go-to-Hell. So we quit the salt marsh and moved clear up to Catahoula Bayou, where the man had a big sugar plantation.

We lived good for about a year, plenty to eat and Momma made good money, considerin' we got a free place to live. I went to school and was doin' okay, though them teachers were rough on a boy like me. I couldn't sit still for one minute. I'd fight easy as I'd sweat in summer.

Then one day, just like that, the man's wife, who never liked Momma, fired her.

The man come to apologize for it and I remember Momma cryin'. He said he was sorry but there wadn't nuttin' he could do.

Maybe there was more between them than I knew about. Prob'ly was.

Momma was never goin' back to Bayou Go-to-Hell, so we found us a tiny rent shack back of Augustin Brien's place about five miles below the man's plantation. Momma had saved some money and thought she'd find another job lookin' after people. But she stayed in bed and cried a lot. For a while, the man would come and bring us sacks of groceries, maybe a bit of money, too. Then he just stopped comin'.

I did what I had to do to keep us goin'. I stayed in school but I didn't go all the time and I finally quit in the eighth grade. I stole—chickens mostly, though one time a pig. I caught him at the edge of the woods at the back of Eustace Daigle's pasture. I tied a store-bought bandana 'round his snout so he wouldn't squeal and wrestled him into a wheelbarrow and pushed him through the woods for five miles. I slaughtered him poorly in our backyard and made a godawful mess of things but we did get a few pork chops out of him.

I was good at stealin' and I never got caught, though people always suspected me. Momma was in bed and I was in charge, and I didn't know what else to do.

Momma died of pneumonia when I was eighteen. I didn't even have the money to bury her proper. People from the Relief come and bought the coffin. The Catholic church up the bayou give her a burial plot.

The man come to the funeral and I saw him cryin' in the back of the church. It was only a lot later that I maybe understood them tears. I myself couldn't even cry at Momma's funeral. Our poor luck had made me hard.

I kept our rent shack for a while but I wouldn't clean it or cut the grass or anything and Augustin Brien come down one day and kicked me out. He said he was sorry and I think he was. Maybe he was hopin' I'd say okay, well, I'll start lookin' after the place better. But I didn't care about nuttin'. I moved lower and lower till I was 'bout livin' in the swamp. Toward the end, I'd moved into a tent I'd bought at the Army Surplus. In fact, the swamp's where I wanted to live. I hated roofs and doors and windows, anything that hemmed me in.

I didn't think much of most people, either.

I drank a lot and I fought a lot. Some was 'cause I was drunk and mad and lookin' for a fight. I won, most times, 'cept if I was too drunk.

When I lost, I lost bad.

I roamed the woods and didn't care much for the law or rules. I paid no mind to huntin' seasons. I took what I needed to eat and what I needed to sell. I figgered I was bein' reasonable about it, though them game wardens didn't see it that way. It took 'em years to finally catch me and even then they got lucky. Or, actually, I got stupid.

I come out of the woods with a big spring buck rabbit I'd shot out of season. It was early yet and I sat myself down in a field of alfalfa to have a nip of whiskey in celebration. Next thing I know, I'm bein' nudged awake by some game wardens who'd found me asleep with that rabbit layin' over my chest.

I met Elizabeth when I was twenty-six and feral as the swamp. It was at a softball tournament. I was a pretty good ballplayer—and so is my boy. Some ole boys that I hunted with—my drinkin' buddies at Elmore's, the bayou beer joint—had invited me to come play in some games over at Catahoula Bayou School. I'd got a pretty good reputation in the huntin' department, and some of them boys who wadn't that good at it would sidle up to me and ax me to take 'em. Them that I liked, I would. On a few of 'em it rubbed off. Most not.

Sometimes I think a man is born to hunt, or he's not. Fishin's about the same.

I played left field for the Catahoula Bayou Crawdads. I walked all over Creation and I ate lean so I was in pretty doggone good shape and fast as a deer. I could pretty well cover left field and half of center by myself.

Elizabeth had come with some ole boy who was on the other team, a big strappin' fella named Dugas. He thought he was doggone Babe Ruth and he doggone almost was. He kept tryin' to hit one over my head—and he could hit a softball three hundred fifty, four hundred feet, no foolin'. But he'd never played against anybody as fast as me, and nobody as proud, neither. I'd play him a lot closer in than normal fellas, and this just got him madder and madder, till every time he come up, he'd clobber one my way tryin' to show me what a bull he was. Wadn't no fence—just a cane-field behind me. And I'd sail back and shag it out of the air. Even I'd never played so good. On his last out, he drove a doggone bullet over my head and I chased it hard and dove into the canefield and come up with that ball, and a stalk of sugarcane to boot.

Nobody'd ever seen anything like it.

We beat them seven-to-two and won the whole shootin' match. At the end of the game, Dugas come up and looked me over like he'd just seen a white alligator. I guess I didn't look regulation. I played ball in my work boots, since I didn't have no spikes or even tennis shoes. I wore faded khakis and a T-shirt and a ball cap that looked like it had spent most its life under the drip pan of an Allis-Chalmers tractor.

Dugas just looked me over and shook his head and said mister, I hope you crawl back under the log you crawled out from.

But Elizabeth was standin' right next to him and I couldn't even speak, much less think what to say to this galoot. Normally, I mighta give him one in the nose—I've won many a fight against a bigger man by just cavin' in his nose without warnin'. But she was there, with her dark hair and her brown eyes and somethin' else about her a man like me couldn't come close to sayin'. But I felt it.

Next I know she's told the galoot to apologize and the galoot looks at me and says aw, hey, look, stud, I'm just sore 'cause you robbed me of all them homers.

Elizabeth held out her hand and took mine and shook it and said I'm Elizabeth Toups.

She smiled and said you cover a lot of ground out there, mister. And I've got to apologize for Brett, here. He sometimes forgets his manners.

Ole Brett was annoyed, but Elizabeth just looked at me. She looked at me in a way no woman ever had done before and not like them gals who know their way around a man's jockey shorts. She looked at me like she saw right into the middle of me, and I couldn't take my eyes off her till Dugas got her by the elbow and waltzed her right away from me.

He wadn't a fool. He could tell what was goin' on.

Actually, I wadn't shore myself what was goin' on. I was confused as a squirrel head-dinged by bird shot.

There was a big barbecue after the game and all the teams stayed around and drunk beer and eat chicken and *andouille* and some steaks give by Dugas and his rich daddy. I sat under one of them big oaks next to the field with my beer and my plate shootin' the breeze with a couple of the podnahs on my team when next I know Elizabeth walks right up to me. She says Logan, I'm not actually dating Brett Dugas—he's just an old family friend, though maybe he wishes he were more. I live with my parents on LeGrange Street in Ville Canard. It's Theodule Toups, we're in the phone book. Please call me sometime.

She just walked away and them podnahs of mine had to practically close my mouth for me. They gimme some ribbin' about that, not to mention they cackled like crows how ole Brett Dugas was gonna blow a fuse if he found out about this and come wipe up the ground with me.

I honestly didn't care what Brett Dugas thought. I wadn't afraid of him, though maybe I shoulda been.

I didn't have a phone and I hated talkin' on them. I doubted I would ever find the courage to call her. Plus, what would she think once she learned how rough I lived?

I thought about it for two weeks. Stewed on it. Four or five times, I drove over to Elmore's joint and put a nickel in that dusty pay phone that hung off the back of the store. I musta put that same nickel in that same slot a hunderd times but I could never get the courage to dial all the numbers. One day, after stewin' over it practically all day, I realized I had to do *somethin'*. So I just shined up as best I could, looked up her address in Elmore's phone book, and drove to town. I walked around through what I figgered would be the supper hour, then went and knocked on her door.

Elizabeth answered it, which was lucky, and the smile that come on her face told me it was the best thing I would ever do. She invited me in. They had a nice house, not big, not little, but fixed up good. Her momma was there—turns out she'd been partly paralyzed by polio and was in a wheelchair. She was a nice woman—nice to me, anyway. They had a colored lady workin' for them, lookin' after Miz Toups. Doggone if I didn't know her—it was Elma Mouton from down Catahoula Bayou. I'd known her husband, Bernel, when he was alive. Me and Bernel had hunted frogs together not long after Momma died.

Elma was glad to see me, for shore, and Elizabeth seemed a bit surprised that I knew the family, but happy about it, too.

You still catch them frogs, Logan? Elma said.

I shore do, Elma.

Will you bring us a mess over here next time? I know Mr. Toups will pay good for 'em. We like our frog legs 'round this house.

I said I'd be happy to do that. Then me and Elma had ourselves a bit of a gossip, catchin' up on this or that, and then she went off to make some coffee.

I had to almost pinch myself. This wadn't me, or the me I thought was me. Logan LaBauve didn't sit around in parlors makin' small talk. But there I was, and one thing led to another, and pretty soon I was tellin' Elizabeth and her momma and Elma gator stories, as I had quite a few of them stories to tell. Some of them maybe even didn't seem true, but they were. Elizabeth just kept lookin' at me with this grin on her face—like she had found Tarzan or somethin'. That was okay by me.

Then Mr. Toups come in and I'd never seen the weather change faster. He was tall, ramrod straight, wore a suit and a Stetson hat. Turned out he was an accountant, a money man, serious as winter. And it took him about ten seconds to size up me and size up the situation and he wadn't happy with either. Lookin' back, I cain't say I totally blame him. I was a man astraddle a fence and even I knew I might fall either way. I'm not sayin' I coulda robbed a bank or nuttin'. But I had a wild, ornery streak in me that some people—a certain kind of man, especially—can read like new deer sign.

He was civil to me but just barely. I didn't stay long.

Elizabeth walked me outside and said call me. I said well, I have a hard time callin'. For one thing, I don't have a phone. For another, I don't do very well talkin' on the phone.

She smiled and said then you'll have to visit.

I come over a time or two but her daddy always seemed to be there and he watched us like a chicken hawk. At the end of the second time, he axed to talk to me alone. He wadn't nasty, just businesslike. He said I didn't look like a man who had a real job or could care for a wife and family. He said Elizabeth had a chance to marry well and if I cared about her, I'd go off like a good man and leave her be. He said he was shore when Elizabeth thought about things she'd come to her senses, and then I'd be outta luck anyway.

I didn't know what to say. I just nodded and left.

I laid low for a couple of weeks. I couldn't think straight. Next I know, I'm up at Elmore's havin' a beer and bein' about as miserable as a man can be when Elizabeth walks in. She walks in like she knew just where to find me and she comes up and says what did Daddy say to you that chased you off?

All I could figger to do was to tell her the whole deal.

She said well, I'm moving out of there. What's between us is between us, not between us and Daddy.

I said I know he cares about you. He's only tryin' to do right by you.

She said so, what about you, Logan LaBauve? You planning to spend your entire life running wild in the swamps? All by yourself?

The cat pretty much got my tongue when she said that. But I did manage to say I've never been lonesomer than I've been stayin' away from you.

She said well, I guess you better do something about that before it's too late. It's not like I don't have options.

I said there's somethin' I need to show you first.

I drove her out to my tent site in my ole battered truck, a mess of rusty tools and empty oil cans lyin' on the floorboard. I figgered when Elizabeth saw that I lived in an ole Army Surplus tent and realized I *was* feral as the swamp, she'd come to her senses just like her daddy said.

But she fooled me again.

She got out my truck and looked around and said well, you picked a beautiful spot.

I said you know I don't have a real job.

She said are you trying to get rid of me?

I said it's the last thing I'm tryin' to do. I guess I'm just not shore what kind of man I really am.

She said Logan LaBauve, I guess we're gonna have to find that out, aren't we?

We got married about three months later. It was a small weddin'. I invited a couple of my ball-playin' friends—Beanie Schexnayder, the short-stop on the Crawdads, was my best man. I had no kin, really, 'cept some distant relations way down Bayou Go-to-Hell that I hadn't seen in a coon's age.

Elizabeth's daddy wouldn't come to the weddin', though her momma and a few other relatives did. One of them was her grandpa, Emile Toups. He was a widower and he was everything Elizabeth's daddy wadn't—he laughed and joked and doted on Elizabeth, and he at least seemed willin' to give me a chance. He even come up to me after the weddin' and shook my hand and apologized for his son and said Mr. LaBauve, I have to tell you the truth—I myself am not entirely sure about this marriage. But I love my granddaughter and what's more I trust her judgment in people. So if she believes in you, I must, too, until you prove us wrong. I hope for her sake you won't.

All I could think to do was to look him deep in the eye and nod and shake his hand and say thank you. I wish I were a man who could have thought quick enough to say more. I think more was prob'ly called for.

I thought we might go up to New Awlins for our honeymoon but Elizabeth surprised me again. She said Logan, is that tent of yours still there?

Nobody had a clue where we was goin'. We didn't even make it to the tent, or totally out of our clothes.

We made love in the woods while the moon rose and Elizabeth said oh, God, baby, the stars are falling down on my head.

I held on to her and felt the night shake itself to pieces and I couldn't say a single thing.

That's how Meely was made. He come nine months later and we named him after Grandpa Emile. Maybe it's no wonder he loves the moon and the stars and the woods and the wild places.

I give up the swamp pretty much to become a carpenter. There was plenty of work around and I was good at it, and made respectable money. We bought a nice li'l farm with a run-down but pretty ole house with money that Elizabeth's momma give us. Grandpa Toups give us his car, a

Dodge only three years old, knowin' that my truck was on its last legs. We couldn't afford a motorboat but many a Saturday afternoon, we'd strap that pirogue to the top of the Dodge and slip it into a slough over by Arceneaux's Marsh, and, with ole Meely sittin' between us, go catch a big mess of *sac-à-lait* or goggle-eye. Pretty soon, Meely wanted to go all the time.

Then life walloped us. First Grandpa Toups died of a heart attack. Two months later, her momma died unexpectedly. At the funeral her daddy said the sorriest thing I've heard any man say—that Elizabeth marryin' me had put her in an early grave.

Elizabeth never spoke to her father again, or hardly anybody in her family, for that matter.

A sadness come into her eyes that never quite disappeared.

The ole Logan woulda knocked him to Kingdom Come for doin' such a thing. But the new one knew that doin' such a thing would only make Elizabeth feel worse.

We worked on havin' another baby—we worked hard, and we used to laugh at how fun it was to work so hard at somethin'—but nuttin' took till Meely turned seven. Everything seemed to be goin' okay till Elizabeth went into labor.

The baby was turned wrong and got the cord 'round her neck and suddenly the midwife was hollerin' for me to go fast to fetch the doctor 'cause Elizabeth was in trouble, too. We didn't have no phone as the phone lines hadn't come that far down the bayou yet. By the time I got back with the doctor, the baby was dead and Elizabeth had lost so much blood that she was pretty well gone too.

She died in my arms and I knew right then somethin' had turned in me.

I cussed God, for I couldn't understand why God had showed me this love and then took it from me. I buried my wife and the daughter I never knew and then I just run off into the swamp and into the bottle and I was fightin' mad all of the time. I tangled with them game wardens and I tangled with the police and I wadn't there very much when my boy coulda used my help.

With Elizabeth, I was pretty good at the daddy business, but without her I've pretty much got it all wrong. Meely has basically raised hisself.

He's turned out to be a good boy anyway, no thanks to me. He got his momma's good heart and good sense, that and his daddy's fight. Sometimes I think that's a good combination, though I don't give myself more credit than that.

Anyway, I realize that thinkin' about all this stuff is not for the best right now. I need to be as clear-headed as possible in the mornin'. I need to think about how we're gonna get our next meal.

I need to sleep.

I snuggle down deeper into my mossy blanket and start to shut my eyes when I hear a faint sound off to the left of me.

I turn my head slow, wonderin' if we've got company.

That's when I see the doe, head cocked, standin' still as fog over in a patch of moonlight. She smells our fire but she don't smell or see me.

I think for a second about reachin' slow for my double-barrel, propped up against the tree behind me but then I change my mind. A shot would scare the wits out of poor Chilly, and I'm just too tired to shoot.

I watch her for a long while, then whisper out into the night go on, ole girl. Go on.

She pricks up her ears but she don't bolt right away.

She just stands there lookin' toward me in the moonlight, then slips off into the edge of the dark and disappears, quiet as a star.

4.

I don't s'pose you're cookin' breakfast? says Chilly. Bacon and eggs maybe? Grits and toast on the side?

I look at Chilly and grin.

The sun ain't been up long. It's cool now but it looks like it's gonna be another clear, hot day.

Chilly actually woke me up when he come scrabblin' outta the lean-to to go pee in the woods. I went off in a different direction and did the same.

I'm stiff as a dried muskrat pelt.

I say no, Chilly, son, I'm afraid I've run clean out of bacon and eggs. I'm even outta possum, but generally I don't eat possum for breakfast anyways.

Chilly grins back. Them mosquitoes look like they beat on him 'bout as hard as Uncle and Junior did.

Chilly says well, about dinnertime that possum might start to smell good again in my brain.

I stomp out what's left of the fire and cover it up with a coupla moldy logs and scatter them palmetto fronds best as I can. But any kind of tracker who stumbles on this spot will know folks have camped here. 'Course, them law doggies will prob'ly miss it altogether. I don't know where the police chief gets them that he hires but Uncle's about par for the course. If them ole boys' brains were eggs, you could crack open a dozen of 'em and not get much to scramble.

When I'm done roughin' up the campsite, I walk over and hand Chilly the canteen and say have a swallow but just one, if you don't mind. This day's gonna get hot and we'll appreciate that water even more later.

Chilly takes a swig and hands the canteen back to me. I do the same. I close it and clamp it back on my belt. It's gettin' awfully light.

Chilly says do you actually know where we are?

I say I've got a pretty good idea. If we keep goin' steady, sometime tomorrow or the next we could reach a place called Samanie's Landin'.

Chilly looks at me mournful.

He says tomorrow or the next? Man.

I say I'm 'fraid so.

He says they got food there?

I say the main thing goin' for Samanie's is that it's outta Catahoula Parish. It ain't nuttin' but a boat landin' with a run-down shack that passes for a saloon, but it ain't open reg'lar, just when ole Samanie wants to open it and he's not the most reliable fella. In fack, he's a bit crazy—what the Cajuns would call *craque*. And what they've got to eat would be things like pork rinds or popcorn shrimp in them li'l bitty bags or maybe pickled pig's feet in a jar.

Chilly says right now that sounds like Sunday dinner to me.

I laugh. I say well, we'll keep our eyes peeled along the way. I might see a squirrel or a duck or somethin' that I could take with the rifle and we could build us a hot, quick fire and barbecue it.

He says you know what I like best about squirrels, Logan?

I say the brains, I'll bet. Nuttin' as sweet as that.

Chilly nods.

We walk back toward the pirogue, which I'd pulled into a thicket of palmettos. Soon, we're out in the middle of the slough, headin' north by northwest again.

It'll be a hot day but it's a pretty one, and peaceful, too. We come through a place where the slough narrows and meanders through a stand of giant cypresses of the kind that are mostly gone from these woods. I point out one of them spindle-tops that's about half as big around as a cistern.

I say you realize, Chilly, that this swamp was once filled with these trees and some that were even a lot bigger. Some ole boys from up north come down here about a hunderd years ago and started cuttin' 'em all down.

Chilly looks up at that tree and says I've never seen a cypress that big, ever. It's a shame about them lumberjacks.

I say I feel about the same way. I never met a tree that wadn't better company than a lumberjack.

We come paddlin' slow out of the cypresses and have our first bit of luck. An oak and hackberry ridge comes tumblin' like a pointy finger out of the swamp right in front of us, and I look along the bank and see a jumble of vines runnin' up thick along a couple of scrub hackberries.

I turn us toward the bank and say Chilly, get ready for breakfast.

He says you see a squirrel?

I say no, but I see a great big ole sweet mess of muscadines. Swamp grapes some people call 'em.

Never had 'em before, Chilly says.

I say well, get ready for a treat.

I steer us over to the bank and Chilly steps out and pulls the boat up so I can get out without gettin' my feet wet. I walk over to the trees and look up. The vines are loaded with deep purple muscadines, thick and fat as quail eggs. The only problem is that they're out of reach.

I say Chilly, come over here and give me a boost up so I can get a purchase on one of these vines. He does so and I go shinnyin' up. I get to the first cluster of grapes, snatch off my cap and wedge it like a floppy bowl 'tween my chest and the vines and start pickin'. It don't take long to fill up the cap and I hold it out in front of me and say I'm droppin' her, Chilly.

Chilly sets himself like a center fielder and the cap plops soft into his big mitts. I say find a clean place to pour 'em out and then throw me my cap back up here.

We do this a few times and we got enough muscadines for breakfast and dinner. I shinny down the tree and I see Chilly's already popped one in his mouth.

I say watch for them pits. Otherwise, you eat 'em, peels and all.

Chilly eats another one and spits the pit 'bout as far as some people can throw a baseball. I've never seen anything like it.

Chilly says I never knew the woods produced such sweet things.

I go over and pick one up and taste it. I say well, I ain't never had none sweeter than these. Some of the ole Cajuns used to gather 'em up and make wine out of 'em. I've had me a few nips of that in my day and it ain't bad if you like your liquor sweet. My wife, when she was alive, made a fine muscadine jelly. It was so good Meely would eat it on toast for supper.

Chilly says man, that sounds awful good. Then he looks up at that muscadine vine and says you know, Logan, let's not talk about food too much, if you know what I mean.

I say I know just what you mean.

The sun's up higher now and there ain't a cloud in the sky, and under different circumstances it might be nice to be out here on a warm spring day like this one. There's no green like hackberries and willow in spring and there's wood irises bloomin' along the bank and a small clearin' just off to our right is covered in buttercups and them daisies the Cajuns call *pissenlits*. If I had more time, I'd take a nice slow walk up this ridge to see what's in it. It's prob'ly full of deer and might be a fine place to hunt squirrels in the fall.

Chilly and I eat our fill of muscadines and then he gives me one more boost up the tree and I pick another mess in case we don't find nuttin' else. We head off again in the pirogue.

We ain't gone too far till we hit a sharp bend in a narrow part of the slough. We start to round the bend when I look up to see a man standin' at the back of a flat-bottom skiff with a push pole, comin' right at us.

He's polin' about as hard as I've ever seen anybody pole.

I pull back hard on my paddle and the nose of the pirogue swings sharp left.

We barely miss each other.

He glides by, not two foot away. I notice he's about as big as Chilly. He shoots me a sideways, copperhead look as he goes by—like maybe I was tryin' to run into him.

Then he leans hard into his pole—and falls right out of his boat, almost into ours. The splash is about as big as them monster alligator gar make when they take a muskrat from the surface.

Chilly says what the hell?

I pull back on the paddle again and brake the boat.

The man comes up sputterin'. He dog-paddles over to the boggy bank, just lettin' his skiff drift off.

He looks right at me. He says you pushed me in.

I say no I didn't.

He says you did. That man there saw you do it.

He points to Chilly.

Chilly says what? Nobody pushed you, podnah. You were steamin' along with that push pole and you fell out your boat. You about ran us down.

The man says uhn-uh. I didn't. He looks down at his hands and starts countin' on his fingers. He says nine lyin' bastids today. Nine.

Chilly says who you callin' a lyin' bastid, anyway?

The man don't look up.

Chilly says look at me, mister. You callin' us lyin' bastids?

The man don't answer.

Then he stoops like he's reachin' down under the water for somethin'. He closes his eyes and moves, kinda like a bear, closer to the bank. He suddenly jerks hard—and comes up with a catfish.

He cocks back and throws it right at us. I duck. It goes sailin' right over my head.

Whoa! Chilly roars. Mister! What are you, nuts?

It wadn't much of a catfish but I wouldn't wanna take a catfish in the face—them spines can hurt you.

The man says see, y'all know me! Y'all know me, don'tcha? Don'tcha?

I say mister, I've never laid eyes on you before and I hope I won't again. Your boat's driftin' away and I'd suggest you get in it and keep paddlin' the way you were goin' before there's trouble.

This time he reaches down and comes up with a knife. He says I got this.

I reach down at my feet and come up with my double-barrel. I say I got this.

He cocks back like he's gonna throw the knife.

I jerk the gun up and fire one barrel over his head. I regret doin' it the minute I hear the gun roar. This idgit is gonna give us away to the law if they're anywhere nearby.

He throws his hands up. The knife goes flyin' behind him, clackin' against a cypress tree. It falls with a plop into the swamp. He flops on his back and just floats there—floats there like some bloated dead garfish.

Chilly says you killed him?

I shake my head, disgusted. I say no, Chilly. I fired three feet above him. He's *craque*—gotta be.

We sit and wait. He floats and floats, not movin'. Not an inch.

I say doggone it, what is it with people lately? How come I get to run into all the idgits, huh?

Chilly says maybe we oughta go ever there and check on him?

I call out. I say podnah, cut it out. I didn't shoot you, even though you tried to bean me with a catfish and throw a knife at me. You need to get in your boat and get goin' before you really make me mad. I mean it.

The idgit still don't move.

I say okay, Chilly. Let's go see.

I paddle Chilly's end up first. Chilly reaches down and pokes the man.

He reaches up and pulls Chilly outta the boat, cat quick.

I don't know how I don't go over, too.

The pirogue bucks like a rodeo horse before settlin' down.

Chilly sputters up, fists flailin'. That fella's got Chilly by the right arm but Chilly lands a pretty good left to the side of his head.

The man groans and says ow, you're murderin' me!

Chilly says I am. I gonna murder you, you fool!

Chilly swings again but his fist catches more water than man.

The man lets go of Chilly, puttin' his hands to his face. Ow, he says. Ow! Then he slowly sinks 'neath the water.

Chilly looks at me. He says what the hell, Logan?

I say I dunno, Chilly. Here, grab on to the pirogue and let me tow you away from here.

I paddle us up about twenty yards, to where there's a big log goin' up the bank. I say Chilly, climb up there and I'll give you a hand gettin' back in the boat.

Chilly keeps one eye on the water and inches up that log. Pretty soon he's settled back into the front of the pirogue.

That fella ain't nowhere to be seen.

So what, says Chilly? He's drowned? I popped him once in the head and he drowned?

I say yeah, prob'ly about the way he died when I shot him. Let's just wait a bit.

We wait and wait. There ain't a sign of the lunatic. A breeze springs up behind us and it blows the man's skiff outta sight around that bend.

Once I spy bubbles, but about a minute later a green turtle rises to the surface, his head pokin' out.

Chilly says so what are we gonna do, Logan?

I put my head in my hands. I say this has give me a headache. Lemme think.

I don't think too long. I say there's nuttin' to do but go. We didn't push the fool out of his boat. We didn't shoot him, and we didn't drown him. We only had the bad luck to run into him. Let's just get outta here.

Chilly says I'm with you. The fool woulda drowned me if he coulda.

Chilly hadn't more than said that when we hear a voice. There's a tree leanin' hard over the bayou ahead of us, the opposite way we been lookin'. It's a good forty, fifty yards away.

The man's sittin' in the tree but he stands suddenly. He yells I'm comin'!

He dives in headfirst and disappears under the water again. There's big ripples comin' our way, like gators make when they come off the bank.

Chilly says damn! Get us outta here, Logan!

I say just get Uncle's gun up at the ready. That's a long way to swim— especially if he's plannin' to attack underwater.

Chilly says what, I'm s'posed to kill the fool? I don't wanna shoot no crazy man. I just wanna get outta here.

Chilly does have a good point. I kinda wanna get outta here, too.

I say okay, hold steady, we're movin'.

I turn the pirogue and we start paddlin' back around the bend where we come from.

About halfway around I say okay, far enough. No way can any man swim underwater this far. Not even Tarzan.

We wait and wait and wait some more. The idgit ain't nowhere to be seen.

Chilly says c'mon, Logan, let's just go.

I nod. I say okay. Lemme paddle. You keep your eyes peeled and your finger on that trigger.

Chilly says okay, but you really want me to shoot him?

I say only if he throws a five-pound catfish at you.

Chilly says funny.

I paddle hard and pretty soon we reach the tree he dove out of.

Nobody up there, says Chilly as we glide by.

I slow and take one more look back.

I see his boat comin' round the bend. He's in it, polin' slow this time.

Chilly says damn! Double-damn!

I say okay, look, we got guns and, far as we know, he don't. I'll keep paddlin' and you just cover my back. If he makes any strange moves, put the first shot well over his head. The second? Maybe we'll just have to blow a hole in his boat. Anyway, I hope it won't come to that. I think we'll lose him eventually.

Chilly says I hope not, too. But you're captain and I'm followin' orders. I'll shoot two holes in that boat if I have to.

I dip my paddle hard in the water and we shove off.

The fool follows us for an hour, stayin' well behind.

And then he disappears, as mysterious as he come.

5.

We've put a couple of hours 'tween us and the lunatic, far as I can tell, and the day's got hot like I knew it would be. I ain't wishin' for rain, but a bit of cloud cover wouldn't be too bad. But we won't get any today.

At least them muscadines do a good bit to keep our thirst down.

It's hard to think that the fool will come after us—two men with guns, one who's already put a whuppin' on his head. But it makes a fella a bit nervous.

I've changed my mind about headin' for Samanie's Landin'.

About halfway to Samanie's, there's another bayou, Bayou Snake, that comes in from the west. It's called that 'cause it ain't got a straight mile in it—the kinda place I'm good at navigatin', the kinda place where it's easy to shake people tryin' to follow you. It wanders though a chain of cypress lakes and comes out clear over at a place called Chenier Atchafalaya, quite a bit farther west than I'd like to go. The chenier ain't nuttin' but a li'l knot of trappers' shacks up on stilts and a two-bit honky-tonk standin' on the bayou's edge. But it'll be quiet this time of the year, with them trappers in town, spendin' the money they made over winter.

Unlike the road out of Samanie's Landin', the road outta there won't offer us much cover—there's a bayou on one side and swamp on the other—but it connects to a dirt road used by sugarcane farmers that eventually crosses a highway that runs clear from New Awlins to Baton Rouge. Best as I recall, if we angle east-northeast from Baton Rouge, we'll make Mississippi sooner or later.

I tell Chilly about my change in plans. He says I'm with you. That fella gives me the creeps.

We paddle on through the day without stoppin'. I can tell Chilly's arms have got sore. He's strong but there's muscles you use to paddle that you don't use for nuttin' else. Sometimes Chilly has to stop for a while and I tell him that's okay.

Game seems to have disappeared. We ain't seen a squirrel, rabbit, nor a possum—not even a nootra—since I spied a fox squirrel just after we got shed of the crazy man. I shot and missed—it was a long shot, anyway. Critters tend to lay low in the hot part of the day. We've spied a few ducks up ahead of us on the slough but they're skittish and they flushed before we could get in shootin' range. Oh, we've seen some herons, what the Cajuns call the *gros bec,* and one big flock of *bec croche,* but we ain't that desperate for food just yet. For one thing, I'm fond of them birds. Them *bec croche* are beauties and fly like I imagine angels would fly if you ever saw one. For another, they're protected by them federal game wardens and you'd be in mess if you was caught with one.

We're down to a half-a-cap's worth of muscadines and a swallow or two of water. If I don't see a critter soon, that's supper.

We paddle on and the light starts to fade and for the first time I also wish we had a fishin' pole. In fack, if I'da knowed we'd be runnin' from the law, I'da throwed a stout cane pole in the truck. This is catfish heaven. About now I'd settle for one of them smelly ole *choupiques.* As fish go, they're about the same as possum. About as ugly, too.

I look up at the sky. Ahead, it's bleedin' gold and purple. Behind, what's left of the day moon's hangin' bone-white above the cypresses. I figger we've got maybe an hour of light left. I peer ahead and see a wide bend and I'd bet my bottom dollar that's the entrance to Bayou Snake.

I say Chilly, let's pull hard for about ten minutes and see if that bend up yonder is where we wanna get off this slough.

Chilly puts his paddle to the water and off we go. I gotta say that boy's gettin' the hang of it, and when he ain't tired, we really scoot along.

I'm right, and when we get to the openin', I drag backwards on my paddle and turn us hard left.

I say I know where I am, but I'm not entirely shore how far it is to Chenier Atchafalaya. I know it's a ways—at least another day's paddle, prob'ly two. And I don't really know where we're spendin' the night. But there are trapper shacks in this country and this time of the year we might find an empty one. Otherwise, we'll be sleepin' on the ground again.

A frown comes on Chilly's face and I can tell he don't care to spend another night in the woods. He says well, let's keep paddlin' hard. If we don't find one of them shacks, I'd just as soon spend the night sittin' up in this here boat than bein' smoked like a ham to ward off them mosquitoes.

We go hard at it for about a half-hour and I myself am pooped. The sun is straight ahead of us now and sittin' just above the slough, throwin' a rainbow on the water.

We go glidin' past a big spindle-top cypress and Chilly looks hard right, then says whoa, whoa, Logan. Back up a bit. Do you see what I see?

He points with his paddle and I peer down a li'l *trainasse* that comes tumblin' out of the swamp into the bayou. It's so narrow, I plumb missed it. I look down the slip and spy what Chilly has spied—a cabin.

I say Chilly, you're a hawk-eye, son. That's a fine sight, and just in time, too. Let's go see if it's got room for us.

I steer us hard right of the bayou and we go clippin' along the *trainasse*, which ain't much wider than the width of the pirogue. When we get up within twenty yards I stop paddlin' and just look. Far as I can tell, she's empty. There's no lights on. There's a beat-up pirogue tied up at the dock and about half of it's underwater. There's a pair of white rubber knee boots—what they call shrimper boots around these parts—up on the rickety porch, and they look like the kind of boots that might've been throwed out. There's a rickety rocker and one of them high-backed metal chairs some people put out in their porches. This one is rusted up bad.

I have to say it kinda looks like my house. I'm wonderin' if it's not abandoned.

I take another stroke of the paddle and we glide up to the dock, which prob'ly was a pretty good dock in its day.

I say Chilly, step out careful, podnah. That dock could be rotten.

He does, gettin' out on his hands and knees and then standin' up slow and stiff. He rocks back and forth on the balls of his feet, then steps forward and stomps, but not too hard.

He says she's got some shimmy in her, but if it holds me, it'll hold you.

I say well, the real question is whether it'll hold both of us. I ease outta the pirogue, holdin' on to both sides of the rails as I go, and step out. I hear my knees crack.

That's when the door creaks open.

I see a woman, scraggly and pale as a bleached bone. She says is that you, Laurent? You come back to see your momma, cher? I t'ought you'd run off for good.

She puts a hand over her eyes, starin' out toward the fadin' sun.

She says oh, Laurent, you come in, 'cause your po' momma's so lonesome.

6.

The woman steps out and lets the screen door slap closed behind her. She's tiny. Her dress ain't much and she's barefooted. She's got long gray hair, 'cept for a white stripe down the middle like a skunk's tail.

I don't really know what to say.

She says, again, is that you, Laurent? You know Momma don't see nuttin' no more. C'mon up here, cher.

I decide I better say somethin'.

I say ma'am, it's not Laurent. We're just visitors. We were just paddlin' by and, uh, well, we're runnin' low on drinkin' water and thought we'd stop to see if you might be able spare some. We wadn't shore anybody was home.

She lowers her hand and then raises it again. I see her brow go furrowed and then just as quick she smiles. She's shows strong white teeth.

She could be an old woman or a woman my age who's just lived hard.

She says y'all come close so Miz Dee-Dee can see y'all.

I see Chilly has arched his eyebrows as though he's axin' is this a good idea? I nod at him and we walk up the dock and up a small step to the edge of the porch. I actually wouldn't mind borrowin' a gallon or two of water.

We get up close, standin' there in the last light of the day. I hear a low hum—mosquitoes risin' from the marsh. One is suddenly flittin' around my ear.

Miz Dee-Dee looks us over and then crosses herself. She says colored and white travelin' together. Mais, I dreamed y'all was comin'. Y'all hungry?

I realize there's a few things I am.

Hungry, thirsty, sore, bone-tired. Itchy, dirty, smelly.

She says aw, yeah, I bet y'all hungry. Miz Dee-Dee Fontenot has got a big pot of red beans and rice on the stove. Y'all come in.

She turns and disappears inside, flappin' her arms as she goes.

Chilly looks at me like I'm s'posed to say somethin' clever. I shrug.

He whispers is she—what's that Cajun word, Logan? *Craque?*

I shrug again.

He says you think she's really got some red beans and rice in there?

I sniff the air and for the first time I actually think I pick up a smell. It's a pretty good smell.

I say she could have.

Chilly says well, let's go. He waves his right hand low and says after you, Logan.

I push through the door, Chilly followin' me close.

We see Miz Dee-Dee with a long candle, lightin' a lamp. She lights one, then another, then another, then another. Pretty soon we realize there's shelves that go clear around the shack about midway up the wall and there's lamps everywhere. I wonder if she's gonna light them all.

She stops at about ten.

It's pretty bright in the cabin, suddenly. There's two things I smell— red beans and rice, and kerosene.

I look around. It ain't much of a place—no more than two rooms, as far as I can tell. There's crucifixes about everywhere, and all of them crosses are pink and Jesus is gold. Second, somebody seems to be awful fond of taxidermy. There's about twenty critters hung on the wall, includin' a piti- ful small gator, a muskrat, several ducks, and even a bullfrog. They're stuffed, poorly if you want my opinion.

Other'n that, the place looks like what a fishin' or trappin' shack might look like. Ahead is a curtain over a doorway. There's a sofa with springs stickin' up from one of the cushions, and a rockin' chair with an arm broke off. There's a small table made by sittin' a wide plank on two up-turned tin buckets. Over against another wall is the kitchen table—a wooden picnic table, really—with a saggy bench seat that looks like a fat man's been sittin' in the middle of it.

There's a rusted wire minnow trap leanin' in a corner, next to some beat-up hip boots and a single-shot shotgun with an extra-long barrel that looks so old and weathered that Davy Crockett coulda owned it.

Miz Dee-Dee has now walked to a small propane stove. She's so skinny she'd about have to walk twice in the same place to cast a shadow. She picks up a long wood spoon and stirs it slow in a big black and white speckled porcelain cookin' pot. Them beans smell doggone good, but it feels closed up and musty in here.

Miz Dee-Dee starts hummin' as she stirs. I wonder if she's done forgot about us.

I say ma'am, we didn't mean to invite ourselves in for supper. Like I said, we were just paddlin' by and—

She throws up the hand that's not stirrin' the pot and calls out Earl, Earl, come eat, cher! Them beans are ready and we got some company! Earl, cher! Earl!

Miz Dee-Dee puts the spoon down and turns to us. She's got that bright smile again. Y'all, don't be ashamed. Miz Dee-Dee is happy to serve y'all some supper. Earl, him, he hardly eats no more. He ain't hardly got a word to say. He don't say nuttin' at night. After dark, he just sits there.

She turns toward a door at the back of the shack. Earl, Earl! *Gar ici, compagnie! Viens donc manger, cher!*

I say is Earl your husband?

Aw, yeah, for fifty-seven and a half years. Anyway, y'all don't pay Earl no mind. Like I say, he usually ain't got nuttin' to say to nobody and when he does he's grouchy. Him and my boy Laurent, they fight all the time. Fight, fight, fight. *Toujours fâché.* Mais, I hate to see that, yeah.

Miz Dee-Dee stops and crosses herself. I see tears in her eyes.

Then, quick as the spring weather changes, she smiles again. She says y'all come over and get y'all some plates.

I got to admit this Earl business makes me a bit curious. And nervous.

What if Earl ain't the type who likes strangers bargin' in for supper? I realize we've left our guns in the pirogue.

Chilly don't seem worried. Earl would have to come in with a gun about as long as the one in the corner to keep Chilly away from that pot. He walks past me to the stove.

Miz Dee-Dee looks up at him. Look at you, a giant, she says, smilin' big again. Just like my boy. I better give you double, aw yeah.

Chilly says well, Miz Dee-Dee, you're an angel of mercy. I ain't had nuttin' today but some muscadines.

She loads up Chilly's plate and then she loads up one for me. Then she gets down some glasses—actually, they're old jelly jars—and fills 'em at a tap.

I'm bettin' it's good ole sweet cistern water. Long as there's no wiggle-tails in it, that's my favorite kind.

Chilly walks over and sits at one edge of that bowed bench seat. I take my plate and sit on the opposite edge.

Chilly takes a bite and the boy just about starts shoutin'. Doggone, Miz Dee-Dee, where'd you learn to cook? You musta stole this recipe from God himself!

Miz Dee-Dee turns to look at Chilly and she suddenly looks serious. She says now, you a nice boy, I know, but it ain't nice to take Gawd's name in vain. Oh, no.

She crosses herself. She says aw, no, it ain't nice, and if you do that too many times, Gawd gonna strike you dead. Dead!

She looks straight at Chilly and then draws her finger across her throat like a knife.

I see Chilly's mouth hangin' open.

I say oh, ma'am, I know Chilly didn't mean any harm. It's just an expression he uses.

Miz Dee-Dee crosses herself and says we better pray. Y'all pray wit' me.

She closes her eyes and pulls up a silver chain hangin' from around her neck. There's a small cross on it. She kisses the cross and then holds her hands up high and starts prayin'.

It ain't a language I know.

I'm lookin' at Chilly and he's lookin' at me. This could be one of them times when a fella oughta maybe eat and run.

Just as quick as Miz Dee-Dee comes out of it—she throws down her hands and opens her eyes.

She says y'all eat. Miz Dee-Dee has got plenty. She then turns to the stove and fixes herself a plate. She takes it to the couch and sits down and puts the plate on her lap and eats slow, never lookin' up.

We all go quiet, 'cept for the clackin' of forks on plastic plates. It *is* a big pot of red beans and rice, and Chilly and me don't feel too bad about goin' back for seconds. It's hard to say when we'll find another hot meal. Thirds might even taste pretty good, but I think that wouldn't be polite.

Plus, even though we ain't seen Earl, I figger he could come in any minute hungry as a horse. A man prob'ly wouldn't be happy to be left without supper in his own house.

I see Chilly lookin' around, studyin' them creatures on the wall.

He says ma'am, does somebody in your family do taxidermy?

Miz Dee-Dee looks up from her plate. She says oh, that. Yeah, my boy Laurent. He learned that in town. She waves a hand like she was swattin' a bug.

She says me, I don't like them things. They give me the *frissons*.

I can see Chilly noddin', his hand on his chin.

She says see that frog there on the wall? Laurent says he stuffed him but that thing was croakin' last week, I guarantee. I said Earl, come tell that frog to quiet down. Miz Dee-Dee cain't sleep. Earl, him, he don't listen. That frog, neither. If he starts up tonight, y'all knock him on the head. I don't care if Laurent gets mad. He's always *boudé'd,* that boy.

Then she looks at me and says mister, would you go see if you can talk some sense into Earl? He's out there on the porch. I cain't get him outta that doggone ole rockin' chair.

Somethin' about this gives *me* the *frissons*.

Miz Dee-Dee seems a coupla quarts low and not hittin' on all cylinders. But she's fed us good and a man should do what he can to repay a kindness.

I say yes, ma'am, I'll go. You mind if I take one of them lanterns? It's got pitch-dark out.

I also wonder how ole Earl can sit there. I figger there are clouds of mosquitoes out there now.

I grab a light and go out the back door slow, with the lantern ahead of me. Soon as I step out, the lantern starts to flicker. A breeze has sprung up.

The porch is narrow, not more than three boards wide, and built clear along the back of the shack. It's got a rickety railin', which I latch on to, and it shakes just from my touch. It ain't a railin' you'd wanna lean on.

I look down at the end of the porch and see a man sittin' in a chair. He seems to have on a heavy coat and a cap of some kind. He's dressed a bit warm for this weather. I walk over and am about to say hello when my lantern picks up a reflection from Earl's face.

Earl looks about like some of them critters on the wall inside. His face is as brown and leathery as a baseball mitt.

I'd say he's been dead for a while now.

I walk back in.

Miz Dee-Dee says Earl's comin' in?

I say no, ma'am.

She looks at me and then her eyes droop toward the floor.

I say how long has he been like this?

She says I don't know. Miz Dee-Dee loses track of the time. Him and Laurent was always fussin', then one day they didn't fuss no more. Laurent tried to take care of his daddy, and then he run off and I didn't think he was comin' back. But he comes back. He brings his momma some food and fixin's, and he comes talk to his daddy. Not that Laurent always talks sense. Mais, half the time, I dunno what the boy's sayin.

I nod.

She says I'm surprised y'all didn't see him. He left outta here yesterday, polin' his boat.

It takes about two seconds to hit me—oh, yeah, we saw him.

I say it's a big swamp out there, ma'am. When's Laurent comin' back?

She shrugs. She says mais, I dunno. He probably won't be back for a while, though sometimes he surprises me.

This complicates things as I don't want Laurent surprisin' *me*. On the other hand, it's dark and we'd face a long, terrible night in the boat if we leave now. But if we stay, somebody's gotta stand watch.

That breeze gives me a bit of an idea. A fella could sleep on that porch not too worried about mosquitoes. We could pull the pirogue up and stack it on its side, crossways to the dock where a coupla them posts come out of the water. Anybody tryin' to come up to the porch would have to move it and the racket would wake me—I'm a light sleeper.

I say ma'am, as it's got dark, I was hopin' we might be able to draw a bit of water from your cistern and settle out on your porch till daylight, then we could mosey on.

She looks at me, her eyes sad. She says y'all can stay in here. Ain't nobody gonna bother y'all if you do.

I look at Chilly. I say can we talk? Out on the porch?

Chilly nods.

We get through the door and Chilly says Logan, the fool *lives here*!

I say shhh, yeah, I know. But he's gone, and if we leave, we'll have another night in the woods like we did last night.

Chilly says damn!

I tell Chilly of my plan. I say you just lock yourself in there with your gun and we'll be fine.

Chilly looks at me doubtful as a kicked dog. He says you shore?

I smile. I say it's this or the mosquitoes.

He says okay, but this time let's not mess around. If the fool shows up, just shoot him, all right?

I say okay.

He says and what about this Earl character? He won't come in and cut my throat, will he?

I say no, you don't have to worry about Earl.

You shore?

I'm shore.

Me and Chilly pee off opposite sides of the dock. I give him the canteen to fill and he goes in and I hear the door latch. I fetch them gunnysacks from the pirogue and fold them into a bit of a pillow. I find me a spot under the eaves of the porch. I lay back, the double-barrel across my chest.

I drift off but not for long. I start up, thinkin' I've heard a paddle slappin' on water till I realize it's riffles slappin' at the dock.

I go back to sleep but dark things chase me around in strange dreams. I startle up again, thinkin' I've heard footsteps.

But there ain't nobody there.

I doze again and the next thing I know, there's a dim light in the sky and a brisk wind stirrin' and a sound I'm not fond of.

It's rainin'.

I rap on the door soft and, after a while, Chilly opens it.

I say daylight in the swamp, podnah. Time to shove off.

7.

We been paddlin' steady through the slow drizzle for about five hours now. Our clothes are soaked through and I can tell from the look of the sky that this is gonna be one of them all-day rains. At least it's a warm rain, though even a warm rain gets tiresome when you're stuck out in it without a slicker suit and no place to get in out of the wet.

Chilly, bless his heart, managed to fill up my canteen and two ole gallon bleach bottles with water from Miz Dee-Dee's cistern and then we lit out. Chilly wadn't happy when he saw that drizzle, but when I told him the real deal about Earl, he said Logan, maybe we're paddlin' too slow.

When I get to any place that feels a bit safe, I think I'll try to phone the law and have 'em go see about the ole gal. Maybe that's one thing good the law could do.

It's funny how the swamp can look nice and cheery when the sun's pokin' through the cypress tops and paintin' the water gold, and how awful and gloomy it looks in the drippin' rain. It don't help my disposition, nor Chilly's.

Our stomachs have started to grumble again and I've got no idea where our next meal is comin' from. It'll be hard to make a fire on a day like today, even if we got to a place where a fire might be made. If we keep at it all day, we might get fairly close to the settlement at Chenier Atchafalaya by dark. There's a few farms up along the road that leads out of there and we might be able to steal into a barn or corn crib to at least get out of the weather for a bit.

Chilly ain't said a word all mornin', though I know just what he's thinkin'.

I'm thinkin' about the same thing—there ain't much pleasure in bein' an outlaw.

I've kept my eye on my compass 'cause Bayou Snake, though it wanders west, does so when it wants to. There's a lot of long bends that take you north for a while and then south for a while. Plus, there are plenty of false channels to mess you up. We wandered into one and wound up in a dead end a mile or two up the swamp. We had to back all the way out. It's aggravatin' but I figger we're lucky we've just done that once so far.

A scientist fella from the North come down here once and I took him out in a part of this swamp where he wanted to make some pitchers with a fancy camera he brought along. He told me, LaBauve, this place reminds me of the doggone Amazon River. The way he talked about it, with them snakes and crocodiles that are longer than a pirogue and them wild parrots hangin' from every tree, it made me want to go there. He said our swamp was about as wild and pretty, even if we didn't have them big snakes and parrots.

Chilly and me have been pickin' our way through a big grove of cypresses, and up ahead I see what looks like a wide bay. I figger we'll hug the right shore and hope Bayou Snake picks up there on the other side. Otherwise, we'll just keep circlin' till we find the openin'.

We're about to the mouth of the bay when my ears pick up a far-off sound. At first, I think it might be a boat comin' from behind us.

But then I hear it better—a kind of *thwuck, thwuck, thwuck*—and right away I know it's a helicopter, and it's behind us and comin' on fast.

I spy the closest cover—a cove off the bayou with a thick canopy of cypress. I yell to Chilly, we got company. Paddle hard on the left side!

By now, Chilly's heard it, too.

The pirogue comes around hard right and we beat the water as fast as we can. We go scootin' into the cove and squeeze in between a cluster of four or five cypresses. We ain't as deep as we need to be when that whirlybird thunders out of the gray overhead not more than a hunderd feet above the treetops.

I catch a glimpse of her as she roars by.

I see it's one of them choppers that's got pontoons on it.

I also see it's got a big star painted on the side.

My heart's thumpin' like a revved-up diesel.

Them ole boys must be pretty mad about things if they're flyin' around on a nasty day like today. The cloud cover cain't be much more than five hunderd feet above us.

I look deeper into the swamp. There's a giant thicket of *roseaus* about twenty yards away but no cover between this thicket and there. I figger in a pinch we could pull or pole ourselves way up behind them things. It would take pretty fancy flyin' to squeeze in there, even with a helicopter that can land on the water.

The *thwuck* of the chopper fades as quick as it comes.

Chilly says did they see us?

I say I dunno. I saw them, so it's possible. Let's pull in a bit tighter to the center, against the biggest cypress here, and wait a while. If they come back and it sounds like they're gonna land, we can haul for that *roseau* brake over yonder.

I point with my paddle.

Chilly nods.

We sit fidgety and miserable for about ten minutes, the rain drippin' through the trees, and then pick up the sound again.

I look at Chilly and say get ready.

The helicopter thunders overhead again, the wake from the blades boilin' up the water in the channel. I cain't see it but it's so loud I feel my eardrums rattlin'.

I'm hopin' they'll fly on past again, but they don't. It don't take long to realize they're hoverin' close by, just up the bay a bit from us.

Well, if I cain't see them, I figger they cain't see me.

I look at Chilly and he's got his arms up makin' a sign that I read as what now?

I mouth the words sit still. He nods.

I cain't think of what else to do. If we move three foot in any direction, they could spot us.

The chopper sits hoverin' for what seems like five minutes. I feel like I'm bein' pounded by an invisible jackhammer.

I notice Chilly's dropped his paddle behind him and clapped his hands over his ears.

I'd do the same but I've got my paddle in the water, holdin' the boat steady. Then I realize the wash from them chopper blades has started to kick us back toward them *roseau* canes—and the open water in front of 'em.

This won't do.

I dig in with my paddle to stop our slide—a bad move.

Chilly takes it as a sign to head for new cover. He reaches back frantic for his own paddle and leans too hard. The pirogue bucks like a skittish colt.

Next I know we're heavin' out the boat backwards.

The water ain't but chest-deep and I come up first, sputterin' like my ole pickup truck. Chilly boils up a second after me, lookin' around wild and confused till he sees me.

Even over the thumpin' of that chopper I can hear him yell out I'm sorry, Logan! Damn, I'm sorry!

I put my finger up to my lips to shush him and point in the direction of the bay. I can see the pontoons of the helicopter floatin' down feather-slow past the low-hangin' branches of the cypresses.

That sucker's landin' or I'm a blue-eyed snake.

The pirogue's bottom-up 'tween us and the helicopter, and I grab on to my end and motion for Chilly to do the same to his end. I point to a place to the right of us, where the biggest cypress of all stands, and mouth the words over there. Then I point at myself and duck down low with just my head out the water. Chilly figgers it out quick and does the same and we start bottom-walkin' the overturned boat toward the back of that big cypress.

As we go, I see a worrisome sight—them two bleach bottles Chilly filled up are floatin' away, their necks stickin' up white. I've got no idea where my canteen is, or our guns either, for that matter.

We nestle in snug as we can up behind that tree and I peer out around the corner. I see the helicopter settlin' in, stirrin' up a big ruckus of wind on the water. I pull back and step toward Chilly and pull him close and say, in his ear, under the boat, son. Let's go. There'll be an air pocket under there.

I go first, sinkin' down slow and quiet as a cagey gator, and come up in the dark with my head practically bumpin' up against the bottom. I hear a commotion and thump and then Chilly says ow, dammit that hurt, and I reach over and grab his arm and say, quiet as I can, steady there. Let's just settle down and listen. That helicopter has landed close.

I feel like an idgit hidin' with my head in a bucket. I only hope they haven't already seen us.

The *thwuck, thwuck* of the chopper is muffled now but I can still hear it enough to know that them blades are slowin' way down. Pretty soon they stop altogether and a hush comes over the swamp, 'cept for the soft sound of the rain soakin' through the cypress branches and peltin' the open water behind us.

Sound carries good on open water and soon I hear the clankin' of a metal door openin' and feet rustlin' and a voice sayin' Bobby, you shore you saw somethin' out here? And a voice answerin' Voisin, like I said, I ain't shore of anything. I said maybe I caught a flash of what mighta been a pirogue runnin' through them cypresses. But I wouldn't bet my daddy's cane farm on it. Maybe it was a log.

The first voice says shuh, them bastids could be anyplace by now. I cain't believe we're even out here flyin' around on a shitty day like today. And I can tell you another thing—it ain't gonna get no better.

The other says I hear you, podnah. Did I make you fly out here? No. The captain told me to come with you and be your lookout and that's what I'm doin'.

The voices stop and there's more clumpin' and clankin'. If I were guessin', I'd say them ole boys have climbed down onto the pontoons for a better look around.

I guess I'm right.

Bobby, what's that?

What's what?

Over there, floatin' in the water over yonder. That white thing? In fack, two white things.

I don't see 'em, Voisin. What the hell you talkin' about?

Look, look. Over there toward them *roseaus.*

Oh, that? Jugs.

Well?

Well, what?

Well, what are jugs doin' out here?

Voisin, where you been? This is catfish country. Half the people out here are jug fishermen. They empty 'em out, tie a line and hook to the handle, and throw 'em out random and just let 'em float around. Them that's movin' has fish on 'em. Makes it simple to run your lines.

Well, how come these are floatin' wrong way up?

Hell, I dunno. Maybe they ain't fishin' jugs. Maybe they're just litter. A lotta sumbitches throw everything over the side out here.

Things go quiet for a while.

Then the first man says well, Bobby, what's that? Over there, by that big cypress?

The big cypress on the left or the big one on the right?

The right. The one on the left ain't big.

It's pretty big.

Aw, man, they got two cypresses side by side. One's big and one's little. What, you blind?

No, I ain't blind.

Well, you actin' like it. Look at the tree on the right. What's pokin' up over by the end of it?

Hell, Voisin, I don't know. Could be a log. Could be a sunk box of some kind.

Could it be the bottom of a pirogue, Bobby?

Things go quiet for a bit. Then Bobby says hhm, shuh, I dunno. I guess it could be. But we ain't lookin' for a sunk pirogue. We lookin' for one with maybe two fellas in it.

Well, what if that's the pirogue you think you saw?

Well, it cain't be 'cause if I did see a pirogue, I saw it floatin', not sinkin'.

What if it sunk 'tween the time we flew by here and come back?

Well, why would it sink if it was floatin' before?

Damn, Bobby! I dunno. How the the hell would I know? I'm just axin' what you think.

There's quiet again for a pretty good while.

Then the one they call Bobby says it's a log.

Well, maybe we should go check it.

How? You gonna paddle the bird over there?

No.

You gonna swim?

Hell no.

Well, me neither. I already feel like a fool standin' out here in this rain. Look, I got an idea.

What's that, Bobby?

You got some cards?

Cards?

Playin' cards, says Bobby. I know you a gamblin' fool.

Yeah, like you ain't, says Voisin. 'Member that night I took you and them boys for four hundred dollars in *bourree*?

No, Voisin, I done forgot about that, same as I'll bet you forgot about the night I kicked your ass big-time in poker by drawin' a straight flush to your boat. Anyway, you got some cards?

I might have some cards, says Voisin. Who's axin'?

Me, podnah. What the hell we doin' wastin' time and police fuel flyin' around out here for nuttin'? I think we oughta climb back into the cockpit where it's nice and dry and play some guts—kill an hour or two like we coverin' this damn swamp like red aints on syrup and then haul ass back to town.

You know what I think about that, Bobby? I think you finally said somethin' that makes sense today. Let's go.

I hear clumpin' and clangin'. I hear the door open and shut. I hear the engine come on and go 'round slow.

We sit and sit and sit and sit till it's got so stuffy under the pirogue that I'm startin' to get woozy. I reach over to Chilly and whisper we better go up for air. But let's go slow and quiet.

We come up, suckin' in the air like a drink of cold water.

I take a few deep breaths, then peer around the corner.

That chopper's sittin' there, *thwuckin'* away. It seems to have drifted up the bay a bit—just the back end of the tail and part of the pontoons are showin'.

All of a sudden I realize how wet, soggy, and totally beat I am. I look at poor Chilly and he looks like a dog locked out in the rain. We ain't got no choice but to wait.

Thwuck, thwuck, thwuck goes the chopper.

Now and then I hear a whoop over the *thwuck.*

Them ole boys seem to be havin' fun.

We wait and wait and wait some more. The afternoon grows late and the wind and rain pick up and finally I hear a whoop and then the motor rev. The *thwuck* ratchets up quick to a whine and then a roar and the chopper lifts up quick and I see its underbelly, pontoons stickin' out like stiff goose feet.

It drones off and in a minute we're alone in the quiet with our sunk boat and the day fadin' fast.

I look around, takin' inventory, and the only thing I'm shore of is that our guns are somewhere at the bottom of the swamp. My bulleye's gone, as is my canteen. I don't even see a paddle anywhere.

I do manage to spy them water jugs, and a li'l cheap green bucket that held a few rusty tools. They've all floated up hard against that *roseau* patch.

Well, that's somethin'.

Chilly looks at me and I'm guessin' I look about as pathetic as he does.

He says sorry about flippin' us over—

I hold up my hand. I say Chilly, you ain't the first person on earth to have flipped a pirogue. I did it all by myself one night with two big gators in my boat. Same thing—I just reached back to get my water jug and over she went. One of them gators come to and swum right over me, tryin' to get away.

I look around and don't like a single thing about our situation. But I know I gotta act like it ain't no big deal.

I point toward that big cluster of *roseaus* and say we'll bed down in there for the night. Them *roseaus* are so thick that if you bend enough of 'em down, you can sleep high and dry above the water. We'll try to prop up the pirogue on one side and use it as a lean-to. At first light, we'll see if we can find our guns and paddles and then we'll head out.

Chilly says what if we cain't find 'em?

I say oh, we'll find 'em. Them guns ain't crawlin' nowhere—they have to be restin' on the bottom close to where we pitched over. As for our paddles, the wind from that chopper blew everything toward that *roseau* patch. If they've drifted anyplace, I'd guess it's that way. They're wood and they float.

Chilly looks up into the gray, wet sky. He says what if it don't stop rainin'?

I say well, lucky, rain won't kill you.

Chilly nods—like he don't entirely believe me.

He says no way we're both gonna fit under that pirogue to keep outta the rain.

I say prob'ly not.

He says any chance of a fire? Or supper?

I say I got matches in a safe but I doubt there's anything to burn—them green spring *roseaus* won't, that's for shore. As for supper, I doubt it.

He says what about mosquitoes?

I say well, this is the swamp. Maybe this rain will keep 'em away—

Chilly says no, I mean, you ever eat 'em?

I smile. I say not on purpose, though I've swallowed a few by accident.

Chilly looks down like he's thinkin'.

He says are you worried, Logan?

I say about what?

He says oh, I dunno—starvin', drownin', dyin' of thirst. That kinda thing.

I say we ain't gonna drown, and we've got water, and we're hungry but a coupla days away from starvin'. So the first thing we need to do is right the pirogue. Gimme a hand.

Chilly's so strong we do it quick.

He says even if we find our guns, what about the shells. Wet ammo don't shoot, right?

I lie and say you know, sometimes it does. Or sometimes you just need to dry it out for an hour or two and it shoots fine.

We slog and swim our way over to the patch of *roseaus*. I scramble up the bank, mashin' down a place to stand. I grab the bow rope to the pirogue and pull it up behind me. Chilly grabs our water jugs and sloshes up himself.

I look around and say let's beat our way to the back side of this thicket and build us a nest.

These roseaus are thick but they sit on swamp and the ground trembles when we walk. I mash down a thick mat of reeds and pull the pirogue on top of 'em. I flip it over and plop down on the bottom.

Chilly settles in beside me and I feel the pirogue sink down into the spongy ground. I already see water poolin' about my feet. Well, I guess that matches the nice steady rain that's fallin' on our heads.

I say I think we deserve a drink of water, Chilly.

He hands me one jug and keeps the other. We unscrew the caps and drink slow. This might be the one moment of pleasure we'll have all day.

Chilly says so what now?

I say this is home. Let's see if there's a way to turn this boat into a bit of a lean-to.

We scrabble around and come up with two soggy, half-rotted cypress sticks, but they're sturdy enough to prop the boat up on one side. I say Chilly, crawl under there and see what it feels like.

Chilly crawls under and lays on his back, his legs stickin' out.

He says Logan, think about throwin' your mattress in a muddy, stinkin' bayou, then sleepin' on it. Oh, and put a few sticks in it so it digs into your back. That's about how it feels.

I say well, that's good, son. You should sleep fine under there.

He says what about you?

I say I'm gonna stay out here and enjoy the nice weather.

Chilly laughs. He says by the way, if any food comes walkin' your way, would you lemme know?

I say I will.

We go quiet and it gets dark soon. A few mosquitoes buzz out of the swamp but it suddenly starts to rain ferocious and that rain seems to beat them mosquitoes away. I've built up a clump of *roseaus* and I cain't think what else to do but sit in the wet, my head on my lap.

Well, I think, this is about the worst of it.

But a man don't know nuttin' sometimes.

I must've dozed 'cause next I know I hear a crack and see a flash and watch as a zigzag bolt of lightnin' splinters the top of one of them cypresses we hid under. Another bolt follows, strikin' the water and rollin' our way in a ball of fire.

Next I know, the hair's standin' up on my head and I hear Chilly screamin' run, Logan, run!

And I hear the thump of the pirogue as he kicks it away and goes gallopin' forward, blind in the dark.

I feel him rush by me and I rise quick and grab for him, tryin' to pull him down. He's so strong that I'm yanked off my feet but I've broke his momentum. We pitch forward, splashin' hard to the wet, muddy ground.

He's squirmin' to get up but I yell, just stay down, Chilly! Just stay down!

I yell and yell as the lightnin' zips and pops everyplace and I feel the slow fire of current runnin' up my leg.

And I hear Chilly sayin' oh, God, please, I don't wanna die.

8.

I would say that I've never been happier to see a mornin' come, but the mornin' comes just like the last one did—rainy, gray, and miserable.

I find Chilly sleepin' facedown on the *roseaus,* his head cradled in his arms. I go over close to make sure he's just sleepin'.

We had a lotta close calls last night.

I guess that shows a man can sleep almost anywhere if he's half-dead already.

Four times the lightnin' popped within fifty yards of us. It knocked the top out of a second cypress tree in that cluster we was under. Twice I was jolted by current and my heart raced like a butt-shot dog.

I've never heard thunder so loud—I felt like we were pinned down in a war.

I wade on out in the water to about where I figgered we flipped the pirogue yesterday. I pee as I go. No use wastin' time.

When I get to where I'm about waist-deep, I stand around, hopin' I can feel stuff with my foot but I cain't. So I dive down a few times and grope along the bottom. I find my shotgun and the one Chilly took from Uncle and a half a box of shells for my gun. Meely's li'l rifle has gone missin' and I realize I'm too pooped to keep lookin'.

Meely shore was fond of that gun. He won't be happy I've lost it.

I look around and see a clutch of cypress knees and slog over and prop them guns up on 'em just outta the water. I figger we'll get 'em when we leave.

I wade back to the *roseau* patch and find one of the missin' paddles but don't see my canteen anywhere.

I clamber back up the bank just in time to see Chilly lift his head. His eyes droopy and bloodshot. There's raccoon circles 'round 'em.

He says what's for breakfast?

I say the same as dinner.

He says how do you like your water, Logan? Over easy? Scrambled?

I appreciate that Chilly's got a sense of humor. We both know there wadn't nuttin' funny about last night.

I say well, Chilly, the good news is that I've found my gun and yours and some shells. I cain't say they'll shoot right away. I've got one paddle and we still have this drinkin' water. And my ole tool bucket. Didn't lose a single rusted tool. About all we can do is shove off and keep goin' the way we was goin' and hope them fellas in the chopper don't come back for another card game.

Chilly nods. He says did you listen to the weather report this mornin'?

I say no, the radio in the pirogue is broke.

He says I figgered. I was just wonderin' if it was gonna rain all day, and how long it takes before a fella's feet start to rot.

He stares off toward the distance. He says I got it—let's sneak up on a squirrel or a coon or a possum and *then* I'll take off my shoes to air out my feet. You won't need a gun then. Them suckers'll be fallin' out the trees.

I'm too beat to laugh.

We right the pirogue and slip it in the water. Chilly takes the front and I take the rear. I paddle us over to our guns and then we make a tight right turn in the bay.

I'm not scared yet but I *am* worried. It's hard to think jail would be worse than this.

We pick up Bayou Snake at a big meander on the right shore.

If anything, the sky's got darker and the rain's got harder. A wind has kicked up and—of course—it's in our face.

We push on for a coupla hours. Time don't seem to mean much. I try to keep the paddlin' steady but my arms feel like their scoopin' molasses and my neck's killin' me. My head's about as fogged in as the day. Except for redwing blackbirds and a few *gros becs* we ain't seen a single thing to shoot, not that we could shoot anything with our wet guns or cook it if we shot it.

My stomach long ago quit growlin'. It's pretty much barkin' now.

We come pullin' around another bend and hit a short stretch of marsh. I don't like this much, 'cause that marsh ain't nuttin' but low prairie of saw grass and alligator grass. It won't give us cover if we have to make a run for it. I look right and spy a small canal that comes tumblin' out to the left of us. It's a beeline canal, which tells me it was dug for a purpose and when I look down it way in the distance, I spy a structure of some kind.

I point with my paddle and say you see that thing way down there? That's one of them oil-field platforms built up off the water. There could be a pump house up there, and if we can get inside, it wouldn't be a bad place to dry out. At the very least, maybe it sits high enough off the water that we could paddle under it and sit out this rain for a bit. Maybe somebody's strung a trotline down that canal and we could borrow a fish.

Chilly says I ain't got a better plan.

I say the only problem is, once we start down that canal, we're in the open. Plus, I'd bet my bottom dollar that the canal dead-ends back there. Them oil companies don't dig more than they have to. There's always a chance one of them oil-field crewboats will come back here checkin' on things and if we're down at a dead end we're pretty much sittin' *poule d'eaus*. What I know of it, they don't man them things, but they do send fellas out to check on 'em pretty often.

Chilly looks at me. I've got to say he's a sad sight—clothes plastered down to his skin, his ball cap soaked through, a sheet of water runnin' down the bill. He's muddy everywhere.

He says Logan, about now I'd do about anything to get dry. I don't care if we are seen. Bring 'em on—crewboats, helicopters, the law, whoever. What the hell! We gotta figger out how to get the hell outta this swamp.

I nod. I say look, I've already thought about how nice a night in a dry warm jail would be. Jail food sounds delicious about now. The only problem is that it prob'ly wouldn't just be one night.

Chilly looks at me and goes quiet for a bit and says I know that. I'm just sandblasted tired is all.

I say I know. I feel the same. Let's just go down there and see if we can get out of this wet.

I paddle along as fast as my sore arms will let me. About halfway there, I see somethin' else that makes me smile—a trotline strung between some rickety posts set up against the canal bank. Normally, I'd never raid another man's trotline, but there ain't nuttin' normal about now.

I ain't never ate raw catfish but I ain't far from decidin' that I could.

I tell Chilly what I see and he about yelps woo, hoo!

I say well, there ain't no guarantee. I get us to the line and grab one end and start pullin' it up. The first six hooks are empty and I'm about to cuss our poor luck when I feel a tug. I pull harder and the next hook has a fine-lookin' six- or seven-pound *goujon* on it.

Chilly says damn, that fish is better-lookin' than my girlfriend right now.

I reach down careful and get my hand around the back of his head, makin' sure his front fins are held fast by my fingers. Catfish are slippery and if one flips and hits you with one of them fins, you'll swear you've been snakebit.

I take the fish off and toss him down on the floor of the pirogue. I reach around me to get my gator hammer from my tool bucket and knock him once on the head. A fish out of water suffers if you don't do such.

I paddle us over to that platform. It's about what I thought it would be, a tin pump house, not more than about fifteen foot by fifteen foot, restin' on a planked deck set on creosoted pilings about three or four foot above the water. There's an iron ladder that goes up to the deck. I see that the house has a metal door, latched with a padlock.

I'm even gladder now about savin' that tool bucket. A screwdriver and a hammer's a pretty good combination for jimmyin' a padlock.

I paddle the pirogue so my end is up against the ladder and tie us up with a double half hitch. I say hold steady in the boat, Chilly, while I go up and see if I can let us in. What I know of such places, there's usually a catwalk that runs in an L-shape alongside the pumpworks so that a mechanic can get at the pumps and valves and such. That catwalk would make a hard bed but it would be out of the rain.

I climb up with my tools and make short work of that lock. I pull open the door and peer in. The layout's about what I figgered. There's plenty of room for me to stretch out one way, and Chilly to stretch out the other.

Chilly comes up for a look. I slide past him and go back down the ladder to claim that catfish and our guns and shells. I've got no idea what I'm gonna do with him 'cept gut him right away so that even if we cain't figger out how to cook him, he won't spoil, least for a while.

I'm glad to find my pocketknife stayed put in my wet britches pocket. I take it out, flip the cat over, and run the knife up his belly.

I reach in and pull out the entrails and find a treat—this fish's got a coupla big sacs of yellow eggs. I pare out the eggs, a double handful, and lay 'em gentle on the platform, then toss the rest of the guts into the water.

I call out to Chilly and say you want a snack?

He comes out of the pump house and says what?

I say fresh fish eggs.

He says raw?

I say well, I'd prefer 'em deep-fried but I've knowed quite a few ole boys who've eat 'em like this. In some places, they'd call this caviar.

Chilly looks down at the eggs. He says I never thought anything raw would look so good.

I say here, have half. I'm hungry as a broke man's dog.

I slice me off a nice chunk of eggs and, stabbin' 'em with my knife, take a bite. They're a bit slimy goin' down but I gotta say they're not half bad. I remember my Tabasco is in a zipped pocket of my huntin' vest. I take it out and sprinkle the next slug. There ain't nothin' a bit of Tabasco won't improve. This bite goes down a lot better.

Chilly wolfs his down in one gulp.

I wonder if we'll be hungry enough in a while to eat raw fish, too. That would even be a new one for me.

We walk back in the pump house and Chilly says this seems like a pretty comfortable motel but don't you think it's a little warm in here?

I realize he's right. I look at the pumpworks and see a big rust-colored pipe, maybe twelve to fifteen inches in diameter, comin' up through the floor and runnin' the length of the L-shaped walk. It's got some valves and gizmos comin' off of it down at the far end. I put my hand on the pipe and it's hot to the touch.

I say there's the reason. This pipe is either carryin' hot oil comin' right out the ground, or else there's some sort of boilerworks in here. Maybe the oil that comes through here is that gummy kind and they've got to steam it up to get it to flow through the pipeline.

Chilly says well, I guess we can leave the door open, provided we don't get swarmed with mosquitoes.

I say I 'spect we'll have to. Otherwise, we'll be sweatin' like sinners in church.

Then another idea strikes me. I say Chilly, what do you think about steamed catfish?

He says how—I don't—?

I put up my hand. I say all we got to do is figger a way to lash that fish to that hot pipe, first one side, then the other. I'll bet she'll be cooked in an hour or two.

Chilly smiles at me and then looks up, puzzlin' this over. He says we could wash out that ole gunnysack in the pirogue and use that.

I say didn't that fall out the boat, too?

He says no, it was wedged up under a seat.

I say that's a doggone brilliant idea, son. It won't be the fanciest catfish you've ever eat but we won't be eatin' raw fish, neither.

Chilly fetches the sack from the pirogue and I hear him scrubbin' it out good in the bayou. This is what they call sweetwater—the way water gets after it's flowed through untamed marsh. It's black as tea but clear enough so that you can see five, six foot down. I've drunk such water in a pinch. It tastes just like rain.

While Chilly gets the sack, I finish dressin' the fish, takin' off the head and the front fins. Normally, if I had my fish pliers, I'd skin a catfish before cookin' it, but I ain't got 'em, so steamed catfish with the skin on will have to do.

Chilly comes up and I douse the catfish good with Tabasco, then roll it up tight in that sack. I then fetch some twine from my huntin' vest and tie the sacked fish, belly down, to our makeshift cooker.

It don't take long before the warm aroma of catfish rises up. I'm droolin' like a deer dog.

Then Chilly says I got another idea. This is a long pipe. It looks like a pretty good clothes dryer to me.

I have to say I hadn't thought of that.

I say I'm glad I took you along, Chilly. You're a doggone genius. We'll just hang everything on that pipe and it'll get dried out in no time.

Chilly says well, first, I'm gonna take off my shoes and I'm gonna take me a nice hard swim in that bayou with my clothes on. They'll smell better, and so will I. Hell, if we had soap and a razor, we might even come out lookin' respectable.

I say Chilly, I'll bet you a quarter I can beat you in a swimmin' race to the canal bank and back.

He says you're on.

It's a wonder what the promise of food will do to a person's attitude.

We shuck our shoes and go scramblin' out the door, each tryin' to get ahead of the other. Chilly don't even pause. He whoops and then dives in headfirst.

For a guy big as he is, Chilly's light on his feet. He swims strong as an otter, too.

He beats me to the bank, though I manage to make up some time comin' back and we come splashin' wild back to the pirogue and touch it at about the same time.

Chilly says I guess that's a tie and I say I guess it is, too.

Chilly looks at me and for the first time since we've run he looks like the kid he really is. His eyes still got them raccoon circles under 'em but he's laughin'. He says Logan, did you forget to take your billfold outta your britches like I did?

I reach back of me and pat my wet britches. I laugh and say you know,

I hadn't thought about my billfold since we flipped the pirogue. I ain't got but fifteen dollars in it but I guess it'll dry out okay.

He says well, I think I've got seven dollars, but I do have a pitcher of Cassie that I'm fond of. It's prob'ly ruint.

I say well, I guess we'll find out.

We climb up that ladder and go into the pump house and strip down to our skivvies. We drape our wet clothes all up and down that pipe and put our wet shoes up there, too. We take out our wallets and our pitiful amount of money and set them to dryin' too.

That pitcher of Cassie is all washed out though, and I feel bad about that.

He says she'll send me another one. No problem.

I realize how fond I've become of the fact that Chilly's an optimist.

It's still warm in here but about right, actually, for sittin' around in your wet drawers. I look down at my legs and feet and they're pale and wrinkled as a drowned man's. I look out the door, and the sky, if anything, has got blacker and that rain has got harder.

But I smell our catfish steamin' and I don't feel too bad about things.

Chilly and I take a seat with our legs stretched out and our backs against the wall and he says well, we're livin' in luxury now. I think we should name this place the Steam-Pipe Motel.

I say that's a fine name. Mighty fine.

We go quiet and I find myself dozin' off. I see Chilly's head bobbin' up and down the same way. A good nap wouldn't be a bad thing if I wadn't worried about bein' trapped in here by visitors or the law.

I force myself to stay awake. I get up and go flop our catfish over. I settle back in and doze in and out and soon enough I figger it's done. I unwrap it careful from the sack and sit it between us with its belly down and I've got to say it smells pretty doggone good, though a bit fishy. That sack might have somethin' to do with it. Polite people would never eat such a thing but we ain't got that luxury.

I nudge Chilly awake and say dinnertime. That half's your half and this'll be mine. I guess we'll excuse ourselves and eat with our fingers.

I take a pinch, enough so that I can start to strip the skin off, but it's hot and I pull back my hand. I say she'll have to cool off a bit. We wait, but not long, and then go after that catfish and in no time we've picked it clean down to the bones.

Some salt and pepper would've helped, of course. A hot skillet, lard, and cornmeal batter woulda been better.

I say well, if we had some hot coffee and a coupla slices of hot apple pie we wouldn't have a single thing to complain about.

Chilly says you won't hear me complainin'. We could be still sittin' in the pirogue in the rain. Or stuck in the lightnin' on a *roseau* patch. Or wrasslin' with that Laurent back at the crazy lady's.

I look out again and realize another day is startin' to fade. You'd think it'd rained itself out by now but it ain't. Rain starts to rap hard on the tin roof. I feel a blow comin' on.

I say Chilly, given our luck with weather so far, maybe we'll shut that door and let this squall pass. Why don't you rest and I'll keep watch. We'll swap in a coupla hours. Long as it's stormin', I don't see a reason to leave.

Chilly says Logan, I don't think I could get back in that boat right now. But you shore? I could stand guard while you rest.

I say no, you go first. I ain't that sleepy anyway.

Actually, I feel drowsy as a coon sunnin' in a hackberry.

Pretty soon, I hear Chilly snorin' away.

I think I'll just put my head back against the wall and close my eyes and rest without sleepin'.

I guess I ain't much of a sentry 'cause the next thing I know I'm comin' out of a deep fog and I hear somethin' dronin' in the distance and I startle awake wonderin' how long I've been asleep.

It takes me a minute to get my bearin's and when I do, that sound makes perfect sense to me. It's a boat—a crewboat, I'd say—rumblin' down the bayou.

I jump up and nudge Chilly and say quiet, son, I think somebody's comin'.

He looks at me with confused eyes and then focuses and says oh, shit!

I shush him and say I think they're a ways off yet. I'll see.

I go to the door and crack it open and look in the direction of the sound.

It's about nightfall and I see a spotlight sweepin' the water. It's definitely comin' our way. And fast, too.

9.

I think Chilly and me break the record for puttin' on our pants in poor light. For a second, I think we might have a chance to make a run for it. But I hear the throb of that boat and I realize it ain't more'na quarter-mile away and comin' on full speed. If it's one of them oil-field crewboats, they can run forty miles an hour.

It could be the law, too, for all I know.

We're stuck.

I snatch up my double-barrel and toss Uncle's 10-gauge to Chilly and say well, I think we've got to make a stand here.

He says it would help if we had guns that would shoot.

I say maybe they will. Anyway, whoever it is don't know we've got soggy ammo. You take that side of the door and I'll take this one and we'll hope our visitors don't come in shootin'.

One thing I noticed when I come in here—this place has lights, a rack of big reflectors hangin' from the tin ceilin'. The switch is just off to my left. This gives me an idea.

I say Chilly, when the door opens, I'm gonna flip these lights. Maybe it'll discombobulate whoever it is and we can get the drop on 'em.

Chilly looks at me and says you know, as a kid, I loved playin' cowboys and Injuns. But playin' it for real ain't no fun a'tall.

I nod and then press a finger to my lips for quiet and point to myself to show Chilly how I'm gonna scrunch up hard against the wall. He does the same.

In about two minutes we hear the boat slow and come rumblin' up to the deck. Whoever's drivin' it will see our pirogue right away.

Through the crack in the doorframe, I can see that spotlight sweepin' back and forth.

Then the spot goes off and the engine dies and we hear footsteps clankin' up the ladder. It sounds like one person, though there could still be others on the boat.

Suddenly, another light goes on—I'd guess it's a flashlight—and I hear a man say now, what the hell is this? Damn. Either more vandals or Badeaux left the damn lock undone.

Then the flashlight seems to focus right on the door and we hear footsteps comin' on fast. Suddenly the door is flung open and I flick that switch.

Chilly and I step out, guns raised.

There's a guy with one of them big metal flashlights. He's standin' there like a rabbit froze by a bulleye.

I see right away he's got on them coveralls that oil-field companies give to workers.

At least he ain't the police—or carryin' a gun.

I say okay, podnah, just step inside slow and don't cause no problems. We ain't gonna hurt you. We're just two guys a bit down on our luck who needed a place out of the rain.

The man blinks and steps in. Soon as he sees our guns, he's got his hands up.

I say you can put your hands down and we'll put our guns away. Like I said, we're not interested in hurtin' nobody.

I look him over. He's average-sized, about thirty, I'd say, trim but built solid like a man who looks after himself. He's got a crew cut and a mustache.

He says this is a hell of a deal. I come to check on well pressure and I'm met at the door by Jesse James and his gang.

I say if a gang is two I guess we could be a gang. But like I said, we've had a bit of bad luck and spent pretty much a night and a whole day in the rain pushin' that pirogue you see out there. There wadn't any other houses around, so we thought we might borrow this one for tonight. We haven't monkeyed with anything, 'cept that lock.

The man looks around and sees our shirts, shoes, and billfolds laid out on that hot pipe. He sniffs the air. I know he smells that catfish.

He says the brass at Big Tex wouldn't appreciate your problem, but since they're not here, I guess what they don't know won't hurt 'em. I generally don't get in arguments with outlaws with guns, anyway.

He looks at Chilly, who's still got his gun up to his shoulder.

Chilly looks at me and I nod. He lowers the gun. He says I'll put it away if you promise you won't do nuttin' foolish.

The man says podnah, my momma drowned all the dumb ones.

Chilly almost smiles.

For the first time I see a named stitched into his coveralls. The name is Prosperie. That's a pretty common name around these parts but I figger it's worth a question.

I say I don't guess you know a John Prosperie?

The man looks at me funny. He says what's that to you?

I point to his name. I say I know there's prob'ly more than one Prosperie family. But I used to know a trapper who worked the lower part of this swamp down by Catahoula Bayou. Him and me used to hunt together a fair amount.

The man says did he wear a red ball cap, summer and winter, and those white shrimper boots?

I say he did.

He says that was my great uncle. We called him Nonc Jack. What's your name, mister?

I think for a second whether I should tell him. Then I can't think of a reason why I shouldn't.

I say Logan, Logan LaBauve. This here is my friend, Chilly Cox.

The man reaches over and offers Chilly a hand and says I'm J.J. Prosperie—'Ti-John to my friends.

Chilly shakes.

Then he takes my hand. I shake, too.

'Ti-John says I think you might be the fella Nonc spoke about a few times. Said you were a crack shot and one of the best trappers he ever met. Oh, yeah, and a bit of an outlaw. 'Course Nonc didn't always follow the letter of the law himself.

I say well, I take that as a compliment. How is the ole fella, anyway? I ain't seen him in a coon's age.

'Ti-John says he passed away two years ago—the doctors were never quite sure what it was. We found him dead in his pirogue, peaceful as a baby. He was eighty-six and still out polin' that boat, lookin' for the last muskrat in Louisiana.

I say well, I hadn't heard and I'm sorry. He was a good man. And wadn't nobody knew the swamp, or critters, better than your uncle. In fact, it's partly 'cause of him that me and Chilly have got as far as we have on our trip.

He says how so?

I say your uncle showed me a shortcut outta Catahoula Bayou. It runs north and west through a good chunk of Catahoula Swamp.

He says I know it well. You fellas come all that way in a pirogue?

I say well, we been at it for a while. We got caught out in some bad stuff last night.

He says I didn't wanna insult a coupla guys with guns but you do look like Momma Nature's rubbed you hard on her washboard. I can tell you this much. They're a lot of guys who wouldn't try that trip in a mudboat with a fast engine. There's about a million ways to get lost.

I say well, we were countin' on that bein' the case. We had a bit of a problem back a coupla days ago and there's people who'd give ten sacks of crawfish to find us. We've been tryin' hard not to get found.

'Ti-John says the law?

I look him over good. I say you alone in your boat?

He says no, actually. I got John Wayne up on a deck with a rifle waitin' for you boys to come out.

I say you know, 'Ti-John, me and Chilly are a just a bit too beat up to 'preciate jokin' right now.

He smiles. He says look, okay, I'm just an oil-field podnah tryin' to make a livin'. I'm not used to surprises and I don't like 'em very much. But, yeah, I'm alone.

I say well, take a seat and we'll tell you the whole deal.

He don't stop me till I get to the part about cookin' that fish on that hot pipe. He laughs like a *poule d'eau* at that.

I say did you come over from Chenier Atchafalaya, or the other way?

He says the Chenier. I make a big loop out here checkin' wellheads, then run back in.

I say you see any law snoopin' around?

He says come to think of it, I saw a sheriff's patrol car down near the boat launch as I was comin' out. 'Course, that don't mean anything. They come back there now and then on patrol.

I tell him my plan, best as I know it—how I'm hopin' to slip unnoticed up the road from the landin' and get on a highway headed for Mississippi.

'Ti-John nods. He says well, you'll have a hard time slippin' up that road unnoticed. We've got crews comin' in day and night. There's no shoulder and it's deep swamp on one side and, for about half of it, the Coppersaw Canal on the other. And it's ten miles to the highway.

I take in this information and start to puzzle over it. There could be problems with my plan. That seems to happen with my plans, come to think of it.

'Ti-John sees me mullin' this over and says okay, how 'bout this? The engine room of my crewboat's nice and roomy. We can stash your pirogue down there and, if it comes to it, we can stash you down there, too. I come in and out of the landin' all the time and the sheriff's guys would never think to stop me. I'll take you boys a half-mile above the landin' and drop you off. Then I'll come back with my pickup to get you. The pirogue can go up top and I've got one of them camper tops over the bed. You can ride back there and nobody'll know you're there. I can't take you any farther than the highway, but I can at least get you that far.

I look at him and say well, I wouldn't want to get you in trouble with the law on our account. If they did find us hidin' in your boat or in your truck, that wouldn't be good for you. But we're swamp beat and I don't know how many more nights sleepin' rough we could take. This is the first time we've been dry in a while.

'Ti-John smiles. He says first of all, they won't find you. Second, if they do, I'll just say you were two guys who were broke down. Your pirogue was leakin' and I gave you a lift. I know you wouldn't tell 'em any different.

I nod. I say no, that's right. We wouldn't.

I look at Chilly and say so, what do you think, podnah?

Chilly says let's go, Logan. I'm tired of that durned ole wet pirogue. I'm tired of sleepin' on the ground and in the mud. I'm tired of mosquitoes and helicopters chasin' after me. I'm ready to get out of this doggone swamp.

I say well, if the truth be told, I'm ready to get out, too.

I say 'Ti-John, you're a mighty good man. I don't know how I could ever pay you back but if I find a way, I will.

He bats his hand at me. He says no problem, podnah. You just take care of the next fella you find down on his luck. That's how it works. Now, y'all give me about twenty minutes. I've got to log in this station, then we'll get the hell out of here.

I nod. I say okay, Chilly, let's go get that pirogue stowed away.

We square away the pirogue and gather up the stuff we've got dryin' on the pipe and settle in the crewboat cabin, out of the rain. In about twenty minutes 'Ti-John comes aboard. He cranks up them twin diesels and switches on them big spotlights that sit above the bridge. The canal lights up like Mardi Gras. He tells me to go untie the boat and I do. He turns it around and pushes down the throttle and the boat shudders up and soon enough we're speedin' down the canal toward Bayou Snake.

It's still rainin' hard but it don't matter. This boat has got windshield wipers. And we're not havin' to paddle in it.

'Ti-John is some captain. He makes the turn into Bayou Snake at full speed and we go clippin' down the bayou, his spot sweepin' the black waters in front of us. There's somethin' soothin' about the throb of them diesels, or else it's just nice to know where we're goin' for a change.

In the dim light of the cabin, Chilly looks at me and I look at him and we grin.

10.

Maybe it's cause I'd never ridden in such a big boat before. Maybe it's cause for about two hours, I didn't have to worry about where I was goin' or catchin' food or keepin' us out of rain and lightnin' or out of the hands of the law or God knows what else.

But that mighta been the best boat ride I've ever took, and the minute I got off that boat, I missed it.

'Ti-John not only drove us up that tight Chenier Atchafalaya road to the highway but, when we got there, he decided to keep goin'. We caught a twisty ole blacktop country lane that snaked north, more or less the direction we wanna go, and stayed on it a dozen miles or so till we got to a two-bit settlement called Pierre Point. He pointed out a tumbledown beer joint sittin' across from the bayouside and said most of the people who hung out in it were trappers or trotliners or jug fishermen of a kind who had about the same attitude about game wardens and the law as I did. He said if we wanted his opinion, Pierre Point might be a good place to spend a coupla days dryin' out and catchin' up on meals and figgerin' out how to cover the three hundred fifty, four hundred miles to Tupelo.

I about choked when he said four hunderd miles. I had no idea a place in Mississippi could be so far away.

It crossed my mind again that a white man and a colored boy travelin' them highways with guns might stick out like yellow crawfish. I'd imagined us hitchin' up to Mississippi but that actually seems like an idgitotic plan.

'Ti-John dropped us off at the edge of a sugarcane field that sidles up to the big lonesome side lot of the Pierre Point beer joint. We stashed the pirogue and our guns outta sight between two cane rows. He done one other good deed before he left—he took a crisp twenty-dollar bill out of his wallet and give it to us.

A loan, he said. You can pay me back when you come back this way.

I said what if I never do?

He said you will. I think you're good for it.

I shook his hand and said I'll do my level best.

Maybe with such money we could flag down the Greyhound to Mississippi, though I ain't never been on the Greyhound and got no idea what she costs. On the other hand, them law doggies might be sniffin' 'round them buses.

I've been thinkin', too, what I'm gonna do after I get Chilly up there to Tupelo. I feel a powerful need to come back down and check on my boy, though I'm not shore what I'll do if I find him in jail. I've done a pretty good job so far gettin' myself into jail. But I cain't say I'd be any good at gettin' people out. I guess that's a bayou I'll cross when I come to it.

One thing I pretty much know—I'm done with livin' in Catahoula Parish. I've had it with idgits like the Guidrys. I don't need Francis Hebert frownin' down on me one more time. The law down there has got on me like fleas on Patin's coondog and I'll just never get 'em off.

Maybe I'll find Tupelo to my likin', though I know a few Cajun folk who've gone to Mississippi and said Logan, them people up there thump their Bibles like we eat crawfish. There's some places you cain't even drink beer! There's more churches than barrooms!

I dunno—I've opened a Bible a time or two but I ain't never wanted to thump it. And as for givin' up beer and crawfish, you might as well ax a man to give up love. On the other hand, Chilly did tell me that a singin' fella that I heard on the radio a few times named Elvis Presley lives up in Tupelo. I gotta say I liked ole Elvis. I wonder if a fella like me could ever meet Elvis? Far as I know, those who get famous tend to start lookin' for a better class of folk.

I've thought about Florda, too. I don't really know any more about Florda than I do 'bout Mississippi. But one time a gator man from Florda come up to our part of the swamp and looked me up. We've got white alligators in Catahoula Parish—just a handful—and far as I know they're the only white alligators on earth. This fella, Arthur Johns was his name, wanted to see 'em and he'd heard I was one of few people who knew how to find 'em. I took him after he promised he wouldn't try to catch or shoot one. While we was gator lookin', he told me he operated a gator farm and a tourist place in the crook of Florda where he comes from. He axed me if I wanted to come down there and help him run it. I didn't then but maybe I do now. That ole boy said there's beaches in Florda where the sand's white as sugar and the water's bluer than the sky. A swamp man like me has a hard time imaginin' such a thing.

'Course, for all I know, maybe they thump Bibles and outlaw beer down in Florda, too, and I didn't think to ax that fella if they've got crawfish. But that ole boy was a character and liked his beer 'bout as much as I do, so maybe Florda folk are differnt.

Just thinkin' about runnin' up and down the country gettin' to and from all these places makes my head hurt. I didn't realize bein' an outlaw involved so much travelin'.

Right now, I'm thinkin' about supper and how glad I am I don't have to shoot it or skin or steal it. I can tell Chilly feels the same way.

I'm just tryin' to figger out what kind of joint this really is—and whether Chilly and I should try to go in there together.

I look out from where we are across a jumbled-up parkin' lot paved, if you can call it that, with oyster shells. There's a streetlamp throwin' dim yellow light on a buildin' that's leanin' so hard it looks like a breath of wind could knock it over. There's a lit sign above the front door that should say Jax Beer, 'cept the x and the eer are burnt out. There's about ten pickup trucks pulled up hard against a rusty iron railin'. They're all dented or dinged up or rusted out, like they've run into each other at some time or another. I know just the kind of ole boys who drive trucks like that.

Chilly's lookin', too, and it's like he's read my mind. He says you know, it might not be a bad idea if you go in there first—check it out to see if it seems okay, you know what I mean? Just in case there's, say, five or six guys like Junior Guidry sittin' at the bar.

I say that ain't a bad idea. It looks like it could be a rugged kind of place.

Chilly says what if it is? What we gonna do about supper?

I say I s'pect it's the kinda place that at least has snacks—pickled pig's feet and maybe pork skins and some bags of them dried shrimp. I'll load up on stuff and be out of there quick as a mink. Then we'll try to go find someplace to spend the night. Since that rain's quit, we could prob'ly even sleep in this sugarcane field if we have to.

Chilly looks at me like I'm crazy. He says Logan, no offense but I've had enough adventure when it comes to sleepin'. Just find out where the colored people live around here, if there are any. I'll find us a bed for the night or at least a hayloft or corncrib out of the weather. Guaranteed.

I say you know, I think you've struck on a doggone good idea. Now, just wait here and lemme check this out.

I get up and go amblin' across the shell parkin' lot.

There's one thing I'm sorry to see as soon as I hit the door—a sign that says Whites Only. It sits just below a bigger sign, faded and peelin' in spots, that says Noonie's Bar—Welcome.

I've almost got to laugh at that, and would 'cept the whole deal is so doggone ignorant and aggravatin'. I've got the Wild Injun in me and I figger if they knew that, they prob'ly wouldn't let me in, neither.

I'll just rustle up a coupla bags of pork rinds and some drinks and we'll get the heck outta here.

I push through the door and the place is about like I expected. I've been in quite a few saloons, some more beat-up than this. There's a wooden bar along the right wall with stools lined up and a coupla people sippin' beers. There's a coupla them curvy neon beer signs—one says Pearl—over the bar. On the counter, over at the far end, is one of them big ten-gallon jars full of them pig's feet. Usually it's about fifty cents per foot. Them things is mostly fat and salt but I like 'em.

On the far wall is a jukebox playin' soft and some ole boy is standin' there puzzlin' over the songs. There's a Cajun waltz on there now—one I kinda know, I think by some fellas named Balfa who come from the Cajun prairie over west of us. Long ago, me and Elizabeth danced to that song.

Along the left wall are some wooden booths. There are about six or seven guys scrunched up in the one farthest away from me. They're playin' cards—*bourree,* I'd bet. The place is smoky and smells of sawdust and stale beer.

I notice a man behind the bar, a stumpy fella with a thick neck wearin' an apron with a big crawfish across the front. He's talkin' to a guy who, I can tell by the way he's dressed, is a fisherman come right off the boat.

The other person at the bar stands suddenly and stretches and I see it's a woman—a handsome woman, too. She's tall and willowy and dark-complected like somebody who spends a lot of time in the weather. The other thing I notice is that she's got on hip boots.

She does a doggone favor to hip boots, I gotta say that much.

If it weren't for that ignorant sign on the door, this might be the kind of place I could pass an hour or two, or more—sip me some beers, and shoot the breeze with some of the local boys, and find out how the fishin' is and listen to Cajun music on the jukebox.

I walk in and squeeze onto an empty stool 'tween the woman and the man the bartender's talkin' to. The bartender don't bother to look up from his yakkin' but the woman looks at me and smiles. She says y'all did any good out there?

I look her over careful. I'm a believer in first impressions, even though I never make a very good one myself. She's got bright brown eyes of a kind that are full of life and, if I was guessin', a bit of mischief. What she mostly looks like is somebody who's smart and knows what she's about. The way she's dressed, she also looks like a gal who knows her way around the swamp.

I say well, we weren't really fishin'—mostly passin' through on a scoutin' expedition.

Scoutin' fish? The trotliners have been haulin' in some big cats lately. I took one off my line today that weighed thirty-two pounds. A *goujon.*

I say hhm, that's a fine fish. I've only took a few that were better. But, no, actually I mostly hunt gators for a livin', though I do a bit of everything when it comes down to it.

She nods. She says I used to hunt gators years ago, too. But they're fairly scarce up in this part of the swamp—too many hunters. But there's a big stretch of swamp about midway between here and the Catahoula Bayou where I've heard you can still find some big ones. Not too many people hunt it 'cause it's a far run and it's one of the easiest places in the world to get lost.

I say I know that part of the swamp some. We've just come through it.

She says you came all the way from Catahoula?

I say yes, ma'am. In a pirogue.

She says well no wonder you look like you've spent a few days sleepin' rough. I guess you have.

She laughs soft when she says it and I don't take it wrong. For the first time in a while I think about what I must look like—unshaved and rumpled, a fisherman back from a hard trip, or an outlaw on the run. I'm suddenly glad me and Chilly took that swim earlier and at least knocked the mud off our clothes and some of the sweat off our bodies.

The woman sticks out her hand and says I'm Annie, by the way. Annie Ancelet. Most people call me Catfish Annie, or some by my Cajun nickname, *Poisson Mee-noo*.

This makes me laugh. Only Cajuns could come up with such a nickname. *Poisson* is fish and *mee-noo* is the sound a cat makes.

I give her my hand and say I'm Logan.

She's got the firmest grip of any woman I can recall. Her hands are nice and warm.

She says you keep sayin' we. You travelin' with someone?

This ain't a question I was expectin'. I glance around and then look back at her.

I guess you could be fooled easy if you decide too many things just by lookin' at a person. But I find myself sayin'—though not too loud—I am. My podnah Chilly is outside. He's a young guy and about as good a fella as you could meet. But he's colored and, well, I saw that sign out front on the door. Now, myself, I don't agree with that sign and under different circumstances I might have said a word or two about it to somebody. But we're just passin' through and don't care to stir up the *roo-garou*. So I figgered I'd just get us some drinks and maybe somethin' to eat, then be on my way.

Annie looks at me careful and then rolls her eyes. She says you know what? I'm sorry about that sign, too. I've told Noonie there—she points to the bartender, who's still gabbin' away—to take it down, but he's a hard-headed cuss. He owns the bar but I own the buildin', such as it is. I'm his landlady.

Then she nudges me on the shoulder and leans close.

Somethin' about her leanin' close raises the hackles on my neck, but not in a bad way. She smells like a breeze comin' off a freshwater lake.

She says let me tell you a little secret about ole Noonie here. He's got a colored girlfriend—a young gal, cute as she can be. She comes in the afternoon when it's slow and nobody's around. They drink beer and dance to the jukebox and do who knows what else. Everybody in Pierre Point seems to know this except maybe Noonie's wife, 'cause if she did she'd come in and take a hatchet to his hard head. Lemme tell you somethin' else. His girlfriend's brother? He's sittin' over there playin' *bourree* with his pod-nahs. He's one of the best fishermen on this whole side of the swamp. Okay, he's one of those light-skinned colored people who could pass for white in town but everybody knows who he is. He's a Daigle—Rabbit they call him—and belongs to the big family they call the Daigles *noirs* as opposed to the other big family out here they call the Daigles *blancs*. They've all got the same great-great-grandpa, ole Anise Daigle, who bought up a big chunk of this swamp before the Civil War and passed it down to his relatives, who eventually found oil on it. Those that have hung on to their money are way past rich, though you might not know it from lookin' at 'em. Half of 'em still live back in the swamps in some beat-up cypress shacks, though they do have mighty fine boats. Now Anise's first family was white. He had six children. But when he was in his sixties, his wife died and he took up with the young colored woman who'd been the housekeeper. He had several children with her—he never tried to hide it.

When Anise died, he took care of all his kids, white and black. Anyway, Rabbit talks French and drives a pickup with one of those squirrel tails on the radio antenna just like every other guy on this bayou has. Noonie's like a lot of the swamp rats livin' out here. Now, Rabbit, 'cause he looks white and talks Cajun and dances to "Jolie Blonde," is considered a Cajun. The black folks from the prairie who pass through here on the way up to Mississippi to work the truck crops are considered trouble-makin' Creoles and they get shown that sign if they try to come through the door. It's stump-headed ignorance, Logan, but I've given up arguin' with Noonie over it. You know what they say—you can always tell a Cajun, but you can't tell him much.

She laughs when she says this. I laugh too.

Noonie, the bar owner, hears us laughin' and looks up. He sees Annie, then me, and he smiles bright. He says hey there, mister, I didn't see you come in. I was tryin' to get the scoop on crawfish season from my bro' Boudreaux here. The water's been low this year and I'm kinda worried we gonna end up short. I do a damn nice boiled crawfish business in season and it's gonna be bad if them mudbugs is scarce. What can I get you?

I look Noonie over. He don't necessarily look like a bad sort, though I wouldn't say he's the sharpest saw on the wall.

I look at Annie and then at him and say well, I just need some drinks to go, if you don't mind, and maybe a few bags of them pork skins you got hangin' back there. And maybe a couple of them pig's feet, too.

Noonie says shore enough. How many of each?

I say I'll have one Jax, three *pop rouges,* and six bags of pork rinds. Two pig's feet. If you could spare a paper sack to put 'em in, I'd appreciate it.

He says no problem, podnah.

Noonie turns to fetch my order and Annie says Logan, you know, you don't have to run off like this. Really, if you want me to, I could have a word with Noonie about your friend. I could just say you're both ole podnahs of mine and I know then he wouldn't care.

I nod and say well, that's awfully nice of you. Problem is, Chilly will see that sign and it'll just make him feel bad. He's already got hisself in some trouble on my behalf and I don't wanna cause him any more. We prob'ly should get on, anyway. We need to figger a way to get on up to Mississippi, where Chilly's got kin he can stay with.

Annie says what sort of trouble?

I glance over at Noonie and see he's bent halfway down into the beer cooler, rummagin' around. I look back at Annie and I hesitate.

She says look, I'm not tryin' to be nosy. You don't have to tell me a thing. You just look like somebody who might need a hand.

I've got to smile at that. I say well, if you catch catfish as well as you can read a man, you must be some fisherman.

Annie laughs and I remember back to what 'Ti-John said about the way people around here feel about the law. I tell her a quick version of the deal that got us here.

She looks down at the floor and then looks up at me, her mouth pursed, and says that's just an awful story, Logan. You must be worried sick about your boy. What did you say his name is?

I say his proper name is Emile but we've always called him Meely. He's quick on his feet and thinks fast and I doubt that the police are so low that they'd harm a boy. But you never know. I'm shore they've carried him to jail, which I regret. I wanted him to come with us but he was beat and his leg was broke and hurtin' and he said somebody should stay and stick up for our side. But I couldn't stand the thought of jail myself—'specially knowin' it would be the lies of them Guidrys that got me there. 'Course, I'm a bit experienced with jail already. Me and beer's got ourselves throwed in jail a few times, and arguin' with them game wardens has got me put in there once or twice besides. I ain't never been in more than a day, but I'm a mink in a trap about to gnaw off a leg after about two hours. I was just afraid of what I might do if I got locked up serious when all I did was rescue my boy from some galoots. Anyway, soon as I can get Chilly up safe to Tupelo, where he's got kin, I'm comin' back down to check on Meely. Not that I'll be able to do him any good. If they catch me, we'll be in a worse fix.

As I say this, I see Noonie comin' back with my order. I realize how much I've said in so little time and somethin' about that surprises me. I stand up from my stool and reach for my billfold to pay. Annie stops me and says no, no, you put away your wallet and hang on to your money. This one's on me.

I'm about to say she shouldn't be doin' that and I'm about to think maybe it wouldn't be so bad to talk to Annie some more if only I could get Chilly in here comfortable when there's a commotion at the door and I see a thing I don't expect.

Chilly's come in.

But he's got his hands up and a man wearin' a tall hat and holdin' a pistol is walkin' behind him.

11.

Hey, y'all, look what I found me, the man says. One of them no-account, cabbage-pickin' out-of-towners loiterin' right here on the side of Noonie's lot. Man, you'd think the word would get around that these people ain't welcome here.

I can see the man clear for the first time. He's a short fella, skinny as a *gros bec,* with a pinched face and bowed legs. His hat's about the biggest thing about him, 'cept for the gun he's got pointed at Chilly.

As pistols go, it's a mighty, mighty pistol.

Chilly's lookin' straight at me. It's one of them looks that says *do somethin', Logan.*

Not havin' a gun, or knowin' anything about this fella or much about this place, puts me at some disadvantage. Even if I could get over there and take this character's gun away, we'd still be in a mess. For all I know, that knot of fellas playin' *bourree* might come over to try to help him out.

What if they're all carryin' guns, too?

That's when Annie steps off her stool and speaks up in a voice that means business.

She says doggone it, Lester Benoit, put your gun away and stop actin' like you're the stud duck in the puddle. That there is my friend Chilly and he's an alligator hunter from way over at the Catahoula end of the swamp and him and my podnah Logan here are just out on a scoutin' mission. These are fellas who earn their money 'bout the same way we do out here, and there's no cause for you to be comin' down on this man like the cav-alry. Your momma taught you better than that.

I see ole Lester look up. He goes boiled-crab red but he don't put the gun away.

He says now, Catfish, you stay out of the law. Ladies should know their place. This fella had a whole pile of guns stashed in a pirogue hidden in the canefields. But I got the drop on him before he could pull one on me. So—

Chilly, soundin' annoyed, says pull a gun? Mister, you're crazy. I was sittin' there mindin' my business. You didn't get the drop on me. You come up like you was gonna ax a question and—

Annie pops out laughin'. Stay out of the law? Lester, c'mon, you're a *special deputy.* Everybody knows what that means.

Lester just turns one more shade of red.

Annie turns to me and gives me a wink. She says Logan, I'm not posi-tive about your parish, but over here in St. Madeline Parish *special deputy* is one of those titles you get if you give more than fifty dollars to the sher-iff's election campaign.

She turns back to Lester. And I happen to know it wasn't even you who gave the fifty dollars, Lester. It was your rich uncle, Roy.

Then she says as for ladies stayin' out of things, why don't you tell Logan here what happened last time Pierre Point held a skeet shoot? As I recall, you came in second and I believe, well—

Annie then looks around and says uh, Noonie, who came first?

Noonie's lookin' this situation over good. He says I think that would be you, Catfish. As I recall, you took ole Daniel Boone there to the ninth round and he missed two. You never missed one. Of course, you never do.

Noonie looks at me serious. He says I mean it, she don't. *Poisson Mee-noo* never, ever misses.

Lester looks around and by this time everybody in the saloon is lookin' at him. He sputters doggone it, Catfish, why you so hard on a man!

He puts his pistol in his holster, though it does take him a few tries to get it right.

Annie walks over and snatches off Lester's hat.

I see Lester's plumb bald.

With her free hand, Annie goes to shinin' up Lester's head.

I can tell that ole Lester don't know whether he's s'posed to laugh or get mad.

I see Chilly lookin' back at Lester, still not shore whether he's actually free to go. He decides he is and comes walkin' toward me.

Lester is sputterin' somethin' fierce. He stomps his foot. He says it's not over, Catfish! This ain't fair! I was just tryin' to uphold the law and keep—

Annie looks at me and Chilly, her hands throwed up. She says y'all have to excuse Lester, here. He practices a strange form of Pierre Point hospitality. He's actually a sweet fella most of the time. Ain't that right, boys?

Some of them fellas playin' cards at that table look up. One of 'em says aw, hell, Lester's so sweet his nickname is Sugar Cane.

Lester says Annie, see what you started?

The fella says just don't try to wrassle him. Ain't nobody on this bayou wants to wrassle Lester no more. He don't look like Dick the Bruiser on the TV, but he is. He shore in hell is.

I look at Lester and he resembles a wrassler about like a chicken resembles a bulldog.

Annie says Lester, come over here and get introduced properly to my friends.

Lester's lookin' sheepish but he ambles over, walkin' like a bow-legged movie cowboy.

Annie tells who we are. Lester's grinnin' now. He says how y'all doin', fellas?

He looks up at Chilly. He says aw, I hope you're not sore.

Chilly looks at me like he don't know what to say.

I say Lester, we've come a long way and had us some bad luck with mosquitoes and weather and such, so ole Chilly here ain't his usual cheerful self and prob'ly feels a bit sensitive about havin' a gun pointed at him. But if Annie here vouches for you, then it's nice to meet you, too.

I give Lester my hand and we shake. Just by that, I can tell Lester's stronger than he looks.

He offers his hand to Chilly. He says no hard feelin's, podnah?

Chilly shakes his head and sticks out his hand. There's the beginnin' of a grin on his face. He says pleased to meetcha, Lester.

Lester says awright, Chilly! How 'bout y'all have a beer? On me.

I say shore, I'll take one.

Annie says I'll take one, too, Lester—a Jax.

Chilly says I'll have a *pop rouge,* if you don't mind.

Lester orders and Noonie rustles up our drinks. We go to sippin' but Lester 'bout gulps his beer down. He says another one, Noonie.

Noonie says you better slow down, Lester. I know you 'bout to get in a wrasslin' mood.

Lester says maybe I am, maybe I ain't.

Noonie delivers the second beer and Lester goes to workin' hard on that one.

I nudge Annie. I say what's this 'bout Lester and wrasslin'?

She says you know, he doesn't look like much but about twenty years ago he was state champion at ninety-seven pounds. He *was* the Pierre Point High School wrasslin' team. His claim to fame is that one time he wrestled the entire team from Our Lady of Grand Isle High School down the road here and he beat every kid in every weight class above him except some giant named Guidroz. And that kid weighed about three hundred pounds.

He weighed two ninety-four, says Lester.

He then crooks his arm to show a muscle.

Whatever, says Noonie, chimin' in. Lester woulda prob'ly beat that ole boy too 'cept he was tired and the galoot got Lester in some hold and then stumbled and fell on top of him. Shuh, we thought we'd lost Lester that time.

He cheated is what it was, says Lester. That hold wadn't legal. That sumbitch about squashed me.

Lester looks over at Annie sheepish. He say oh, Catfish, sorry about the cuss word.

Annie says don't worry about it, Lester. I'll try not to fall over.

He takes another deep swig of beer and drains his can. He says but you know what? I think one of your podnahs here oughta wrassle me.

He points to Chilly. The big one there would be best.

I look at Annie. I say is he serious?

Annie gets a funny look in her eyes—a look that could be mischief. She says oh, Lester's very serious.

She leans in close to me and whispers I feel like certain kinds of men need to be humored sometime. If you know what I mean.

I'm not entirely shore what Annie means. But I like somethin' about the way she's said it. Or maybe it's just her leanin' in close that I like.

I look over at Chilly, who's sippin' his *pop rouge* real slow—like he might not ever get another one.

He comes over to me and says, quiet, I'm not gonna wrassle that li'l fella. I'd squash him like a stink bug.

Lester says y'all talkin' 'bout me over there?

Chilly looks up sheepish. He says aw, no, Lester. We're just tryin' to figger out which one of us wants to go first. And it's Logan here.

Lester says aw right!

I say thanks a lot, Chilly. Maybe I shoulda left you back there in that *roseau* patch.

Annie laughs. She says trust me, it'll be easier if we just get this over with.

I turn to see that Lester has took off his gun belt and laid it on the bar and is now strippin' off his shirt. I guess I should do the same. I take off my huntin' vest and shirt and lay 'em over my bar stool.

Annie's lookin' me over good. I realize that's pretty much okay with me.

Noonie looks at me like this is somethin' that goes on here every day. Maybe it is.

I go out to face Lester. He ain't much bigger'n my boy Meely and it's hard to see how I won't be able to pin him quick.

Just goes to show you what a man knows.

Lester moves in fast as an oiled cat, grabs me by the arm, and I'm flung over his back on the floor faster than a *choupique* takes a shiner. Lester pins me and maybe I could throw him off but I ain't inclined to even try. I hear Noonie bangin' on the bar one-two-three, Lester!

Lester hops up and holds up both hands like I've seen them TV wrasslers do. He goes hoppin' up and down like a bow-legged crow. Them boys in that *bourree* game are clappin' and whistlin' and snortin'.

I pick myself up off the floor feelin' a bit like a man who's been bit by his best rabbit dog.

Annie looks at me with a wide grin. When I dust myself off and get over there, Lester announces I want that Chilly one next. C'mon, galoot!

Chilly looks around. By this time, all them ole boys who'd been playin' *bourree* have got up and walked over. They're all lookin' at Chilly.

I can tell Chilly don't know whether to be embarrassed or annoyed at bein' called a galoot.

He looks at Lester. He says look, podnah, I don't want nobody to get hurt.

Lester cackles. He says well, don't worry, Mr. Chilly man. I won't hurt you!

The whole bar busts out laughin' then.

Chilly nods but he don't grin. He takes off his shirt real slow and after he does he does a few flexes hisself.

I have to say Chilly might be the strongest-lookin' guy I've ever seen.

Lester don't look ruffled, though. He looks calm as one of them hell diver ducks in a hurricane.

Chilly walks out to the center of the floor and goes down into a wrasslin' crouch. He says Lester, oh, by the way, I gotta tell you somethin'. I'm state champ up at my school in the two-hundred-thirty-pound class.

Lester nods, then looks down like he's thinkin' somethin' over.

Then he comes flyin' at Chilly like a rooster with his spurs up. He tries for that same hold he got me with. 'Cept one thing is different. Chilly just steps aside and Lester stumbles over Chilly's feet and goes sprawlin' across the wood floor.

Them podnahs from the *bourree* game all crouch down around him and start yellin'. C'mon, Lester! Get up and show that fella what you're made of! Go on, podnah!

Lester gets up and dusts himself off and gets back into his crouch. Chilly does the same. They circle around two or three times and Lester darts in again like a blur.

This time he dives between Chilly's legs and then somehow bucks himself up as he goes under.

Chilly's like a shortstop who's just let a hot grounder get through his legs.

Lester flippin' up like he does knocks Chilly forward and he sprawls onto his belly. Lester's atop him in no time.

Noonie starts bangin' on the bar but at two, Chilly, realizin' he'll be pinned, bucks like a rodeo bull.

Lester is flung off like a horsefly and goes floppin' on his belly toward the front door.

Chilly springs up chicken quick before Lester can recover, but instead of going for a pin, he reaches down and grabs Lester by the back of his belt. He lifts him up and then, lookin' around, spies somethin' on the wall to the left of the front door.

It's a metal hat rack mounted on a big plate, and screwed into the wall. Chilly walks over and hangs Lester up by his belt.

Lester's flappin' his arms somethin' fierce. He says no fair, podnah! No fair! This ain't wrasslin'!

Chilly is grinnin' now. He says okay, Lester, here's the deal. It's a draw, what you say? You got me once, I got you once. How's that?

No fair! Lester says again. No fair a'tall!

Lester keeps tryin' to reach behind to get a purchase on the wall so he can unhook himself. But it ain't workin'.

Annie walks over. She says Lester, you done good, son. Look at this guy—he's three times your size. And you just about pinned him. Didn't he, boys?

Noonie and them others all say oh, yeah, Lester. Oh, yeah.

Lester's still flappin', but not as hard.

He says I did, didn't I? I about pinned ole Chilly. Okay, let me down. It's a draw. I'm gonna buy this podnah a beer.

Chilly helps Lester down. He dusts himself off and says get this man a *pop rouge,* Noonie, and get me another Jax.

Noonie says comin' right up. And this round is on me.

I hear them guys from the *bourree* game say our round, too?

Noonie shakes his head like he might be disgusted but you can tell he ain't really. He says yeah, why not. The whole lot of you freeloadin' sumbitches. You too, Annie, you too, Logan. And yeah, you, too, Boudreaux. In fack, why don't we invite the whole damn bayou to come down and join us? On me!

Annie laughs. She says I'll call 'em, Noonie, if you're serious.

Noonie shakes his head, like he might be disgusted again. He says hell no, I ain't serious. It's enough I got this pack of leeches spongin' off me.

Noonie starts to rustle up that round of drinks and Annie goes off to talk to Lester.

Chilly leans over and says Logan, you get this whole deal? You understand why a man who puts a sign on a door like that wants to buy me a *pop rouge?*

I say no, I wish I did but I honestly don't.

I tell Chilly what Annie's told me—about Noonie's girlfriend.

Chilly nods again and it's a serious nod. He says doggone it, white people are weird.

I say that's another thing you and me can agree on, Chilly.

Annie comes over about the time Noonie delivers our drinks. She's ordered a whiskey and soda herself. We clink cans and glasses and Catfish says look, I know y'all are hungry. When we're done here, why don't we all pile into my wagon and go to my house? I cooked up a big turtle *sauce piquante* yesterday and it's just sittin' in the icebox waitin' for somebody to eat it.

I can see Chilly's face has lit up and mine prob'ly has, too. I say well, Annie, that's awful nice of you but you shore you want us swamp rats invadin' your house?

She says well, Logan, true, I don't normally pick up strays, but this is your lucky day. Anyway, some of my best friends are swamp rats—come to think of it, all of 'em are.

We sip our drinks slow and talk about fishin' and then Annie tells Noonie we're goin'. She says goodbye to Lester and them *bourree* boys. They all come over in a knot and shake our hands.

We go out the door, and as it slams shut behind us, Chilly says oh, wait. One more thing.

He turns around and gets his hand on that Whites Only sign and pries it off the wall like some men would peel a banana, then tucks it under his shirt.

A souvenir, he says. When I get up to Tupelo, I'm gonna tack it to my aunt's ole outhouse. She'll get a laugh outta that.

We go find Annie's car—it's a new-lookin' Ford station wagon, actually—and she pulls up to our pirogue. We load up our stuff and off we go.

12.

Here we are, gents, says Annie. Home sweet home.

We've been rattlin' up the bumpy, crooked Pierre Point Road for about twenty minutes when Annie slows her wagon and pulls into a narrow shell driveway marked by a stand of big cypresses. The wagon bounces through a couple of potholes filled up by the recent rain, then Annie turns hard right into a tight blacktopped space just wide enough for the wagon.

It's dark out here in the country and I don't see a house anywhere, though I do see about a million stars crammin' the sky. Annie reaches down under her seat and comes up with a flashlight. She switches it on and says we've got a bit of a walk.

We pile out of the wagon and she tells us not to worry about the guns or the pirogue, they'll be fine out here. We follow Catfish, her light makin' crazy circles on the ground in front of her. We come to a set of narrow wooden steps with a gate at the top. She looks back at us, keepin' the light ahead of her, and says it's single file up to the house. This boardwalk makes a couple of zigs and zags, so watch your step. The railin's are in pretty good shape but, still, I don't want anyone fallin' into the swamp.

We push through the gate and go cloppin' along the narrow walkway. As we walk, Annie says when we built this house—my husband Luke and I—we wanted a view of the bayou, but we also wanted to keep every possible tree on our property. So we set the house up on stilts at the edge of the treeline and built this walkway through the cypresses to connect us to the road. It's a bit inconvenient to be luggin' groceries out here, but we saved every last cypress.

About a hunderd yards later, we come upon another gate. Annie pushes through that one and we find ourselves on a broad porch—I guess it's actually a deck—that seems to go clear around her house. There's a dim yellow light atop a door and about a million bugs buzzin' 'round it, the kind my boy Meely calls tickle bugs. But 'tween that and the starlit sky and a moon just startin' to rise in the distance, I can make things out pretty good.

Annie has a nice house, built out of what I'd guess is rough cypress left to weather. It's two stories, with lots of windows and, when my eyes adjust more, I can see it's set right over the bayou. It would be the kind of house a rich person with simple tastes might build. I know Elizabeth would'a loved it.

About then I hear a terrible racket—the deep bawlin' of dogs close by.

Next, I hear 'em scramblin' our way, paws clickin' on the wood deck.

Annie hollers oh, hush, pups, it's just me. C'mon, Duke, c'mon, Daisy, settle down.

I look and see two giant dogs roundin' the corner. When they get to Annie, they jump up on her and just about knock her over.

They're good dogs, I can already tell—full of dog kisses.

Annie says boys, meet my family, Duke and Daisy.

The dogs look over at us, like they've just understood every word Annie said, and they come boundin' over. One of 'em hops up on me and puts his paws on my shoulder. The other one has hopped up on Chilly.

I say steady there, pooch. I don't think I've ever danced with a dog before.

That dog licks my face 'fore I can stop it.

Annie laughs. She says Daisy and Duke, get down and mind your manners. You know better than that.

Them dogs do just what she tells 'em and go waggin' over to her again.

Chilly says I've seen big dogs before but none this big. What kind of dogs are they, anyway?

Annie says Great Danes. They're big and goofy and they can make a lot of noise but they wouldn't hurt a fly, though any strangers comin' out here wouldn't necessarily know that.

Chilly says yeah, well, I wouldn't care to be a flea on a dog that big. You could get lost in the tail and never find your way to the head.

Annie laughs. She says let's go in and have some supper.

We go through the door, the dogs followin' us in, and Annie switches on a coupla lights. The inside of her house looks even better than the outside. We're standin' in a narrow hall that leads out to a big, bright open room with high ceilin's and a coupla fans hangin' down. Over across the way is a fireplace. There's an ole-timey gun stuck up on the wall above an oak mantel and a coupla of stuffed wood ducks, froze in flight, on either side. Whoever was the taxidermist did a whole lot better job than Laurent back at poor Miz Dee-Dee's. Them things look real. I look around more and see the floors are wood and shellacked bright. There's a coupla comfortable-lookin' sofas out in the middle of the room facin' each other, plus an easy chair, all sittin' on a rug of a kind I've never seen before. It's a rug of fancy patterns and colors I couldn't come close to namin'. There's a long, wood coffee table in the middle. On it sits a carved painted decoy that, good as I can make it out, looks like a green-winged teal.

It's not too hard to see that, in the winter, a person could crank up that fireplace and sit in the easy chair and think pretty easy thoughts, maybe with a glass of whiskey in his hand.

I say well, Annie, you shore got a nice place here.

She says thank you, Logan. Luke designed it. He wasn't really an architect—in fact, Luke never finished high school—but he was good at a lot of things. So he drew out the plans and built a lot of it himself.

I look around wonderin' if we'll get to meet Luke.

Annie seems to again read what I'm thinkin'. She says oh, well, I guess I should explain, Luke's gone. He died seven years ago. After he died, I thought about sellin' this place—I wasn't sure I could live here anymore. So much of *us* was tied up in it. But another part of me couldn't bear to part with it. Plus, my boys—they're men now, actually, and both off in the Army—loved the house so much they'd've been heartbroken if I'd sold it. So, I thought about it long enough to talk myself into keepin' it.

I say well, I'm awful sorry about Luke. Do you mind if I ax what happened?

Annie looks at me and Chilly and I see somethin' sad come in her eyes and I think I've done a wrong thing by axin' that question.

She says Logan, he was struck by lightning one day runnin' a trotline. It was one of those freak thunderstorms that flashed up out of the north.

I say I know exactly the kind—me and Chilly got a taste of one of those ourselves.

She nods. He was caught out on open water in our small jo-boat and I think he was tryin' to run for cover. At least it was instant, or so the doctors said.

It's hard to know what to say even though I know I should say somethin'. But I'm not good at such times.

She says you know what's stupid about it? Luke didn't have to fish. He had family money—oil and gas royalities on about a thousand acres of swamp passed down by his trapper great-grandfather. We weren't exactly rich but we could've lived comfortably off the royalties. But neither Luke nor I could imagine our life without our work, and our work has always been out there, on the water, in the swamps. I guess mine still is.

Things go quiet, then I see Annie shake her head like she's shakin' a thought out of it. She smiles and says okay, here's the deal. I don't allow any dirty dogs at my table, or men, either. Chilly, let me show you the shower down here. Logan, you can use the one in my bedroom upstairs. There are plenty of towels in the cabinet below both sinks and plenty of hot water and soap. You gents clean up and I'll get the *sauce piquante* on the stove, and a big pot of rice, too. Maybe fix a salad or slaw.

Somehow I find this a bit awkward but Chilly says Annie, I've been dreamin' of a hot shower ever since we left Catahoula Bayou. Momma and Daddy put in one of them shower stalls just last year and it's about the best thing that's ever happened to me.

I'm feelin' a bit embarrassed, as I myself have never been in one of the durned things. We'd always just stuck to a bathtub at home.

Annie goes off to a back room to pull off her hip boots, then she takes Chilly over to the downstairs shower and points the way. She comes back and says Logan, you follow me.

The stairs are them fancy spiral kind made of wood and I go cloppin' up behind her in my ole work boots.

Maybe I shouldn't be noticin' such things but Annie is wearin' blue jeans, and what I thought about her when I first saw her stand up at Noonie's in them hip boots is definitely right.

I'd guess Annie's in her early forties—about my age—but she wears her age well and is nicely made.

When we get upstairs, I see her bedroom is about twice the size of any I've ever seen, though, true, I ain't spent a lot of time visitin' people's houses. She draws open some white accordion doors and says here's the shower—towels are under that cabinet. Now hold on just a second.

She walks over to another door and opens it and I can see it's a closet. She rummages around for a bit and then comes out with a T-shirt, a long-sleeved shirt that's green, and a pair of dungarees. There's even a pair of boxer shorts. She comes over to me and holds them up real close like she's measurin' me, which I have to say for some reason gives me the *frissons* again, though not of a bad kind. Them clothes have a friendly smell, though I couldn't tell you just what that smell is.

She says these should be pretty close to your size. You're a trim one. You either walk a lot, or you lay off the red beans and rice.

I laugh. I say well, I do walk a lot and, as for eatin', I tend to eat what's handy.

She says and what would that be in your house?

I gotta think about that. I say my boy Meely's a pretty good cook, though I'm not always there to eat what he makes. I myself have been known to make a pretty good *sauce piquante,* though I don't cook often.

She says well, now I know I've got an expert eatin' my *sauce piquante.*

Annie stops for a second and says and what of Meely's mother? I don't mean to pry but—

I say unfortunately, she died some years ago. I guess a year before your husband did.

She says oh, Logan, I'm sorry, I—

I put up my hand. I say you could'na known about that any more than I coulda known about Luke.

She says do you mind tellin' me what happened?

This time it's me starin' up at the ceilin'. I say lemme get cleaned up and maybe we can talk about it after supper.

Annie nods. She says have a nice shower and I'll see you downstairs. And, oh, by the way, if you look in one of those side drawers, you'll find an unopened toothbrush. In fact, there are a couple in there—lemme fetch one for Chilly.

She goes into the bathroom and rummages through a drawer and comes up with the toothbrush. She walks past me out of the room. I hear her cloppin' down the stairs.

I go into the bathroom, carryin' the clothes she give me. I close those accordion doors, though they don't close like most doors I know about. I set the clothes across a stool and undress and slide open a glass door to the shower. There's a funny-lookin' handle that I guess controls the water. I fiddle with it till the water gets nice and hot and step in.

I have to say it feels pretty good. I guess a man could get used to a hot shower same as he could get used to a warm fireplace. Prob'ly lots of other comforts, too.

I realize how I've got used to livin' without much comfort at all.

After a few minutes I turn off the water and step out onto a mat and grab my towel. It's nice and thick—not like the kind me and Meely use that we get out of soap-powder boxes. I lay the towel aside and put on them clean clothes. They fit okay. The jeans are a tad loose, the shirt just right. I look in the mirror and realize if I had a razor, I could spruce myself up good. Sometimes I don't look too bad spruced up.

I run my old comb through my hair, find that toothbrush she told me about, brush my teeth, and amble on downstairs.

The smell of that *sauce piquante* meets me about halfway down the stairs and I have to say it smells doggone good. I wander toward the direction of the smell and end up in a nice round room with windows everywhere. Chilly's already sittin' at a table set with a blue checkered tablecloth, talkin' away to Annie.

We pile up our plates with *sauce piquante* and rice and a salad Annie's made. Everybody's so hungry that we eat silent, 'cept for the clinkin' of our forks and knives, through the first helpin'.

About halfway through the second, Annie says to Chilly, so Logan told me a bit of what happened back down there in Catahoula Bayou. I'm very sorry, but I have to say it doesn't completely surprise me. What's your plan, Chilly? You both are welcome to stay here for a while and lay low if you want to. I had a little word with Lester before we left Noonie's. I didn't tell him any more than you were old friends, but I also asked that he not say anything to the law here, such as the law is.

Chilly says it's kinda up to Logan but I'm pretty anxious to get on up to Tupelo, where I've got kin. My Auntie Belva and her husband, Uncle Cane, live out in the country west of town at a place called Endville. Daddy says Uncle Cane is one of the few colored farmers in Mississippi who ain't a sharecropper—he owns his own farm where he grows a bit of cotton and soybeans and some vegetables. Anyway, they don't know I'm comin', which is best, 'cause they'd be awful worried, but I know they'll put me up for a while till I can figger out what to do. It's a doggone shame, in a way, 'cause, till I come across that moron Junior Guidry and his moron uncle, I was about to graduate from high school at Greenville Colored High, and me and Cassie—that's my girlfriend—we were thinkin' about maybe gettin'—

Chilly trails off and looks at me.

He says Logan, I'm sorry. I don't mean to make it sound like it's soundin'. Wadn't Meely's fault Junior picked on him and wadn't nobody's fault but Junior's that he sicced that Klan-headed uncle on us. It's just that, well—

I stop Chilly. I say look, you don't need to be apologizin'. You stepped in and prob'ly saved my boy from a bear-sized whuppin'. But the fact is, 'cause you stepped in on our side, you're in a bunch of trouble. I cain't tell you how sorry I am about that. I'll do whatever I can do to help get you out of it and put it right, as much as us outlaws can make things right.

Chilly says well, I crossed the Great Catahoula and the law ain't caught me yet. That's pretty good already.

Annie says well, just let me know what I can do to help.

Chilly says you're helpin' now. This beats steam-pipe catfish, don't it, Logan?

I say it does, Chilly, and burnt-roasted possum, too.

Annie smiles slight. Then she raises her glass of iced tea and says well, here's a little cheer for a safe trip up to Tupelo. She leans across the table toward Chilly and me with her glass held up and we all clink.

She says you know, though I don't always go to mass anymore, I'll say a little prayer for you boys before I go to bed. On the other hand, I think prayer only goes so far, and it helps to have a plan. So here's one idea. There's a truck farmer, a colored man, who grows late winter cabbages down at a wayside called Broussard's Bend. Harris Daigrepont is his name—nice fella. He trucks his cabbages north to Mississippi this time of the year, where there won't be cabbages harvested for at least another month. Harris and I have a little barter arrangement. I keep him in catfish and he keeps me in greens. Anyway, I could call him tonight and see if he's got a trip planned. He'd probably give you a lift, plus you'd have some cover. You're Harris's field hands, ridin' up-country to help him unload.

I say well, that sounds a lot better plan than walkin' all the way up Mississippi. But I'd shore hate to get this Harris person mixed up in our trouble—I'd feel like we'd need to tell him we're on the run.

Annie nods, like she's thinkin' this over. She says I know Harris pretty well and I doubt that's gonna be a problem. He's an independent-minded fella, plus he knows just what roads a colored man drivin' through Louisiana and Mississippi should take to minimize trouble.

I look at Chilly, then at Annie, and say that beats any plan I have for gettin' up to Tupelo.

Annie says okay, I'll call him after supper.

Things go quiet and we go back to eatin'. Annie's a righteous cook. I don't normally make my *sauce piquante* with turtle, since rabbits are a whole lot easier to dress. But I do love turtle meat, 'specially snappin' turtle, which is what this is made of.

Chilly himself has three helpin's plus a ton of salad and then says y'all, I'm beat as a snake in the chicken yard. Annie, if you'll show me where I'm sleepin', I'm gonna hit the hay.

Annie dabs her napkin to her mouth and says oh, of course, Chilly. I know you boys have had a tough one out there. You'll sleep down here in the official guest room. Logan, I'm putting you upstairs in my son Jeremy's room. If you're tired, too, I could—

I raise my hand and say I'm fine but Chilly here should definitely go get some shut-eye.

Chilly smiles. He says if I fall asleep before I get to the bedroom, just zombie-walk me to the bed.

He gets up, as does Annie, and they clop across them wood floors. I hear a door open and their voices go soft and then a door close. Pretty soon Annie's back.

It feels a bit strange bein' alone again with a woman—at least one I ain't paid for. Annie seems to sense that, too.

She says Logan, how 'bout a nightcap of Gentleman Jack. I don't drink a whole lot of bourbon but it's all I drink when I do.

I actually have to think about this for a second.

I say well, Annie, as you might've already figgered, I'm a man who likes a drink. Sometimes I like it too much, and more'n once likin' it too much has got me in trouble.

Annie smiles. She says I've got carried away a time or two myself. Luke liked to drink, too. That's how I acquired my taste for whiskey. But you're among friends here and I doubt there'll be trouble. And I keep a club in the hall closet, and some rope, just in case there is.

I gotta laugh at that. I say okay. In that case, I'd love one.

She says let's move into the livin' room. It's a bit more comfortable in there and, frankly, I don't get to use those couches much.

She gets up, goes to a cupboard and rustles up two fancy-lookin' glasses with ducks etched into them, and the bottle of Jack Daniels. We go over and sit on one of them soft couches I'd noticed before. We sit close but not too close.

She pours the whiskey and puts the bottle on her coffee table and hands me my funny li'l glass. She picks up hers. We clink glasses again and she says *salut*.

I say that's a word I don't know.

She says I picked it up in Paris. Luke and I went to France one year. All it means is cheers.

I say cheers back and take a sip. Annie does the same.

This is a lot better whiskey than I'm used to drinkin'.

Annie says I loved France. We saw Paris and a glittery palace called Versailles where a king once lived and we traveled to the coast where, long, long ago, the people who became the Cajuns came from. Logan, you wouldn't believe what they can do with roasted chicken over there. It's the best I've ever eaten. Luke was country, like I am—he was born and grew up about twenty miles from here—but we both had an *envie* to travel, see places we'd only dreamed of. In fact, we were plannin' a trip to England the summer he was killed.

I say I'm a bit of a wanderer myself, though not to places nearly as far as you've gone. But I think I might've walked over every stretch of woods in Catahoula Parish that ain't got a Posted sign on it. I just never thought much about far-off places—back down where I grew up, about the best you could hope for was to get off that bayou one day or have enough food to eat or have a house that wadn't fallin' down. Elizabeth talked about far-off places, though. She'd read magazines and books and such, and I think she'da loved to have gone over to France or Germany where some of her folks come from long, long ago. She spoke good French—Cajun, and French she'd learned in school. But she never ever axed to go anywhere far. Elizabeth knew she coulda married a lot richer than me. She never cared to talk about things we couldn't afford, lest it would make somebody feel bad. Actually, she never wanted to make *me* feel bad.

I stop for a second and realize I'm tellin' Annie a lot more than I've told anybody else about Elizabeth.

I say anyway, goin' over there must've been somethin'. I don't think I know anybody else who's ever done such a thing.

She nods and takes another slow slip of her whiskey.

She says what happened to Elizabeth, Logan? Do you mind tellin' me?

I say I don't mind. She died in childbirth, along with our baby daughter.

Annie shakes her head and that sad look comes into her eyes again. She says oh, I can't imagine such a thing. How awful for you, and how awful for your boy.

I say that about describes it. If you wanna know the truth, my boy's done a bit better than I have, though I know it still makes him sad.

Annie says well, the way you talk of her, I know you must still miss her.

I say I do. I miss her every day. Sometimes I think I miss her too much for my own good.

She says it's the worst thing, isn't it? Tryin' to live without your other half?

I can only nod to that.

She says I'm amazed at the people who ask me if I've gotten over Luke's death. I know most of them are only tryin' to be kind. It's just their way of wonderin' if I'm okay. But I know now I'll never *get over* Luke's death. I've just learned to manage the sorrow of it all. I get up every day and I eat a nice breakfast and I run my jug lines and thank God for another day out *there,* on the water. I go down to Noonie's now and then for a drink or when he puts on a crawfish boil. I try to be grateful for what I've got and not dwell on what I've lost. Those people in Paris would probably think I live in some godforsaken, lonesome bog, but I don't think there's a more beautiful place on earth than the deep of this cypress swamp under a blue sky with the sun shinin' on the water. But there are some days—and nights, especially—when I would trade everything I have, except my boys, to have Luke back.

I look at Annie and see that thing in her eyes that I know sometimes comes into mine.

I say yes, I understand how that feels. I guess I'm about in the same boat.

We go quiet for a while, sippin' our whiskey.

I drain my glass and Annie picks up the bottle and pours me another one.

I say in a way, I'm glad you told me about Luke and how it is with you. Sometimes I've got the feelin' that I was about the only person in the world who carried around old grief that always felt like new.

Annie smiles. She says Logan, you and I are hardly the only ones. Maybe we just feel it more, but if you scratch the surface of people very much, you'll find that most people are carryin' some sorrow deep inside. There's a poet who talks about how practically everyone leads lives of quiet desperation. And that's exactly how it feels for me sometimes. The impossible loss of him, the impossible sadness of it all.

Annie drains her glass and pours herself another, too.

She says tell me about Meely. I know you must be terribly worried.

I manage a small smile myself. I say Meely? Well, he's got a bit of my hound-dog ways and a lot of his momma's brains and book smarts and her sweet disposition. But he's a scrapper, too. He's only in trouble 'cause he wouldn't tuck tail like some whupped dog when that Junior Guidry got after him. Heck, when Junior and his gang of idgits come to throw rocks at the house, Meely run 'em off with my shotgun. They like to drove their car in the bayou runnin' from him. He's pretty near fearless, far as I can tell.

Annie says I'll never understand bullies like the one you describe, but there's a stretch that boys hit where bullies seem to be a fact of life. My own sons went through it, though nothing that sounds quite so nasty. But Meely sounds like he's turned out fine. He sounds like a fine young man.

I say well, I might be braggin' but I think he really is. But not much of it is account of me. After Elizabeth passed, I stumbled bad and I've pretty well kept stumblin'. Meely's spent a lot of time lookin' after hisself, not to mention more than he should frettin' over me.

Annie says he probably frets over you 'cause he admires you. I'm sure, when your wife was still alive, you did everything a good father could do and more.

I say we did, all of us, have a pretty good time. Heck, Meely was a doggone good fisherman by the time he was six. He killed his first squirrel with a .22 rifle I give him when he was seven. Him and me would go bull-eye them coons at night and he got to be almost as good as I was at findin' 'em. He likes to ramble, too. On them nighttime coon hunts, we woulda walked all night if Elizabeth didn't get after us to come home by ten. And a frog hunter? That boy has the fastest hands on Catahoula Bayou. Wadn't nuttin' for us to come home with a hunderd doggone big ole bullfrogs in the sack, and Meely would've caught almost all of 'em. It got so I'd just paddle and watch him catch.

Annie says Logan, what you've just told me is that when Meely was at that age when all boys need a daddy's time and attention, you gave yours. You probably think that about all you really taught him was huntin' and skinnin' or swamp lore. But I'd bet my bottom dollar he picked up all kinds of other lessons, too. A kid that bright would.

I say well, that all could be true. But anybody can be a good daddy in good times. I know Meely needed me more than ever after his momma died and I, well—I just fell down into someplace cold and dark. I swear, Annie, some of those years seem totally lost to me. I can hardly remember a thing, though I guess this—I hold up my whiskey glass and tap it with my finger—didn't help me none.

Annie nods.

She says you mustn't be too hard on yourself. I can't say, after Luke died, that I was much of a mother for a while, either. My boys took it as hard as I did, maybe harder, but half the time they were havin' to pick me up. And they weren't much older than Meely is now. Anyway, I'm sure I don't know everything there is to know, but the way you talk about Meely, it's clear you love him and he loves you. And that's the rock of everything.

I nod. I say problem is, I ain't much of a rock to him now. He's back there, in jail, I'd imagine, tryin' to explain our side to people who won't ever believe him, and I'm headin' to Tupelo and, after that, Lord knows where. Somehow, though, when things cool down a bit, I've got to slip back down there to check on him.

Annie nods again. She says I wouldn't totally give up on justice. If that

Junior fella is such a troublemaker, people would know that, right, and step forward and tell the law? Didn't you say that a friend of Chilly's, a girl, saw what Junior and his gang were doin' to Meely? She'd be an eyewitness, she—

I say Cassie—that's her name. She's Chilly's girlfriend. And, yes, she did see everything, and I'm shore she'll tell what she saw but, you know like I do, Annie, that the law treats colored differnt than it treats whites. They'll take the word of that knucklehead Junior and his knucklehead uncle over hers, and that'll be that.

Annie says I agree what you say is often true. But I wouldn't rule out an honest judge or an honest jury. Meely sounds like the kind of kid who is totally believable.

I say that's nice to think of, but I'd bet my chances are better of seein' a blue alligator one day than of seein' the law do right.

She smiles slight at that. She says well, if it would make you feel better, I could make a phone call or two before you leave tomorrow to check on Meely. They might at least tell me how he's doin'. Unless you think it's better not to know, uh—

I say oh, no, I'd appreciate it if you could do that. I want to know, no matter what.

She nods and takes another sip of whiskey.

Then she says okay, here's the deal. I'm gonna go see if I can raise Harris Daigrepont and get you boys a ride to Mississippi. In the meantime, you just relax. And help yourself to more whiskey if you want it.

I look at my glass and see it's about two-thirds empty. I say I might have one more for a nightcap.

She says good, I was hopin' you would.

Then she winks at me and gets that look in her eye like she had when she told me I should go ahead and wrassle Lester. She says you know, Logan, sometimes I think a little trouble around here might be good for a girl. And by the way, you clean up pretty well for a swamp rat.

She walks off to make her phone call. I'm sittin' there with my drink half raised and my mouth open. I drain my glass with one big sip, then pour myself another two fingers of Gentleman Jack and sip it and look around Annie's house. There's interestin' knickknacks and gizmos everyplace.

I figger she must've got Harris 'cause I hear her yakkin' away for about ten minutes.

She comes back and says your luck couldn't be better. We're to meet Harris in the parkin' lot behind Noonie's around eight in the mornin'. And Logan, he's goin' all the way up to Tupelo, though he won't be goin' too fast. You'll probably spend a night in Natchez and another in Vicksburg before he cuts over to Tupelo.

I say that sounds plenty good to me. And you're shore this poor ole fella don't mind that he'll be truckin' a coupla outlaws?

Annie smiles. She says when I told Harris your story he said Annie, I know they'll be better company than them cabbages.

I laugh at that.

We go quiet for a while and sip our whiskeys slow. We don't say much but it don't feel like much needs to be said. There's somethin' *comfortable* about Annie.

After a bit, Annie stretches and yawns and says I was up at four this mornin' runnin' my lines and I'm startin' to flag. I think I'm gonna hit the hay.

I say I'm of about the same mind. I'll go with you.

Then I realize how that came out and I blush. I say I didn't mean it that way.

Annie smiles. She says don't worry, I'm afraid I know what you meant.

I bust out laughin'. I say Annie, you better be careful.

She looks at me quiet and says I guess I should.

She gathers up our whiskey glasses and the bottle and totes them to the kitchen, then we go cloppin' up the stairs. Up top, we go left past her bedroom. She comes to a door and opens it and switches on a light. She says this is my son Jeremy's room. Sheets are clean and there's a ceilin' fan to keep you cool if you wanna switch it on. I think I could even rustle you up some pajamas if you want 'em.

I shake my head. I say I ain't a man who's spent much time in pajamas.

She smiles at that and says I bet you aren't.

Then she does a surprisin' thing. She steps up to me and gives me a hug. It ain't a hug like you'd get from a gal friend, but it ain't a hug like you'd get from your sister, either.

She pulls back and says sleep tight, and I'll see you in the mornin'.

That whiskey has made me dumb and drowsy and I cain't think of a thing to say.

She goes off to her room. I shut the door and undress and drape my clothes over the end of the bed. I turn off the light and slip beneath the sheets and close my eyes. I ain't slept in a bed this nice in a coon's age.

I feel myself slippin' away but I'm still thinkin' about that hug.

Sometime later, I hear a rustle and I'm in a fog and then it seems someone has their hand on my forehead real soft.

I wonder if it's Elizabeth and though I cain't open my eyes, I reach out and find somebody soft and snuggle up close. And the sad of my life and the glad of my life all seem mixed up together, all seem like the very same thing.

I drift on and on and on and on and she says my name soft, till I'm asleep again, and when I wake up in the mornin', I'm alone.

I'm alone and all hopped up as a man often is in the mornin' and I feel drowsy and dreamy and good. I lay there for a good while watchin' the sun come in my window and thinkin' it musta been one of them dreams.

PART TWO

The Road to Tupelo

13.

Harris Daigrepont is climbin' down from his truck. He's a small man, stout as a cypress, serious as church from the look of him. He comes toward me and I see that he walks cane-stalk straight, nuttin' slouchy about it. He's got on a John Deere ball cap and coveralls over a short-sleeve khaki shirt, and sturdy steel-toed boots of the kind I wear. 'Cept his are in a mite better shape than mine. He might be my age or older but with colored people it's hard to know, as he's hardly got a line on his face. As Elma Mouton from Catahoula Bayou is always tellin' me, black don't crack.

Harris comes over quick and shakes hands like a man who knows what he's about. We're standin' on the far edge of the empty oyster-shell parkin' lot back of Noonie's, next to the canefield. I'm still fidgety enough to be on the lookout for the police.

Annie's dropped us off—we've already made her two hours late runnin' her lines, so she said her goodbyes at breakfast, which is prob'ly best.

I ain't the best at goodbyes. Besides, I think there's a fair chance I'll see Annie again sometime down the road. At least I wouldn't mind, and she said she wouldn't mind, either.

She called the jailhouse this mornin' early and told whoever it was up there that answered the phone that she was a friend of Meely's late momma and she was worried about the boy. They hemmed and hawed but Annie softened 'em up and they finally told her that, yes, Meely had broke his leg but it wadn't real bad and he had been fixed up at the hospital and was now in a part of the jail for juveniles. They also said they were still lookin' for them outlaws that got away.

Meely havin' his leg patched up made me feel a bit better.

The other thing I axed Annie to do was to have the law go and check on Miz Dee-Dee. I know she thought at first I was pullin' her leg about Earl bein' dead out on the back porch, but she finally realized I wadn't. She also solved another problem. She said she'd sell my pirogue for me, as I knew I couldn't take it with me and I could use the money. She knew of some ole boy who'd prob'ly gimme twenty, twenty-five dollars for it and she'd hold on to the money for me. She also talked me into leavin' Uncle's shotgun with her. She said if I sold it or if the police found us with it, it would just be one more thing they could get after me about. She said one day, when things blow over, I could give it back to the police.

Annie's got a level head on her shoulders.

Noonie's ain't open at the moment. Annie told me he opens at four in the mornin' to serve coffee, eggs, grits, and *boudin* to the trotliners and sport fishermen, then shuts it down at seven and don't open again till eleven.

Harris Daigrepont is up close now and says Logan, is it?

Yes sir, Logan LaBauve. Pleased to meet you.

He says Annie's told me all about you. Where's the other fella, Chilly?

I say he wandered off into the sugarcane there. Nature called. He'll be back quick.

Harris nods. He says you ever been a farmer?

I say I've been a bit of everything, though farmin' ain't what I do best, though my boy is pretty good at it. I make most of my livin' huntin' and fishin'.

Catfishin'?

Some. But I fish and hunt about anything I can eat or sell.

He says is there anything better than catfish fried up in an egg, milk, and cornmeal batter, with hush puppies on the side? My wife sometimes throws mustard in that batter when she wants to get fancy.

I say I ain't tried the mustard part but you're right about the rest.

Harris says I guess I'm a man with simple tastes. I stick to my catfish and fried chicken and potatoes done any which way, though it might surprise you to learn I don't eat cabbage. It rubs my belly the wrong way. Now, I do enjoy them crawdads in season as long as they're not too spicy. Over west of here in the prairie, them Creole and Cajuns put enough cayenne in their crawfish pots to make the sun sweat. I cain't eat 'em that hot. Now ole Noonie here, that man can boil crawfish. He doggone can.

I look at Harris. I say you go in there to eat 'em?

He laughs hard. He says hell, no. You must've seen that sign on the door.

I say I did, though it ain't there no more. Ole Chilly took it last night for a souvenir.

Harris arches his eyebrows. He says he did?

I say he did.

He says has Noonie said anything?

I say no. He prob'ly ain't noticed yet.

Ha! Harris says. We'll all get to see how long it takes him to put up another.

I say well, maybe he won't. I guess Annie has told you the bit about Noonie havin' a colored girlfriend.

He says mister, every colored person from here to Mississippi knows that story. Now, myself, I don't approve of the young lady's taste in men, all the more 'cause Noonie is a married man. Of course, havin' seen Noonie's wife, I have some sympathy for the devil. On the other hand, I'm a churchgoin' man, though not the Bible-thumper my missus wishes I was. So I don't approve, based on what Scriptures say. But, face it, a white man sweet on a colored gal probably won't be puttin' one of them sheets over his head any time soon, if you know what I mean. Now, I'll allow that maybe Noonie is bein' led to the cause of righteousness by his Johnson, but we all come to the Truth in our separate ways.

I laugh out loud.

I say I've been led that way a time or two myself but I doubt anybody would call it righteousness.

Harris Daigrepont haw-haws deep as a mule when I say that.

I gotta say I'm already fond of Harris.

I look over at his truck. It's a Ford flatbed, red, and kept nice and shiny, with a high, shellacked maple railin around its bed. It's heaped up with more cabbages than I've ever seen in one place. It would take an awful big garden to grow that many cabbages.

Harris says well, maybe we oughta holler to your friend Chilly. I've got miles to make and cabbages to sell.

Just then, Chilly comes scrabblin' out of the cane. He sees us and smiles and walks over and shakes hands with Harris.

Harris says I'm pleased to meet you, Chilly. I understand you might need a ride all the way to Tupelo. That's close to four hundred miles, if I'm readin' my Texaco road map right.

Chilly nods.

Harris says by the way, just so you'll know, we're gonna stick to Loosiana roads till we cross the Mississippi River over to Natchez. What I know of Cajuns, most are like Noonie, too busy foolin' around or drinkin' their beer or boilin' their crawfish to bother joinin' some of them outfits that mess with colored folk. Now, even though some do put signs on their beer joints, it's better to stick with them devils we know than the ones we don't.

Me and Chilly nod. A man would have a hard time arguin' that point.

I say Mr. Daigrepont, one thing. What would you like me to do with my shotgun?

He says first things, you just call me Harris. Second, you just give it to me and I'll stick it in my gun rack. Even if we're stopped by the po-lice— and I hope we won't be—they won't think nothin' of it. You know it's the rules in Loosiana. If you got a truck, you gotta have a gun rack. Even a cabbage truck.

I fetch my gun and my huntin' vest from behind an oak where I stashed 'em. Harris says now both you fellas can squeeze into the cab if you'd like, though it will be a bit tight in there. I take up half a space but I can see ole Chilly here takes up about two. So I've laid in a nice space over on the left just inside the tailgate with a bunch of burlap bags. A fella could even stretch out and take a snooze if he wanted to. The weather's good today so we won't have to worry about rain.

I say Chilly, if it's all the same with you, I'd like to ride in the back. I'm kinda partial to the fresh air myself.

Chilly says you shore, Logan? I'm happy to ride back there, too. In fack, we can trade off if you want to. Maybe when Mr. Daigrepont stops for gas or food.

I say well, we can think about that. But don't worry about it for now. I'll be happy as an oyster at risin' tide.

Chilly says okay.

Harris walks around to the back of the truck and unlatches the tailgate. It swings open smooth and easy, without so much as a creak, and I see that nest of burlap he's made. It looks totally comfortable. I hop in and settle down. Harris closes the gate and goes around and hops in. Pretty soon the truck rumbles to life and off we go.

Harris is a pokey driver, which is all right with me. We go bouncin' up the Pierre Point Road, passin' a few scattered farms, some with cow pastures, some with fenced lots where folks keep horses or mules. Then we hit a stretch where everybody seems to have a vegetable garden squeezed in between the road and the bayouside, same as we've got at home.

One ole boy already has Creole tomatoes on his vines the size of baseballs. Another has okra in bloom. Another has some of them *mirliton* vines runnin' thick up a willow tree and they're heavy with *mirlitons*. Some people call them things alligator pears 'cause they got ridges on 'em just like a gator hide. Elizabeth used to smother them things with onions and garlic and spices and throw in some ground beef and, man, a fella could make a whole meal of that.

In about an hour, the road narrows and goes through a long stretch of low country, with the swamp edgin' clear up over the shoulders. Harris slows down even more. This is flat land but a road built through the swamp is a road that tends to settle, and this one is a bit like ridin' up and down on the backs of big turtles.

We slide on by and I gotta say this particular swamp is handsome—spindle-top cypress, swamp maple, gum trees wearin' spring leaves, that deep, dark sweetwater lit up like a gold mirror where the sun strikes it. Cypress knees pokin' out everywhere. We drive past a break where a broad pond lays flat and smooth up against the treeline and I look out and see an eagle spring from the top of a big mossy cypress. There ain't many of them birds in this country, far as I know, but this one's a sight to see.

In about an hour, we break outta the low country and are back in cane land, the fields green and waist-high and rollin' on and on far as the eye can see. It's still a tar road but it gets wider and smooths out, 'cept in places where them cane-haul trucks have beat potholes into the blacktop.

There ain't many houses but the ones we see are somethin'. We pass one clearin' where there's a yard about as wide as a football field is long, and it seems to go back as deep. The grass is St. Augustine and cropped short as a golf course I seen one time. Whoever the fella is who cuts it has a big job. The house is one of them gingerbread kind, wood painted bright white, with a porch clear around it, and so big that a normal man might feel lonesome in it. It's got five or six oak trees that must go clear back to the Civil War or before.

It's a pretty sight. I only know of one other house like it—the one that Francis Hebert lives in on Catahoula Bayou.

The day's got warm and there ain't a cloud in the sky. 'Tween the warm sun and the bouncin' and rumble of the truck and all the lookin' I been doin', I realize I've grown a bit sleepy. I been sittin' up, my back against them cabbages, but I decide maybe stretchin' out some wouldn't be bad.

I do and I close my eyes and think about things.

I think mostly about last night. How I slept like an angel. I wonder about that.

Maybe them warm hands and arms really were just a dream.

I think about Annie, then Meely, then Elizabeth, who is always the last person I think about before I go to sleep.

And pretty soon I'm noddin' off.

14.

I'm rattled awake by the bouncin' of the truck and realize we've pulled off the road into a gravel parkin' lot about as jumbled up as Noonie's. The truck groans and creaks slow through a coupla big potholes, stops, then groans forward again, then bounces to a stop.

I see we've pulled up to a gas pump at a store of the kind you find every fifteen or twenty miles in this country. I hear the truck doors open and I try to shake the sleep from my head.

Chilly appears around the back and he unlatches the gate and opens it. He says you wanna stretch your legs, Logan? How you doin' back here with all them cabbages?

I say I'm doin' just fine, though a stretch would be good. I've met chickens that don't have a better nest than the one Harris has made back here. I guess I'm catchin' up on that sleep we lost out in the swamp.

Chilly smiles. He says that's good. I dozed off myself, though ole Harris could talk the sweat off of a mule—not that he don't have lots of inter- estin' things to say. He's gone over to find whoever it is pumps the gas.

I say where are we?

He says we're about ninety miles north of where we started—gettin' close to bein' halfway to Natchez, I figger.

I say well, that's as far as I've ever been from Catahoula Bayou.

Chilly nods. He says I came up here to Tupelo when I was small to see my relations but I don't remember much of it. I do recall there's someplace you get to and you start goin' up and down some hills and the dirt gets as red as the sunset.

I say as a flatlander all my life, it might be nice to see some hills.

I step down from the truck, a mite stiff, and see Harris comin' over with a slouchy man in khakis about as beat-up as mine, and boots that ain't any better, and a T-shirt that looks like it's been used to check a few dipsticks in its day. The man's bald as a duck egg and he's got a moon face as red as that dirt Chilly was talkin' about. He's got about three chins and his jowls bounce up and down when he walks.

He and Harris seem to be yakkin' it up.

The man goes to the pump and cranks it up with that ringin' sound and comes around back with the nozzle. He fiddles with the gas cap, sticks the nozzle, and starts pumpin'. I don't know why but gasoline smells pretty good to me. I look over at the pump and see reg'lar sells for twenty-six cents a gallon, which seems expensive. I've bought it for nineteen in town.

I say to Harris, can me and Chilly help you pay for this?

Harris bats the air. He says heck, no.

He looks at the gas pumper and says to me I'll take a share out of your pay when we've dropped our cabbages.

I say okay.

The man pumpin' the gas says where y'all goin'?

Harris says to Natchez, sooner or later, to try to unload some of these cabbages. You wanna buy some?

The man says I dunno, how much you take for 'em?

Harris says all of 'em, or just some?

The man laughs. He says my wife's about as big as your truck, Mister, and she likes her supper, but I doubt if even *she* could eat all these cabbages.

Harris says I get twelve cents a pound normally but it's a dime to you.

The man says why, that's doggone nice of you. I'll take three of them cabbages. By the way, my name's Shine, Shine Trosclair.

He puts out his greasy hand, thinks better of it, wipes it on his greasy shirt, puts it out again. We all give it a shake.

Harris says tell you what, Shine, I'll swap you four cabbages for three soda pops and three bags of popcorn shrimp, if you've got any.

Shine looks up, like he might see somethin' in the sky, and starts countin' on his fingers. He does this for a while and then says awright.

It takes about ten minutes to fill up Harris's thirsty truck, then Shine says y'all come on inside.

Harris looks at me, then Chilly, and then shrugs, like what the heck.

This is a white man, and it's not easy to forget that sign at Noonie's.

We follow him in, though Chilly first rustles up four cabbages. He carries them in the crook of his arm like a baby.

It's another poor place, the grocery on one side and a small bar on the other. The store is cramped, two or three narrow isles stuffed with canned goods and vegetables in crates, and it smells like country stores often do—like bread and pickles in jars. The bar ain't no better. It's got a scuffed-up wood floor and rickety tables all wedged in tight. It smells of stale beer and tobacco, and maybe of catfish that was fried last night. We go over to the bar counter, which ain't but rough plywood, and Chilly lays them cabbages down. I see there's about a thousand places where fellas have laid their cigarettes and burnt streaks in the countertop.

Shine lets himself in behind the bar and yanks three bags of popcorn shrimp off a rack and tosses 'em on the counter. Those things are salty but good. I've always heard it was Chinamen livin' down in the salt marsh long ago that invented them things. Shine goes off and opens up a cooler and bends way down into it till he about disappears. I hear him clinkin' ice and bottles aside. Soon, he comes up with the soda pops held between the fingers of his right hand.

He comes over to the counter and sets them down, then comes up with a church key from under the bar. He pops the bottles open quicker than you think a man could. They're fizzy and frosty.

Harris reaches for his billfold and says how much for that gas?

Shine says five sixty-nine is the total.

Harris hands him a ten-dollar bill and he goes over to a old-timey cash register, the kind that cranks open, and comes up with the change. He comes back and lays the money on the bar.

Shine says y'all followin' this road all the way to Natchez, then crossin' over on the ferry?

Harris nods.

He says well, y'all know about the jailbreak?

Harris says no, what jailbreak?

He says well, if you're goin' up that road, you could run into some police roadblocks 'cause there was a jailbreak last night and they're lookin' for some runaways.

Chilly looks at me. I look at Harris. He arches his eyebrows.

Harris says you don't say?

Shine says well, not a jailbreak, egzackly. There's a gals' reform school way out in the woods ten miles up this road and some of them girls broke out last night.

He bends across the bar and looks around and says now, I ain't s'posed to know nuttin' but there was an ole boy who come in late last night who works as a guard up there. He says one of them girls managed to smooch up the warden and while he was all smooched up she stole his gun out of his drawer and he didn't even know it. They pulled the gun on one of the guards later and threatened to kill him and every other guard if they didn't let 'em out of there.

No foolin'? says Harris.

No foolin', Shine says. Hell, I already heard they stuck up the ole boy who drives the beer truck around here. He's a local podnah. He was pulled over takin' a nap and next thing you know, them gals come up like bandits in a cowboy movie and put that gun in his face and laughed while they did it. He says there were four of 'em.

Harris says they sound like bad girls.

Bad is right, says Shine. They stole his wallet and everything. Lawd, what's the world comin' to when you've got wile womens runnin' 'round all over Creation stickin' up bayou people with a gun? They prob'ly some *putains* if that's how they act. Tell you what—they come in here and try to stick me up? Shuh, they can have it, have it all. I'll point 'em right to the cash register and I'll even give 'em the keys to the place as I slip out the back door. Yes sir. This ain't my joint. It belongs to ole man Crank Lirette.

I just work for the drunk ole bastid and I ain't gonna take a bullet for him, that's for shore.

Harris nods. He says well, I guess a man couldn't blame you for that.

Shine swats the air like he's goin' for a horsefly. Hell, no. This ain't my real job, anyways. I'm a mechanic is what I really am. I've got me a li'l shop over behind my house about five miles up the bayou. I fix cars mostly but I can fix about any damn thing that's broke. Lawn mowers, tractors, radios, refrigerators, toasters. I even fixed one ole boy's telephone one time when his ole lady yanked it out of the wall and give him one with it. That was Bataille Benoit, y'all know him?

Shine stops for a breath and knits up his brow. His face looks like it's made of rubber.

He says well, I guess y'all wouldn't since y'all not from around here. Anyway, so said, Bataille's wife went through his wallet one day and she found a rubber in there and, man, oh, man, there was hell to pay. Now don't ax me what Bataille was doin' wit' a rubber in his wallet. I got me a one-eared hog in my back pen that's better-lookin' than that sumbitch. And me? I'm a good Cat'lic man. Me and Myrna, my ole lady, we don't believe in that birth control stuff. You ain't never gonna catch me wit' no rubber, no siree. We got nine kids, and if we get some more, like Father says, Gawd will provide.

Shine stops and wipes the back of his neck.

He says that's the only reason I work here. I got me plenty mouths to feed. Ain't enough broke cars around here to keep that many kids in food and clothes.

I see ole Harris noddin' at this, his hand on his chin.

I see Chilly lookin' at Shine, his mouth hangin' open. It is kinda surprisin' what perfect strangers will tell you.

Harris says well, Shine, if I'm ever in this country and need a mechanic, I know who to call.

Shine says you shore do. 'Cept I ain't got no phone. I don't believe in phones, even though I fix 'em. But if you come by the store here, you'll prob'ly find me. And if you don't, ole man Crank will know where I am. 'Less he's too drunk to stand up. Then he won't know his own name. Tell you what, when I'm not around? They got some boys down the bayou—the Champagnes, about ten of them li'l bastids—who come in here and steal him blind, I'm not lyin'.

Harris nods. He says well, Shine, you stay outta the way of them girl bandits. And you and your missus enjoy them cabbages.

Shine smiles at the last part and when he does his face moves up and down, like the moon would do if it was made of *boudin*.

Shine says I will.

Harris says one other thing. You got some facilities we can use?

Shine jerks his thumb toward the back door. He says we got an out-house, a double-seater. Hep yourself.

We go in there one at a time, then collect our drinks and bags of dried shrimp and go.

15.

Back at the truck, I don't wait for Harris to tell me what's obvious.

I say look, if this jailbreak stuff is true, these roads could be swarmin' with cops. You might be better off just droppin' Chilly and me here and goin' on about your business. You done took us this far and it's a lot farther than we figgered to be by now, anyways.

I see Chilly noddin' in agreement.

Harris says well, we cain't really change our route—that would mean drivin' back all the way down about a hundred miles to cross the Mississippi. But two men on foot out in this country *would* seem suspicious. And, we may not get stopped. Even if we do, they won't be lookin' for you two. Of course, it could make the po-lice up this way a bit suspicious that a white man is travelin' with two colored ones unless the white man is drivin' the truck. But that prob'ly ain't a good idea 'cause they might then want to see a driver's license and this particular white man wouldn't care to show 'em one. On the other hand, the white man don't need to be present, if you know what I mean. I believe we could manage to rearrange some cabbages and some of that burlap and a tarp I've got so that a man could be back there and not a soul would know. Chilly, here, on the other hand, could pass for my boy. He's 'bout the right age and we're roughly the same size.

Harris pokes Chilly in the ribs. Chilly grins, even though I can tell this has made him a bit nervous.

Harris looks at Chilly. He says that okay with you?

Chilly says hell, let's go.

Harris decides the rearrangin' of the cabbages ought to be done without Shine seein' it. So we all squeeze into the cab and go down the road to the first cane-haul turnout, places where tractors pullin' wagons drop their cane so that them big cane trucks can pick it up and carry it to the mill. Harris backs the truck in, with the truck bed facin' the canefields, then pops open the hood of his truck.

He says we can always say we've got motor trouble if anybody comes snoopin' around. Then we go 'round back. Chilly unlatches the gate and we all stand there for a minute, puzzlin'. Then Harris says I've got it. Y'all climb up and gimme a hand.

Pretty soon, we're cloppin' down the road again and I'm sittin', facin' backwards, in a kind of a bowl, way up top of the cabbage pile, with a jerry-rigged peephole to look out of and a tarp over the top of it all.

If I didn't feel like an outlaw on the run before, I do now.

We clop along for maybe an hour and I figger if we were gonna run into a roadblock or any kind of trouble, we prob'ly woulda already done it.

Shows what I know.

I'm about to come up for a look around, since my seat up here ain't nearly as comfortable as that nest I was in before. That's when I feel the truck brake hard and the tires start to squeal and then suddenly Harris has thrown her into a lower gear.

I'm knocked backwards and we lurch to a stop.

A bit harder and these cabbages might've spilled out, me with 'em.

From what I can see outta my peephole, it does seem like a peculiar place to stop—ain't nuttin' but woods on either side of us. The first thing I'm thinkin' is that we've run up against a deer boltin' across the road.

Next I hear Harris shoutin' girl, are you crazy! I coulda killed you!

And then I hear a girl or woman gigglin'. She says oh, hell, mister, I'm just lookin' for a ride. C'mon, pretty please. Just as far as the very next town. *Please!*

Harris says ma'am, you just scared the sweet potatoes out of me and I don't even know you. And I'm sorry, but as you can see, there's just no room—not in here or back there.

She says no room? Oh, c'mon, sweetheart. There's always room for Della LeBlanc. Always!

I think I hear a bit of whiskey in Della's voice.

There's a moment of quiet and then Della says now, it's just not proper for a gentleman to refuse a stranded lady a ride. It's *impolite.* I'm gonna have to bring this up with my boyfriend and he won't be happy, no he won't.

She says Burl, Burl! Help! Help! *Darlin'!*

Harris says lady, I'm sorry. I wish I could help you but I cain't. But I will send somebody back for you at the very next town.

I suddenly hear another voice, a bit distant but deep as a Cajun bull-frog's.

The voice says why Della, my flower, is there a problem here? Is someone treating you shabbily?

I hear the tromp of boots comin' up across the graveled shoulder of the road, though I still cain't see nobody.

Della says yes, yes they are. It's him, that colored man there. I asked him nice for a ride but he said no.

Did he now? Well, perhaps I should have a word with him.

I hear Harris say mister, there's no reason to point that gun at me.

I hear the man haw-haw. He says oh, friend, how else should a modern-day highwayman comport himself? You see, boys, we—my ladyfriend here, not to mention some compatriots back in the woods—are indeed in dire need of transportation. And I see that you have some, though it isn't exactly the model I was hoping for.

Harris says what, you're gonna steal my truck?

Steal? the man says. Ah, how crudely you put it. Well, as you can see, first we were hoping to persuade you to give us a ride. And since I know I don't look entirely presentable, I sent my sweet Della out to try to flag you down. You stopped, but now you refuse her.

Harris says well, hold on a minute. For one thing, she about made me wreck this truck by runnin' out in front of me. For another, it's nothin' personal but we got word at a country store back the way we came that some girls had broke out of a reform school near here. For all I knew, your ladyfriend could've been one of them girl outlaws. We'd been warned not to stop for anyone.

Burl haw-haws again. Della, he says, the man flatters you! I can assure you, mister, that it's been many a moon since Della's been accused of being a schoolgirl. Now, as for her status with the law, it *is* true that Della's line of work sometimes does attract the attention of those factions of the police who cannot be persuaded by monetary remuneration. Isn't that right, darling?

Della says Burl, *please*—don't be crude.

Burl laughs. He say ah, but now, as to the matter at hand. Yes, sir, I think we need to appropriate your truck. Perhaps you and your friend will be kind enough to step out and move around to the back. I wonder what's keeping my confederates in the woods?

I hear the truck door open and I feel the springs creak as Harris and Chilly step out, both on Harris's side. I hear the shuffle of footsteps comin' toward the rear of the truck. Pretty soon, through my peephole, I've got everybody in view.

The woman is a tiny thing. Her dress is shiny and short and she's all made up. Her hair's yellow and piled up high and lacquered in a way that certain kinds of ladies I've known wear it. There's one big curl that looks like it's about to give up and fall over. I notice, too, that her ankles are muddy and her shoes are a mess.

The big voice belongs to a tall, rangy man with a face as wide and wild as the swamp. He's standin' on the right. Chilly, Harris, and the woman are on the left. He's got a shotgun in his right hand, finger on the trigger, the barrel cradled in the crook of his left arm.

It's just the way I carry my gun huntin' squirrels. You can be ready to shoot quick that way.

I shore do regret not takin' my double-barrel with me into my hidin' place up here.

The man's got a beard, which is unusual in these parts, and his hair is combed over in a peculiar way so as to hide a big ole bald spot. I can see now why he sent the woman out to flag down Harris. I've seen *carencros* that are better-lookin'. He's got on suit pants with a rip in the right knee and trouser legs that are tucked into muddy rubber knee boots. His plaid suit jacket don't come close to matchin' his pants. There are blotches—grease, blood, or mud, which, it's hard to tell—all over it. He's got big saddlebags of sweat under each armpit.

Harris speaks up. He says look here, mister, let's talk this over. I'm just a farmer tryin' to make a livin'. My boy and me have got to make Natchez before dark. We got this big load of cabbage sold and another one, too, if we can keep on schedule. If a ride's all you need, then, well, I'm shore we can make some space for you. I was just worried that she was an outlaw. Plus, I don't have to tell a smart man like you that it might seem, well, a bit strange to some folks hereabouts to see a white woman travelin' with two colored men.

Burl guffaws. I see you are a generous man after all and I understand your reservations. But, alas, your offer will not do. By the way, as you may have heard, my name is Burl—Professor to my friends, of which there are, admittedly, few. I'm traveling with my brother Ferlin and an acquaintance, all of us from the Mississippi side of the river. We invade Louisiana from time to time on poaching expeditions. We've spent a long, hot time traversing these woods with a couple of deer that we had harvested, illegally of course. But, a man must make a living, don't you agree? Having already traded our venison for whiskey, and having bartered our whiskey into companionship with Della and two sisters of her craft, we've gotten quite used to living the high life. But the rich life requires money, and our supply needs to be restocked. So we've been thinking about a certain bank up the road from which we are considering withdrawing funds. Ah, well, I shouldn't give too much away.

Professor Burl stops long enough to flick a horsefly off his nose.

Harris speaks up. He says mister, just hearin' you talk, I can tell you're a smart man. Surely a smart man like you don't need to be runnin' up and down the country stealin' cabbage trucks from honest farmers just goin' about their business. Why you—

The Professor raises his free hand and butts in. He says now, now, no tired lectures on morality. But you *are* observant, my friend. This is not my original line of work. I actually *was* a college professor, and dear departed MaMa spent a large part of her meager assets on my elocution lessons and generally trying to educate me. To some extent, she succeeded. True, I never rose past being a *junior college* professor. But I taught literature, and well, too—the Bard was my specialty. Alas, I ran afoul of the academic authorities, who did not appreciate my fondness for drink and young female students. I did *not* actually trade sex for grades, as I was so crudely accused of doing. My relationships were much more complex than that, but difficult, I admit, for small and conventional minds to grasp. At any rate, I was literally run out of town by the Yahoos and had to resort to another livelihood. So I became an outlaw, which is really but a label society often foists upon its renegades and freethinkers. And my conversion was easy enough, as my brother Ferlin, whom I expect you will meet shortly, was already well engaged in such enterprises. Ferlin is actually my half brother and not well endowed when it comes to critical or learned thinking. But he makes up for it with his rugged determination and—ah, how should I put it?—his raw anger and spite. Believe me, in our little gang of reprobates, I am the nice one.

Della says Burl, what a blowhard you are! I'm hot and tired, sweetheart, and you promised me and the girls a ride back to the Crossing. Let's get going.

I see Burl turn toward Della. He says impatient, are we, my magnolia? In your line of work, you do yourself a disservice by rushing a man. It does not augur well for repeat business. Now, please stop whining and behave yourself or another spanking may be in order.

Burl goes to haw-hawin' one more time.

I see Della shoot him a kicked-cat look. Myself, I don't generally kick cats, 'cause they always find a way of scratchin' back.

Burl says anyway, we're not going anywhere until Ferlin and Stack arrive. I can't imagine what's keeping them. Surely they are not still basking in conjugal bliss? But then again, perhaps your sisters-in-trade are more gifted at prolonging the loving arts than some people we might name.

Della all but spits. She says well, maybe your brother and friend aren't so quick on the trigger as some people *we* might name.

Burl don't haw-haw this time. Even from where I am, I can see his face go red and blotchy. The cat's got his tongue, for a second at least.

Then he says, in a hard voice, Della, my darling, one more word out of you, and you and your girlfriends will be walking back to Mississippi. Or perhaps crawling, if you're not careful.

And why would we have to crawl? Della says.

Because if I ask Ferlin nicely enough, he will be happy to break your legs. Now, I've suffered enough of your insolence. Quiet, please.

Burl holds up his hand to make the point.

Della stamps her foot and raises her hand, too. She gives Burl the bird finger.

I'm tryin' to stop myself from laughin'.

I'm watchin' poor Harris, who's just standin' there with his hands in his pockets, lookin' down and noddin' away, like he's puzzlin' somethin' over. I can tell from Chilly's posture he would love to go after the big fool, 'cept for that gun.

Harris speaks up. He says now, mister, given the smart fella that you are, how could I change your mind? What about money? A man could put say, two hundred, three hundred dollars in your hand and drive away and forget that he was even here. We could even take this woman with us, just to keep her from aggravatin' you.

Burl frowns and says my good man, you wound me with such a trifling offer. Also, I'm afraid I don't believe the driving-away-and-forgetting part. I believe it highly more likely that you would get to the first pay phone you could find and summon the authorities, such as they are. I'm afraid what I must do is take you fellows back with me to the spot of our spring dalliance and confer with my brothers in arms, assuming I can roust them from their recreational pursuits. Then we will tie you up and be on our way, though—he motions toward the truck—we may have to dump these cabbages. In fact, I think we will have to dump these ladies, too. Thievery is man's work, and driving them hither and yon would slow us down.

At that, he raises his shotgun with one hand and points it in the direction of Della.

He says there, sweetheart, see what your tongue has wrought. Now come and stand with these two gentlemen and then we're all going to take a little walk in the woods. Perhaps they will enjoy your company better than I did.

Della says you *wouldn't dare*!

Burl raises the gun a little higher.

Della stomps her foot again and walks over to Harris and Chilly.

She says you're a bastard, Burl. You'll get *yours*!

Burl gets his haw-haw back. He says ah, Della, that's among the kinder disapprobations normally applied to me. Now, gentlemen, please, don't try to do anything foolish or heroic. As a learned person, I carry little prejudice against men of any kind, but I must tell you that my half brother, Ferlin, is not fond of the Negro race. You do not wish to get cross-wise with Ferlin. He travels with a Bowie knife and he can skin anything that walks or crawls in about two minutes. It is both a phenomenal and strangely pleasurable thing to watch.

Up from where I am I cain't say I totally know how to read Burl.

A man with a mouth like his could be blowin' smoke or he could be mad as a cut snake. Anyway, I gotta decide quick what to do—go after him now, or wait till he's marched off and try to slip up behind him in the woods.

Maybe the fool hasn't noticed my 12-gauge up on the gun rack. It would be helpful if he hadn't.

Harris decides for me.

He says Professor, I see you're a hard bargainer, so before you march us off into the woods, what if I upped the stakes? What if I could offer you, say, three *thousand* dollars stedda just three hundred? How would that sound?

I can see Burl arch his eyebrows.

He says ahem, let me get this straight. You are telling me that you're a Negro farmer traveling up through Louisiana with three thousand dollars in cash? I find that rather hard to believe.

Harris says well, believe me. And I can tell you for a fact that three thousand dollars from a Negro farmer will spend just as good as three thousand from a white one. And of course, you could have that three thousand dollars for yourself—nobody back in your party would have to know the difference.

Burl looks hard at Harris and his forehead knits up like overcooked snap beans. He says somehow, sir, I think you're one of those clever Negroes of a kind I've encountered who delight in trying to pull a man's leg.

He stops and, click, pulls back the hammer of his shotgun. He says all right, for grins, where do you have that kind of money?

Harris points up at my hidin' place. Up there. You see that tarp up on that heap of cabbages? I travel with a steel safe hid away there. I only keep gas and food money in my wallet. That way if I'm stopped by crooked police or bandits, I'll only be out of a little, not a lot. You probably know better than I do that a colored farmer who's made a bit of money cain't be too careful with it goin' up and down these highways.

Burl flicks another horsefly off his face with his left hand, then reaches back and scratches his rear end the way I've seen some hounds go after ticks.

He says you know what? I've got a better idea. Why don't I just take your three thousand dollars *and* your truck?

Harris says a gentleman wouldn't do such a thing.

Burl haw-haws, louder than ever.

Harris says well, suit yourself. But you'll never open that safe without me. I'm the only one who knows the combination and now that I know what kind of man you really are, I'm not tellin'.

Burl snorts. He says actually, I could simply stick this gun to your head right now and tell you to give me the combination or else. I don't think you fully appreciate your predicament. In fact, I want you to climb up there yourself and open that safe and get that money for me *now*.

Harris says I'm not goin' up there. You'll just shoot me in the back soon as that safe's open. No, sir. I'm not goin'. You can forget about it. And you know what else, mister? We're known in these parts. We checked in to a li'l country store not too far back down the road and our friends back there will call the po-lice for shore if we don't call from Natchez tonight.

I see Burl's face turnin' all red and splotchy again. He barks out we're wasting time here. Why—

Then I hear Chilly speak up. He says mister, mister, please, calm down. Daddy here—he points to Harris—is hardheaded sometimes. Look, nobody needs to get hurt. We don't care about the money or the truck. Here, take the keys.

Chilly reaches over and grabs the truck keys from Harris. He pitches 'em to Burl, who catches 'em clean with his left hand.

I see Harris give Chilly a hard look.

Chilly says now, you seem like a sportin' man. Here's my idea. Why don't *you* go up to the safe? Daddy will call out the combination when you get to the top. You pop that safe open and start rakin' out your money and me and Pops here will beat feet for the woods. We'll take our chances in a footrace. I'm not tryin' to insult you or nuttin', but, mister, you don't look like a man who's spent much time runnin' track. Pops here, he's old but he can still run like a pony.

I hear Harris say I am *not* old, son! What you mean by callin' me *old*? Chilly shrugs.

Burl's noddin' again. He says I can tell bullshitting is an art in your family, but perhaps you've struck on a worthy compromise. I actually deplore physical violence myself—I leave all that to Ferlin. But, all right, to humor you, I'll go up and loot the safe. You can have your fair start. I may or may not give chase—though if there is no safe or money up there, my gun here is loaded with long-range buckshot and I *am* a gifted marksman. And, oh, you can escort Miss Della as well.

Della says Burl, I'm not going with *them*!

Burl says Della, you'll go where I tell you, darling. Now, gentlemen, I'm going to ease up there and it won't be pretty if you've been lying to me.

Burl walks to the truck and swings open the tailgate, keepin' his eye on Harris and Chilly. He then backs in and gets his butt up on the trailer bed and stands up, his back to me, his shotgun in his right hand. Then crouchin' down, he starts to feel his way up the cabbage pile.

I let him get about halfway up the mound, then I give a mighty kick with both feet, pushin' cabbages away with my hands as well.

There's enough grade to the pile to set off a pretty good cabbage land-slide.

I come boilin' out behind the cabbages, givin' a Wild Injun whoop.

Burl turns quick but not quick enough.

He tries to get the gun up but the first wave of cabbages catches him at the knee and knocks him backwards. I see the shotgun pitched up in the air and floatin' end over end off the back of the truck.

I'm airborne myself and I come down on Burl's belly with both feet and I know when I hit I've done him some damage. I hear the whoosh of his lungs goin' flat and I see fear in his eyes.

Then I'm on my back, tumblin' in a big knot of cabbages to the ground. I hit hard on my left shoulder and the wind pretty much goes out of me and I come stumblin' up in a panic.

I don't need to worry.

Burl's lyin' facedown on the ground, all but one shoulder and his head buried in about two foot of cabbages. He's moanin' low.

Chilly's standin' over him with Burl's gun.

I feel the Wild Injun rise in me again and I go over to Burl and rake those cabbages off him and turn him over hard and grab him by his beard and yank his face right up to mine.

Burl's eyes cain't focus quite right.

I say well, Professor, for bein' such a smart guy, how'd you get to be such a complete idgit?

Burl shakes his head like he don't quite get it.

I yank his beard hard. He says oww, mister, you're killin' me.

I say Burl, you better listen to me. You know your brother Ferlin? Well, I can tell you one thing for shore—Ferlin ain't a better skinner than me, and he don't have a bigger knife, neither.

I yank on his beard again. I say now here's what you're gonna do. You're gonna pick your sorry self up and you're gonna apologize to my friends here for threatenin' them. 'Cause, see, Professor, there's one thing you oughta know. I'm already on the run from the law for doin' things a site worst than you've ever done and if you don't do as I say, I will skin *you* like a gator and laugh while I do it.

Burl is focused on me now and I can see there ain't much fight in there.

I hear Harris say Logan, it's all right. I know this kinda man and there's nothin' to him. When a rat apologizes, it don't mean much anyway.

I look over at Harris, who's standin' there calm—a lot calmer than me. I feel myself cool down a bit.

I say I appreciate what you say, Harris, but I'm just sick of people who act this way. This here's a mad dog, and you know what you need to do with mad dogs—put 'em down.

I see Burl lookin' at me serious now.

I say get up.

He says I'm not sure I can. I think perhaps you've damaged a rib or something.

I say well, we'll help you, Burl. Chilly, give the gun to Harris and gimme a hand.

Chilly checks the shotgun and clicks it on safety, then hands it to Harris. He then grabs Burl by one arm and I grab him by another and we lift.

Burl groans.

I pull his face close to mine again with his beard. I say you know, Burl, I'm gettin' awful doggone tired of idgits. I've been up against more idgits in the last few days than I have in years. I'm kinda sorry I didn't break your idgit neck, and I still might. Now, you better start talkin' and talkin' fast.

Burl says oh, come now, be a reasonable man. I can see you're a fellow of character and stature. Why are you traveling up-country anyway with a couple of clever Negroes? I know these men can't be your friends. Throw in your lot with your own race—join my band! Assuming there is a safe up there, you and I could spring it and split the proceeds.

It's hard to believe I'm hearin' this.

I turn away for a second, then yank Burl's beard hard toward me and give him a head butt and let him go.

I coulda done it harder but it does the job.

Chilly lets go of him and Burl crumples like a sawed-down oak.

I'm standin' over him and I just feel a whole river of bad feelin's bottled up in me about to give way. Harris steps over and says calm down,

Logan. I understand how you feel. I might give 'em a kick myself 'fore it's over. But there's no use makin' things crazier than they are.

I look at Harris, annoyed at first, 'cause when the blood rises in a man, it tends to rise against all men in the way of it. But Harris talks easy, and I know a lotta men who mighta cracked or tried to run or fight in this situation.

I say you're right, Harris, no reason to make this any crazier than it is. I say Chilly, let's just get a rope 'round his wrists and legs so he don't give us no more trouble. I don't know what to make of his story about his confederates out in the woods.

I look for Della, figgerin' she might sort that out for us.

But that's when I hear the truck door slammin' and I see Della comin' around the corner.

With my shotgun.

At first I think she wants to pay ole Burl back, but that don't seem to be the plan.

The gun, sorry to say, is pointed right at us.

16.

But not for long.

Harris is annoyed and starts yellin' at Della, sayin' lady, are you crazy! Then we all hear cacklin' off across the road.

Chilly says holy shit, Logan, we got more company.

I look up and we shore do.

I have to say I'm gettin' awful tired of company. Especially fellas with guns, who are pointin' 'em at us.

There's two of 'em at the edge of the woods with shotguns at the ready. One of them shouts out now what've we got here? Stack, it looks like Burl's rose has gone and pulled a gun on everybody. Now ain't she *somethin'*. And what the hell happened to you, brother? You look like you tangled with a catty-wampus.

I hear Burl moan.

Ferlin, he says, is that you? Ferlin, come over here now and get me untied. I need to settle a score with these gentlemen.

Ferlin says I'm a-comin', brother. Jest you keep your shirt on. Now, I want everybody to drop them guns, then I want you boys to step far away from my brother.

I hear Della sneer. She says you got it all wrong. You better drop *your* guns or I'll plug ole motor-mouth there.

She steps toward us and pivots the gun so it's trained on Burl.

I look at Della good. She wouldn't weigh ninety pounds slathered in syrup. But her jaw is set and her eyes look hard. That curl that keeps wantin' to fall down off the top of her head is bobbin' like a coiled spring.

My gun's way too heavy for her to hold steady, and it's already weavin' in pretty good circles.

There's somethin' else she needs to know about my gun.

It ain't loaded. I made sure the chambers were empty before I put it in the truck, and I've got all the shells with me.

I decide I better tell her this before she gets her fool head blowed off. Maybe ours, too.

She looks at me like I've just killed her dog. She says you are just one lyin' sack of pig-doo, mister. Now, step away from Burl so that when I shoot him, I don't have to shoot you, too.

Just hearin' her talk, I'd say there's quite a bit of whiskey in that statement. That might help explain that weavin'.

Ferlin snorts. He says oh, boy, this is gonna be fun!

Rattlesnake-quick, he whips up his shotgun and fires off a round toward Della. I know in a flash he's aimed high over her head—but not so high that we cain't hear them pellets whizzin' by.

Della's spooked and jerks her gun up high and wild, pullin' both triggers as she does.

Click, click.

She loses her balance and falls over backwards, the double-barrel clatterin' out of her hands to the road.

I do feel bad about my poor gun.

She looks at me and says what kind of fool travels with an unloaded gun, huh? I'da took that three thousand dollars and moved myself to Memphis. Bought me a Chevrolet. And a big ole Catahoula Cur dog. Taught him to bite people like him.

She points to Burl.

Ferlin laughs. He nudges the other man and says send them other gals over there with that one.

The man turns away from us and for the first time I see he's got a rope in his free hand. He tugs on it and two women, all tied up with ropes around their wrists, come stumblin' forward.

They are a sorry-lookin' sight.

He lets go the rope and they fumble ahead. The back woman stumbles into the first and they both go down.

The man says aw, now looka there, they've fallen down, Ferlin. I shore hope they didn't hurt their tender selves.

Both men bust out laughin' at that one.

The gals struggle up and come stragglin' over, their heads down. They look muddy and sweaty.

Della picks herself up and goes rushin' toward them.

Burl says Ferlin and Stack, I was wondering what was keeping you boys. And why have you tied up your lovely roses?

Roses my ass, Burl, says Ferlin. That's the last time I listen to you about women. Next time I'll just give my money to a spider, I shore will. These two ain't give me and Stack nothin' but troubles. You *know* what we had to pay 'em, brother, and mine wouldn't even gimme a little *kiss.*

One of the women over by Della looks at Ferlin. She says we don't kiss, you hillbilly moron. I offered to keep my part of the bargain but you wanted to get all lovey-dovey. Don't you know *anything*?

Ferlin says see, Burl? This is what I'm talkin' 'bout? She said, yeah, I could have a poke but she'd keep her eyes closed, thank you. Now, for twenty-two dollars and fifty cents you'd think a gal could keep her eyes open and a man could get a kiss. I mean, they were treatin' me and Stack like *dirt*! Dirt, Burl!

The woman says, mister, you don't bathe and you don't brush your teeth. You don't comb your hair. You don't wash your clothes. You've got little funny things growin' in your ears. You talk nonsense. You could pay me twenty-two *thousand* dollars and I still wouldn't kiss you.

Ferlin says see! See, Burl, what I'm talkin' about. That's why we had to hog-tie 'em. They were gonna run away 'fore we even got to first base. We figgered we'd drag 'em over here and maybe you could talk some sense into 'em. That's about the one thing you're good at, Burl. Talkin'. Y'all, Burl could charm the yolk off an egg, he could.

Burl says now, now, little brother, sarcasm isn't your forte—just stick to revenge. You see, I thought I had solved our transportation problems. I got Della to flag down this truck, but things degenerated. Regrettably, these gentlemen got the upper hand on me through cunning and treachery.

Ferlin says Burl, we're gonna rob a bank with a cabbage truck?

Burl says please, Ferlin. Chess is not your forte, either. A cabbage truck is the perfect feint in a situation like this.

I hear ole Della snort. She says he's lyin'. This is about as lonesome a road as there is and he was afraid nobody else would come along. Plus, boys, he was plannin' to steal three thousand dollars and not even cut you in on it.

Burl says ah, see, boys—I fared no better in my choice of tarts than you. This one is bitter and dry as Mother's fruitcake.

Three thousand dollars? says Ferlin.

A figment, says Burl. A web of lies. That cunning Negro there—he points to Harris—offered three thousand dollars in exchange for his freedom. But when I went to secure it—for all of us, of course—it turned out to be a trick. Now come over here and free your brother from his chains. Perhaps you will be kind enough to break a few of their ribs in return for the bruises I have suffered.

Ferlin chuckles. He says Burl, you shore do get yourself in some messes, don'tcha? I'm a-comin'. I'm a-comin'.

Ferlin ain't much to look at. He's skinny as a starved chicken. His eyes are set close together and he's got a waddle of skin at his neck. He's wearin' a spotchy-colored cap of the kind I've seen welders in these parts wear, and it's pulled down low across his eyes. He's wearin' the same kinda rubber boots that Burl has on, with tattered dungarees, a checked shirt with a tore pocket, and a huntin' vest over it. He's totin' a pump-action shotgun and I do see he's got a big ole knife hung from his belt off his left hip.

I'd figger to whup Ferlin easy in a fair fight, but I gotta feelin' Ferlin ain't spent much of his life fightin' fair.

He comes over to where Burl is standin'. Keepin' an eye square on me, he whips out that big knife of his and makes quick work of the ropes.

Ferlin says which one did you say did this to you?

Burl points at me. That tall one there, he says.

Ferlin chuckles. He says doggone it, Burl, how come I'm always havin' to settle your scores?

Burl says we all have our roles in life, little brother. I am the brains and you are the brawn.

Ferlin says here, hold this. He hands Burl his shotgun, then turns to the other man and says Stack, keep your scattergun on 'em.

Stack nods.

Ferlin comes walkin' right at me, that big knife out in front of him.

I've been in one knife fight before and I won that one. I didn't have a knife then, either, but I did have the advantage of havin' a broke beer bottle.

I hold out my hand and say whoa, podnah. I wouldn't come no closer if I were you.

Ferlin slows but don't stop.

He says you must be kiddin', mister.

I bend quick and pick up one of them cabbages lyin' at my feet.

I say I ain't kiddin'. One more step and I'll clobber you with this.

I wave it around with both hands. I say I kilt a man with a potato last year.

Ferlin caws like a mad crow. He says Burl, are you listenin' to this?

Ferlin gets a crazy-goofy look on his face and goes into a crouch, wavin' that knife out in front of him. He looks pretty good doin' that.

He charges.

Snake-quick, I chuck that cabbage hard as I can like a man chest-passin' a basketball.

It catches him by surprise and thumps him hard in the chest and I hear him suck for air. He drops his knife hand down low, clutchin' at his stomach as though this might help him breathe. I go in and kick at the knife with the hard toe of my right boot and smack it clear out of his hands. Then I use my long arms and grab Ferlin up by the straps of his huntin' vest and pull him down on top of me, keepin' him between me and Stack.

I put a knee in his balls as we go down and he moans like an overloaded cane truck. I give him a head-butt just to make shore. I hear him cuss me, then go slack.

I just hope that fool Stack don't shoot us both.

I start to push Ferlin up like a shield, bargainin' chip, but I hear the fast clop of footsteps on the road and a shadow falls across us.

He says let Ferlin go, you dirty-fightin' sumbitch, and get up and get over there by your nigger friends 'fore I blow your brains out.

I rise slow and then feel a foot in the small of my back.

Stack kicks me hard and I go floppin' forward on my face toward where Harris and Chilly and them women are.

I know I've scraped up my knees good and when I push myself up with my hands I see a trickle of blood from where I've gouged my wrists. I feel the heat rise up in me again and I'm about a flash from turnin' and goin' after Stack, whether he shoots me or not, when I feel a hand on my shoulder and it's Chilly sayin', low and steady, now, Logan, no use gettin' yourself killed. We might need your help later on.

I turn back toward Stack, who's still bent down over Ferlin. He looks up at me with razor blades in his eyes and says you've screwed the pooch, mister. You don't know Ferlin. When he comes outta this, he'll come after you like a bobcat on moonshine.

I say Ferlin got about what he deserved. Now, why don't you boys just take me and let my friends and these women here go on about their business. I'm a man on the run from the law myself and I ain't gonna be missed much by respectable folk. But these folks will, and you'll have a army of police, not to mention a few other sorts, after you if you mess with 'em.

Stack ain't much bigger than Ferlin, though he don't quite have the same ornery, porch-dog look. He's got ruddy skin like a drinkin' man and seems a bit cross-eyed. He's wearin' muddy, mismatched cowboy boots. He wouldn't win a prize at the county fair.

He stands and raises his shotgun right at me.

He says mister, you talk big for a man about to get a supper of buck-shot.

Then I hear Burl speak up. He says easy there, Stack, easy. I'm intrigued. Let's have the gentleman tell us exactly why it is he's a fugitive from justice. He does seem to have talent in the manly arts—at least of fighting dirty.

I look at Burl and he don't look too hot. He's leanin' on the gun Ferlin had him hold like it's a crutch.

I gotta think about this for a second. Then I say well, a few days back, I robbed a bank back down the other side of the Catahoula Swamp. Took twelve thousand two hunderd and twelve dollars in broad daylight. Shot two lawmen and a nosy so-'n-so who tried to keep me from leavin' town. Didn't shoot 'em good enough, 'cause they're still breathin' in the hospital down there. I'm a swamp man and I paddled and slogged clear across the Catahoula over about four nights, sleepin' in the daytime. One time, so many mosquitoes landed on me that I weighed twenty pounds more than I do now. I got me a bit of an outlaw network myself, which is how I run up against these two once I got over to this side of the swamp.

I point to Chilly and Harris.

I say Harris here talks like a churchman but he's one of the best smugglers in this part of the country. Outlaws or whiskey, it don't matter to him. He hides it all under them cabbages. I buried most of my money way back in the swamp but give him three thousand dollars to get me up to north Mississippi—Tupelo.

I point at the truck. I say up in those cabbages—that was my hideout. See, ole Harris wadn't lyin' about havin' that kinda money, he just don't have it on him. He give it to the man he works for for safekeepin'. You boys heard of Bobo Cenac? Baddest man on the west side of the Catahoula Swamp. He runs a gang of about ten big Cajun sonuvaguns all biggern' ole Chilly here. They poach gators and deer and seine redfish illegally and rob rednecks who come outta them saloons around Yankee City all drunked up with that oil-field pay in their pockets. My name is Hank, Hank Jones. If you boys kill me, don't go braggin' to nobody that you did it. Bobo and them fellas will come find you. I pay them boys good money to hide me out and hook me up with characters like Harris here. I'm a steady customer and Bobo don't like losin' customers.

I look straight at Stack.

Stack don't put his gun down but he slacks it off a bit.

He turns toward Burl and says Professor, I think we've just heard a big pile of bullshit, don't you?

Burl's lookin' down like he's thinkin' somethin' over. Then he looks up at me and says it may well be, Stack, but I can appreciate a man who tells such a fine story. True *raconteurs* are exceedingly hard to find. Ah, so let's see. How should we proceed?

Burl looks down again for a long while and nobody says nuttin', 'cept Ferlin, who's comin' to slowly and mumblin'. I hear him ax Stack where am I?

Then Burl says all right, Hank Jones, I'll accept at face value that you're an outlaw on the run from robbing banks. So I'll make you an offer too good to turn down—because, well, I won't let you. Up this road about twenty miles is a lovely little town called Cypremore with two spots of particular interest to me—a brothel and a bank. We will save the brothel for another time. As for the bank, we scouted it once and I'm of the opinion that it can be robbed, though not without moderate risk, which is where you come in. As you are a fellow experienced in such matters, we are going to let you go in there and rob it. The other charm of Cypremore is that the Mighty Mississip' runs right through it. A person or persons who could, by stealth or guile, secure a boat could slip away down the river little noticed carrying all manner of things, including money taken from a bank robbery. One of the things that would make that work is a feint. Ah, there again, we have you, Hank. We'll cover outside. You go in and rob the bank. There is only one way out—the front door. You hand off the money to us, shoot your gun in the air a few times and flee in this truck, cabbages and all. As part of the feint, we become outraged citizens shouting out your trespass and inflaming any and all nearby to call the authorities. Then we slip off to the river and dash away. Now, speak up and tell me what you think of my little scheme? Tell me, Hank, is it not particularly brilliant?

About now, I'm feelin' like I did when I got myself into wrasslin' Lester back at Noonie's—a bit too clever for my own good.

I say Burl, that sounds like a good plan for you boys but what do I get out of it? Generally, when I rob banks, I'm used to gettin' a payday.

Burl says it's quite simple, really. *If* you get away, you have your freedom and your life. You would even be free to come back here and rescue your companions in arms. And these lasses, too. They will all be tied up together out in the woods. Who knows? Perhaps these ladies, having spurned our affections, will smother you with kindness if you return to save them. Or, for twenty-two fifty you can at least get a poke.

Burl haw-haws when he says this, then grabs at his ribs.

Ow, he says. Hank, you do know how to hurt a man. Now, what say you? *Tempus fugit* as they say.

I don't get the last part of that but I look at Chilly and Harris. I got to admire their poker faces.

I say you drive a heckuva bargain, Professor.

Burl says well, all right, let's get going. Ferlin, you okay to travel, my brother?

Ferlin hobbles to his feet and looks at me. He says Burl, cain't I just give this one a fist up the side of the head before we go?

Burl says Ferlin, be patient, brother. Why, who knows what calamity may befall our friend as he comes out of the bank with his shotgun? Now, Stack, take all but Hank and go tie them securely in the woods. He looks at Della for the first time in a while and says don't worry, flower. I'm sure you'll be rescued before the mosquitoes suck you *completely* dry.

Della says Burl, I'll get you for this.

Stack says no more whinin'. He points with his shotgun across the road at the woods and says okay, everybody get a move on this way. There's a big ole hackberry about a quarter-mile out there that's got your name on it.

I look at Harris and Chilly and say well, I'm sorry about this.

Harris looks at me steady and says Hank, I appreciate your business. You just try to take care of my truck. If there's a scratch on it, I'm gonna get Bobo Cenac to come collect the fixin'-up money from these characters.

Stack shakes his head. He says you boys talk awful brave for people on the wrong side of a gun. Now, get goin', the whole lot of you. Off to the woods.

I watch 'em go and realize the best I can hope for is that that fool Ferlin don't decide to shoot me on the spot.

17.

A man can accumulate a fair number of things to worry about in his life.

I've accumulated a fair number to worry about in the last ten minutes.

I'm in the cab of the truck, squashed in between Stack, who's drivin', and Burl, who turns out to have another trick or two up his sleeve.

Actually, what he's got is one of them tiny pistols, the kind they call a derringer. I thought them things were somethin' out of a cowboy movie or a storybook. But he's got a real one in his right hand tucked inside his coat and pointed right at me.

He's got another regular pistol tucked into the waistband of his britches. He says when we're ready, he'll give me that one—unloaded—to go rob that bank, 'cause, now that he's thought about it, carryin' my shotgun into the bank might stir a ruckus before I can get the money out.

They've stowed their shotguns, and ours, up top in my hideout with Ferlin.

The day's grown hot and I worry about Chilly and Harris and them ladies all tied up out in the woods without food or water.

I wonder if Harris regrets ever meetin' up with me and Chilly. In that cabbage spill that toppled ole Burl, I bet we lost about a third of them cabbages. That don't seem like a thing a guy should worry about, considerin' everything else, but I do feel bad about it.

Plus, though it is true I once stole a pig as a young man, I ain't got a lick of experience when it comes to robbin' banks.

We go bouncin' down the road.

Not that I'm over fond of bathtubs myself, but it *is* a bit rank in here. Burl's wheezin' like a broke-down accordion.

Burl says now, my good man, tell me about your life of crime. How does one, say, graduate from petty crime to bank robbery? Unless, perhaps, you skipped all those petty steps in between and went straight into more felonious pursuits?

I puzzle this over. True, I've always liked to tell stories. But this is gettin' to be ridiculous.

I say I've always stole stuff to support myself 'cause I don't take to reg'lar work too well. Since the law was chasin' me anyway, I figgered I might as well get chased for big money as little. The other thing about bank robbin' is that, if you're not greedy, you don't have to do it that often. Heck, with the money I've got stashed away back in the Catahoula, I wadn't plannin' to do nuttin' for a while but go fishin' and drink beer.

Burl nods. He looks at me like he expects me to keep goin'.

I say you know, stedda robbin' this bank, we could all turn around and go down to Chenier Atchafalaya where I got me a boat stashed away. I could take you boys out to where my money is hid and we could split it up four ways. Save us all a lot of trouble. You boys would get nine thousand dollars plus some change. That ain't bad money. The only thing I'd ax is that we first go untie my friends and them gals out in the woods.

I see Burl smile at that. He says Hank, my friend, you are a charming schemer. Under better circumstances, why, I believe you and I could share many a lively escapade. However, let's see—you lead us way back into some godforsaken swamp that you know like the back of your hand and we don't know at all. Then what happens? We get separated? You tip over the boat? That gang of rogues you told us about—Bobo whomever—is lying in ambush for us? No, I don't think that's in the cards. I think we will stick to the plan to have you liberate Cypremore First National of some or all of its money. Plus, I am keen to see you in real action. Now, back to the topic at hand—your life of crime. As a man who has come somewhat late to the trade myself, I'm eager to hear more of your experience.

I can see Burl ain't gonna let go of this easy.

I say well, there ain't that much more to tell. I rob two or three banks a year at the most. I got me a few hideouts in the swamp and I move around quite a bit. I use a sawed-off shotgun for the jobs. I wear me a cowboy hat and a Mardi Gras mask, a differnt one every time. Down there, them police know me as the Mardi Gras Kid. I dress in black clothes, 'cause one time I heard a fella say a man dressed in black always looks bigger than he is, and it's harder to make out what he really looks like when he's switched back to reg'lar clothes. I go in there and draw my gun and say if you don't gimme all your money, I'm gonna kill everybody in this bank and feed 'em to the gators. Usually, they gimme the money.

Burl nods.

Impressive, he says. And how do you get away?

Sometimes on foot. I wear reg'lar clothes under my robbin' suit and I generally try to shuck my uniform before anybody's really knowed what happened. I've gone through a lot of black clothes that way. Sometimes I've worked it out with a podnah who don't mind drivin' a getaway car. One time, we drove off in one of them airboat do-jiggies. It was stolen, too, and we sunk it way out in the swamp, down in one of them sinkholes. They never found it.

I see Burl keeps noddin' his head.

Even I don't know where I'm gettin' this stuff.

I say you bein' an outlaw and all, you shore you never heard my outlaw name? Down there, every law doggie knows it, as do all the other crooks I run with.

Burl says no, but we tend to run our whiskey and do our poaching and thieving up around here, where things are familiar. Frankly, I find the outlaw life rather taxing sometimes, which is why I'm interested in your theories on bank robbery. You make crime sound all so, well, efficient.

I say well, one of the things I've learned is that it's usually good to stick with what you know.

Burl nods at this, like I've said something important.

I say you and Ferlin shore are different for bein' brothers.

He says yes, but perhaps you didn't catch what I said earlier. We're actually half brothers. The same derelict father but different mothers. Papa was a charming but crooked gambler who was found pistol-whipped, floating facedown in the Mississippi one day when I was but a lad of twelve. Mother was a college-educated beauty from the East. Her parents had money and had come voyaging, as they called it back then, and made a fateful stop in New Orleans. Papa played poker in only the finest hotels, and they met that way, in the salon of the Roosevelt. At any rate, the fever struck and before anyone could know it they'd eloped and I was the result of their wedding-night madness. My mother's parents promptly disowned her and my father soon basically abandoned her for one of a number of mistresses of ever-declining quality. Ferlin was the fruit of one of those unions. Mother took him in out of pity, though my mother's lot had by that time devolved into near poverty. However, at one point she did have a small sum she inherited from her grandmother and she invested it in my education. I actually *am* a learned man—I studied literature at Tulane. At any rate, in the spate of about a year we lost both Papa and Mother, and it was just Ferlin and me, tossed to the fates. I basically raised the lad.

I say I can see you did a good job.

Burl actually laughs at that. He says Hank, my good fellow—such a wit for a backwoodsman! Though what you say wounds me, I take your point. Still, Ferlin was born with a feral nature that I don't think a loving home would have done much to improve. God knows my poor mother tried as best she could to make a gentleman out of me. And you can see how that worked out.

The Professor goes quiet for a bit. Then he says there you have it, my friend, one of the major themes of literature—life as but the torturous crucible of destiny.

I say you know, Professor, I don't quite follow that altogether but I see the notion of it. It makes me wonder, though, why a fella smart as you couldn't go off and do somethin' else with your head, even if you got fired by that college. Not that I haven't met smart crooks—I have, and I like to think that even though I don't have a lot of book learnin', I might be one of 'em. But let's face it—a lotta crooks I know are crooks 'cause they're too stupid or mean or lazy to be anything else.

Burl smiles again. He says I thoroughly share your observations, Hank. Look at my brother Ferlin. And our comrade in arms Stack here. Not a man destined to run a bank or teach Sunday school, are you, Stack? Not the sharpest sword in the scabbard.

Burl reaches past me and nudges Stack on the shoulder.

Stack just nods and keeps drivin'.

I don't think Stack even knows he's been insulted, though it's true—with the Professor slingin' around them big words, it's not always clear where a man stands.

Burl says well, much like you, Hank, I'm not a man who easily abides authority. At Judah P. Fox Junior College, where I taught, I did not enjoy easy relations with my superiors. You might be amazed at what cauldrons of political intrigue these places are. Strip away the thin veneer of academic civility and you find nothing but scheming and petty jealousies and hostility. Absurd! Judah P. Fox is a rural junior college whose mission is to take thick-headed farm boys and try to pump a bit of oxygen into their brains before they go off to agricultural school, where they learn pig management and cotton-planting techniques and such. The only thing that made it bearable were the farm girls—the smart ones, at least. The girls were blessed with the good fortune of *not* inheriting daddy's ten acres of hardscrabble paradise, and thus they were free to actually study and learn meaningful things. The challenge was to keep them out of the clutches of the farm boys, who were constantly trying to bed them and wed them and keep them barefoot and pregnant so that the tragic breeding cycle that has created generations of hicks and hayseeds and mindless rednecks could be replayed, over and over again.

I say Professor, it sounds to me you're bein' a bit harsh on farm folk.

Burl laughs. Ah, probably so. I do have a tendency toward hyperbole. Have you noticed, Hank? Nonetheless, there's more than a glimmer of truth in there. But, where was I? Oh, yes, the lilies of the field. What made teaching worthwhile was looking out over all those vapid faces at the beginning of each semester and discovering the one winsome lass who would be sitting, wide-eyed, drinking in every word I spoke—a girl of intelligence and wit herself who would be charmed by my knowledge, wit, and erudition—a connection, if you will. That, my friend, is all that made my dull, dull, dull academic life worthwhile. It was finally my undoing, as well. Actually, her name was Charlotte, Charlotte Flowers. Lovely, flaxen-haired, blue-eyed Charlotte. She was my truth, my beauty, my soul. Unfortunately, she was also only nineteen, and her father, an unpromising lawyer in town, did not cotton to our affair once Charlotte, in a lapse of good judgment, told him about it. Of course, fraternizing with a student at Judah P. Fox is extremely frowned upon and her father complained to the authorities and before long I was in the dock, and Charlotte was there—coerced by her father, I'm sure—to testify against me. Well, yes, she had gotten an A in my Advanced Shakespeare course, but only because she was an A student. That I was sleeping with her mattered not a whit to me but, well, the way things go at these sham tribunals, the outcome was preordained.

Then Stack nudges me and says don't take the Perfessor serious, Hank. He'd poke anything in a skirt, and it wouldn't necessarily have to be a person. We've seen the Perfessor in love many a time.

Stack says haw, haw—haw, haw, haw!

I look at Burl. He's shakin' his head but he looks serious.

He says do you see, Hank, what I put up with? Low-grade humor. Sophomoric attacks upon my character. Men like Stack know nothing of the torment of the tormented soul. Suffering is the true art of all men, yet so few men divine this. At any rate, the tragedy for me was not losing my lousy little teaching job, Hank. It was losing my Charlotte—my soul mate.

Stack chuckles again. He says me and Ferlin spied 'em one time in the barn, goin' to town. She was a horny li'l gal, we'll give her that much. Why, she had the Perfessor tied up to the—

Burl reaches across me a lot quicker than I expected he could move and whacks Stack on the side of the head with that derringer.

It ain't a real hard whack but Stack hollers oww, Burl, stop it!

The truck swerves sharp to the left and Stack jerks it back hard to the right and for a second I think we're gonna lose control.

But he straightens her out.

I'm just glad that midget pistol didn't go off.

Burl says Stack, my good man, I can take a joke as well as any man, but, as I've said many times, Charlotte Flowers is off limits. Please don't make me tell you again.

Stack shakes his head, like he's tryin' to shake some cobwebs out. He says doggone it, Burl, that smarted. I was just jokin' you.

Burl says it's not funny, so don't joke me anymore.

Stack says okay, okay. Doggone it.

I cain't say I know what to make of Burl.

I say well, as a man myself who's had his head turned a time or two and don't live very well without the comforts a woman can give, I can see your point. But honestly I think nineteen is a bit young for a man your age.

Burl says you certainly aren't the first person to condemn May-December relationships. But there are certain young women who flourish under the attentions of a more seasoned man. And, well, the salutatory effects of young, winsome women on the conditions of middle-aged men such as myself are well known.

I say if you're tellin' me men grow up slow, I'll buy that. And if you're tellin' me a man can be perked up when a young gal flirts with him, I'll buy that, too. But I'm not shore young women, even the smart ones, know what they're gettin' into when they run up against fellas like you or me. Some of 'em might even want us to be daddies to 'em, but a man in that position might decide he'd have more fun if he was a sugar daddy. Usually, there's trouble down that road.

Burl looks at me kinda funny. He says Hank, I've never known a thief who could be such a moralizier!

I'm puzzlin' that over when I hear Stack say doggone it, Burl, we got serious problems.

Burl says what do you mean, Stack?

He says check out your rearview mirror. The po-lice are comin' up fast.

Burl bends his head so that he can see out the mirror on his side. He says regrettable. Quite regrettable.

He says all right, Stack. Pull over slowly. We're clearly not going to out-run the law in a cabbage truck.

Burl shifts in his seat and looks hard at me and tucks that derringer in his coat in a way that lets me know it's pointed at me again. He says Hank, I'm starting to like you, but don't even try to say a word.

18.

Cramped in the middle, I don't see a thing, myself. I hear a coupla doors slammin', and then I look out and see two deputies standin' just outside Stack's window.

One of 'em, a kinda big fella, has his hand on the grip of his pistol stuck in his holster. The other one, a short skinny guy wearin' sunglasses and a big deputy's hat pulled down low over his face, has got his arms folded and is starin' hard into the truck.

When I look 'em over good and realize what I'm seein', I just put my head down.

This might be the most peculiar day yet.

The small fella, who's closest to Stack, says hey there, boys, where y'all headed?

Out the corner of my eye, I catch Stack glancin' at Burl. It's Burl who talks up.

He says why, Officer, we're heading to Mississippi to sell our cabbages.

The deputy nods. He says y'all are farmers?

Burl nods. As you can see, we're proficient in the finer arts of agronomy.

The deputy nods again. He says I can see that. My wife makes smothered cabbage with potatoes. Y'all ever had any?

Burl says no, I don't think I've ever had the pleasure.

The deputy says you pour a little pepper vinegar and sprinkle on some Tabasco and man, oh, man, that's a meal in itself.

Burl says how fascinating. Now, Officer, do you mind if I ask what the problem is? Certainly we weren't speeding. This truck simply doesn't go that fast. As for the rest, well, I think everything is in order. We did swerve a bit back there but we were just trying to avoid a pothole. I—

The deputy gets his face right up in the window and says to Burl, we're lookin' for a fella who might have been travelin' up this road today. We picked up a hot tip this mornin'. From a snitch.

He leans farther in and gazes hard at Stack, then at Burl, then at me.

He steps back and says Galjour, come up here and take a look at the podnah in the middle there. It definitely ain't them other two. They're uglier than a gator's ass but they don't look like Hank Jones.

I look at Burl and see his eyes go wide.

The big fella steps forward and looks in. He says well, ain't Hank Jones kinda ugly, too?

The skinny guy says I guess it depends on who you axin'.

The big podnah looks hard at me. He says well, I'll be doggone. The one in the middle here looks just like Hank Jones to me. Just like that pitcher on the post-office wall. Take another look, podnah.

The skinny guy leans into the window again—then whips out his pistol and points it at me.

He says now fellas, everybody sit still and don't make a move.

He looks first at Stack, then at Burl. He says y'all know this character here? He a friend of yours?

Burl starts to sputter. He says well, actually, no, Officer, well, no he—

The deputy says uh-huhn, pickin' up hitchhikers, right? Man, oh, man, the number of dumb sumbitches who still pick up hitchhikers these days. People must think we're still livin' in the fifties, but there's crooks and crazies all over the roads these days. Anyway, boys, you've managed to give a ride to Hank Jones, the most wanted bank robber in Catahoula Parish history. Now, Hank, you packin'?

I say no, Deputy, I ain't packin'. I ain't even sayin' I'm Hank Jones.

I got to hand it to ole Lester Benoit. He ain't just good at wrasslin'. He's a pretty doggone good actor, too.

He says well, okay, everybody out of the truck, nice and slow. We don't want no trouble. I don't have no truck with you other boys, but this one here is comin' with us.

Lester steps back and opens Stack's door with his left hand.

The only thing I'm worried about is that derringer Burl's got. I hope the fool ain't got so fond of me that he'll try to fight the law on my account.

As Stack steps out, I look right at Lester and, holdin' my fist close to my stomach so that Burl cain't see, I flash him a finger, then a thumb pointin' up. Nasty ole Ferlin, hid like a snake in them cabbages, could cause serious problems.

Lester nods. I see the one he calls Galjour looks up, too. He walks, with his pistol down, toward the back of the truck.

Then it hits me—he's one of them fellas in the *bourree* game at Noonie's.

We all get out.

Lester, pointin' with his pistol, waves Stack to the left, then me to the right. Then Burl climbs out slow. I can tell he's still hurtin' some.

Lester backs up a bit and, wavin' his gun, says over there with your friend, mister.

Burl has no sooner stepped over by Stack when Lester trains his gun on them. He says okay, you two, hands up, and don't make me tell you twice.

Burl says wait, just a minute, Deputy—

Lester keeps his pistol on them and then, reachin' behind him, draws another pistol and flips it to me.

I catch it nice and easy.

He says doggone it, Logan, you had us worried for a while. These two cottonmouths have guns?

I say the big one there does for shore, a tiny pistol tucked up under his coat and a bigger one in the waistband of his britches. There's one more up top, where they've stashed my shotgun and his up in the cabbages.

Lester says thanks. He drops down in a crouch and gets both hands on his pistol and says okay, podnahs, drop your guns or you'll be sorry.

Lester, I got to admit, has got this deputy thing down good.

I hear Galjour yellin' you there, up in the truck, c'mon down with your hands up and there won't be no trouble. You're surrounded.

Burl throws me the kind of look that's hard to figger out—oh, there's some disgust in it, but somethin' else I don't quite recognize.

Then he says well, Hank, I guess there really isn't any honor among thieves. He eases the derringer out of his coat and drops it on the ground. He does the same with the pistol he was gonna give me to rob the bank with.

Now kick 'em over here, says Lester.

Burl does so. The pistols skitter on the blacktop. Lester picks 'em up and says Logan, would you mind holdin' these? In fack, you can keep 'em if you want.

I say Lester, I've been collectin' guns ever since I left Catahoula Parish. I don't need any more. I think we'll just drop these in the river at the first chance.

Lester says okay, you two boys turn around and put your hands on the hood of the truck.

I hear Galjour say Logan, you shore he's up there?

I say well, he was, unless he fell out on the road someplace. But you'd've seem him if he had.

He says come around here and cover me. I'm goin' up there.

I walk back and watch Galjour pick his way slow up the cabbage pile. He gets to that tarp and snatches it back quick.

He says aw, looka here. Sleepin' beauty. C'mon, fella, climb on down. You're under arrest.

I hear Ferlin moan low. Then he says in a hurtin' voice, Burl, Burl, you down there? What the hell's goin' on here, brother?

Burl yells up Ferlin, it is just like you to fall asleep on the job.

I see Galjour give Ferlin a hand. He comes up out of them cabbages lookin' beat as a bear-whupped coon dog.

Ferlin says don't yell at me. My head hurts like I've drunk a bottle of poisoned moonshine. Anyway, you the one got us caught.

Burl says oh, shut up, Ferlin. They tricked us in the most disingenuous fashion. Again.

Galjour guides Ferlin down off the back of the truck by the scruff of his shirt and brings him around and steers him over to Stack and Burl.

I say Lester, doggone, son, you're about the last person I expected to see.

Lester grins. He says me and Annie talked it over. I knew all about your troubles and them plans to go with Harris. Annie thought it might be a good idea if I kinda tagged along, least till you boys got out of Loosiana. Good thing I did, too.

I say well, bless your heart, and Annie's, too. So you been followin' us the whole way?

He says yep. Well, except for the part where we caught a flat tire and worried we'd lost you. But we got rollin' again and, from way back, saw Harris's truck stopped in the middle of the road. We pulled over and slipped up quiet in the woods and, well, we got turned around for a bit. I don't care too much for the woods myself. Then we come upon that tree where Chilly and Harris were tied up with them womens. They told us all about the famous bank robber Hank Jones.

I say Lester, are Chilly and Harris all right? And where'd you get the police duds? And that car?

Lester says we untied Chilly and Harris and they're fine. Them wild womens we left tied up. And as far as the car and uniform, well, this here's a reg'lar police car and I'm a reg'lar deputy. So is Sergeant Galjour here.

Galjour grins and says I thought I was a captain. Oh, well, sergeant's okay. Anyway, I moonlight for the sheriff's office now and then. As for that car, I think you met ole Shine Trosclair back down the road? He's my cousin and he had that car in his repair shop. It was one of them that the sheriff's office had sold and—

Lester puts up his hands. He says Sergeant Galjour, I don't think you should be discussin' po-lice business in front of crooks. Now, Logan, what do you wanna do with this lot here?

The Professor is lookin' at me funny again.

He says so, Hank, my friend, you really *are* a *raconteur.* So what are you going to do with us? It's abundantly clear that these men are just cronies of yours, not the law.

Lester gives Burl a dirty look and says I'll tell you what we're gonna do, Mr. Big Mouth. We're gonna turn you in to the real law.

Burl says on what grounds, my good man?

Lester looks at me. For the first time, he's flustered. He says well, Logan, uh, what did they do to you?

I say I guess you could say they kidnapped me. Burl there tried to rob Harris. And since I know Harris and Chilly didn't care to have guns pointed at 'em and be tied up out in the woods, I guess you could make a ruckus of that. Them gals prob'ly have a claim, too, though it is true the one they call Della tried to rob us, too.

Lester brightens up. Robbin' and kidnappin'! I'm gonna run you buncha nootras in for both.

Burl nods. He says ah, well, now if you're going to accuse us of kidnapping, let's think about the ramifications. I'm willing to wager that our man Hank—I mean, Logan—here *is* actually a fugitive of some variety. So if you turn us in for kidnapping him, we'd feel honor bound to report that little matter to the law. We could give them a very accurate description of the notorious Hank Jones.

Lester looks at me. I shrug.

I say Lester, as much as I hate to admit it, ole Burl here is right. Besides, Chilly needs to get to Tupelo and Harris needs to get what's left of them cabbages sold. If you turn 'em in, we'd all have to go tell the law what we saw, and who knows what kinda mess that could turn into.

Poor Lester looks like a hungry hound that's just had a fat T-bone steak snatched right out of his mouth.

He says Logan, this was my first real collar!

I say I know that, Lester, and nobody is happier about it than me. But the other thing you might wanna think about is that the law 'round here might not appreciate you as much as I do. What I know of the law, they sometimes don't take it friendly when other police come bargin' into the places that they're in charge of.

Lester nods and then he frowns and then he says so, what are we gonna do with 'em?

I say my advice is to take their guns and knives and let 'em crawl back under the rock they crawled out from under this mornin'. Them gals, too, though I s'pose we could offer the ladies a ride to the next town. Best as I can tell, the honeymoon is over 'tween this lot and them gals.

Lester don't look happy but I can tell he ain't gonna argue.

I turn to Burl and say there is one more thing. You boys got any money?

Burl says what, Logan, you're going to rob us before you let us go?

I say no. But y'all owe Harris a bunch of money for them cabbages that got spilled. And you owe Lester here for gas—all the way from Catahoula Parish. I'd say altogether we're talkin' two, maybe three hunderd dollars.

Burl says why, that's highway robbery!

I gotta laugh at that.

I say Professor, you got you some weird notions in that head of yours. But, okay, I'll be reasonable. I figger we spilled a hunderd cabbages, most of them bruised or ruint. If you add in the time we've lost and the cost of bein' tied up, a dollar a cabbage would be fair. If you've got a hunderd between you, plus another twenty for gas, we'll take that and call it even.

Burl shakes his head.

Lester says Logan, I think you're lettin' 'em off, easy. But what the hell. Okay, boys, that'll be a hundred and twenty dollars. Let's see those wallets.

Stack reaches back for his. Burl reaches up behind him, too.

Miserable ole Ferlin says I don't have no billfold. I keep my money in my drawers.

Lester says podnah, you know, that's somethin' I didn't necessarily wanna know. But I'm gonna take your word for that. You better hope your friends here have enough to cover you, 'cause nobody wants money that comes outta there.

Lester goes over and gets the wallets and starts rummaging through 'em. He says skinny here has got sixty-two.

Stack says you could at least leave me the two. I shore could use a beer right now.

Lester nods. He says it depends. Lemme see how much big ugly here has.

Burl says really, there's no reason to stoop to insult.

He pulls a buncha bills outta Burl's wallet and starts countin'. He says let's see, he's only got forty-four. I guess that'll have to do.

Lester takes the money and gives the wallets back.

He says I left skinny two but big ugly gets nuttin'.

Stack says how come I gotta give sixty and Burl only has to give forty-four, huh?

Burl says Stack, don't be daft. We're being robbed and it's just your misfortune to have more to contribute than I do.

Stack stomps his foot. He says I want my money, Burl! I doggone well do!

So litigate, my good fellow, says Burl.

Do what?

Burl says, aggravated, so sue me, you fool! You'd think a man could find companionship with those who have at least a rudimentary vocabulary.

I say okay, you girls knock it off. Lester, you and Galjour should search 'em one more time, then we'll get on our way.

They take a fair-sized skinnin' knife off Stack.

Stack whines. He says that's my best knife. I give twenty dollars for that knife. You owe me for that, too, Burl!

Burl says God, what an idiot you are, Stack.

I say Lester, give it to me—it'll be a souvenir to remember these fellas by. Now, you boys best get goin'. You obviously know this country, so you'll find a way back to where you come from.

Burl starts to turn away but turns back and says any chance you'd give us a lift? At least to the spot of our first encounter? It's such a long way, and the day's turned so hot—

I laugh loud. I say Professor, I think we've seen enough of each other for a while. And if you want my advice, I'd go back to where you come from and clean yourself up and try makin' an honest livin'. Based on what I've seen, I don't think you're goin' very far in the outlaw business.

Burl looks at me like he might smile. Then the three of 'em turn and walk slow down the road. They head down an embankment and disappear into the woods.

I let Galjour drive Harris's truck back and I ride with Lester. Chilly and Harris are waitin' by that pile of spilled cabbages. I don't see them gals but Chilly explains it quick.

We untied 'em after Lester sprung us, he says, and before we knew it, they'd run off into the woods. Hell, I wadn't gonna chase 'em. Harris figgers they ran 'cause Della thought we'd turn her over to the law.

I puzzle this over for a bit and say you know, that's prob'ly a good thing for Della to think.

I can tell poor Lester's disappointed.

We all pitch in and reload them spilled cabbages and I give Harris the money we took off of them outlaws. He's tickled.

Then we all shake hands, and Lester says I'm happy to follow you all the way to Tupelo if you want.

I say Lester, I actually think we got it licked now. I appreciate a lot what you and your podnah Galjour done. You be shore to thank Annie Ancelet for me. And one more thing.

He says what's that?

I take out Stack's knife and say I'm sorry all your crooks have got away. You take this as a souvenir of the day you rescued Hank Jones from the bad guys. I had a chance to look it over on the drive back and figger there must be fifty dollars worth of turquoise in the handle.

Lester takes the knife and looks it over and says aw, are you shore, Logan?

I say I'm totally shore. Anyway, I'm headed to Tupelo, where I s'pect I'll do farmin'. I doubt I'll need to skin anything for a while.

Lester smiles and says awright, Hank. You keep well.

I say I will.

We shake again and I climb back up into the burlap nest that I rode in when we first took off, and up the road we go.

19.

Tupelo is a nice li'l town, what I've seen of it in the four, close to five months I've been here. It's got a pretty ole courthouse with a shiny dome on top. There's a cluster of brick houses with wrought-iron porches off the square like the kind you'd see back in Ville Canard.

It's September and I been earnin' my keep workin' on Chilly's uncle's farm. It's out in the rollin', red-dirt hills at a place called Endville and what work there was has pretty much been done. I helped 'em pick melons and tomatoes and beans in the early summer. Then the okra come in and then the cotton, then finally the feed corn. I did okay in everything but it turns out I'm not much of a cotton-picker. Boy, is that hot, awful work.

I hadn't spent much time on a tractor before but I turned out to be pretty good at tractorin', and so I plowed up the stubble in the back forty.

Cane Duggins has got a nice enough place, plain but comfortable. It's in a break in a long stretch of ramrod pines along a rutty tar road, and most of that corn grows up on a red-dirt hillside that catches the sun a good part of the day.

Cane's a good fella, a bit younger'n me, trim with a shiny bald head and a nice sense of humor. 'Cept on Sunday, I've never seen him in anything but dungarees and khaki shirts and steel-toed boots and a straw cowboy hat. Now and then, he'll slip away from the missus and come find me with a couple cans of Pearl beer and we'll go up on that hillside around sunset and drink us a cold one slow and watch the sun go down and just shoot the bull.

His missus goes to a Baptist church up the road three or four times a week, not countin' about all day on Sunday, and she don't think much of drinkin', or those who do it. She says it's the devil's work and I had to laugh at that, mostly 'cause there might've been a time or two I thought that was true myself.

What I know about churches, I don't know how anybody could spend so much time in one. Cane says he goes on Sunday 'cause if he didn't he would hear about it Monday through Saturday. We both laughed, but I could tell there was some truth in that.

The missus—Belva—even axed me to come along one Sunday. I said thank you but I'm just not the churchgoin' kind, though the truth is I did go some to the Catholic church when Elizabeth was alive. After that, Belva ain't had a lot to say to me, which is all right as I'm not a man who always cares to talk. There are churchgoin' people of a certain kind who take it personal that you're not one of 'em.

I live in a pine shack fixed up nice a coupla years ago when Cane thought his ole momma might come to live with him. But she died before he got it done. It's got a small porch with a rockin' chair and there's a view of the farm pond down the hill a ways. Inside, it's a bit tight but I don't need much room. It's got a tin roof and a nice soft bed and a table next to a window with a screen on it so the mosquitoes cain't get in.

Some days I sit out on that porch till it gets dark, then I go to bed. I sleep with the window open, with the crickets for company. Them crickets love to sing on warm summer nights. In the early summer, a man could find his way around in the dark by walkin' in the light of the fireflies, there was so many of those things.

The shack's got one of them tiny stoves that at least lets a man make coffee in the mornin'. I'll make my coffee and sit there and watch the sun come up and it ain't a bad way to start the day. On the other hand, a man cain't buy good coffee in Tupelo, far as I can tell. Nobody here sells Community Coffee, nor dark roast of any kind. I guess that's a Cajun thing. So no matter how much coffee grinds I heap up in my drip pot, it still comes out weak and bitter, like I've brewed it from pinecones.

The outhouse ain't a far walk, either, and as Cane has indoor plumbin' in the main house, I'm the only one that uses it—funny, since Chilly's hung that Whites Only sign he took from Noonie's on the outhouse door. It's a two-seater and I'm of the opinion that the right seat's a bit more comfortable than the left. Cane has left some old Sears-Roebuck catalogues out there and though I've not spent much time lookin' in catalogues, I gotta say I don't mind browsin' 'em. Elizabeth would order stuff from them catalogues now and then.

If I want a bath, I go down that half-acre pond I can see from my porch. It's filled up natural by a cold spring and from a distance it looks deep and black, like that sweetwater in the Catahoula Swamp. After a hot day, a dunk feels good. I've seen fish in there, though I ain't tried to catch 'em. They look like fingerling bass.

Cane keeps a horse called Nugget and he comes down to that pond to drink. He seems like a fine ole horse and he'll let me rub his nose, even though I gotta say I ain't much of a horse man. Sometimes there's an apple left over from my lunch bag and I'll save it for Nugget. I think he likes apples a whole lot better than I do.

Cane don't pay me much but he lets me live out here free and he feeds me, breakfast and supper inside, and dinner out of a lunch pail out in the fields wherever it is we're workin'. So I don't need much pocket money for now. In my opinion, Cane wouldn't have to pay me nuttin' at all, but he said white people once had slaves but he wouldn't ever have a man, white or colored, that he worked for free.

He ain't axed me one single thing about what chased us outta Catahoula Parish, though he did ax Chilly.

I eat breakfast and supper at the kitchen table in the farmhouse. The missus cooks it, and Belva's a good fry cook. Cane eats breakfast with me. We get eggs, bacon or homemade sausage, grits, and biscuits every day.

The farmhouse ain't very big but it's painted bright white and kept nice. A young woman named Flora comes out once a week to scrub this and that for the missus. She's the daughter of Jackson, one of the ole boys who works with me in the fields. She changes the sheets on my bed.

Flora's pretty as a swamp iris and sweet as a preacher's cat and one time she smiled at me and I got a tingle all over. I don't think I had the wits about me to smile back and it's prob'ly best I didn't.

I realize I've been thinkin' some of Annie Ancelet. Funny how certain women can get on a man's brain quick like that. Actually, I've been thinkin' of her a lot.

Chilly stayed out here about a month then moved to town and lives with a cousin called Booty. Chilly's not a farm type a person and his cousin runs a garage that fixes up a lot of the colored cars around Tupelo, as most of the white mechanics won't work on colored cars. Chilly helps Booty out and, what I hear from Cane, Chilly seems to have a knack for mechanickin'. Chilly's plannin' to work there till he can save enough money to go to a colored college some place not too far from here. Chilly, seems to me, can do just about anything he puts his mind to.

That's, of course, if the law don't catch up to us. But we laid real low when we first got here, and I mostly stay outta town even now.

One day about an hour before dark, I sat on my porch lookin' at a hill across the way with a solitary oak on it. I saw a man come up on that hill, a white man I'm pretty sure, and just stare my way for the longest time. I didn't stir at all. I just sat there still as the day moon. He left at dark. It give me a bit of a scare but nuttin' come of it.

Even though he's moved to town, Chilly and me still get together now and then. He comes out here with Booty to see Cane and Belva. Twice we've gone with a few of their podnahs to a saloon on the outskirts of Tupelo where on Saturday night they've got fellas who play music of a type I hadn't heard down in the swamps. Chilly says it's blues music and only colored people will ever play it 'cause only colored people have got a proper notion of what the blues is all about. I pretty much agree with Chilly on everything, though I think I could tell him a thing or two about the blues.

There's this one ole skinny colored boy who wears sunglasses even inside and he makes his guitar cry like a baby. Doggonedest thing I've ever heard.

Chilly says goin' to that saloon ain't a thing I'm s'posed tell his Aunt

Belva about 'cause she would get on him day and night about it. Me, too, I s'pect.

They serve beer in there, and moonshine, too. I stuck with the beer that night.

Another night I went and, well, one thing led to another. Chilly says he got me outta there when I started dancin' on the floor in a way that wadn't regulation with some young gal who kept makin' eyes at me. He said that gal was the girlfriend of the drummer and he was a fella known for his nasty temper.

I guess I argued a bit with Chilly about leavin'—I don't really remember. Anyway, we got outta there and I woke up on the floor of my shack with a mule steppin' on my head. Cane, when he saw me, tole me just to go back to bed but I went on to work.

Seems to me I used to like gettin' drunk but there wadn't nuttin' I liked about it that time. I think Chilly was aggravated with me and I was sorry to have made him so. We patched it up.

I hitched into town one time by myself and went to one of them white saloons but I didn't stay long. The bar man was friendly enough but there was some other ole boys in there that I could tell didn't think much of strangers, at least ones that looked as rugged as me. I left Catahoula Bayou with the clothes on my back and I haven't been inclined to spend what bit of money I've got on clothes, though I did buy a pair of dungarees and a shirt and some socks. I pretty much wear the same thing every day. One time Flora volunteered to wash my clothes but I said no. I hate to be trouble for anybody, so I wash my clothes now and then in the pond and spread 'em on the porch of my shack to dry. I don't use soap, as I'd be worried about them fish, so my clothes dry stiff in the sun, but they smell okay. They smell like the country air.

Anyway, I mighta stayed in that bar a bit longer but I heard one of them fellas say, loud to the other, that he'd heard there was a white fella workin' for a nigger farmer outside of town and what the hell was the world comin' to.

In different circumstances I mighta said somethin' about that. But I didn't even look up. I drained my beer and left.

Cane Duggins acts like I've always been here livin' in his shack. He says I can stay here long as I want. He says after the crops are laid in and what needs to be plowed is plowed, he's got a barn and a corn crib he wants to start workin' on 'cause they both need new roofs, and since I seem to be handy, he could keep me on through the winter.

That's awful nice of him. But truth is, I'm a swamp man and farmin' ain't what I'd be doin' if I had me a choice. I'm gonna let things cool down a bit more and then I'm gonna slip back down to Catahoula to check on my boy.

I miss him big as Christmas.

I guess I coulda called Annie on the pay phone to check on him some more but I haven't. Me and phones, you know.

After I go check on Meely, who knows? But I'm still thinkin' serious about Florda. Arthur Johns, the man I showed them white gators to, gimme his card and I've carried it in my billfold ever since. It got soggy crossin' the Great Catahoula but I can still read the phone number. I just hope I won't sound like a tongue-tied moron when I get up the nerve to call.

Now, he did describe his operation as a gator farm so maybe I'd just be tradin' one kind of farmin' for another. But I figger anything to do with gators has got to put a man closer to the swamp. And that's where I wanna be.

Chilly says it's about as long to that place down in Florda as it was from Catahoula Bayou to Tupelo. I wish it wadn't. I've decided I like bein' places more than the gettin' there.

One night as I was 'bout to go to bed, Jonelle Lackey come to my door and knocked on it. I didn't really know her or any of the Lackeys though I'd seen her some. There must be about ten of 'em—a dozen countin' the momma and daddy. They're poor white folks who live down the road a mile from Cane in a beat-up house with a beat-up barn full of rusted tractors and such. Cane told me early you better watch them Lackeys. He said Earl Lackey, the daddy, made whiskey and sold it and his whiskey once blinded a man.

I don't know why Jonelle come over. I'd said hello to her walkin' down the road a few times. She's a looker, made real nice, but she dresses poor in shoes and clothes that better-off folks throw away.

She come to my door and said mister, how are you?

I said I'm okay.

She said can I come in?

I said what for?

She said maybe you need the company, stayin' way out here by yourself with nobody but colored. Must be lonesome out here.

I said I'm okay in the company department.

She stepped in anyway.

She said for five dollars I'll give you a poke.

I laughed at that. I said you know, I had not heard that word used that way till I run into some Mississippi folk a while back. And, well, thank you, cher, but I'm old enough to be your daddy. You need to go find some boys your own age.

She said you'd like it, I know you would.

She hitched up her dress and showed me what she had. Just like that.

For about two seconds I thought about it, and she saw that I was thinkin' about it and she put one leg up on my table to gimme a better look. She wadn't wearin' her drawers. She run her hands up and down her legs in a certain way.

I turned away and then I turned around. I went to her and gentle took her foot off my table and pulled her skirt down proper. I said missy, it ain't like you ain't pretty, you are. And it ain't like I don't need such a thing, I do. But I cain't do it.

She got huffy and said what's wrong with you, mister? Five dollars ain't much money for what I got!

I took out my billfold and fetched five dollars and said here, it ain't about the money, and I can see that you prob'ly need some. Now, you should just go home and think about better ways to make you some money. A pretty girl like you has lots of advantages in the world, and this is only one of 'em.

She didn't say nuttin'. She just come to me and rubbed up against me like a cat and kissed my neck and rubbed her hands in a certain place and

I have to say, them things lifted my blood and I almost fell over the edge, same as I sometimes fall when I'm drinkin'.

But I rocked back on my feet and pushed her away, a bit harder this time, and said really, darlin', go on home. You're just a girl, confused as some girls are.

She threw me a snakebit look and balled up my five dollars and threw it at me and said she was a woman and I was just too stupid to know it. She run out and slammed my door hard and she wadn't gone a minute when I was of a mind and state to chase her down. But I didn't, and I tried to be glad that I didn't.

I crawled into bed a bit later but I couldn't sleep. I was all hopped up, the way men like me sometimes get, and I realized I hadn't been with a woman since ole Velma had set fire to my bed that night out on Catahoula Bayou.

I finally pleasured myself the way lonesome men sometimes do.

I cain't say if it helped or hurt—it feels like it feels.

But I did go to sleep and I woke up thinkin' of Elizabeth, who I'd loved, and then of Annie Ancelet, and wonderin' if she might be feelin' about me the way I was feelin' about her.

Not that I could name all those feelin's.

But I knew I needed to get on down to Loosiana. And I knew I had another reason to go, besides seein' 'bout Meely.

20.

It's the sixth of October, early yet. It's cool but clear, 'cept for wispy fog hangin' in the cypresses. The sun's easin' its way into the woods. There's nothin' quite like the October mornin' light when it lays out all golden in the treetops.

It's so quiet I hear a squirrel, prob'ly fifty yards away, cuttin' an acorn in a pin oak and droppin' the shavin's, plip-plop, onto the soft carpet of leaves.

That squirrel's lucky I've already had my breakfast. Anyway, I've got other business today. Maybe I'll find my boy.

On the first of October, I said goodbye to Cane and the missus and Chilly and his cousin Booty and caught me a ride clear down to Chenier Atchafalaya. I was lucky—Harris Daigrepont happened to come up to Tupelo on more farm business. He come out to Cane's to see me and offered me a lift, as he was headin' back down that way the next day.

Before I left Tupelo, I took twenty-five dollars of the money I'd made workin' for Cane and I give it to Booty to give to Chilly after I was gone, as I knew Chilly wouldn't take it from me directly. A man who's gonna go to college will need money. I won't ever come close to payin' Chilly back for helpin' Meely, and gettin' me hid out at Cane's all that time. But I fig-gered that was a start.

About a week before I left, and things had slowed down on the farm, I managed to call Arthur Johns, the gator man, c'lect on the pay phone.

He said LaBauve, I'm tickled to hear from you. C'mon down soon as it's convenient for you.

Me and Harris had a nice drive down to Loosiana—not a bandit in sight—and he dropped me off not too far from where 'Ti-John Prosperie docked his crewboat that rainy night he rescued me and Chilly from that pump shed. Harris woulda took me to Noonie's or Annie's but I said no, thank you, temptin' as it was. I felt like people had done too much for me already, and I was feelin' anxious 'bout Meely in a way that was hard to pin down. Maybe, as Meely's daddy, I felt like gettin' down to Catahoula Bayou was somethin' I needed to figger out on my own. And now that I had one foot in the swamp, I also had a hankerin' to see the Great Catahoula again—assumin' I didn't have to paddle the whole way. Plus, I could take the double-barrel with me and shoot my food.

Down at the landin', I run into a man named Tregle who said he could take me about two-thirds of the way across the swamp, to a point called Chacahoula Ridge. I said I'd give him ten dollars for his trouble as I could see he was a poor man like me. He didn't wanna take it but I insisted. We went slow and spent the night in his shack. He made trapper's jambalaya for supper outta rabbit and some *andouille* he'd brought along, and it was good. Nobody cooks like Cajuns do.

Chacahoula Ridge is a long, skinny snake of high ground that, if you stay with it long enough, comes out in Catahoula Parish, though far north and west of where I would prefer to land. But I had a compass and my gun and my bulleye and plenty of matches to make fires. And I'd put together a bit of a hobo's bedroll, with a small pot for boilin' my drinkin' water.

I've walked four days through these woods, shootin' squirrels and rabbits for my dinner and sleepin' on the ground. The weather's nice and cool at night, but not cold yet, and there are a few mosquitoes around but not them swarms that got after me and Chilly. I haven't seen another soul, though yesterday mornin' I heard the boom of shotguns far off and I figgered some squirrel hunters were in the woods, as the season always opens the first week of October down here.

I come out on a snaky, potholed tar road that I knew was the Gibson

Bayou Road that runs east and hooks up with the Catahoula Bayou Road eventually. I walked and walked, out of sight in the canefields, or in the grassy tractor roads—what we call headlands—that run up against the tar road, shielded by the cane.

I spent last night in the woods not too far from our farm.

I've been awake since first light and had my coffee and chewed on a rabbit leg leftover from my supper. I've been sittin' on a stump thinkin', watchin', and listenin' as the woods wake up. It's my favorite time of day.

I get up and get my bearin's and figger I ain't more than twenty minutes from my back door.

Somethin' about this makes my heart beat faster and it ain't 'cause I'm worried about bein' caught. Maybe I'm afraid of what I'll find—or won't find.

I no longer try to deny that I've been runnin' from more than the law.

I hit the edge of the woods soon enough, cross over a log, and take a narrow, grassy headland I've walked a thousand times. The dew's so heavy I get my britches wet clear up to my ankles. About a hunderd yards from our house, I duck into the canefield on my left and push through a coupla rows so I've got plenty of cover should somebody come travelin' along or be hangin' around our place. The cane's horse-head high this time of the year. It smells sweet.

At the edge of our yard, I look out and it's a sad sight. The grass is tall and raggedy and the cypress garage looks saggier than ever and the house is all boarded up. I walk through the wet grass and up the back porch. There's some signs nailed to the door by the law tellin' folks to stay away, and another about taxes.

I sit on the porch just thinkin'. There ain't nuttin' in there that I need and I just don't feel like goin' in—it feels too lonesome. I realize I've sat there for a while, my mind just wanderin', when the sun catches the porch and lights it up. I've gotta get goin'.

I'll cross the bayou and see if Henrietta Lirette might be around. She was Meely's teacher and always seemed to treat him nice and she'd know what's become of him. And she might be the one person who, if she sees me, won't call the law.

I walk up toward town in the cover of the canefields to the Waterproof Bridge, cross it and the paved highway on the other side, then duck into the fields again. I head back down the bayou. It's a good hike—two miles at least—and I can tell this day will work its way up into one of them warm Injun summer days.

I get up to the edge of Miz Lirette's house. It's a nice ole place, set under big Spanish oaks, with a circular driveway paved in clamshells. It's two stories, painted white with green trim and shutters. There's a broad porch that runs around about half of it. The yard must be three or four acres and the grass is mowed short and there's one of them gizmos that Catholic ladies put in their yards—a statue of the Virgin Mary—over by the front-porch steps.

I stand there for a while at the edge of the field, just lookin' and tryin' to figger out if anybody's home and wonderin' whether I should really go up and knock on the door. I don't see no cars in the driveway.

Then I hear footsteps comin' up the yard along the edge of the field to my right. I move back deeper into cover.

A boy walks past, headin' toward the porch, a beagle followin' him. He's carryin' a mess of squirrels in his right hand—fox squirrels from the look of 'em.

It's Meely.

He plops them squirrels on the porch, then skips up the step and disappears into the house. The dog follows.

I'm too surprised to move. Before long, I hear a screen door open and Meely walks out, that dog right behind. He settles into a big ole rocker on the porch with what looks like a cup of coffee and that dog curls up at his feet. I hear him say this is some day, ain't it, Rascal. Ain't it, boy?

I find my legs and walk out, leavin' my gun propped up against some cane stalks. Meely puts his hands over his eyes tryin' to make me out. Then he smiles big.

I say hello, Meely.

He says Daddy? Is it really you?

I say it is. That's shore a nice mess of squirrels you got.

He says I got my limit—every one a fox squirrel.

I say you're prob'ly a better squirrel hunter than me now.

He says I doubt that.

I look at that dog. I say that's one fine good-lookin' beagle you've got.

He says Rascal's his name and he's a good dog, for shore.

I say c'mere, pup. He comes over and gives my hand a lick.

Meely says Miz Lirette give me that dog.

I say looks like she picked a good 'un.

Meely says are you all right, Daddy?

Fit as a fiddle, I say.

How'd you know I was here?

I say I didn't. I was comin' to ax Miz Lirette about you. I figgered she'd know where you were and, even if she didn't, she'd be the one person I could ax who wouldn't turn me in to the law.

Meely says that's true, she wouldn't. But there's one thing you oughta know—the police ain't really lookin' for you no more.

I think I musta misheard him. I say how could that be?

Meely says 'cause you're dead.

I'm dead?

Yes sir. A gator drowned you. Or else you drowned and the gators and crawfish pretty much ate you up.

I say you better tell me this slow, son.

He says well, they come to get me one night from the jail. Nasty ole Sergeant Picou said he was sure they'd found a man drowned in the swamp, about the same size as you. He was awful shore it *was* you. I had to go look at the body.

I say I'm sorry about that, Meely.

He says don't be. It was some poor fella but he had a tattoo on his shoulder and the second I saw that I knew it wadn't you.

So what did you do?

I cried.

Doggone, son.

It worked. As soon as I started cryin', the police thought it *was* you. So they give you a funeral and everything.

They did? Where am I buried?

He says in the Catholic church cemetery.

Not next to your momma, I hope?

No sir. You got a poor man's space over by the back fence. People passed the hat and the church where Momma used to go give some money, too. Daddy, you wouldn't believe the number of your friends who come to the funeral. And about every other one of 'em wanted to know if you'd found God before you died.

What did you say to that, son?

I said if God was lost, you'd be the one to track Him.

I bust out laughin' at that. I say and you're tellin' me I've got friends on Catahoula Bayou?

Meely says I'm serious, Daddy. 'Bout everybody on the bayou came to your funeral. Even the police come. I think some of them ole boys were cryin' 'cause they were wonderin' who they were gonna chase now.

I say well, Meely, had I knowed dyin' was so much fun I'da tried it earlier.

Meely smiles and says just don't try it again anytime soon.

I say I'm not plannin' to. Now, for truth—is my name on the tombstone and everything?

He says it is. I woulda put your middle name on there, too, but I didn't know it.

I say it's Earl.

Meely says well, next time I'll know.

Things go quiet for a while. When I tell him all the coffee up in Mississippi tastes like pinecones, he goes in the house and fixes me a cup of Community just the way I like it. I sit on the edge of the porch and sip my coffee in the warm sun while Meely tells me his story about jail and how Joey Hebert, Francis's son, finally stood up before the judge and told what he knew about Junior's and Uncle's lies. Joey had been in a stall in the bathroom at school and overheard Junior and his gang braggin' 'bout the whole deal. The judge pitched a fit and sprung Meely and almost put Uncle and Junior in jail. He tells me how he still might'a had to go to the orphanage 'cept Miz Lirette offered him a place to live here in this nice ole house. He tells me how she's got him to study and how he actually don't mind it and how, since he's makin' good grades, he might even try his hand at algebra. He says Miz Lirette even told him he should start thinkin' about college.

This about knocks me over.

I say Meely, if you go to college, that would do your momma proud.

We talk pretty much about everything else. I give him the dope on how me and Chilly crossed the Great Catahoula and how we got rained on and bug-bit and how we had to wait out that helicopter and how we got waylaid by the Professor and his bunch on the way to Tupelo. When we're about talked out, I tell Meely I'm thinkin' about goin' down to Florda to work for that gator man as I still wadn't shore I'd get a fair shake by the Catahoula Parish law.

He says you should go, Daddy. Even though Junior and Uncle have been proved liars, the police could still get you for shootin' up that police car.

I say I guess I shouldn'ta shot it up.

Meely smiles. He says I'm glad you did. I shoulda helped you.

When I say I'll prob'ly hitch to Florda, he tells me I should get the bus and stay off the roads at least till I'm outta Loosiana as I still cain't be too careful about the law. Then he tells me to wait and he goes in the house and comes back with thirty-five dollars, remindin' me it was money I give Velma that night she caught the mattress on fire. She give it back to him the next mornin'.

He says that should get you a ways on the bus.

I want him to keep it but he won't.

I say well, bless Velma's heart. If she were here I'd kiss her.

Meely says if you paid her thirty-five dollars again, I bet she'd let you.

I have myself a belly laugh. It feels pretty good.

We go quiet, then Meely says did I tell you 'bout Junior's cantaloupe problem?

I say no, *what?* Was he caught stealin' some?

Meely says no. Them fire aints Chilly put down his pants ate him up and he's allergic. His pecker swelled up so big, they had to take him to the hospital so they could shrink it.

Haw-haw, son! Could that be true?

Meely says I think it is. I heard it was the size of a cantaloupe. But Joey Hebert, whose cousin is a nurse there, heard it was a watermelon.

I double up and about fall off the porch. Meely comes off of his chair laughin' so hard he has to steady himself against a porch post. It's good to see my boy laugh so.

We go over a few other things, though for some reason I don't tell him about Annie Ancelet. Pretty soon I realize I should go or I might not go at all. I realize how much I've missed my boy.

I say when I get settled in Florda, I'll send you a bus ticket. You know, that ole boy down there says there's beaches white as sugar and the ocean's as blue as the sky.

Meely says I wouldn't mind seein' that one day.

We have ourselves a hug and I walk off into the fields.

Then I find myself doublin' back and comin' up to the edge of the yard, just out of sight, and watchin' him for the longest time just drinkin' his coffee and scratchin' his pup's ears and lookin' out into the Injun summer sky.

Then he goes inside and I slip away.

I go back to the woods and stretch out for a nap. In the afternoon, I shoot me a squirrel and roast it for my dinner. Just before dark, I go by the churchyard and stop by the grave where Elizabeth and our baby are buried. I stand there for a long, long time.

Then I walk back to find my own grave.

It's a strange thing to see and my heart does one of those fish-flops and I get the shivers when I read my name on the tombstone. I ain't a prayin' man but I say a li'l somethin' for the ole boy buried in there, whoever he is.

Then I slip back across the bayou by way of the Mandalay Bridge and walk back to our ole house. I spread out my bedroll and sleep curled up on our back porch. I dream of wild, wild woods that go on forever.

When the sun comes up through the fog in the mornin', I head off, keepin' to the cover of the canefields and the woods, in the general direction of Florda.

21.

I guess it's harder to leave Loosiana than I thought. Maybe it's 'cause, 'cept for runnin' up to Tupelo, I ain't never left it before.

Maybe it's 'cause of the way I'm leavin'.

Anyway, I ain't left yet.

I'm standin' at the gate to Annie Ancelet's place, feelin' like a bashful schoolboy. Seems like a man would get over that one day, same as he might learn to talk on the phone without feelin' like a tongue-tied moron. It's a Monday mornin', not too early, cool, the sun burnin' gold through the last of the fog in the cypress tops. There's a big ole black and yellow banana spider that's strung a web about three foot square between two willow saplings. It's caught a whole rainbow of dew.

Annie's wagon's here, so she prob'ly is, too.

I got here on the Greyhound. It took forever. I decided I don't like the bus. I get car sick.

I push through Annie's gate and go cloppin' up her wooden walkway.

About halfway through, them dogs of her start bawlin'.

By the time I get to the gate, Annie's standin' there, them pooches with their paws way up on the gate posts. They've sniffed me out and remembered who I am. Dogs are smart like that.

Annie smiles bright when she sees me. She's wearin' a simple blue dress, with her hair pulled back. She says why Logan LaBauve, I thought maybe you'd forgot about your old friends. I heard you'd come down this way not too long ago.

I smile back. I say no, nuttin' like that. I just had an *envie* to go check on Meely is all.

She says well, far as I know, your boy's okay. I called down there not long ago and they said there had been a development in court and he'd been released of all charges. I would've told you, 'cept I didn't hear from you.

Annie opens the gate and I step through.

I say Annie, I just come from seein' Meely and he's fine—real fine, in fack. He's got him a good situation down there, livin' with a nice lady who was his teacher. And it's a hard thing to explain about me and phones but, basically, I don't like 'em. I'm afraid of 'em, I guess. So that's why I didn't call or anything. I, uh—

She laughs and waves her hand. She says well, come on in here and tell me about how you've been. I got bits of it from Harris Daigrepont.

I go in and Annie fixes us some coffee. It's hot and strong, like I like it. She stirs two teaspoons of sugar in hers. I take mine unsweetened.

I give her the dope about my time up in Tupelo and what I'm thinkin' I'll do.

She says Logan, you won't find gumbo or turtle *sauce piquante* in Florida, or good coffee, either. Or Cajuns to drink beer or go fishin' and huntin' with.

I laugh and say no, but there won't be no Catahoula Parish law doggies lookin' for me, neither.

She says have you thought about goin' in and gettin' things straight?

I say I have but I don't trust the law down there, even if there is one honest judge who sprung Meely. Maybe one day. But even Meely doesn't think I should take a chance now.

She says this is all just a shame. To have to be separated from your son and, well, your friends.

She stops and smiles. She says you've made some down in this part of the swamp, too, you know.

I say well, ole Lester Benoit shore come through. I 'preciate you sendin' him after us. Lord knows what woulda happened otherwise. I was on the verge of becomin' a real bad outlaw, by accident. If I ever run into

Lester again, I might even wrassle him, though I don't necessarily look forward to bein' thrown around the floor like a rag doll.

Annie laughs. She says you know, seein' Lester again could be arranged. How big of a hurry are you in to get down to Florida?

I say well, I dunno. It's not like the gator fella gimme a timetable. But I figger I shouldn't hang around too long, all things considered.

She says okay, I've got a proposition for you. Why don't you come with me to Noonie's tonight? I'll invite Lester and his crowd and we'll have a little party.

I say Annie, I'm not shore I'm a party fella but I don't mind sittin' around drinkin' a beer or two and shootin' the bull, if that's what you've got in mind.

She says that's exactly what I've got in mind, so, good, that part of my proposition is settled. The second part is how 'bout, tomorrow, or the day after, I drive you down to Florida?

I hadn't expected this.

I say doggone, are you shore? It's a ways down there, far as I can tell. I've got me a map I picked up at the Texaco along the way but I ain't studied it much. That fella lives in the crook of Florda, what they call the Panhandle. My boy gimme some money for the bus and I was thinkin' it was enough to get me most of the ways down there. But I just come up here on the bus and didn't think much of the bus.

She says there's no reason to spend that money. In fact, remind me—I've got twenty-five dollars for you. I sold your pirogue to Coon Chiasson, an old trapper who'd banged his up on a cypress stump towin' it from his camp a couple of months ago. Anyway, it's a slow time for me. I'm gonna trap this winter but I've already scouted my place and staked out my traplines. This trip would be a little adventure for me. Unless, of course, you don't care for my company.

I say your company is plenty fine with me, Annie. I just hate to be a bother, is all. You've done way too much already.

Annie smiles big again and says Logan, while you might be trouble, so far you're no bother.

That cat's pretty well swallowed my tongue on that one.

She says well, you just think about it and let me know.

I nod.

She says now, how 'bout more coffee, or even some breakfast? And maybe a shower?

I say all three sound good, maybe startin' with that shower.

We go inside and I like how the mornin' sun filters through the cypress tops and lights up her windows and her rooms and turns everything cheery. I follow Annie upstairs and find my way to the shower and undress and she says, through the door, I'll put out some clean clothes for you on the bed. I say okay.

Mine *are* pretty grungy.

I turn on the water and step under and knock the woods and swamp off of me. I take my time and it feels pretty doggone good, and when I'm done I step out with my towel around me.

I come out lookin' for those clothes and Annie's got a surprise for me.

She's still here, sittin' on the bed.

One thing I notice. She's got a bathrobe on and not anything else, far as I can tell.

Oh, I say. I didn't know you were—

The next thing I know, Annie's slipped into my arms and she nuzzles up against my neck. She says you didn't know that I'd be here?

I say right.

She says I wasn't sure I would be. But Logan, here I am.

She nuzzles me some more. I nuzzle back.

I say well, that's somethin'.

Somethin'?

Oh, it's better than somethin'.

She says you smell nice and clean.

I say that's prob'ly good.

She says that's *very* good. I like a freshly showered man.

Hhm.

She says you know that breakfast I promised you?

I say yeah?

Well, here it is.

She steps soft out of my arms. That robe floats to the floor.

She comes close again and kisses me on the neck. She whispers I know this is crazy, but would you mind comin' to bed with me? I'm just not a person who can beat around the bush.

I would say somethin' if I could find my voice.

I feel her hands around my waist and her thumbs in the fold of my towel and pretty soon that towel's down around my ankles.

I wonder if we'll even get as far as the bed.

We have a kiss and then another and then another.

She says you know, I haven't wanted to do this with anyone since Luke died. For a lot of years, I thought maybe I was done with it.

I say I can understand that.

She says have you loved anybody since Elizabeth?

I say well, it depends on what you mean by love. A bit like you, I figgered I was done with the love business. Oh, I've been with a few women but they haven't been the kind of women inclined to fall in love, or me with them.

Annie snuggles in against me.

She says well, it's been so long, don't expect too much from me.

I laugh at that. I say it's been awhile for me, too. I'm afraid I could go pretty quick.

She giggles. She says hhm, well, maybe I have a few tricks up my sleeve to keep that from happening.

She cradles my head and next I know, there's a nipple, hard as a spring blackberry, on my tongue. I manage to get the other one hard, too. Annie moans, a hand feathery on my neck. Then she takes my hand and puts it in a certain place. She lifts my head and kisses me again and says you know what would be nice?

I say no, what?

She says if you kissed me there, too.

She has a rug on the floor. I kneel and it's soft on my knees. I haven't done this many times, though I like it.

She's wet and warm and sweet, all folds and softness, and I take my good ole time.

I feel her hands soft in my hair.

Oh, Logan, she says. Oh, you sweet, sweet man. Oh, that's so, so righteous.

Seems to me I could do this forever but she pulls me up and we tumble into bed. She holds me and strokes me in tender places. She returns the favor of those kisses and I float off someplace far off where the pleasure of it all almost drowns me.

Women always mystify me with what they know and what they can do.

When I'm finally inside her, it's as if I'm bein' picked up and flown by angels. And when I come to that place where there's no goin' back, I cry out like some shot animal—the sweet, awful pain of it breaks me in two.

She says oh, sweetie. Oh, poor thing. It's okay. I've got you. I've got you right here.

She snuggles me in close.

Things go slow and quiet for a while. I don't mind.

A breeze comes blowin' through her big open window and it flutters the tops of the sheet.

Then Annie says this was nice, Logan. Maybe this is just what I needed.

She pokes me in the ribs.

She says by the way, you weren't so quick on the draw after all. And I've gotta tell you, you have what just about every gal really wants.

I say what could that be?

She says a slow hand. And a warm heart.

A man, after he's had love, is usually a man with a muddled head. Mine's muddled most times anyways. I wonder about the last part, but I don't really know what to say.

After a while, she says what do you think? Should we lie around here some more and see what happens? Or are you starved for the bacon and eggs I promised you?

I don't have to think too long about that.

I look at her and say why, Annie, I wouldn't mind breakfast but when

I get down to Florda, I might have me some bacon and eggs every day. But I won't have you. Plus, I don't think we'll have to lie here too long.

I smile when I say that but I see somethin' come into Annie's eyes.

She leans over and kisses me and looks at me and says no, that's true. Down there in Florida, you won't have me.

PART THREE

The Storm

22.

Them blue skies that have accounted for October so far have give way to gray and slow rain. For the last hour, we've been cloppin' down the highway through the piney woods of Alabama, windshield wipers floppin' back and forth.

I'm so ignorant of geography, I didn't even realize there was another state, other'n Mississippi, 'tween us and Florda.

It's a cool day, late in the afternoon. Annie's runnin' the defroster to keep fog off the windshield and she has the radio tuned to a country music station, which is about all you can catch around here 'cept stations where people are preachin' about the Lord. She plays it fairly low and some ole boy named Ernest Tubb is croonin' a song about a man waltzin' clear across Texas.

Actually, I don't mind the rain all that much. We've had a pretty long dry spell and, anyway, it feels kinda cozy here in the wagon with Annie. It's a nice wagon, white with wood panelin' on the doors and springs so cushy it feels like it floats over the road.

We went to Noonie's last night and had ourselves a fine ole time. We got fairly drunk, which is a term any drunk would understand. I didn't wrassle Lester though some stranger drivin' an oil-field hotshot truck come in the bar and did, though he done it after he was 'bout half-*chaqued*.

He was a big ole boy, with lots of muscles, and he laid fifty dollars on the bar, though Lester told him he'd just be givin' his money away.

Lester pinned him in no time. He went out of there mad.

Me and Annie went home and spent the night together. We slept late and didn't get started till a bit after noon.

A man can wake up after a night like that in two ways. He can wake up feelin' all perked up, which I did. He can also wake up feelin' some weight tied 'round his heart, which I also did.

Annie hadn't said what she thinks, or much at all. But she could be thinkin' the same thing.

It seems like life would be easier if a man could just feel one way or the other.

What would Elizabeth think of this, I wonder?

I never even axed that question when I slept with the likes of Velma. It's not that I didn't like Velma or appreciate the comfort she give me. This just feels differnt.

A while back, we come through a place in Mississippi where the highway scooted along the Gulf of Mexico and even though it's a gray day, the beaches still shined white as sugar. The man on the gator farm in Florda tole me I'd see such beaches down there, but I didn't expect to see 'em so soon. There was a pretty stiff wind out on the sea and it was white-cappin' good.

We had a late breakfast and skipped dinner altogether and, though it's early for suppertime, Annie is lookin' for a place to stop to eat, though this stretch of road we're goin' down seems pretty lonesome. But we round a curve and come upon a road sign that says Pinky's BBQ, two miles ahead, and Annie says what do you think?

I ain't had much barbecue but what I've had I've liked. I say sounds good to me. Them people who come from Texas to work the oil fields barbecue just about everything. Cajuns don't do it so much.

We spy Pinky's pretty soon, and as we're pullin' in the man on the radio comes on and says there's a tropical storm in the gulf that's accountin' for all the rain up and down the coast from Loosiana to Florda. He says it's stalled out there about two hunderd miles off the coast and it ain't expected to do much of anything except get bigger over the next few hours. People need to keep an eye on it. If it gets much bigger it'll be a hurricane. He cain't say where it will go.

Annie pulls up to the front of Pinky's, which ain't but a ten-by-twelve wood shack set down on blocks in a pine clearin'. There's picnic tables, a bit bent by the weather, set up under the pines. I can see smoke pourin' out of a pipe that must go to the smokehouse. Even with the wagon windows closed, it already smells doggone good.

Annie says Logan, I'm not sure I like this news. We don't need a hurricane blockin' our way to Florida and we don't need one sneakin' up on Chenier Atchafalaya, either. I don't think I even locked the doors to my house. And what about my poor dogs? Lester is lookin' after them but they'd go crazy in a hurricane.

I say look, if you're worried about that and think we should go back, that's okay with me. Or you could even just let me out here and I could—

Annie leans forward and touches my arm. She says shush, Logan LaBauve. I wouldn't just let you out here, no matter what, and if I go back there, I'd just drag you with me. It would be a big job boardin' up all my windows by myself.

I say it shore would, but you wouldn't have to drag me. Of course, down there where you live, I'd be a lot more worried about water than wind. Your house seems like it's built stout. And though I've seen oaks blowed over by hurricanes, I ain't never seen a cypress blowed down.

She says that's all true. We built on stilts about six feet above the bayou with hurricanes in mind. The rest is up to God. We'll just keep the radio on and hope that storm heads way out into the Atlantic.

I nod.

We scurry outta the rain into Pinky's. The inside's about like the outside, simple and a bit cramped, with a long counter and a coupla small tables wedged up against the wall and not much room in between them. There's a woman, short and wide, behind the counter. She's wearin' a stained white apron over a pink dress and her hair is scrunched up under a pink hair net. The menu is scribbled in pink on a chalkboard on the wall above her. Above that is another sign that says Jesus is Coming. It's in pink letterin'.

We read the menu, then order two large pulled pork sandwiches and two glasses of lemonade, though I'm not entirely shore what pulled pork is—I don't necessarily like the sound of it. But I figger anything that smells this good won't be bad.

The woman don't bother to write nuttin' down. She opens a tiny slot that must go to the smoke room and hollers out Pinky, two pulled piggies and two lemonades.

The woman rings it up and it's $2.87 with tax. I reach for my billfold but Annie stops me. She says I'm payin', Logan. You can catch me next time you're back down.

I say you've paid too much already.

She smiles. She says hhm, I probably have.

She hands over a five-dollar bill. The woman makes change out of her apron.

The woman says y'all heard about the storm?

Annie says well, yes, just now on the radio—

The woman says it's comin' this-a-way, I can tell you that. We been seein' the signs for weeks, me and Pinky. And October storms—well, lemme tell ya somethin', you don't want to be around when they blow through this country. Fifty-seven years ago, one come through and killed my great-grandpa and nine of his ten children. Only my grandpa survived. Ain't that right, Pinky?

A man yells through the slot oh, yeah, honey-bunch, that's right.

We nod. I say we come from down in Loosiana and we've lost people that way, too, though none of 'em were my relations.

She says y'all accept Jesus Christ as your Savior?

I look at Annie. Annie says well, we—uh, I'm Catholic. We do, but—

The woman says me and Pinky do, don't we darlin'? That's why we're not afraid of one single thing. If this place burned to the ground or blew down with us in it, praise God. Pinky got a cancer last year. Some men woulda cried. Pinky said praise Heaven—it just puts me one step closer to God, punkin'. Didn't you say that, Pinky?

Pinky hollers out I did, woman. I did.

The woman says Pinky meant it, too. He ain't one of them backslidin', beer-drinkin', Sunday-go-to-meetin' types who praise God but secretly love sin and Satan.

The woman says after Pinky got sick, we went to the tent meetin' over in Eufalala and the preacher put the Holy Ghost in Pinky and it drew the cancer right out of him. He's healthy as a fat baby now, ain't you, darlin'?

I am, Pinky says loud. I doggone am, woman.

She says we fed the whole congregation for a week after that for free. Just about broke us but God told Pinky to do it. Now, I know them Jews ain't got no use for the pig but us Christians digest it just fine. Pork's good for the liver. We musta gone through four, five hogs feedin' them people. Ain't nothin' dirty 'bout hogs. Our neighbor raises them in a pen with a concrete floor and sells 'em to us on credit, don't he, Pinky?

Pinky says yes, Myra, he shore does.

She says we only barbecue pork. We won't touch beef. You ever look a cow in the eye? If you have, you already know what I'm fixin' to say.

Annie and me look at each other.

I just nod at Myra.

Pinky opens that slot again and says sandwiches are up, darlin'. I'll come around with the lemonade.

A tray appears through that slot and I gotta say them sandwiches look doggone good, piled high with juicy barbecue.

Myra grabs 'em and hands 'em over.

Pinky clatters outta the kitchen holdin' a lemonade in each hand. He's a tall man, slouched over. He's got on a white cook's outfit and a kerchief 'round his bald head. His face is crawfish red and shiny as melted butter.

He comes over and puts them lemonades on the counter.

He says y'all Cajuns, I'll bet.

We nod.

He says I been to New Orleans street-preachin'. More sin there than catfish in the Mississippi, I guarantee you. I've never understood why any group of people could love the Pope more than they love God, or say prayers to statues. But I'm Pinky and any man or woman, Pope-lover or pagan, is welcome in my tent. Ain't that right, Myra?

Myra says Pinky here's a holy man, yes he is.

Pinky says y'all enjoy.

He buries his sweaty face in the lap of his apron.

I see Annie's about to say somethin' but thinks better of it.

We gather up our lemonade and sandwiches and head over for a table.

We dig into those sandwiches and they're spicy and good. The lemonades are sweet and cold. We eat without talkin' and then make our way out.

I notice the rain's picked up some.

Pinky hollers out y'all be careful out there. Myra's right—that storm's a-comin'. Praise God! Praise God!

Out in the wagon, Annie wipes a splatter of rain from her cheek, cranks the ignition, and switches on the radio. She turns a knob and sets the windshield wipers to flappin' again. The radio comes on and it's a country song. She punches a button, then another, then another. All the stations have got music or preachin' or people sellin' flour or soap or trucks or whatnot. She turns the dial. The stations squeak and squawk in and out.

She looks at me a certain way, a way that I like. She's thinkin', and when Annie's seriously thinkin', she might be the prettiest serious woman I've ever seen.

She says well, I hope they're wrong.

I smile. I say well, you heard 'em. Both are crazy as moonstruck *poule d'eaus*.

She says Logan, what was that cow stuff about, anyway?

I say I've got no idea.

She nods and fiddles with the radio dial some more.

After a bit she says if that storm was comin' this way, surely the radio would be full of news, wouldn't it? Let's get out of here and get on down to Florida.

23.

We drive slow and steady for three more hours or so and leave Alabama and head into Florda but the land don't really change much. It's got dark and there's a steady wind bendin' the pine tops and whiskin' the rain across the road, but I can see well enough to know that the country we're in is about like the country we left—pine trees and rollin' hills.

That's the thing I've noticed 'bout maps. A man can draw a line or a dot on a map and call it one thing, but it don't change the land one way or another. The Mississippi River prob'ly don't care which side of the state line it's on.

We've heard two more things about that storm. The man come on and said it had gotten bigger and it was now a hurricane, wide across but not yet too powerful, and that it had got a name—Belva. But he also said it was now nosin' out to sea, trackin' pretty much due south and might march clear out into the open Atlantic Ocean.

I realized that Belva was Cane Duggins's missus's name and I thought to myself that might be a pretty good name for a hurricane.

Annie seemed relieved by the news.

We soon come upon a road sign that reads Articola Island Causeway, 10 miles—and though I'm pretty shore Articola Island's a town I seen on the map, I'm not entirely shore what a causeway is. Annie thought we should take that route 'cause it looked a quite bit shorter to where we're goin' and might be nice to drive along the coast, though this ain't the best weather to sightsee in. But I'm kinda excited to see that blue ocean.

Annie seems to read my mind and says a causeway is just a fancy name for a long bridge over a bay or a lake. Logan, I don't know about you but I'm gettin' tired of drivin' and could use a break. If we spy a convenient place in Articola, I'm of a mind to pull off for the night. These roads are slick and we're probably still three, four hours from where you're goin'.

We drive on and there's not much traffic and soon enough we hit a spot where the road starts to go up and I look out and realize we're on that causeway. Out to my right, I see a line of lights at the edge of the water and can just make out that it's a dock of some sort with boats tied up all around. The winds kickin' up a bit higher out here in the open and them boats are bobbin' up and down pretty good. They look like fancy boats, of a kind rich fishermen would have.

Even though my window's rolled up, I can smell the salt water mixed with the salt marsh and it's a smell I've always liked.

We go cloppin' over that causeway for a long ways. It climbs gentle to a place where there's steel arches markin' a drawbridge, and then we start down again. Tugs could prob'ly make it under that drawbridge okay, though ships couldn't.

About two or three miles down the road, we hit a sign that says Articola Island City Limits, pop. 1,423. Annie slows down and we crawl though the town. There don't seem to be much to it, and though it ain't that late, it looks like it's been rolled up and put away for the night.

I figger we'll just have to keep headin' on when, on the outskirts, 'round a sharp curve, we run upon a blue neon sign that says Bay Motel and Cabana Bar and Grill.

Annie flicks on her turn signal and says well, Logan, isn't this convenient—grub, drink, and a bed, all in the same spot.

I look over and she's got a pretty nice smile on her face.

For some reason, I hadn't thought much about sleepin' arrangements. I'm thinkin' about 'em now, though.

Annie pulls into a blacktop parkin' lot. There's a fair number of cars and a few pickups pulled up against an iron railin'. The motel is a line of tiny houses with thatched roofs, each with a porch light out front. The restaurant and bar is propped up on stilts and seems to be a big version of them huts. It's got a porch that looks like it goes clear around it. We wheel into an empty spot and Annie shuts off the motor and switches off her headlights.

We sit for a minute in the quiet, 'cept for the rain shushin' against the window.

Then Annie says look, Logan, I don't want to presume a single thing about us. Yesterday and last night were great, but as far as I know, I could drop you off tomorrow at that gator farm and never see you again. I know you're lousy with the telephone and probably not much at writing letters, either. And beyond all that, I just don't want you to feel like you're betraying anyone—well, betraying Elizabeth is what I mean.

I say well, I guess most people would say you cain't betray the dead.

She nods. She says they probably would say that but neither you nor I are most people.

I smile and say that much is true.

She says to be completely honest, I'd say that even before I met you I'd been thinkin' some about that very thing—about Luke and my feelings for him and what it might feel like to be with someone else. And maybe it's a bit like comin' out of a fog, but I know Luke simply wouldn't want me to live without passion of any kind for the rest of my life. He would understand that, in my heart of hearts, I'm a sad girl without love—the deeper kind, and yes, the physical kind, too.

She looks at me in that thinkin', pretty way of hers. She shifts around to face me.

She says so, here's the deal. I'd like to go in there and rent us one of those little cabanas. Don't reach for your wallet—don't worry, I'm keepin' track and you can pay me back one day after you get settled. Then you and I can go into the Cabana Bar and Grill and have us a drink or two and then some supper, and, dependin' on how we're feelin', maybe even a drink after supper. Then we can go to bed and we can just hold on to each other or we can swing from the rafters, whatever comes to mind. And in the mornin', we'll just take care of the mornin'. I can't put it any more plainly than that, and if I've gone too far, well then—

I look at Annie and hold up my hand and some feelin' comes up in me, that thing again that feels like gladness and sadness all mixed up to-gether but a feelin' maybe less tangled than it's been before. And I find my-self doin' somethin' that even surprises me. I reach over and take her in my arms and say well, I'm not shore how good I'd be at swingin' from the rafters, but I like how you speak plain and say what's on your mind, and I might learn to get better about the telephone now that I've got somebody like you to call.

And then I kiss her square on the mouth and realize how much I like the way she kisses and somethin' else rises up in me and I know exactly what that feelin' is.

I pull back, still holdin' on to her, and I say look, Annie, I cain't say how the mornin' will feel, either. I know I've been hidin' out, in the bot-tle and in the swamp. Some of it's 'cause I've been feelin' sorry for myself. Some of it's 'cause I think sadness is contagious and I didn't think it would be proper to give what I have to anybody else. I guess I figgered if I just whittled my life down, there wouldn't be much the world could do to me anymore, or me to it. But I will admit one thing—it's been a pretty lone-some place.

We go quiet and Annie pulls me close and tousles my head and says it's okay. I know your sufferings, Logan. I know them like my own.

We hold on for a good while and I breathe Annie in and realize I like holdin' her so. I like the feel of her and the warmth of her and the way she smells. I like how I don't feel the need to say more than I already have.

Then Annie looks out and says you know, I didn't think to bring an umbrella. I guess we'll have to make a run for it. That rain's comin' down pretty hard.

I look out, too, and say I'm ready when you are.

We scoot out of the wagon, slammin' the doors behind us, and go scramblin' up some wide steps onto the porch. Annie's rabbit quick and it's all I can do to keep up with her. She's got on dungarees and cowboy boots and a kind of western-lookin' shirt tucked into her britches and I gotta say she looks doggone nice that way. At the top of the steps, we prac-tically bump into each other and Annie stumbles and I grab her and keep her from fallin'. We laugh and head, arm in arm, for the door to the restaurant.

My experience in restaurants is pretty well limited to the kind of places where a man can get a cup of coffee and a plate of eggs and biscuits for a dollar or a dish of red beans and rice for about the same. This one seems fancy to me. It's got round tables with white tablecloths on 'em and candles in fancy glass jars in the middle. There are baskets with plants in 'em hangin' from the ceilin'. There's a real palm tree growin' up toward the ceilin' right in the middle of the place—a fair-sized tree. It looks like there's even a hole in the roof, till I realize it's actually a window of a kind I've never seen.

A woman wearin' a dress with yellow and red flowers comes over and takes us to a table right under the palm tree and when I sit I realize there's more knives and forks than I've seen around any plate. She gives us menus and it's filled with dishes of a kind I've never heard of—fish with names like wahoo and mahi-mahi.

I notice, too, that a man could have eight or nine plate lunches of red beans and rice back at Alma's in Ville Canard for the price of supper here.

I ax Annie if she's gonna need some of my money but she smiles and says no, this is her treat.

If she is keepin' track, I'm gonna have to help that fella wrangle a lot of gators to pay her back.

Annie says let's have a drink first. Do you have an opinion of gin and tonic?

I say no, I cain't say as I've ever had one.

She says you up for somethin' new?

I say shore, why not.

Those drinks come in tall glasses with lots of ice. Them glasses have tiny paper umbrellas stuck to a wedge of lime floatin' at the top in ice.

We sip our drinks real slow and I gotta say mine ain't bad. I like how it fizzes. Then we order supper. I ax for mackerel—at least I've heard of it. Annie orders a fish called a sand dab, which don't sound like a fish I'd wanna eat. Annie wants to know if I'd like to try some wine. I ain't had wine but once and I know it wadn't the kind of wine you'd get here but, well, I say okay, why not.

The wine comes, a whole bottle of it, and it's yellowish and a bit sour, but it's a taste that seems to grow on you. Them sand dabs come, too, and Annie offers me a bite and they're fried up tender and good with butter drizzled all over 'em. Shows you what I know. My mackerel's not bad. Turns out they cooked it on a barbecue grill.

Annie tells me not to worry 'bout all them forks, knives, and spoons— just to grab the nearest one and start eatin'. I know my manners ain't the best.

We drink that wine and talk and talk and then move over to a big round bar that's up on a kind of stage higher than the restaurant.

The place is pretty well empty 'cept for a few fellas and a young couple sittin' close to each other on high stools down at the other end of the bar. Annie orders whiskey of a kind I ain't had, neither—it's called Irish whiskey and I gotta say it's tasty.

The bartender is a friendly fella who wears a name tag that says Jack. He's got on white britches and a flowered shirt made of the same stuff that the waitress's dress was made of. Seems like a lotta trouble to go to, though it does look pretty sharp. Even though them other people filter out, he tells us there's no hurry. He keeps pourin' that whiskey and we keep sippin' it slow and then after a while time rumbles down like a truck shifted into granny gear and I realize I'm way out in some warm, cozy place and the world and all its troubles seem a lifetime away. And I look at Annie and think, God, how pretty she is and I lean over and say you know, I'm thinkin' pretty seriously about them rafters right now.

And Annie smiles and leans close and says Logan, I thought you'd never ask.

We pay our bill—well, Annie does—and she axes about a room and the bartender says he can sign us in right here.

He says just tonight?

Annie says just tonight, and we collect a key and he says follow the porch down all the way 'round the bend. It'll be the cabana straight ahead of you. I've given you a room with a view of the bay. You won't see much of the bay on a night like this but at least it's away from the road and should be nice and quiet. Well, except for the wind and rain.

Annie says thank you and we stumble out, arm and arm, and walk across that porch, not totally steady on our feet, and race out into the rain and under the tiny overhang of our cabana, where there's a porch light shinin' down. It seems to me the rain and wind have both picked up. We fumble a bit with the key and laugh the way only drunks do when they think everything's funny, includin' gettin' rained on. We open the door and switch on the light and it seems like a fine place, with a round bed about as big as a bed could get and a pitcher window and color pitchers of birds and fish on the wall.

I shut the door and Annie falls into my arms and we have a kiss and then another and then another.

Clothes just seem to fall away.

She turns from me and walks toward the window and reaches up and pulls the drapes to and says no use invitin' the world to have a look.

When she reaches up and I see how nicely she's made, I'm like a deer staggered by buckshot. I think my knees could buckle but I walk to her before she's able to turn around and snuggle her up in my arms, and she moves in a way that tells me there won't be no time to make the rafters.

She half-turns and I kiss her on the mouth and I love the warmth and taste of her and my arms go 'round her and her nipples rise hard against my palms. Annie moans and twists around to face me and I lift her up on that windowsill and she opens herself to me and I am inside her and I know it don't matter whether I last a minute or forever, there is no place better and sweeter than this.

At some point we make it to the bed, not botherin' to turn off the lights, and lie cuddled and drowsy atop the covers, listenin' to the wind and rain peltin' the window. For the first time, it seems I can hear the grumble of waves on the beach behind us, but I don't think much of it 'cept that a certain kind of rainy, blustery night can help a man sleep.

Not that I need help. Lovemakin' and whiskey have me spent as a bluetick hound after a night chasin' coons. I fall asleep in Annie's arms, and then we dream and wake, and make more slow love and finally I fall into one of them dead sleeps where a man slips way down into his soul and seems to shed years and worries.

It takes an awful racket to drive a person from such a sleep, but the next thing I hear is an awful racket.

There's a poundin' on our door and a man yellin' anybody awake in there? Anybody awake?

I straggle up, bleary-eyed, and find my britches and hitch 'em up and open the door.

I'm a bit cross till I see the man at the door is the bartender from last night. He's holdin' a soggy ball cap in his hands and his hair has been blowed all over his head and he looks about as red-eyed and rumpled as I must look. He says I'm sorry to bother y'all but we got big problems. That storm whirled around in the middle of the night and is chuggin' this way like a downhill freight loaded with dynamite. The radio says the road back to the causeway is already underwater from tides and there ain't but one other way outta here and that's over Tarpon Pass Bridge, seventeen miles south. The sheriff has put out an evacuation order and I'm gettin' the hell outta Dodge. And you better, too.

I look at a clock on a bedside table and it says noon. I got no idea what time we got to the room, but the combination of wine and whiskey and lovemakin' and deep sleep has put a whuppin' on my head.

Annie is sittin' up in bed rubbin' her eyes. She looks about in the same shape as me.

She says oh, my God, this is awful news. Well, I guess I don't have to worry about my house on Chenier Atchafalaya—that storm's practically in our lap.

I say I like how you look on the bright side of things. That fella seemed pretty anxious so I guess we better get a move on.

Annie swings out of bed and goes to the window, draws just enough curtain back so that she can peek out. She's still naked. Even hungover, I realize how much I enjoy lookin' at her.

She clucks her tongue and says that wind must be blowin' fifty knots already. If that tide gets any higher, there'll be waves lappin' at our doorstep.

I say well, I guess we better go quick.

She turns and comes to me and snuggles into my arms and says by the way, good mornin'.

I kiss her and say good mornin', too.

It's more of a kiss than I was expectin' to give or get and pretty soon we have another and pretty soon Annie's fingers have figured out the snap on my dungarees and they're down around my ankles with a little help from her.

She says that was nice last night.

I say it was a lot better than that.

She smiles. She says I'm no good without a shower, hurricane or not.

I say well, I've been in storms before. I respect 'em but I ain't necessarily afraid of 'em. It's just that these ain't our stompin' grounds. Back on Catahoula Bayou, I'd know just where to go to ride one out. Here, I, uh—

Annie puts her hand in a certain place and says I know. Just five minutes in the shower, what do you say?

I smile and say hey, you're drivin'.

We ain't in there long and I gotta say love and a hot shower ain't a bad way to wake up. It's definitely cleared my head some. We dress quick in what we wore yesterday, though Annie does trade her cowboy boots for sneakers, and head on out.

24.

We hustle out to the station wagon, the wind whippin' the rain sideways, and we're pretty well drenched by the time we make the front seat. I had to snatch my ball cap right off my head to keep it from bein' blown away. Annie wipes her face on her shirtsleeve and puts the key in the ignition and cranks the Ford to life. She switches on the windshield wipers and the headlights and turns on the blower.

I notice the clouds are low and dark gray, and as we back out and steer toward the road, losin' the lee of the buildin', a gust of wind comes shriekin' off the bay and rocks the wagon.

Annie looks at me and says well, Logan, maybe that shower was a bad idea.

I run my hand through my wet hair and smile and pat her on the arm and say I think it was a great idea. We'll just get on the road headin' south toward Tarpon Pass, like that fella said. Once over that bridge, we can prob'ly find a road inland and a place to ride out the blow. Maybe we'll even outrun it. I ain't worried too much about wind. It's water that'll get you.

Annie nods and turns on the radio. She fiddles with the dials but mostly gets static, 'cept for one station where a man's preachin' the Lord again.

She says you'd think these people would give up Jesus long enough to give us some news.

Annie steers the wagon toward the highway and makes a slow right turn.

I can tell this ain't gonna be easy drivin'. It's not just that the rain is comin' in at a slant, it's also that we're catchin' spray blowin' off the bay to our right and that salty water is streakin' the windshield up good. There's whole sheets of water blowin' across the road. The waves out there must be pitchin' six or eight foot already. They're comin' in fast and they're churned up frothy and white like the spittle off a mad dog.

I was in a hurricane once where the wind blew one hunderd and forty miles an hour. I don't care to be in another like that. I'd guess this wind is kickin' up at seventy.

We go on like this for about fifteen minutes, passin' a scatterin' of bay-side motels and a few houses up on stilts near the beach. In between are big open spaces, some of it marsh, like we have down by the Loosiana gulf. Some of that marsh is thick with alligator grass or saw grass and that wind has blowed it flat, like hair plastered down with Brylcreme.

It's kinda spooky that there ain't nobody around and we ain't seen another car on the road. Some of those houses are all shuttered up. But most of them small motels are just sittin' there empty, their curtains drawn open. Some have lighted signs that say Vacancy. Some have tape across the windows, which I guess would help keep glass from shatterin' every which way if the windows got blowed out.

It's pretty clear folks have left in a hurry.

Annie plays with the radio dial some more and some stations make a *wee-ooo* sound and fade in an out. We finally manage to catch a fella sayin' somethin' about a hurricane warnin' but it's all staticky and we only catch bits and pieces.

A severe hurricane watch . . . Florida Panhandle . . . Winds gusting to one hundred and ten miles an hour . . . Moving fast . . . Belva expected to intensify and reach land . . .

I look at Annie and for the first time I can see she's plenty worried.

Well, I guess I am, too.

We've got no choice but to poke along like this for another half hour.

I doubt we're makin' more than ten or fifteen miles an hour. The road hugs the bay and sometimes the mix of rain and spray blinds us and we're forced to stop altogether. We come upon a place where there's a pretty good-sized boat dock sittin' in the shelter of a big rock jetty. It's empty 'cept for two boats, one a fair-sized shrimp boat. I see a man in a green slicker suit on the deck, totin' a bundle of rope. It's clear that a boat that ain't left by now ain't leavin', and I guess he's tyin' her down. I give a wave as we go by but he don't ever look up to see us.

We leave the dock behind and hit a stretch of road that runs right along the beach. It's a big, broad beach but them waves have already lapped up to the roadside and in some places already flooded our side of the road, though not deep. Annie drives careful around them puddles.

We come around a bend marked by a big oak tree and I can see that tree leanin' hard against the wind. But then there's a welcome sight—a sight I normally wouldn't welcome. It's a truck, sittin' up high in the oncoming lane, with red police lights flashin'. Standin' beside it are two deputies in yellow rain slickers and tall police hats, wavin' long flashlights at us.

Annie pulls up and stops and rolls down her window. The wind goes *wooo-wooo-wooo*, like them mournin' doves we've got back in Loosiana.

The deputy looks in with his light—it's got pretty dark out—and leans in close. He tips his hat and says ma'am, sir.

He don't look happy to see us.

He says y'all are a little late gettin' off this island. You need to keep movin' and go as quick as the weather allows.

I nod and say yes sir, we're tourists from back Loosiana way and we spent the night at a motel last night back there in Articola and last we heard—

He interrupts. He says sir, I'm aware the storm has turned quick. But the beach road between here and the Tarpon Pass Bridge is already under two feet of water. Your wagon will never make it. There's one way around—about two miles up on the left is a blacktop spur called the Indian Rise Road. It runs over some dunes and Indian mounds on the back side of the island and then comes back down and connects with this road just above the bridge. I wouldn't wait another second to get goin'. We've got reports that Belva's already spun off tornadoes ahead of and behind us.

Annie says but officer, what about once we're off the island? What do we do then?

He says head for Spanish Town, ma'am. The Red Cross has set up a shelter in the courthouse. Keep on the coast highway for about twenty miles below Tarpon Pass, then turn left at the blinkin' light. That's Spanish Town Road. Follow that eight miles into town. You can't miss it.

She says well, that sounds simple enough. Can you tell us any more about the storm?

He says it's headin' right for us is all I know. One-hundred-and-twenty-mile-an-hour winds by dark. Now, I can't sit here and gab—we've got some people already stalled out down this road that we need to go see about. You need to get goin', too.

Annie nods. She rolls up the window and puts the wagon in gear and off we go. She looks at me with a bit more worry in her eyes.

We rock along slow and steady and come to the Indian Rise Road turnoff. Annie makes a left. It's a narrow road, slicked with rain, and not much of a shoulder on either side. It's also full of potholes, which are hard to see 'cause they're filled up with water.

We rattle right over a few and Annie says ouch, this isn't doin' my wagon any good. I don't know why I just didn't buy a pickup. It's what I drove before.

In a few minutes the road starts to climb a bit and we enter a glade of woods, mostly pine and oak pressin' up against the shoulder, with palmetto brakes in between. I see a few palm trees of a kind I've only seen in pitchers. Them trees are sashayin' in the wind and there's leaves and small branches flyin' every which way across the road. It's clear the wind's kickin' up stronger than ever.

As we round a bend, one fair-sized branch breaks off and comes twirlin' down at us.

It ain't bigger round than a broom handle but it's long and leafy and it hits the windshield with a *thwuck* and then sticks.

It blocks our view and Annie brakes the wagon. There's a scary second when the back end starts to skid on the slick blacktop, even though we're not goin' very fast.

We slide to a stop.

The windshield wiper on my side has gotten tangled in a knot of stems and is all jammed up.

Annie looks at me and shakes her head. She says damn, this weather is startin' to aggravate me.

I say don't worry. I'll get it off.

I ease open the door but the wind seems to shift and the handle just jerks out of my hand and the door blows forward, *sprong*. I hop out quick and am almost blown down myself. My cap goes sailin' off my head.

I grab on to the top of the door with my left hand and make my way around to the windshield and lift the branch best I can and try to push it off. I get some help from a gust of wind and that branch goes *pop* and flies off into the sky like some big green drunk bird.

That's when I realize that the windshield wiper of my side got snapped off with it.

I don't know why I didn't try to untangle it first.

It's a tussle just to get back in the wagon. I settle into my seat, about as happy as a rained-on rooster.

I say I shore was fond of that cap. And I shore am sorry about that wiper.

Annie shakes her head. She says don't worry about it. If we had to lose one, that was the one to lose. Are you all right?

I say wet is all. I guess I won't be much good at helpin' you navigate. Unless I sit on your lap or somethin'.

Annie smiles. She says I guess we better save that for later.

We head off again, even slower than before. I'm gettin' downright uneasy. On a clear day, we could walk faster than this.

The road starts to climb and twist, though it ain't much of a grade. It's gettin' darker by the minute.

The Ford has a bench seat and I scooch over next to Annie so I can look out of her side of the windshield. I figger, in this weather, two pairs of eyes on the road are better than one. We bump along like this for a while longer, steerin' around potholes, and round a sharp bend. We come up to the top of what looks like a crest, only to see that it's just a spot where the road levels out before it starts to climb gentle again. There's a short wooden bridge just ahead of us—it looks like it crosses a small creek or bayou—and beyond that is a long straightaway with the woods still close in on each side. It almost looks like we're in a long tunnel, what with them clouds pressin' down hard upon the treetops.

I peer out through the flappin' wiper and see some kinda movement up above the treeline way off on the horizon.

I say Annie, do you see that? Is somethin' flyin' in this weather?

I point with my left hand and Annie brakes gentle and looks out, too. She suddenly grabs my arm. I see her jaw clench up and she says Jesus-God, Logan—a tornado!

I look out hard just in time to see the downspout rip out of the clouds and touch down on the road in the distance, a whirlin', puffed-up devil that seems to be suckin' up everything in front of it and spittin' it out the sides.

Suddenly, there's somethin' like a hum in the wagon and slowly the hum builds until it sounds like the choog of a far-off freight train.

The hairs rise on my neck.

I ain't never been in a tornado before, though I have seen waterspouts out on the Gulf of Mexico. I don't know what to do.

Annie, lookin' around, thinks quicker than me.

She yells let's get under that bridge! Run for it, Logan! Run for it!

Annie scrambles out of her door, me followin' her, and she's blown down the minute her feet hit the blacktop. I pile out on top of her and grab her and lift her up, and yell are you all right?

She nods and then I put my back to the wagon door and it takes every bit of strength I have, plus Annie pushin', to get it closed.

Holdin' on to each other, we scramble ahead toward the bridge, the wind knockin' us about like a boxer. We're almost to the bridge and I look up. There's somethin' that looks like a ten-story buildin' barrelin' our way, maybe a quarter-mile ahead.

It's a monster, with a giant head and a long body, black and awful, full of moans and shrieks and a kind of hissin', poppin' sound I ain't never heard before.

I'm ahead of Annie and I see a narrow cut down the bank to the right of the bridge and I point and yell down there!

I lurch forward, holdin' on to Annie's hand, and as I hit the cut my feet go out from under me and I drag Annie down, too, and we go slippin' down, me on my backsides, Annie on her stomach.

We tumble down with a plop into a shallow slough of some kind and I realize I've somehow got turned around and am sittin' in shallow water, ooze way up past my ankles.

Annie, basically, has landed in my lap, facin' me.

She's lookin' up over my shoulder and I'm lookin' up at the bridge, tryin' to figger out what cover there is, and then I see her eyes widen and she yells God, it's gonna come right over us!

I struggle up and grab Annie by the hand again and we start churnin' up the bank, runnin' as hard as we can for the eaves of the bridge. It ain't far but by now the wind's roarin' like an airboat in my ear and I feel like we could be snatched up like a cat at any second and just tossed into the clouds.

I spy some latticework under the bridge up close and tight against the embankment—posts tied together with rounded beams—and I know that's our only hope. We have to scramble up there and wedge ourselves in and hold on and hope the whole bridge don't blow away.

I point and yell that beam, Annie! We gotta get there and dig in!

We dive forward, the deck of the bridge givin' us a bit of a lee from the wind. The bank here is rock and concrete mixed with mud and it's all slicked from the blowin' rain and we claw and kick our way up, ignorin' sharp things that gouge at our knees and elbows and hands.

I manage a hand on one of the cross beams and throw the crook of my arm around it and look back and give Annie my hand. She grabs my wrist with both of her hands and I pull hard. She loses her feet but I somehow find the strength to pull her up to me.

She grabs on to the beam, too, and I'm about to say use both hands when a sickenin' blackness roars over us and the wind shrieks like the *loup garou* and I feel myself go weightless and I realize I'm basically bein' stood on my head.

I feel the heels of my boots smackin' hard against the deck of the bridge above me, *rat-ta-tat-tat*, and then there's an awful weight that slams my feet to the ground and I think I'm gonna be ripped away from the beam.

Then, just as quick, the shriekin' stops, like some runaway balloon that's puffed out all its air, and the blackness passes and a calm seems to come over everything.

And I look toward Annie and I'm struck dumb.

Annie's not there.

25.

I scramble out from under the bridge, my work boots sloshin' with water, my heart thumpin' hard in my chest, and notice a few other things.

Annie's wagon ain't here, neither.

There's trees flung everywhere up and down the road, some of 'em heaped up in big mounds, some snapped in two, like a man might snap a green bean.

The sky has a hole in it, with a chimney of light slantin' down. I cain't explain it any other way. It's as though that tornado sucked up the clouds from right above me and took 'em away.

The rain seems to have stopped.

I look ahead and notice somethin' else—somethin' that wadn't on that road before.

It's a house. Not a big house but a house just the same.

A white house with what looks like a small porch.

I feel my heart hammerin' hard in my chest and somethin' awful start to roar in my head and I'm about to call out when I hear her voice.

It's calm and low and seems nearby.

She says Logan, Logan, are you here?

I look around, a bit panicked, wonderin' if I'm hearin' things.

I say Annie? Yeah, I'm here. Are you okay? Where are you?

I hear my voice rise. Where *are* you!

She says it's okay, Logan. I think I'm okay. I'm down here on the bayou bank. Or maybe in the marsh. I'm not sure.

I walk over to the cut we went down and look around. I don't see a thing. I turn and walk onto that bridge and look over the other side.

I still cain't see her, though there is a big tumble of brush sittin' down to the right of me, across that bayou, off in a small, shallow-lookin' pond. It kinda looks like one of them beaver dams.

I say I still don't see you.

She says well, I can see you, or some of you, up on the bridge. I'm under a pile of stuff—mostly branches, I'd say, though I'd swear there's a bale of hay mixed up in here somehow. I can smell hay. Anyway, I'm stuck, Logan. I'm on my back in shallow water and my legs are pinned by somethin' or other and I can't get enough purchase on these branches to pull myself loose. You'll have to come get me.

I rush, slip-slidin' down the bank, and wade into that slough. It's boggy but not deep and I'm about up to my thighs in ooze when I reach the brush pile. I go to pitchin' off branches but it's harder than it looks. It's a jumble of pine and scrub and oak branches, about ten foot round, all knitted together pretty doggone good. I take out my pocketknife and start cuttin' my way through. I've always kept a sharp knife and now I'm glad of it.

I say Annie, I'm here and this is a real mess you're in and it may take me a while to get through. Are you hurtin' anywhere?

She says no, not really, though maybe there are parts I can't feel yet.

I say that's good, you just hold still.

She says I can't hold any other way.

She says I flew, you know. I really flew.

I say it's obvious you did.

She says I can't say I enjoyed it any.

I say no, I can see how a person might not.

She says I should be dead, you know.

I say it's a good thing you're not. Then I'd have to feel bad about us lollygaggin' in that shower.

She says well, maybe that saved us. Who can say? Had we not lollygagged, we might've been out on that straightaway with nowhere to hide at all.

I say that's true.

She says how's my wagon?

I say I hate to tell you this but it flew, too.

She says it did? To where?

I say I've got no idea.

She says the Ford's gone?

I say it is.

She says well, damn. Double damn!

I say lemme just get you outta here and we'll figger out what's next.

Annie's right about that hay smell. I cut my way through the thicket of branches and come upon a bale of hay, about two-thirds of it intact. When I throw it off and pull away a coupla more branches, there's Annie.

She looks up at me, rubbin' straw out of her eyes.

She says there you are.

I say it's nice to see you, too.

She says good thing I plopped down in this marsh instead of on the road. Otherwise, there might not be much to find.

I look at her close. Her face is covered with long, thin scratches—like a passel of cats have got at her.

I say okay, I'll get you out.

I see the problem. Basically, there's an oak log, about as big around as a fence post, over her legs. It didn't mash her only 'cause some other branches are holdin' it about six inches off the ground.

It's heavy but I get the log off and pull Annie slow to her feet.

She's a mess—scratched up, her dungarees and shirt soaked through and through. I cain't even see her sneakers, they're so caked in ooze. She's muddy as a marsh dog.

We could change clothes 'cept our clothes are in the wagon.

Annie makes it to her feet and tries to take a step. She says hold it, Logan, my left ankle is a bit tender.

I say here, put your arm around me, and let's go on up to the bridge.

We make it up there slow and when she gets to the bridge, she lets go of me and walks like a cat testin' hot blacktop.

She limps a little at first, then walks reg'lar.

I'm wonderin' how long it'll take her to see that house. I was hopin' it might be gone—maybe I'd just seen things. But it's not.

Annie says Logan, is that what I think it is?

I say I'm afraid so.

She says we're in a big mess.

I say well, a mess, true. How big I'm not shore.

She turns and looks past me.

She says how could my *car* blow away? A whole *car*?

I say any wind that can blow a house onto the road could suck up a car, easy.

She says well, I guess so. Jesus, the whole road we came in on is gone.

I say not gone, just covered in trees. That twister just mowed them pines down like grass and heaped 'em up on the road. Kinda the way they cut the sugarcane in Catahoula Parish.

She says well, what now? Should we try to hike back down to those policemen?

I say you see the road back plain as I do. No way, I don't think, to claw our way through there. And them deputies, I'd guess, are long gone. I think we gotta keep goin' the way we were goin'.

I point to the house in the road. I say at least one person lives up here. Maybe there are others. Maybe there's somebody up here with a car who ain't left yet. Maybe we can at least find shelter.

As I say this, the wind gusts up again. That hole in the sky has disappeared and the clouds are pressed in low and dark again. The rain's started up, though not quite as heavy as before.

I don't wanna say what I'm thinkin'—we're caught out here in the open with only this bridge for poor cover, and them tornadoes might not be finished.

I'm lookin' past Annie toward that house and I notice one other thing, too.

Somebody's walkin' real slow on the road toward us, leanin' into the wind. And she's carryin' somethin' in her arms.

26.

The old woman says can y'all help me? That's my house back there. Buster here is hurt and Mr. Pike's gone missin' on me. He was standin' on the back porch shooin' Buster through the screen door and then it got black—a tornado, I reckon?

I say yes, ma'am. A bad one.

She looks down, then up, and shakes her head, like she's tryin' to shake somethin' out of it.

She says it got awful black. I got spun around and all jumbled up.

I look at her good. She's a small woman, white hair in a bun that's been plastered down by the rain. There's a hickey on her forehead and a cut on her arm. She's wearin' a black dress with small white checks that's been soaked through. There's a trickle of blood runnin' down her right shin. One of her shoes is missin'. She's holdin' hard to a tiny dog. He ain't movin'.

Her eyes are dull and milky and her face is as wrinkled and innocent as a baby pig's.

She says I told Mr. Pike we should 'vacuate like them men come told us to do. He said Bernice, I'm too old to 'vacuate, and you are, too.

She looks at me, then Annie, and says I didn't think I was too old, my-self. I'd've gone to the shelter at Spanish Town. But Mr. Pike, he don't even listen to the radio no more. He says no use lettin' what's wicked and fool-ish in the world come into our house. Lord, he has his notions.

She says there's somethin' wrong with Buster here. She looks up at me. She says do you know dogs, mister?

She holds Buster up for me to look at.

I say well, ma'am, I've had some dogs but I cain't say I'm a dog doctor.

She says here, look at him. I don't see so good anymore.

She hands me the dog. It ain't but a bitty dog, brown with pointy ears and a bobbed tail and of a kind I couldn't name.

I take Buster into my hands and have a good look. He's still warm but I couldn't swear he's breathin'. I notice quick that he's got a broke back leg and there's a trickle of blood comin' out his ear. Buster's been banged around good.

I say he looks pretty beat up to me.

She says is he gonna die, mister? When the black come, that old house got shook up pretty good, and us with it. I don't know why I'm still standin'. Mr. Pike was on the back porch just comin' in. I was in the kitchen. I don't know where he went off to.

For the first time, I see she's got tears in her eyes.

I say well, ma'am, Buster needs a vet, I'd say, but I doubt we'll find one out here.

She says Mr. Pike would know what to do. He can fix anything. Dogs, too.

She looks past me and Annie, like she's scannin' the horizion. She says can you see him anywhere? My eyes ain't what they used to be. He's gotta be 'round here someplace.

I say no, ma'am, I don't see 'im. But we'll go look for him.

Annie steps forward and says oh, you poor thing. You poor, poor thing.

She takes the woman into her arms and hugs her. She says I'm Annie and this is Logan. What's your name?

She says Bernice. Bernice Pike. Mister is Harold. We're long retired. A fella up at the top of this road works our farm. We've got citrus—mostly satsumas. I've got two grown boys all the way out in California, and great-grandbabies, too. I don't see any of 'em much anymore. Mr. Pike says he never lost nothin' in California and won't go to visit and, well, I don't feel steady enough to go by myself.

Annie says well, I can understand that. How old are you, Bernice?

Ninety-one, she says. Mister is ninety-four.

Annie says I think the thing to do is to go have a look for Mr. Pike and then find someplace to get out of this weather, don't you, Logan?

I say that's a good plan, Annie. Are you okay to walk, Mrs. Pike? Unfortunately, the station wagon we drove up here with got took away, too.

She says do tell? Well, I don't walk like I used to. But I can walk if you ain't in a hurry.

I'm thinkin' to myself that we prob'ly should be in a hurry. But there ain't no way to hurry now, unless I sling Mrs. Pike over my shoulders.

I say okay, we'll take it slow.

I point to the house over her shoulder. I say now, just where was your house before the tornado?

She turns and puts her hand over her eyes, looks, and says it used to be up a gravel track up on the right, a good hundred yards from this road.

She calls out Harold. HAROLD! Where *are* you?

Annie pats her gentle on the back. She says don't worry, Mrs. Pike, we'll go have a look.

She says all right. But what about Buster? He was a yappy dog, but him and Mister were the best of friends. What are we gonna do about that dog?

I look at poor Buster again and I can see now that he is breathin', slow but steady. This ain't the best time to be totin' a dog around but he ain't much of a dog and I don't know what else to do. Anyway, I'm partial to dogs. At least he ain't a Great Dane.

I cradle Buster in one arm and we all turn and go slow toward the house.

Up close, it's easy to see that it's banged up, too. The windows are all broke. It's got a tin roof and some of the sheets have been peeled away. Mrs. Pike walks along the side of the house and says oh, my, I come out the front porch. I didn't realize the back one is gone. Like I said, that's where Mr. Pike was.

She puts her hands over her eyes again, looks over toward the woods.

She says again, but not loud, Harold, where on earth did you go off to?

I look at Annie and say why don't you take Buster here and walk with Mrs. Pike. I'll scoot on up ahead a bit quicker and see what I can find. I'm lookin' for a gravel track shootin' off to the right, is that right, Mrs. Pike?

She points ahead. She says yes, somewhere up that way.

I hand Buster over and say watch his sore leg. Annie nods and takes him from me.

I head on up the road at a brisk walk and it comes a bit clearer what that twister did. It come down from the grade through the woods, zig-zaggin'. When it hit the road, it come barrelin' straight down on us.

There's a patch of woods just off to my right that looks like it's been lawn-mowered. The trees on the other side ain't even been touched.

I get up maybe a quarter of a mile and see a gravel path goin' off to my right. I figger this is gotta be it. I walk up and start to call out as I go.

Mr. Pike. Mr. Pike. You here, Mr. Pike?

Nuttin' answers but the wind moanin' in the treetops.

In a bit I come to a bend and just around it is a big oak tree—or was.

About half that tree has been ripped away and is lyin' across the gravel track about fifty yards ahead. Up in a tangle of branches in the part that's still standin' is what looks like the back porch of Mrs. Pike's house.

I walk up to the tree and circle it, lookin' up.

On the back side, I see Mr. Pike.

He's pinned way up in that tree to a sharp, broke-off branch that's speared him clean through, same way a shrike pins a lizard to a barbed-wire fence.

I look away.

There ain't a thing I can do for Mr. Pike now—not even get him down.

I walk on around the fallen part of the tree to see what else I can see. I find the spot where the house was—a bare concrete foundation. About all that's left is a toilet sittin' lonesome on the back edge.

I notice two other things—a barn still standin', and a car parked near it. It's an old car, a Buick if I'm guessin' correctly, but it might drive us all out of here if it still runs. I could send the police back for poor Mr. Pike.

I turn and head back down the gravel drive and meet Annie and Mrs. Pike just turnin' up the path.

I look at sad Mrs. Pike and I lie.

I say I found where your house was but sorry to say, no sign of your mister. I looked around pretty good but obviously not everywhere he might be. I think the best we can do is to try to call the police or get to where they are and send 'em back so they can have a good look.

She says do you think Harold's dead?

I say I don't know, ma'am. It was an awful thing that come through here and we're all lucky just to be standin' here.

Mrs. Pike buries here face in her hands and starts to sob. She says there's nothin' lucky about this. Nothin' a'tall. You know, it wouldn't be right for me to be alive without Mister. We were married for seventy-one years last July.

Annie puts her arm around Mrs. Pike's shoulders. She says there, there, it'll be all right. I'm sure we'll find Mr. Pike.

I look at Annie and shake my head.

She mouths the word dead?

I nod.

She puts her head down and shakes it slow and holds Mrs. Pike tighter.

I say Mrs. Pike, does that car in your yard run? Maybe we could borrow it to get ourselves outta here and fetch the police.

She says that ole Buick? It runs sometimes but the key was in the house. I never drove and Harold got his license took away four years ago 'cause he couldn't see no more. But he kept the car and sometimes he would get in it and drive it up and down our driveway. He'd say you know, Bernice, if I wanted to go to town, I could go and who'd stop me? He even once got out onto the road, but he turned around and come back. He didn't talk for the rest of the day. Harold took it hard that he couldn't go where he wanted to.

I look at Mrs. Pike and say you know what? Harold sounds like my kinda fella. I had my license took away once 'cause I wouldn't pay for insurance—well, I was broke, but I know how he felt. It just goes to show that a man should never have the bad luck to get poor, or too old, neither.

Mrs. Pike looks up and wipes her eyes and manages a smile. She says you know, that's somethin' that Harold would say.

Then she looks down like she's thinkin' of somethin' and says we do have a tractor. Did you see our barn? It's in there. It's an old tractor and it don't need a key to crank. It's got a little wagon on the back of it. But I don't know how far we could get on a tractor.

I say well, how far is it to the top of this road?

She says about three miles. There's a little settlement up there called Indian Rise. Jack Hanks, the fella who works our citrus, lives up there with his wife. Old Bull Crawford does, too. He was a fishin' fella in his day, retired now. There's a new family moved in a few years ago—Oakleys, I think, but we never met 'em. The Oakleys have got a bunch of children, I hear. That's everybody.

I say well, I know a bit about tractors. Lemme go up there and see what I can do. Even a tractor pullin' slow up the road will beat walkin'. That's assumin' that tornado didn't pile up the road up that-a-way with trees. Or houses. Anyway, we need to find someplace to get everybody out of this weather.

Mrs. Pike nods. She looks up at the sky, just as the rain starts to fall in buckets.

I hike on up quick.

It's a small barn, with a wide door held fast by a turn latch. I go in and it smells musty the way a place does that's been closed up for a while. There's cobwebs everywhere and the floor's dirt and smells like chickens have scratched around.

I spy the tractor, a smallish John Deere. It's pretty much an antique and that wagon hitched to it is rusty and a bit beat-up but it looks like it'll hold a coupla people sittin' still. One of them trailer tires is low but ain't nuttin' I can do about that.

I crank the tractor and she coughs and choogs but finally sputters to life. I push the barn doors open, which ain't that easy in the wind and I'm about to get on up in the seat when I spy somethin' useful hangin' from wood pegs on the wall—two tattered yellow slicker suits. I get 'em down and throw' em in that trailer. They'll help keep the wind and rain off of Annie and Mrs. Pike.

I put the John Deere in granny gear and crawl on out.

I ain't a prayin' man but I'm prayin' now that we'll find somebody up at the top of this road, and a ride off this island.

27.

We get one good surprise.

The road is pretty much clear up to the top of Indian Rise, though I have to steer around a fallen branch or two, and I come upon a dip in the road where muddy red water, about two foot deep, has come racin' from a small slough and created a flood.

I crawl through that, hopin' the tractor don't stall.

The rain seems to come and go. It rakes at us like needles one second and it drizzles the next. For a while, I thought the wind might be slackin', but it's actin' like the rain—it blows hard in fits and starts.

Even if the road ain't blocked, it's hard, slow goin'. It's gettin' on toward late afternoon now, and darker than it would normally be, when I see a house, and a fair-sized house, too, risin' out of the gloom up about fifty yards away on my left. I don't see a light on, nor a soul around, but the sight of anything that looks like shelter cheers me up.

I look back at Annie and Mrs. Pike, sittin' in that wagon and wrapped as best as they can, in them ole slicker suits. They're a sad sight and them suits prob'ly ain't helpin' much—we're all soaked to the bone. But Annie's able to cradle that poor dog under there.

I steer the tractor toward that house till I spy a driveway and pull in to a nice level spot.

My spirits sink when I see what I see—the owner has boarded up the front windows, though there's a kind of open garage on the right side that will get us out of the rain.

I'm hesitant to shut the tractor off 'cause we might not be stayin' here long and it'd be bad if she wouldn't crank again. So I put her in neutral and set the hand brake and hop off and go back toward the wagon.

I see Mrs. Pike has pushed the hood of her slicker back and is pointin' toward the house.

I get there in time to hear her tell Annie this is the Hanks place but they must be gone. They've got a red pickup and a brown station wagon, and I don't see either one.

I say well, why don't y'all hop down and get outta the rain under the carport there and I'll knock on the door to make shore.

I unlatch the gate to that wagon and help Mrs. Pike down first, then Annie.

They shuffle outta the rain and I go up some front steps and bang hard several times on the door but it's clear this house is empty.

I go 'round and find Mrs. Pike settled onto the wood stoop of a side door.

I say where do the rest of them folks you talked about live?

She points the way we'd been headin'. She says Bull Crawford lives in a shotgun house around the next bend on the right. It ain't the kind of house you'd want to ride out a hurricane in. That place where that new family lives is stuck back up in the woods just as the Indian Rise Road starts to fall toward Tarpon Pass. It sits on the back side of this ridge, facin' the bay behind us. It ain't all that far, as I recall, but like I said, I ain't been up there in a blue moon.

I nod and say okay, why don't you and Annie just hunker down here outta the rain while I take the tractor and see if I can find someone or at least try to figger if the road's open beyond us. No use all of us bargin' about out there if we don't have to.

Then I think better of this for a second. I say Annie, have you tried that door?

She says yes, but it was locked.

I say lemme just see what kind of lock it is.

Annie moves aside. I go up and jiggle the handle and look close.

I'm pretty shore it's the kind of lock that can be jimmied easy with a screwdriver—actually maybe with my pocketknife. I take mine out and open it. I've gotta whittle away a bit of the wood to work the knife in between the latch and the jamb. But I manage it and turn the handle and put my shoulder gentle to the door and it swings open.

Mrs. Pike says bless you, Logan.

I say well, if I don't get to meet the fella who owns the place, you'll explain to him why I did it.

Mrs. Pike comes up the steps on Annie's arm and says I won't have to. He'da done the same thing.

I say y'all get dry. I'm gonna go see if this road is open and if anybody might be around with a car. I'd still like to get outta here before dark, if possible.

Annie says me, too. But *please* be careful out there.

I nod. I head out the door, mount the tractor, and back out slow. I put her in forward and head off down the road.

Soon enough I come upon Bull Crawford's house and Mrs. Pike was right—it ain't nuttin' but a shack up on blocks, with a small yard overgrowed in weeds. A post to his front porch has gone missin'. There's an ole green easy chair pulled up next to the door, springs stickin' out, and a faded wood rockin' chair next to that.

There ain't a car around, though there is a wrecked motorcycle leanin' with a crumpled wheel up against a tree next to the driveway. I go up and knock anyway and even try the door handle. The door opens. I call out but my voice just echoes through the house. It smells in here, of stale cigarette smoke and bacon grease. I don't need to be thinkin' about bacon right now.

I climb back up on the tractor and go on.

I poke down a long straightaway and the road opens up. Them woods we come through give way to low scrub on the gulf side and, without the lee of woods or houses, that wind comes a howlin'. There's a line of telephone poles as far as I can see in the distance and them wires are whippin' up and down and singin' an awful tune.

This tractor is fairly heavy but it sits up high and I can feel it bein' knocked about. Even as slow as I'm goin' it ain't easy to keep it from bein' driven off the road.

I get up another fifty yards and look out to my right and realize that even that scrub has give way. This road now sits up in the open maybe fifteen foot above a marsh that sprawls as far as I can see toward the horizon.

That wind's shriekin' in from my right. There are low woods off to my left and the trees moan and creak and grumble.

I brake the tractor to a full stop and grip the wheel hard and hold on for a long minute, just seein' whether I oughta even try to go on.

Next I know, a big gust comes—the strongest I've felt so far—and I hear a terrible pop, and then a screechin' sound like tin bein' dragged across asphalt.

I look back in the direction of the sound and see that wagon's been wrenched from the hitch and is skitterin' down the road.

Then a gust lifts it up and it tumbles twice and flies up and smacks a tree.

Cussed wind.

I was gettin' fond of that wagon, figgerin' that's about the only way we'd be able to drive Mrs. Pike off this island if we had to make a run for it on this tractor.

I look ahead into the gloom. I desperately need some notion of whether this road is open to the Tarpon Pass Bridge. I still think goin', even on this pokey tractor, is better than stayin', even in Hanks's big ole house.

I inch forward, thinkin' I'll try to at least make it to the end of this straightaway and try to see what lies beyond. I nose along, wrasslin' the tractor through the gusts, and I cain't remember any trip bein' slower. Nuttin' feels good about this.

I badger my way to a place where the road curves sharp left. I realize I'm back in the woods, and the wind, though it's still bawlin', ain't nearly as strong here.

I speed up a bit and steer around another curve and know right away I ain't goin' any farther.

Up ahead, there's a big tree down across the road, and a telephone pole, too. And when I look close I realize I'm seein' somethin' else—two dim red lights shinin' at cockeyed angles in the tangle of branches.

Somethin' about this ain't right.

I crawl up and see right away it's a car basically buried in that tree, turned partly on its side. The back end looks okay but the front, from the driver's door forward, has been smashed by a giant branch.

I scramble off the tractor and pick through the tangle and press in close enough so that I can peer in through the right rear window.

My heart does a fish flop—there are three kids in there, two boys and a girl, huddled together in the backseat against the far door. The girl cain't be more than three, four years old.

I look forward and see the driver is a man. He's pinned hard to his seat, the steerin' wheel pushed tight against his chest. His head is back but canted toward me and his eyes are closed. There's a big gash in his forehead and blood runnin' out of his mouth.

I notice about half the windshield is gone and the rest is shattered into glassy spiderwebs.

I know right away him and Mr. Pike are in the same place.

The car is tilted up on its side and I try the back door handle but it don't work. The light's not good but it's good enough that I can see the door latch seems to be pushed down.

I rap hard on the window and say is everybody in there okay?

It's like them kids have been in a trance and ain't seen me till now.

Two of 'em turn to me and start to bawl but what looks like the oldest, a boy maybe ten or eleven, startles up and gets a hand on the back of the front seat and pulls himself up to my door. He pulls the latch up and I yank but it don't do no good.

He says, through the window, it's stuck, mister. I don't know what's wrong with it but it's stuck.

I say well, can you roll down the window, son?

He says no, I cain't. The handle's broke off. Daddy was gonna get it fixed in town, but—

I see him lookin' at me good. He's got blond hair and big, sad rabbity eyes and a pretty good hickey on his head.

He says, soft, can you get us outta here, mister? Please? My sister and brother are scared. Real scared. And Daddy won't talk to us.

I say okay, I'm gonna have to break through. Gimme a second to find somethin'. Scoot on back against that door where you were.

I make my way out of that tangle and look around, hopin' to find a stout, short log I can use as a batterin' ram.

I find one and claw back in and say again, okay, scooch back far as you can. I don't want nobody gettin' cut up.

I pound that window hard but she's tough and it takes about a half-dozen blows. Even then, it don't break clean and I gotta knock away the shards around the openin'.

I've made quite the racket and them two youngest ones are cryin' again.

I guess I don't blame 'em.

I say to the older boy, okay, son, now be careful but I want you to help your baby sister there to the window by holdin' her steady. Then I'll lift her out.

He says okay. Bonnie, you need to go with that man.

The girl looks at me from around her brother. She'd stopped cryin' for a second, but when she sees me, her lip goes to quiverin' and she starts to bawl again.

It takes me a second to realize what I must look like—some over-growed, half-drowned swamp rat would be close.

I say soft it's okay, Bonnie, I'm just here to help you out. I know I must look rough but I don't bite. I'll get you out and then your brothers and we'll all go on together. Okay?

She says I don't wanna go nowhere, Billy. I wanna stay with Daddy.

Billy looks at his sister, then at me, and says Daddy's sick but he'd want us to go. He wouldn't want us to sit in this stupid ole car with a hurricane comin'. This man's come to help us.

She throws her arms around Billy's neck. He gets both arms around her bottom and scoots up slow on the seat toward me. I reach in with both hands and Bonnie lets go her brother. Soon she's got me 'round the neck, and I lift her out slow.

I can feel her warm tears on my cheek.

I look around and find a place to put her between the branches.

She says it's rainin', mister. Rainin' hard, and you're wet. I will be, too.

She says Momma don't like us in the rain. She'll be mad, yessiree. Won't she, Billy?

Billy says I don't think Momma will be mad this time.

I say Billy, help your little brother next.

The other boy says I'm Bobby and I'm not little and I don't need help. Watch out, Billy.

He grabs hold of the back of the front seat and comes forward quick. He's a strong, wiry li'l cuss. I give him my right hand. He takes it and puts a foot on the window frame and pulls himself out.

Billy follows the same way.

He says mister, you got a car?

I say son, I'm sorry to report that I don't.

He says you walked here?

I say no, I do have a tractor.

He says a tractor?

It's a long story. I come originally in a station wagon but, well, it got lost.

He says we need a car. There was a twister back at our house and part of it fell down. Momma's stuck in there, with our baby girl and my older sister. They got trapped and my sister's hurt and the baby's cryin' and Momma's gone half crazy. We couldn't get 'em out. Daddy and us were goin' to find help at Tarpon Pass when we run into this tree. Or it into us. I dunno. It got black again and the tree fell and Daddy slammed on the brakes.

He stops and looks around, like he still cain't quite believe he's here. He says Momma wanted us to go earlier 'cause she knew that hurricane was comin' quick but Daddy didn't think so. They were arguin' about it and then—

He looks at me and shrugs his shoulders.

I look at him and think what a mess we're all in. The ole Cajuns would call this a *roo-garou*.

I say I think the first thing we gotta do is get everybody inside. I've left a coupla people back at a house up on the rise—the Hanks place, I think it is. Do you know it?

Billy nods.

I say well, there wadn't nobody home but we've let ourselves in. We'll get everybody out of this weather and then I'll come back to see if I can help your momma. No way can we fetch help now.

He says okay but we have to go quick, mister. Momma was sayin' how Barbara—that's my older sister—was in a bad way. She'd cut her head and was bleedin' bad.

I say that tractor won't go too quick, we'll do the best we can. I'm shore everybody's gonna be all right.

I'm actually not shore of anything right now. All I wanna do now is get these kids up on the tractor and see if we can make it down that straight-away without bein' blowed clear into the bay behind us.

I say okay, everybody hold hands and follow me out of this thicket. Careful 'cause there's sharp branches everywhere.

Next I know, Bonnie gives me her left hand and Billy her right one. Bobby grabs hold to Billy's other hand.

Bonnie says I'm ready. Y'all ready?

I say I am, missy, let's go.

Bonnie turns and looks back. She's says Daddy's sleepin', right?

I look at her and nod.

We pick our way out from the tree and back to the tractor. A big gust of wind comes up and the rain kicks up at a slant again. I think about the seatin' arrangements and figger there's room for the boys to stand on ei-ther side of me, holdin' on to the back of my seat. Bonnie can sit in my lap.

We settle in and I back the tractor around and head back toward the Hanks place.

Bonnie grips the wheel like she's gonna drive and looks back at me and says are tractors dangerous, mister?

I say that's a funny question but no, tractors ain't normally dangerous.

She says that's good. Momma says hurrycanes are dangerous and there's one after us. Is that right, mister? Are hurrycanes dangerous like Momma said?

I look at Bonnie good for the first time.

Even plastered down wet, she's cute as a bug's ear and has the gab to go with it. I would laugh 'cept for a few things.

I'm wet and tired and hungry.

Her daddy's dead in the car there.

Her momma and sisters could be dead, too, for all I know.

We're stuck on this island for the night.

And hurrycanes *are* dangerous.

Belva's a killer, and we ain't even seen her fangs yet.

I put the tractor into gear and we nose out into the open. I say everybody hold on tight.

The wind comes beatin' down on us like God's own bully and a big branch from a tree someplace comes sailin' over our head, loud as an airplane.

Five or six times on that straightaway I feel the tractor grow light and unsettled and I think, well, this is it, it'll be me and these kids, up in some tree like Harold Pike.

I fight us out of that straightaway and, in the bit of a lee that the woods along the road give us, I look at those two boys. Their eyes are shut and their fists are clenched so hard in a grip on that tractor that they've turned white as a catfish's belly.

28.

We pull up to the Hanks house about the time the last drop of light drains from the sky. Good timin', as the tractor ain't got lights.

In fact, there ain't lights nowhere. I'd guess that tornado pretty well took care of the power lines. There's a weird gray glow in the sky. The wind and rain still seem to come and go in bands.

Them boys scramble off and I hand Bonnie down and climb off myself. The front door to the house opens a crack. I can make out Annie standin' there with a kerosene lamp. She opens the door a bit wider and says everybody, quick, in this way.

We tumble in. Annie's lookin' quite a bit better than when I left her. Her hair is in a towel and she has on a T-shirt and what could be men's britches.

She says Logan, I was gettin' awful worried about you. I see we've got company. Come on through the house back to the kitchen. That's a better floor to drip on. I've got some towels ready in there.

We traipse on to the kitchen. Annie sets the lamp on a small table and I see she's got two candles goin', too. I walk over to her and say I would hug you, but look at you, you're all cleaned up.

She says I don't care what kind of mess you are, I'll take a hug anyway.

We hug like people dancin' far apart.

Annie says the main thing is that you're here. And, yeah, about the first thing I did after I settled Mrs. Pike down for a nap is take a bath.

Then she looks around. These poor kids—what on earth?

I say Annie, this is Billy, Bobby, and Bonnie. Y'all, this is Annie. The kids were goin' down the road in a car toward the pass lookin' for help and had a run-in with that tornado, too. Their daddy is back there stuck in the car 'neath a fallen tree—no way I could get him out. No way we can get off this island now, either. The road's blocked solid behind us and solid ahead of us and the wind stole that wagon right off the tractor. Lucky, this group didn't get hurt other'n some hickies and scratches. Billy here says his momma and two sisters, one of 'em a baby, are trapped in part of their house that got knocked down. I'm goin' back out to see what I can do, but I thought it was best to get these youngsters inside first.

Annie says oh, you poor kids. Let's get everybody dried off. I don't know what we'll do about those wet clothes but we'll figure somethin' out.

Bonnie says this ain't your house, is it? This is Hankses' house. They got a dog named Mackerel and I come see him sometimes. He's a big dog but he don't bite.

Annie smiles bright. She says I've got me a coupla big dogs at home myself—Duke and Daisy. They're big but they're silly. And you're right, the Hankses are gone and we're kinda stuck like you are, so we've borrowed their house for tonight.

Annie passes out towels to everybody. She looks at the kids like she's sizin' them up and says maybe I can find some dry clothes—T-shirts, at least. You can even go back into the bathroom and take a warm shower if you want to. But let's try to be a little quiet. We've got two other guests, Mrs. Pike, who's very old and who's sleepin' on the couch, and her dog, Buster. He's a tiny dog and he's been hurt and they both need their rest.

I see the kids, towels around their shoulders, noddin'.

Billy says I don't need a shower or to get dry. He points to me.

He says I want to go with him—to help Momma. I know she must be real scared. My sisters, too.

I say I'm goin', son, just as soon as I've had a word with Annie about how we're doin' here. Plus, I ain't ate since last night and I'm feelin' on the shakey side. No use goin' out there weak-kneed. Now, I don't think you need to come with me. You saw what it's like, 'specially when we hit any place in the open. We don't need to risk more people than we have to, plus your brother and sister will need you here.

Billy says please, mister, I have to come. You won't know how to find it. And you'll need help when you get there. The house is a mess. It's—

He stops and looks down.

I look close at Billy. He looks pale and tuckered out, and if I'm guessin' right, I'd say he don't *really* wanna go out there, same as I don't.

He just knows he has to.

I know if it were me stuck in that house, that's just what Meely would do.

I say all right, I'll think it over. In the meantime, why don't you take your brother and sister down to that bathroom and get them dried off proper. Annie will come in in a bit and try to figger out dry clothes. Meanwhile, I need to talk to her.

Billy nods and says okay. Just, please, don't be long.

They go off down the hall.

I turn to Annie and say I see you've found lanterns and candles. Anything else useful?

She says well, it could be a lot worse. I've found four lanterns and a two-gallon jug of kerosene out in the garage and some candles and two flashlights. One I'd say has fresh batteries. The other won't last too long. The power's out and the phone's dead. But the stove's gas, and it works, and there are canned goods in the cupboard and leftovers in the refrigerator—they seem to be awful fond of Beanie Weenies in a can. We won't starve, at least for two or three days. And there are boxes of oranges everywhere to snack on.

I say well, that's some good news.

She says sorry to say that may be the only good news. I found somethin' else—a fancy kind of transistor radio, one of the kinds that can pick up stations all over Creation. Unfortunately, the batteries were old and I could only get it to work for about ten minutes. But I caught a storm bulletin. It said Belva was packin' winds of one hundred twenty miles an hour already and they could reach one hundred and forty—or more—by late tonight. It said tides ahead of the eye could reach ten to *thirty* feet above normal.

Annie stops and looks at me in a way more serious than I've ever seen her look.

I don't guess I have to tell you where they said the eye was headin'?

I say Articola Island?

She says right over the top of us.

I nod.

She says in all your days, have you ever heard of a thirty-foot tide?

I say no.

She says well, I have. I read a book once about a hurricane that struck Galveston, Texas, back around 1900. It killed six thousand people and basically wiped out every building on Galveston Island.

I nod again. I say well, we seem to have decent elevation here—right where we are might be the highest point around. Even a thirty-foot tide might not get up this far. We've put quite a few miles 'tween us and the gulf.

She says I hope you're right. Anyway, there's somethin' else I wanna show you. Follow me.

Annie grabs a kerosene lamp off the table and goes down a hall. I follow, moppin' my face with that towel. We take a left into a big room with a high ceilin' that kinda reminds me of the big room at Annie's place. It's even got those ceilin' fans.

We walk between an easy chair and a coupla sofas that sit together in an L. Off to one side, against a wall, there's a big TV with some of them rabbit ears sittin' on top of it. We reach a set of windows that runs the width of the room. There's a double door in the middle, also made of glass. These windows ain't boarded up but, in the lamplight, I can see big strips of tape runnin' every which way across 'em.

Annie says there's a deck off the back of this room and, while it was still light, I could see pretty far out. There's a broad marsh and what looked like a bay beyond. I think I might have even seen the lights of cars goin' slow on a highway in the distance.

I say that should be the direction of the mainland. Maybe if we had a boat—

Annie stops me. She says that's what I want to show you. There's a boat on a trailer out there in the backyard. Not a particularly big boat, maybe a sixteen-, seventeen-footer, but a sturdy-lookin' fishin' boat that could easily hold six people, maybe more.

I say what, you think we could maybe get out of here in that boat?

She says no. A, I think it's too late for that, and B, it's just a boat, no motor. Besides, I don't see how we could launch a boat. This house sits up on what I'd say basically is a sand dune overgrown with grass and trees. There's a fairly steep decline to that marsh, and it looks like a good quarter-mile across the marsh to the water. And the way those whitecaps were kickin' up, I'd say that bay is awfully shallow. No, what I'm thinkin', Logan, is that we oughta try to pull that boat up close to the deck and rope it to the railing and have it so we could cut it loose quick in the middle of the night if we had to.

I look at Annie careful. I say what you're really thinkin' of is a lifeboat, right?

She says right.

I walk up and push my face up against one of those glass windows. A willow in the backyard is bent double. But near it, I make out the white outlines of a boat.

I say havin' a boat out back ain't a bad thing.

Annie nods. She says are you scared, Logan?

I say I got a bit rattled out on that tractor a few times with those kids when I hit an open stretch and thought we might be turned into a kite. But I ain't scared yet, though I guess I am worried. I have a feelin' we still have plenty of time to get scared.

She says I don't like anything about this, except that you're here.

I say nobody could blame you now if you thought runnin' me down to Florda was a bad idea.

She says Logan, as if. Of course, we could be a lot farther down the road if I hadn't kept that barkeep pourin' Irish whiskey all night long.

I say Annie, listen. Last night was about as good as nights get for me. I don't have a single regret about it. Anyway, given the circumstances, we're in about as good a place as we can be.

She nods. She says I'm thinkin' about those poor children in there. They must be terrified. Is their father—is he dead?

I say yes. That tree fell right across the driver's part of the car and he was mashed in there good. I didn't actually feel for a pulse. I thought it might upset them kids too much, and anyway, it'll take several people with better tools than we've got to pry him outta there. As for that woman stuck in that house, I got my doubts I'll do her any good. I didn't wanna stir up Billy back in the kitchen, but on the way back I tried to get him to show me the road that leads to his place but we couldn't spot it. It looks to me like that tornado hopscotched over this bay behind us and come through the south part of this ridge and then roared down on us. I have a feelin' the entrance to their road is buried in a tumble of trees and who-knows-what-else.

She says well maybe the best thing is just to ride this out tonight and try to get in there at first light.

I say no, I gotta go. If it was Meely in there I'd go, and if it was you in there I'd go. And poor ole Billy—well.

She nods. She says I know, I know. I'd do the same thing. I just want you comin' back in one piece. We've just started to swing from the rafters. There's a lot more rafters out there to try.

I manage to laugh. I say now *there's* a reason for man to lick a hurricane.

She says I'm serious, Logan. Do what you have to do, but no heroics.

I say don't worry. Us swamp rats always manage to crawl out of scrapes okay. Now, I think what I need to do is get a drink a water and wolf down a can of them Beanie Weenies and get goin'. The weather ain't gonna get no better. And, oh, and I'll need one of them flashlights you've found.

She says do you think you'll take Billy?

I say I guess I will. What I'm *really* worried about is that we'll get there and find dead people—no boy should have to go through that. But he's right. He's our best chance of findin' the place. I just need to make sure he understands clear that if things start goin' to hell out there, we're comin' back.

She nods. She says oh, the boat. Let's go see if we can pull it up close to the deck. I'll go grab a flashlight.

Annie leaves and comes back quick, carryin' the light. I put down my towel and notice the door out to the deck is one of those slidin' kinds. I figger out the latch and push it open.

Even I'm surprised at how loud the wind is.

I step out and Annie follows me. She hands me the flashlight and loops an arm in mine and says let's go.

We walk careful across the deck to a set of steps goin' down into the yard and use a hand railin' to ease down slow. We're soaked again in no time and the wind bullies us somethin' awful but we make the boat quick. It's up on a trailer, the tongue of the trailer propped up on a sawhorse. I shine my light in. It's an ole lapstrake hull with a V-bow but seems in decent shape. There's a paddle shoved into a side panel—good to know. I walk to the stern, where the drain plug should be. It's in place. I figger there's already two foot of water accumulated—hard to say since the boat's on an angle. I reach down and pull the plug and set it aside. I motion Annie over and point to the plug. I say if we have to get in this thing, let's not forget to put the plug back in.

Annie knows boats good. She nods.

I give the water a coupla minutes to drain out, then remove a chuck from in front of the left wheel. Annie and me get on opposite sides of the trailer tongue, lift, and pull forward. The tires on the trailer are good and it moves easy.

We hustle it up close to the deck. I toss its bow rope over the railin' of the deck. The wind tosses it back.

Annie sees this and she tromps up the steps and yells I'll catch it.

I throw it again and it comes back again. The third time, she grabs it and ties it off quick. I tromp up the steps after her.

We ease back through the slidin' door and shut it behind us, but not quick enough. The wind has blowed out that kerosene lamp.

We stand for a moment in the dark, except for the beam of that flashlight pointin' down at the floor. A gust rattles these big windows, and I wonder if there's enough tape in the world to hold 'em together tonight.

Annie says don't worry, I'll relight that lamp.

Then she looks out toward the dark and that boat and says it wouldn't be a good night for a boat ride, would it?

29.

In the kitchen, there's a crowd around a table with a kerosene lamp flickerin'. Everybody is temporarily dry, except Billy who won't give up his wet clothes.

Annie has heated up a few cans of Beanie Weenies. She dishes them from a pot and passes a plate to me, and one to Billy. Billy takes his plate but just stares off into the distance.

Annie says Billy, you should eat. You'll need your strength.

He nods and starts to pick at his food with a fork.

I'm hungry as a March alligator and eat like one, too.

Annie says I'm feedin' Logan and Billy first. They're goin' out to try to get to the Oakley house. Everbody else can sit still for a bit. I have drinks—RC Cola or iced tea or grape soda.

Grape soda, says little Bonnie.

RC, says Bobby.

Mrs. Pike has straightened herself up and is sittin' next to Bonnie. I can tell she was a pretty woman in her day. She says Annie, I'll have tea, if you don't mind.

Annie says comin' right up.

Bonnie says you're old, ain't you, Miz Pike?

She smiles and says I'm older than the stones, young lady.

Bonnie says is that older than sixty-one? That's how old my grammy is.

Mrs. Pike says yes, I'm a lot older than sixty-one.

How 'bout sixty-two? Bonnie says.

Even older than sixty-two, says Mrs. Pike.

How 'bout forty-nine?

Bobby speaks up. He says Bonnie, forty-nine is *younger* than sixty-two. Anyway, you shouldn't be askin' Mrs. Pike such questions. Momma says it's not polite.

Bonnie pats Mrs. Pike on her hand and says no, Momma wouldn't be mad. Momma talks to everybody, just like I do.

Mrs. Pike smiles. She says don't worry, Bonnie. I'm too old to get mad anymore. But Bobby is right about his numbers. He's a smart one, I can tell.

Bobby smiles a bit bashful and says I told you so, Bonnie.

Mrs. Pike takes a long sip of her tea and says the last big blow through here was forty-four years ago. We'd just moved into our farm and we stayed put through that one, too. Of course, back then, few people even had radios. We didn't know better. We got heavy surf down on the beach one afternoon, big rollers, and a bit of rain but folks didn't think much of it. Then that night about midnight, it walloped us. It blew and moaned and rattled all night long and well into the next night. We lost a barn and a milk cow but that turned out to be the worst of it. It was an old barn and an old cow. There probably weren't more than a hundred people on the island then and them down by the beach all got up to the schoolhouse before the worst of it come. A few fishin' shacks washed away but not a soul was lost. Not a single one. It's hard to believe.

I look at Mrs. Pike and she looks way off into the distance.

She says Logan, when you go out there, would you keep an eye peeled for Harold? It might be that he just got blown down and is wanderin' around lookin' for a place to sit it out. Harold doesn't ruffle easy, I can tell you that.

I nod.

I wonder how good of a liar I can keep bein'.

Bonnie says is Harold a dog, too?

Mrs. Pike laughs soft. She says no, sweetheart, Harold is my husband.

Bonnie says is he older than the stones, too?

Bobby says *Bonnie!*

Mrs. Pike looks at Bobby and says it's okay, son. I know your sister doesn't mean any harm by it. She just likes to ask questions is all.

See, Bonnie says. See! I'm just like my momma.

I look at Mrs. Pike and say shore, I'll keep an eye out. But it's quite a few miles back to your farm from here. It would be a long way to walk in a storm, especially if a fella's, well, uh—

Hurt? Mrs. Pike says.

I say well, I was thinkin' a fella up in his nineties, is what I meant.

Bonnie says what. Is Harold lost? Is he sleepin' in a car like my daddy is?

Billy speaks up this time. He says Bonnie, stop pesterin' Mrs. Pike. Momma wouldn't like it. They don't know where Mr. Pike is. That tornado hit their house, too, and he's missin'.

Billy looks sheepish at me and then Annie and says well, I think that's what happened. Right?

I say that's right, son.

Bonnie nods and wrinkles up her face like she's thinkin' somethin' over.

She says I'll bet a tornado is the same as a hurrycane. We know where my daddy is. He's sleepin' in the car. And we know where Momma is, too. She's with Baby and my sister Barbara. Barbara's sick. When the house went *kaboom,* Barbara got sick. Didn't she, Billy?

Billy says oh, Bonnie, be quiet. You just don't know *anything.*

He looks at me. He says can we go, mister?

I say okay. Let's go back to the den, where we can make a plan.

He nods.

Bonnie says can I come?

I say no, missy. I need to talk to your brother in quiet.

When I'm shore nobody's followed us, I say okay, Billy, here's the deal. Comin' in here, you couldn't find the entrance to your road yourself and I'm of no use at all there 'cause I ain't set foot in this place till now. That tornado has shook the world up like a jigsaw puzzle in a box. We're gonna go out there and do our best to find 'em. We'll take the tractor as far as we can up the road. You'll hold the flashlight and I'll steer and maybe we'll get lucky and spy the entrance to your road. It's dangerous goin', and knowin' what I know about mommas and how they think, your momma wouldn't be too happy with me if we got out there and you got trapped or hurt. I wouldn't feel too good about it myself. So just you remember—I'm the captain and if I say we gotta turn around and come back, for whatever reason, that's what we gotta do. No ifs, ands, or buts about it. Okay?

Billy nods.

I say okay. Let's go.

At the side door, Annie meets me with the flashlight and says do you want me to get those slicker suits from the garage? They're beat up and about half the fasteners are gone but they're probably better than nothin'.

I think about this a minute and I don't want one. With that wind and rain, no way they'll keep us dry. But Billy, you take one if you want.

He says no, I'm fine.

Annie says you poor things. Keep safe.

I say we'll be back as quick as we can.

She nods and things go quiet for a minute and then I say well, okay, Billy, let's go.

We walk toward the door and Annie follows, with little Bonnie followin' her, and before I get there Annie stops me and pulls me close and says Logan, please, I mean it. I need you back here in one piece.

Then I hear Bonnie say are y'all kissin', mister?

I gotta laugh at that.

I say no, but that's a good idea.

I pull Annie even closer and kiss her on the lips and say see ya soon.

She says you know what the old Cajuns would say, right?

I say what?

She says *lâche pas la patate, neg.*

I smile and head out the door.

30.

The tractor choogs and huffs and backfires once but she does crank, a thing I worried about, given all this blowin' rain and damp.

I climb onto the hard metal seat and Billy climbs up to my left to the standin' place he had before. I glance back at the house and see Annie starin' out of a window, the soft light of the kerosene lamp on her face. I wave but then wonder if she can even see me.

I back the tractor out slow. Billy is tryin' to help out with that light but at one point he shines me in the eyes and I'm blinded like a cat in a flash-bulb.

I say try to keep that light down toward the ground, son.

He says sorry, mister.

The second we get out of the lee of the house, the wind comes down on us loud and blustery, like a helicopter beatin' six feet overhead.

I put her in low gear and off we go.

I realize quick we're just gonna have to crawl along—even goin' slow, the tractor steers skittish as a sore-footed horse. If I tried to run her at ten or fifteen miles an hour, she'd be an airplane.

The wind seems to beat on us from two directions at once, and the rain drives in like nails on my cheek. I'm thinkin' them slicker suits mighta been a good idea after all—we might not get as peppered. Whole sheets of water are blowin' across the road and we hit one patch where the water seems like it's two foot deep.

When I realize I've lost the road entirely, I brake the tractor and bend over and yell for Billy to try to shine the light a bit farther up in front of us. When he does and I still don't see blacktop, I tap him on the arm and take the light from him and rise up off my seat, holdin' on hard with one hand, and shine the horizon as far as the light will go.

I get a glint of blacktop. I keep the light on that spot and sit down and hand it back to Billy and say shine it there if you can. That's the road.

We crawl forward till we're on solid ground again. I'm wonderin' if we'll make a mile, much less the two we prob'ly have to go.

I drive on around a bend and the edge of the flashlight picks up Bull Crawford's house again.

I see somethin' else—that ole beat-up easy chair of his flopped over sideways in the middle of the road. I take the light from Billy again and shine it toward the porch.

About half of it is gone. One post is hangin' free, flappin' like a broke cow leg, and the front door has blowed open.

A roar of wind smacks us head on, then comes roarin' rabbity up behind us.

That door slams shut with a bang, blows open hard again, and smacks loud against the porch wall. It blows shut one more time.

The next roar kicks it open again and I hear a muffled pop even above the commotion of the wind.

We watch the door go spinnin' off, quick as a shot-at duck, into the black not too far above us.

There's another deep grumble of wind and then a hard scrapin' sound.

Billy shines his light up toward the sound and we watch as first one sheet of tin, then another, then another, then another, are peeled slow off the roof and go whirlin' down the road ahead of us like low-flyin' helicopters.

One crashes down and flips over and over like a kicked tin can, screechin' against the blacktop as it goes.

Then it's sucked up into the wet dark and disappears.

The wind drops back to a low moan.

I'm figgerin' that was a small twister.

I'm wonderin' what woulda happened had we been below Bull's house and not above it.

I lean again toward Billy and say son, I think we need to go back. Flyin' tin like that could take a man's head off.

He says no, mister, please. It's not that far, really. Comin' this way, I know I'll be able to find our road. It's at the end of a straightaway and there's a Resume Speed sign just past it. I know—

I say son, that sign coulda been took by the wind a long time ago.

He says there's somethin' else, a big ole cabbage palm just across the road from our mailbox. It's a tough ole tree. It's gotta still be there.

I say look, I know how this must feel to you. But we won't be doin' your momma and sisters any good if we get our fool selves killed out here.

He looks at me and I can see his moon-shaped eyes in the glow of the flashlight beam.

He says well, I've gotta go there, I don't care what happens to me. Daddy would do the same thing if he was here.

I say maybe so. But your daddy obviously couldn't get 'em out of what they was trapped under, and he was *there*. That's why he was goin' for help, right?

He says Daddy has a bad back and he cain't lift no more. It was a mess in there. It—

I stop him. I say look, it sounds like your daddy was tryin' to do the right thing. And I am, too. But it's crazy to be out here. Let's go back and the very minute this blows over, we'll fetch help.

Billy shakes his head. We cain't wait, mister. Don't you see? If we don't go get 'em now, they'll die in there. I know it. Momma begged Daddy to leave. She had a bad feelin' about this storm.

He pulls away from me. He says I'm goin' to find 'em. I don't care if you come.

I see his eyes have filled with tears.

I take a deep breath and look around.

I don't know what kind of fool I am—big or small.

I say Billy, remember I said back at the house that I'm the captain of this here expedition?

He nods.

I say I'm gonna make you one last deal. We're gonna go on slow, but if we hit another bad spot where there's too much water or trees down or power lines whippin' around or things blowin' around in the air, we're turnin' back, no questions axed. And if you don't come voluntarily, I'll have to fix it so you come back anyway. I'm not a mean fella, but I've hog-tied men a lot bigger than you and I won't be sassed about it. Do you understand clear?

He looks at me and his eyes are quiet and soft as a deer's.

He nods his head and says yes, sir.

I say okay, hold on.

The ole tractor jerks forward and I steer us around that easy chair in the road and we poke our way forward. We hit lots of water, but not any deep water. There are limbs down but no real big ones. In a coupla places, I just roll right over 'em.

We finally hit a straightaway and Billy leans close and says this is it, mister. Our road is down on the left at the end of this stretch.

I look forward and, far as our light goes, the road don't look too bad. On the other hand, it's clear that our light's startin' to fade. It'll be hard to get back to the house without any light at all.

We ease on up and Billy shines the light hard along the left shoulder. Then he shouts here it is! This is our road!

I look over and see a muddy red track, about wide enough for a car or tractor, anglin' up through a thicket of what looks like palmettos. There's some bigger trees that I don't recognize sashayin' in the wind.

I nose the tractor to the left and say shine the light on up, son, and see what she looks like.

It ain't good.

There's a small tree across the entrance, which is prob'ly why we missed it the first time. Beyond that, the road looks clear, 'cept for some big puddles, for about fifty feet, then there's a big shadow across it.

I say hold on a second. I'll see if I can move this tree out of our way.

I climb from the tractor and use the wind to wrassle that tree off onto the roadside. I get back up and nose the tractor forward before I see the shadow is another downed tree—about the size of the one that fell on their car.

I say no way we're drivin' around that, Billy.

He says our road ain't that long. We can walk from here.

I look around tryin' to see what else might fall on a person.

I say we can try.

We climb off the tractor and I take the flashlight and get up to that tree and shine the light through the branches. We can prob'ly scramble over it, though there's broke and twisted branches every place that will scratch like a feral cat if you slip or fall.

I say okay. Follow me and be careful.

We scrabble on through and reach a spot where the trunk's canted up at an angle. There's no good purchase above that I can see. I shine the light down and there's an openin', maybe two foot high, that a person could prob'ly crawl under.

I don't care to be wormin' my way on my belly but I don't see any choice. Otherwise, we'd have to back out and try to find a way around.

I tell Billy what to do and he nods.

The ground's wet and oozy but I snake on through. I shine the light and Billy follows.

The road turns sharp and I can already see another log across it. Worse, rainwater slidin' fast around that log has cut a trench that's gouged out a good chunk of the road.

We walk on up and I realize we've basically got to cross a fast-movin' bayou about twenty foot wide.

Billy seems to know what I'm thinkin'. He says it cain't be that deep.

I say, no, but it's fast and there could be sweepers—logs or stumps— big enough to knock us over. But we'll give it a shot. Here, take my hand.

He looks at me like maybe he don't want to.

I say it's no time to be bashful, son. We've got enough problems without either one of us slip-slidin' away.

He nods and reaches out.

We go walkin' slow, like I do when I'm walkin' the marsh back home. When that water gets up to my butt, I look back and see it's clear up to Billy's waist. I feel him grip tighter. We slog on through.

I wish I could do what them wet coonhounds do—just shake this water off my hide.

But the sky just keeps dumpin' buckets of water on our heads.

I peer up ahead far as the light will let me and spy another thicket of knocked-downed trees and brush.

I say that'll be pretty tough goin' through there. How much farther do you think?

In the dim glow of the flashlight, I see him squint and wrinkle his brow like he's thinkin'.

He says it cain't be that far. Maybe we could go around—in the woods.

I say no. If we got out there and this light quit on us and we got turned around, we'd be in a fix.

He says these woods ain't so big, mister. You cain't really get lost. If we walked one way or the other, we'd hit the main road we come in on, or the bay that's behind our house. It's the same bay that sits behind the Hanks place.

I shine my light around and it's pretty clear these woods have been torn up, same as this road.

I say honest, Billy, I think we need to stick to this road and see if we can fight our way through.

He looks at me like he's puzzlin' somethin' over. He says what's wrong with me? We shoulda just come up the back side along the bay. Me and Bobby are always walkin' to the Hankses from our house. The only hard part is crossin' Horseshoe Marsh—a place where's there's a big break in the dune. Momma didn't want us in there 'cause she said there's quicksand in that marsh. But I ain't never sunk down to more than my butt.

I say how wide is that stretch?

He says maybe a football field across.

I say I dunno. That would be a *real* lotta marsh to cross on a night like tonight. Look, let's see if we can fight on a bit. We need to keep movin' or go back.

He nods.

Twenty minutes later we've scrabbled over or under trees and brush and cracked stumps and waded through other washed-out places in the road. We got down on our bellies twice more to wriggle under things when we couldn't climb over.

I'm startin' to think we might actually get to the house when we come upon a small rise and I hear the loud sound of gushin' water, even over the sound of the whippin' rain and wind.

I shine my light, which has really started to fade now, and see a roarin' creek, maybe fifteen foot wide. Muddy ridges of water rise up like giant gator hackles.

I doubt we'd get safe across that in a boat.

I look at Billy and say you didn't tell me about this.

He said well, there was a bridge here. Honest, mister, it's usually just a little creek. Yesterday it had just a trickle of water.

I nod.

He says the house is right there. Really.

I shine the light and I can see he's right.

I can also see it's a mess—far as I can make out, it looks like somebody took a giant hatchet and cleaved it in two.

I say well, I'm sorry, but there's no way across this.

He says we could swim.

I can tell even he don't believe that.

I say no, you'd be a mile downstream in a Mississippi minute. That's if you wadn't already drowned.

He looks down.

He says, quiet, they're in there, mister. Momma and Barbara and Baby.

I say I know that and I'm sorry. If this storm don't get no worse than this, maybe they'll ride out the night fine.

He looks up at me. He says they won't.

I don't know what to say to that.

I say well, we gotta turn back now. I promise you, at the first break we get, we'll come back to see about 'em.

He nods again and looks down, starin' at the dark, muddy ground.

I look back over the ragin' creek toward the wrecked house. For some reason I switch off my light and just stare out at the wet, moanin' blackness.

The hair rises on my neck and I don't have the heart to tell Billy what I see.

Maybe it's just my imagination but, from way down low toward the back of that house, I swear I see the flicker of a dim, dim light.

31.

I've pretty much give up on time. I cain't say whether it took an hour to get back or three.

But we finally drag up on foot to the Hankses' driveway with Belva moanin' so loud that we had to give up on talkin'.

We give up the tractor, too, about half a mile above Bull Crawford's house. Some telephone poles had snapped off and blocked the road with no way around 'em.

We didn't have to worry about Bull's shack blowin' down on us, though.

It was already gone—not even a slab.

We make the back steps and I feel like I been wrasslin' in the mud with a thousand-pound swamp bear.

Annie's standin' at the door, a lantern in her hand. We step in and she shuts the door behind us. She says God, I was worried. Let's get you out of these clothes.

We step in. I'm not shore Billy looks worse than me but I know he feels worse.

Annie says no luck, huh?

I say we got there, Annie—well, almost all the way to the house. But the bridge across their creek was washed out and we couldn't get across. That creek musta been runnin' ten, fifteen, knots.

Annie says I'm so very sorry. Could you see anything?

I say no.

Billy says I don't blame you, mister. You tried. It's my fault. We shoulda tried to go in the back way, along the dune. I don't know why I didn't think of it. I don't—

Annie comes over and bends down before Billy and puts her hands on his wet shoulders. She says it's not your fault, Billy. Mrs. Pike's husband is missin' and I just about got blown away myself. If Logan hadn't been there to pull me out, I'd be stuck like your momma and sisters. This is a very bad storm and we've all had the bad luck to get caught in it.

Billy nods.

Annie rises and says okay, let me try to scrounge dry clothes for you both. Why don't you shuck your wet shoes here.

Billy says if it's just the same, maybe I'll keep my shoes with me. In case we need to go someplace fast.

Annie nods. She says I hope we won't, but I can understand that.

She looks up like she's thinkin' of somethin' and says actually, Billy, why don't you come on through first. I'll get that shower runnin' for you.

Billy says all right.

Annie says Logan, meanwhile, why don't you sit at the kitchen table. I've got one of the kerosene lamps goin' and I'll get you a towel to dry your face.

I say sittin' would be nice.

Annie disappears with Billy down the hall and I shuck my boots and tore-up socks and put 'em on a mat by the door.

I go sit at the table and use that towel as best as I can. I hear the wind moanin' through the boarded-up windows and runnin' wild in the trees. I realize I feel a bit woozy. I close my eyes and feel myself noddin' off.

Next I know, Annie is standin' next to me, runnin' a towel soft in my hair and down around my face and neck. She says your turn. Let's go get you cleaned up.

I say where is everybody else?

She says Bonnie and Bobby are asleep in one bedroom down here and Mrs. Pike is snoozin' in the other. Billy went in to join his sister and brother. I expect he'll be snoozin' soon, too. There are two more bedrooms upstairs but I figured you and I would just man the couches down here till this thing blows over.

I say that's fine with me. About now, I could sleep in a hog trough. I'm past whupped.

She says I know you are.

I say what about that poor dog?

She says you mean Buster the Wonder Dog? I found a cardboard box in a big hall closet and fixed up a bed with old rags and put him in there where it would be nice and quiet. I didn't think the poor thing would last the night. But just after Mrs. Pike went to bed, I heard a noise out in the hall and wondered, what could that be? Well, it was Buster, walkin' in a slow circle, draggin' his busted leg. I picked him up and put him back in the box. He's still there, in a deep sleep, though he still whimpers now and then.

I say I'll bet that dog's gonna be all right. He looks like a tough li'l cuss.

She says I hope so. Anyway, to the shower you go.

I get up groggy and walk down the hall, Annie followin' me.

There's a kerosene lamp goin' in the bathroom and it throws off pretty good light.

The shower runs into a claw-foot bathtub, with a curtain on a rod around it. Annie pushes that curtain to the back of the tub and reaches over and turns on first one spigot, then another.

She walks over and shuts the bathroom door and says okay, Logan LaBauve, out of those wet duds.

I say everything?

She says what, you're bashful?

I'd smile if I weren't so tired. I say well, maybe I was but I'm gettin' over it.

She says you'll need somebody to get your back.

I say oh, I can do that.

She smiles and says yes, but why would you want to?

She helps me with my shirt and then helps me pull my T-shirt over my head. I toss 'em aside and shuck my britches and my baggy wet drawers and step in the shower.

Annie reaches in and soaps me up everywhere, then has me turn around and soaps me up everyplace else.

I might be bone-tired but I guess I ain't dead.

She cups me with her warm, soapy hands and says, well, look at you.

I close my eyes and say see what you do to a man?

She says I see. Nice. We'll have to try this again sometime—without the hurricane.

I laugh at that.

Pretty soon, I'm outta the shower, moppin' off my face and head while Annie towels off my back real soft. She pats me dry.

I realize I like standin' naked in front of Annie. Maybe I like how she looks after me.

She pats me on the bottom and says I'll get you some clothes.

I finish dryin' off and she's back quick. I get dressed, except for socks.

She snuggles up close and says it *is* too bad ole Belva's gotten so nasty about things. She spoils a girl's fun.

We hug, then grab our lantern and head for those couches.

Annie says you must be totally exhausted.

I say I am and you must be, too.

She says I'm numb, actually. Anyway, you should sleep. One of us should try to stay up in case we have to leave quickly. I'll take the first shift.

I say that's prob'ly smart. There's only one place we could go—the boat. I don't wanna have to think about that.

I tell her about that fella Bull Crawford's shack and how it ain't there no more.

I say it's a good thing we found a better place than that.

Annie looks down, shakin' her head. She says true enough. If I correctly understood that snatch on the radio, we'll need every timber. The worst of Belva might not be hittin' us for the next two to three hours.

I nod.

She says Logan, be honest with me—that poor woman and her children in that house. Do you think they're still alive?

I say the worst thing about not bein' able to get there is that they very well could be. I didn't wanna say anything in front of Billy but I saw what I'm shore was dim light flickerin' way back in the broke-down part of that house. *Somebody* was stirrin' around in there.

We go quiet for a while, listenin' to the house shudder and shake.

Those couches are put together in an L-shape. I sack out on one and Annie sits next to me on the other.

I say you know what? We should prob'ly bring them flashlights in here, too.

She says okay, I'll get 'em in a second. Then I feel her hands feathery on my neck and soon I've got my eyes closed. My mind seems to be turnin' round slow, like I'm bein' tumbled easy by the wind.

I say Annie, I'm fadin' out. You call me if you need anything at all.

She says don't you worry, I will.

And that's all I remember till a terrible dream comes upon me and I hear a crashin' sound and glass breakin' and somebody hollerin'.

I try to hunker way down in that deep, deep sleep to get away from that dream, when suddenly I know the truth.

It ain't no dream.

I feel Annie shakin' me hard and sayin' Logan, Logan, God, wake up! I think a window or somethin' blew out upstairs!

32.

I pop up groggy and look around.

Annie's got one of the flashlights, shinin' the beam on the wall.

I see a pitcher go flyin'. It smashes with a bang to the floor. It seems to me the house is swayin', though maybe it's just the shape I'm in.

Annie yells upstairs. Follow me!

We go trompin' up. At the top, the flashlight beam picks up the problem.

There's a door flappin' hard at the end of the hall and a reg'lar gale blowin' down on us.

We fight our way there and look.

There's a tree branch stickin' through a broke window. The board across that window musta blown off or got knocked clean through.

I look around and spot a tall chifforobe standin' in the hall.

I rush past Annie and grab the flappin' door and put my back to it. I get it shut, though with the wind shovin' against me, it feels squirmy as a coon in a burlap bag.

I say you come hold this shut and I'm gonna move that dresser in front of it to get her blocked.

Annie steps over to the door. When it's clear that dresser's too heavy for me to move by myself, she leaves the door and comes over. We give it a big shove and it starts to move, scrapin' along the wood floor.

About halfway, that door bangs open again and for a second I think it's gonna blow the dresser down on top of us.

I wrassle the door shut again and rush back to the dresser. We heave and huff again and get it jammed against that door. It sounds like a Catahoula wildcat has busted into that room, raisin' hell.

We head down—only to be hit by another big gust of wind. I wonder if we've lost another window downstairs.

We get to the bottom, a fierce, wet gale blowin' through the halls, and I get my answer.

Bobby's standin' there, lookin' hangdog, like kids do when they've been misbehavin'. But it ain't that.

He says Billy's gone, mister. He's gone out.

I hear my voice risin' above the wind. I say out? Out where?

He's gone out to get Momma and my sisters. He's gone the back way along the dune.

I can see Bobby's lower lip quiverin'.

He says I told him not to, mister. I told him. It's not my fault.

Annie goes over to Bobby and bends down. She says of course not, Bobby. But you have tell us—how long ago?

He says I dunno exactly. A few minutes ago, I guess. He went out that slidin' door in the den. He told me to shut it behind him but I couldn't. The wind's too strong.

Annie says geez, Billy doesn't even have a light.

Bobby says oh, he does. I gave him my penlight. I didn't wanna give it to him. But he made me. Kind of.

Annie looks at me, exasperated. She says that's not much light on a black night like tonight. But okay, let's go shut that door. You better grab the other flashlight, Logan. It's over by the couch.

She shines her light for me to see and I get it quick.

Maybe Billy wantin' to hang on to his wet shoes shoulda told us somethin'.

I grab that light and we find the back room. That door's wide open and a good chunk of glass has been broke out. The rain's peltin' in hard and there must be a quarter-inch of water on the floor already.

I manage to wrangle the door shut but the wind shrieks through that hole like steam from a teakettle.

Annie walks to a window left of the door. She shines her flashlight down to the floor and puts her face up against the glass and looks out.

I say if I were you, I wouldn't spend much time by that window. If I can find Billy, I think the best we can do is to all hunker down in one of them bedrooms that have the smallest windows. Or maybe even in that bathroom. It's the one room that don't seem to have an outside wall.

Annie nods. She says how on earth will you ever find him?

Bobby speaks up. I hadn't even noticed that he'd followed us into the room.

He points out into the growlin' dark. He says just follow the dune that way, mister. That's the way he's gone.

I say okay, I'll do my best. Now you need to skee-daddle outta here, son, and go back to that room with your sister, okay?

He says okay and turns to leave.

Annie says I can't believe that boy. This is all we need, I mean—

I say youngsters do foolish things, and this is a big one. On the other hand, I can understand why he's done it. I just don't know if I have it in me to wrassle Belva one more time. Anyway, the sooner I go the better chance I have of trackin' him quick.

Annie says well, I guess you'll need your boots. I'll get 'em.

She's back fast. I lace 'em up and head for that slidin' door.

She says damn, Logan, I'm sorry—sorry for you, I mean.

I say me, too. Now, I'm gonna slip out that door. You make shore it shuts behind me.

She says okay.

My flashlight in my left hand, I fiddle with the latch with my right and push. The door slides open a crack. The wind blasts in and I'm about knocked backwards. I put my head down and fight my way out.

I look back to see Annie, her flashlight in the crook of her arm, pushin' with all her might to close it. It *whumps* shut. I get my bearin's and point my light and head down the steps of the deck.

I'm down to the last one when what I see in my light shocks me. It's water.

The yard's flooded.

I step down and go calf-deep. I reach down and dabble my fingers in it—warm.

I put my fingers in my mouth.

It's salt water.

I shine my light far as I can see and all I can see is water. I shine the light at that boat and realize the water's about a third of the way up the tires on the trailer.

I see a slow eddy around the tires.

I race up the steps, squeeze through the slidin' door and run back down the hall toward the kitchen. I find Annie standin', lookin' out the small window in the garage door.

She says Logan, what? I thought—

I say we got big problems. There's already a foot of water in the back-yard and it's salt water.

She says salt water?

I say it's gotta be the storm tides. That bay's crawled into the backyard and it's comin' up quick.

Annie says good Lord.

I say we need to get them kids and Mrs. Pike all ready to go if it comes to that.

You mean, in the boat?

That's right.

What about Billy?

I say I'm still goin'. He could be in a lot more trouble than he thinks he's in for.

Annie says okay, I'll start roundin' everybody up.

I say tell 'em gentle—no need to panic anybody. But they need to be awake and ready to move. Mrs. Pike, especially, since she don't move fast. And I guess we don't wanna forget about that dog.

Annie says oh, right, Buster. It'll be a regular Noah's Ark.

I turn to go and then say oh, if it comes down to the boat, don't forget to put the plug back in.

She says I won't. But you'll remind me anyway.

I say I will—if I'm here.

She says Logan, forget it. I won't leave without you.

I say Annie, I hope you won't have to. But I'll feel a lot better about bein' out there if I know you'll do what has to be done, whether I'm back or not. Now, I've gotta go. Please promise me you won't let yourself get caught here. I need to know that.

Annie gets that serious look in her eye again. She says you know, I hate this. I hate to make any such promise. And if it were just my hide at stake, I wouldn't. But you musn't worry. I'll take care of things here. Now, go quick and come back the same way.

I turn to leave and Annie's suddenly at my side. She looks at me deep and fierce and says I mean it, Logan LaBauve. You've got to come back—I couldn't bear it if you didn't.

I say what, and let all them rafters go to waste? No way. I'll see you again, Annie. I'm shore of it.

Then I turn and go, not nearly as shore as I've said it.

33.

I get outside again, the wind boxin' me about the head, and slosh across the dark, dark yard.

I walk for about fifteen minutes, if you can call pushin' through a hurricane walkin', keepin' the dune over my right shoulder, pickin' my way through stands of tall grass and low-lyin' woods.

Actually, that grass was tall but big stretches have been mowed down flat as fall sugarcane. It's springy to walk on.

I've never been in such wind and the roar in my ears has already give me a headache. I do notice, though, that the rain has pretty much stopped for now.

I hit a boggy spot and shine my light down and see footprints. They're fresh, the heels pooled with water. This is a lot more luck than I'd hoped for.

Well, Billy got at least this far.

I call out his name loud as I can but the wind just swallows any sound I can make.

I press on and come to an open spot and my light picks up the shimmer of whipped-up water. I'm figgerin' this must be that Horseshoe Marsh place that Billy was talkin' about.

It ain't marsh now.

I shine my light far as it will reach and it looks like a broad bayou chopped up by the wind. I ease on in and am surprised to find hard, sandy bottom. But I don't get more than fifty yards when I'm up to my waist in water and the bottom turns soft.

I get my light up high and the bank don't look that far, plus the wind for now seems to be at my back. I make up my mind. I just ease over on my back keepin' my light above me and paddle and kick toward the other side. I feel a current tuggin' me along.

The water's definitely risin'.

I make the other bank and slosh out and get my bearin's and walk on.

I don't actually have a plan, 'cept that if I don't find Billy pretty quick, we're both in big trouble. I'm wide awake now but I realize every bone and muscle in my body hurts like a bad toothache.

I try callin' out again but I know it's useless.

Pretty soon, I come upon a grove of what I guess are sea pines. Several have been uprooted and I'm wonderin' if I can get through. I hear waves lappin' and realize the bay's marchin' up quick. I shine my light and figger a way to shinny through, though at one point I scrape my back against a tree trunk and holler like a pig stuck for the *cochon de lait.*

It's about that time that I pick up a light, real dim, up ahead.

I scramble out of the pine thicket and go half-runnin' toward it, callin' out Billy's name. I kick a root of some kind and stumble and fall flat on my face and my light goes flippin' out of my hand.

I hit hard and feel splinters and branches dig into my palms and realize I've cracked my knee on somethin' hard, too.

I pick myself up and look around in the dark. The flashlight was metal. I see a glint of somethin' ahead and ease my way toward it. It's my light, all right, but it won't come on.

I shake it and rap it soft against the palm of my hand and fiddle with the switch but still no luck.

I peer out in the direction where I saw that light and I see it flicker again, like a distant firefly through the roarin' dark.

I grip my light hard, figgerin' maybe I can fiddle it back to life, and grope my way toward that dim beam. I realize I'm headed gentle uphill, I'd guess up the face of the dune.

I come upon Billy sittin' on a fallen tree, starin' ahead, his light pointed toward what looks like a caved-in roof. It's cocked up at a strange angle and looks like it could just slide down on us, though we ain't on much of a grade.

When I put my hand on Billy's shoulder he jumps and turns to look at me.

I pull him close and say you know you mighta tole me what you had in mind.

His eyes are big and glassy as a whippoorwill's.

He says I heard Momma's voice and she heard me. But I cain't get through, mister. I cain't. It's just a jungle of splintered wood and boards and nails and glass.

I look over to the tangle and say okay, you wait here for now. Take my light—I think it's shot 'cause I fell and dropped it back there—and gimme yours.

We trade lights. He shakes mine and says loose bulb, I'll bet.

I say maybe so.

I make my way toward the wrecked house. It does look like a giant hatchet lopped it in two, and not clean, either. Billy's light is pitiful for a job like this but it's good enough to let me see that it might take ten men with crowbars to pry their way in. I try one spot, a tangle of broke and twisted two-by-fours, and cain't move a thing.

I shine my light a little farther to my left and spy what mighta been a doorjamb at one time, but it's blocked up good. I keep anglin' left, past a pile of jumbled timbers, and then a saggin' stretch of roof that's jammed hard into the ground, and then past another knot of splintered lumber. There's somethin' of an openin' in the knot and I bend down and look.

It's a tunnel of sorts, big enough that a stooped man could squeeze through. Maybe ten foot in is what might've been a window frame, canted to one side. I cain't see farther than that.

I stoop down and slide in, when I hear a noise above the wind.

I straighten' up some, tryin' to figger what on earth such a noise could be, when I feel the ground shake and hear what sounds like thunder.

I turn quick and shine my light out the way I came and there's a giant sloshin' sound, like monsters have thrown tubs of water from the sky. I'm knocked backwards and suddenly I'm knee-deep in a fast-movin' current.

I keep my feet and clamber outta my hole and look up. The dark sky don't give a clue but I suddenly know what's happened—a wave has slammed the opposite crest of the dune.

I run fast as a man can in knee-deep water toward Billy.

I'm amazed to see my light shinin' toward me. Billy's dazed, starin' down at the water rushin' 'round his legs.

He says I fixed your light, mister—it was the bulb. But what was *that*?

I say that was a wave, son.

A wave? From the gulf? Up here on the dune?

I say that's right. Now you listen to me, no back talk. You take that light and run as fast as you can back to the house. If Annie already hasn't gotten everybody in that boat out by the deck, she needs to do it right away. Stick to the highest ground you can. If that really was a wave, there could be another one. I've found a place where I might be able to squeeze in and get to your momma and sisters. I'm gonna try. If I get 'em out, we'll come along behind you on the dune line. But *don't* wait for us. Annie's good with boats. Maybe she can work that boat up along this shore. Look for my light. This is the best chance we've all got. Now, fly, Billy. Go!

Billy looks at me and for a second I think we're gonna have an argument we cain't afford.

But he turns and starts to run, then scrambles back and comes up close and says take your light back. It's better than mine. And be careful, mister, okay?

I say I will. You, too.

He turns and disappears into the dark, howlin' night.

I make my way back to the wrecked house and find that tunnel again. The water's receded as fast as it come, leavin' the ground spongy. I scooch down so I'm about walkin' on my knees and ease into that hole, thinkin' two things—one, I hope the Hanks place sits up higher than this one does. Two, Annie will be lucky to get that boat loaded and keep it afloat, much less steer it over this way to pluck me and whoever off this dune.

If I ever see Annie again, it'll be on the other side of this storm.

With this better light I can see this tunnel goes deeper than I first thought. I crab on in, at one point tearin' away a coupla bent and busted two-by-fours that sag down in my way. I realize my hands are shakin' and I'm sweatin' like a fox in a forest fire.

I claw deeper, to that thing that looked like a window frame, and that's just what it is. This tunnel makes an elbow here.

I lean in and look right. The tunnel narrows but my light picks up somethin' I hardly believe—a face is starin', pale as the belly of a *sac-à-lait*.

My heart does another fish flop.

The face says Billy, Billy, could that be you?

I say no, ma'am. He was here but I sent him for help.

She says I know he was here. I heard him call out.

She says are my children okay?

I say yes, ma'am, they are.

My husband?

No, ma'am, he's not. There was an accident. I got the kids out safe. We're all holed up at the Hanks house.

She says Barbara's dead.

I say would that be the baby?

She says no, it's my firstborn, my eldest. She was knocked unconscious and was bleedin' bad. I couldn't stop the blood.

I say I'm sorry.

She says we don't have long here. I'm trapped and this island is gonna be underwater soon.

She says you have to take the baby.

I look good with my light. The woman's lookin' out from a lattice of twisted boards and rafters and tin. It looks like a cage only God or the devil could build.

I say well, maybe I can get you out.

She says don't waste the time. I managed to claw open this hole I'm talkin' through. I think the baby will just fit, if you can get up here to take her.

I look hard again. It's an awful tight space. I might manage if I go in on my belly.

I say okay, I'm comin'.

I stoop lower and wriggle forward through that window frame. Boards above gouge into my back and I groan.

I wriggle some more and get close enough so that when I reach out my right arm far as it can go, it's about a foot from the woman's face.

She's a pretty woman, pale and freckled, with sad green eyes.

I try to move forward more but I'm stuck. For a second I wonder if I'll be able to wriggle out again. I'm about a nickel away from panickin'. I don't like tight spaces—that was one of the problems with jail.

She says just a little more, mister. Just another six inches.

I tuck my light into the waistband of my britches and I close my eyes and grab ahead at the jumbled lumber and pull hard.

When I open my eyes and retrieve my light, I'm starin' at her face-to-face.

She says okay, hold on.

Her face disappears down into some void, and for the first time I realize she does have a dim light of some kind goin' in there. Shadows flicker. And then the baby appears in the small round openin' where the woman's face was.

At first, I don't see her mother's hands under her belly. She just seems to be floatin' in space.

She's a beautiful baby, pale as her momma, with big, soft, gray eyes starin' straight ahead. She seems to be lookin' right through me.

The woman says okay, sweetie, it's time to say goodbye to Momma.

The baby's eyes blink but I don't hear a peep.

The woman says my husband keeps whiskey in a kitchen cabinet. I gave her some so she wouldn't fight us. I hope I didn't give her too much. Now I'm gonna hand her out headfirst just like she is now. If you can get a hand under her belly, I think we can do this.

I say I'll try. It's awful tight in here.

She says okay, here she comes.

I realize I'll have to do this blind as I won't be able to hold the baby and the light at the same time. I tuck my light back into my pants. I reach forward and feel her tiny head. It's warm.

I manage a hand under her chest, and then her belly.

Her momma passes her out slow, like a baby bein' born.

She's a bitty, warm, soft thing.

I shift best as I can and get two hands under her. I say okay, I've got her pretty good. Now, I'm gonna try to back out.

The woman don't speak. I cain't see her anymore. The baby's blockin' the way.

Time stops. My heart pounds in my chest. At some point, I realize a nail in the tight space above me has hooked my belt. I find myself whisperin' to the baby, now you hold on, sweetheart. You hold on.

I free one of my hands and manage to reach back and unhook myself.

I worm out backwards to a spot where I can stoop again.

I cradle the baby up in one arm and retrieve my light. I look at her.

She blinks her far-off eyes and smiles.

I shine my light back down toward her momma. Her face has filled the hole again.

I say we're gonna make it.

She says thank God. Now go, quick. Before it's too late.

I say I'm sorry, ma'am. I'll try to get back here as soon as possible— maybe tomorrow—

She says don't be sorry, mister. Just take care of my baby and tell my boys and Bonnie how much I love them.

I say okay. I'll do my best.

I realize how spongy my legs are. I back on out slow and stand up and the storm wraps itself around us.

I point my light in the direction of the way I came and stumble forward.

It ain't long before I'm sloshin' in water again. Soon it's knee-high. I'm tryin' to figger where the top of the dune might be. I spy what I think is a rise in the treeline and head that way.

I come out of the woods onto a clearin' and think I see a way forward. I stumble on, half-runnin' on my dead legs, and I keep sayin' hold on, sweetheart, hold on.

But I don't get a hunderd yards when I hear a roar again and more thunder and I look in the direction of the sound and somethin' glints white above me.

Another wave. I'm knocked backwards and I clutch that baby like a man clutches a football and I hold on as hard as I can. I'm on my back, kickin' hard and I lift the baby up above me. I start to sink and I kick harder and harder, tryin' to stay afloat. And when it feels like I cain't kick anymore, my toe catches bottom. I manage to stand with my neck just out of water, the baby lifted above me.

I'm so tired.

I need to catch my breath.

Then I realize the water is risin' again and I say okay, LaBauve, just be calm. I ease onto my back, the baby cradled on my chest, and I kick just hard enough to keep us afloat.

Time slows way down again. I realize we're driftin' along like a leaf in a fast river and we would be fine, perfect, really, if my doggone boots weren't so heavy and draggin' me down. All I can think to do is to try to kick now and then when I feel us sink too low and clamp my hands over the baby's mouth and hope she don't swallow water.

I can only think well, okay, Logan LaBauve. You've wrestled up gators from the deep and tussled with the law and you've fought hard, but this is it, right here—this is the sumbitch that finally gets you.

And then I think how my boy would get a kick out of me sayin' sumbitch 'cause he knows I don't cuss.

I don't think it's right that I have to die on Meely again.

Then we bump hard against somethin' and I feel the current shift quick and we're bein' shoved into a boil of water. Pointy waves rise up all around, I can see 'em even in the black.

I lift that baby up high as I can with my right hand just as my head is sucked underwater and I flail with my left one. My left hand strikes somethin' hard, somethin' that rolls slow toward me, and I realize it's a log. I feel for it blind and I get a purchase on it and I use what's left of my strength to pull myself up.

I'm coughin' up gobs of water, tryin' to keep the baby balanced in my right hand. I look around and see big, dark things floatin' along with us—

more logs, a half-sunk cistern, the roof of a house, somethin' that looks like it might be the roof of a car. We're all bobbin' along on a current, the kind I've seen suck barges down the Catahoula Bayou durin' floods.

I cain't understand how I'm suddenly seein' these things so clear when I look up.

Stars are shinin' and a big wildcat-yellow moon is takin' up about half of the sky.

I know the good news is that the eye of the storm has come right over the top of us and for a while we'll just bob along in the calm. Then that wind will come shriekin' from the other direction, tearin' up this land and the water again.

I wonder if the eye will last long enough to save us.

I improve my purchase on our log and bring the baby around and cradle her with both hands and nudge her up, usin' my elbows, so that her head's restin' higher above the water than I could hold her before. Then I feel a bump behind me and see an even bigger log, maybe even a whole tree, has floated over to us. It looks wide and steady—broad enough for a man and a baby to crawl out on.

I take one hand off the baby and roll slightly and fling an arm over a branch. When I got it solid, I bring the baby around slow and then manage to push her, gentle as I can, onto the oak's broad beam. I see a place where there's a shallow scoop in the tree trunk. I manage to nudge her into there.

I let her go and when I grab that branch harder to try to get myself up, I lose my grip and fall back with a splash. I'm sucked down by the current and I thrash and there's a roar in my head sayin' no, no, no, I've promised!

With the tiny spark that's left I kick hard as I've ever kicked and I feel myself start to rise.

I break the surface with the tree ten yards ahead of me.

The baby's on it, pale in the moonlight. She's not movin', but she's there.

I kick over to the tree and realize that if I pull myself up the back side it'll be steadier that way. There's sharp roots pokin' up, but I squirm between 'em and inch my way up like a worm.

I make it to the baby and curl up beside her.

Her eyes are closed and I cain't be sure whether she's even alive. I touch her and she seems warm, but maybe that's just the gulf water. But I've got her and I won't let go.

I say to that moon, whatcha think, podnah? We gonna make it?

And the moon whispers somethin' quiet and I say you know, I didn't quite catch that.

That's mostly all I remember till I feel somethin' warm on my face and a hand on my shoulder and I realize I'm lyin' faceup on a muddy bank someplace, starin' at a stranger framed by the sun and a deep-blue sky.

And I startle up and say the baby, where's the baby?

And he grabs on to me and looks me in the eye and says its okay, mister, it's okay. We've got her.

And she's alive.

34.

I'm standin' on a sugar-sand beach that looks like it goes on for-ever. It's as pretty a day as a man could want, a day that feels like fall in Loosiana, warm but not too warm, the sky a certain shade of blue peculiar to fall, and not a breath of wind. The ocean is flat and clear and lit up like a green diamond all the way to the horizon.

A big flock of pelicans come by a minute ago, flyin' so close I could hear the swoosh of their wings. One took breakfast not twenty feet away from me and made me glad I'm not a minnow. The way he smacked that water was somethin' to see.

The birds down here in Florda don't seem to be as scared of folks as the birds in Loosiana are. But maybe that's 'cause folks down here ain't shootin' at 'em all the time.

I've come to be an early riser and I walk this stretch of beach pretty much every day just after the sun comes up and I never can quite get over how white the sand is and how green the water is and how, on calm days like this one when the sun pops up in a cloudless sky, the ocean turns colors a man cain't easily describe. I've seen porpoises and turtles and bright-red starfish, and one day a ray so big across that I'd never dreamed such things existed. He come clear out the water, flyin' like a bird, and made a splash that woulda sunk a small boat. Scared the heck outta me.

Arthur Johns, the fella I work for who runs the gator farm, said it was a manta ray. It beat anything I'd ever seen. Even a white alligator.

Well, that's not countin' things I seen in Hurricane Belva.

The weather's been fair pretty much since Belva blew through this country and it's s'posed to stay that way for a bit longer. At least that's what the man on my transistor radio said this mornin'. That's good, 'cause Annie Ancelet's drivin' up today from Loosiana in her brand-new pickup truck she got to replace the station wagon that Belva took.

Not a trace of that wagon was ever found.

My boy Meely's with her and we're all gonna spend Christmas together. We've got two rooms in a pretty nice motel down the beach from here, as the room I board in over at Mr. Johns's place ain't big enough for all of us.

It ain't clear to me yet whether Annie and me are stayin' together or whether Meely and me are stayin' together. Annie was good enough, after she got back up to Loosiana, to look in on Meely and let him know I'd made it safe and sound, since he woulda heard about that hurricane and been plenty worried.

He wouldn'ta been wrong to worry, either.

Belva and her tornadoes killed 227 people, includin' William and Sara Jane Oakley and their daughter Barbara and poor Mr. Pike and poor Mrs. Pike, too. That fisherman fella that stayed—the one me and Annie saw tyin' down his boat—got drowned as well. Most of the rest were killed at a place about fifteen miles south of Articola, where they'd all gotten together in some kind of apartment complex near the beach to have a hurricane party. They thought they were well below the mean part of the storm. They thought a big fancy brick apartment complex could stand up to any hurricane. But that second wave just knocked the buildin' down. Or so the newspapers said.

It's hard to think of a sadder thing than that.

I write Meely once a week and he writes me about the same and we've talked on the phone once since I've been here. We decided we couldn't do this unless we squared it with his teacher, Miz Lirette. She wrote to me sayin' she understood and she was happy to have Meely. But she hoped one day, for everybody's sake, I could come back home.

I'm not shore how much Meely knows about Annie and me. I haven't said a lot.

Of course, I'm not shore myself how much *I* know about Annie and me, 'cept that I think about her every mornin' when I wake up and every night before I go to sleep and I think about her a fair number of times in between, too.

She calls me every Saturday mornin' on the pay phone down the road from the gator farm, as I don't have a phone of my own. I've got better at talkin' on the phone. In fact, I'm always surprised how much I have to say to her.

I offer to send her a money order to pay for half the phone bill but she won't let me. I send Miz Lirette money for Meely and she takes it and puts it in a bank for his college.

I like my job and Mr. Johns seems happy to have me. He got a lot of wind at his place from Belva, though this part of the coast was far enough away so that it got spared the water. But that wind knocked over some of his gator pens and blew a tin roof off a toolshed. It also blew open a cage where he kept a poisonous snake of a kind I'd never heard of called a bushmaster and it got out. We rounded up most of the gators and I've helped him rebuild the pens and that roof but that snake's still gone, though we've set traps with rats hopin' he'll show up.

Mr. Johns says a bushmaster once chased down a man who was on horseback and bit both man and horse. They both died.

I know snakes and I ain't generally afraid of 'em. But I'm keepin' a sharp eye out for that bad boy.

After the storm, the Red Cross put us up in a motel about forty miles south of Articola Island that turned out to be not all that far from Mr. Johns's gator place. We stayed in bed for the first three or four days and just held on to each other. I felt like a beat snake, and some cuts and scrapes I got became infected, prob'ly from layin' in that marsh like I did. Them Red Cross people brought over a doctor who give me salve and some pills to take. I run a fever for a few days and Annie got all worried, but I knew, after what we'd gone through, a few scrapes and some fever wadn't gonna kill me.

When I got better, Annie gimme that proper bath she'd promised durin' the storm. In fack, we gave each other a proper bath about every mornin' and it's a thing a man could get used to, that's for shore.

Annie stayed on another week after I got better, then got herself back down to Loosiana 'cause she had lots of things to take care of down there, too. She missed them dogs somethin' terrible, and she had to badger the insurance company some before she got paid for the Ford wagon Belva stole.

To say that I miss her don't say much about the way I feel.

Before she left, we went to church services for the Oakleys and the Pikes, which they had outside atop the dune where the Hankses' house used to be. There wadn't a man-made thing standin' on the island after Belva got through with it, though she did leave a three-hundred-foot gasoline tanker sittin' about halfway up that road where that tornado bushwhacked us. It's a hard thing to believe, even when you've seen it as I have. Belva washed out one of the bridges and big chunks of the beach highway and took about half the dune, too. Even the slab to the Hanks house was pitched, all broke up, into the bay.

It come out in the papers that the first of them tidal waves was about twenty-five foot high and flipped that tanker over like a bathtub toy and the second one was even higher and just sucked it up and carried it for about four miles inland across the island, leavin' it rightside up. Go figger. The hurricane people just decided to leave it there and build the road around it 'cause nobody can figger out how to move it without cuttin' it apart.

Folks have already started callin' it Belva's Boat.

I don't know how we survived. It does make a man wonder about God or somethin' bigger than himself.

All I know is that I often cussed God when Elizabeth and our baby died, but I won't cuss Him no more. I'm done with that.

Billy, bless him, got back in the nick of time and helped get his brother and sister into that boat. They got tugged along by the roiled waters of the first wave and somehow had got shoved pretty far out into the bay when the second wave come.

Mrs. Pike didn't make the boat.

When that first wave hit, it blew in the front door and some of the windows, and before anybody knew it, there was two, maybe three foot of water in the house, though Annie said the water drained out about as fast as it come in. She saw Mrs. Pike standin' in the hall as she ran past to tend those kids, who were screamin' and terrified. She said Mrs. Pike didn't seem ruffled at all.

Then Annie heard a racket, like wind knockin' open a door, and came back out to see. Mrs. Pike was nowhere to be found and Annie knew she'd gone.

She ran out to try to find her but she'd just evaporated, like she'd been sucked up by the wind. Maybe she had.

Them Oakley kids were hollerin' and Annie knew that she had to make that boat fast. It was all she could do.

It was only when she come back in that she saw a note on the kitchen table, anchored down by a bowl of oranges. It said Mrs. Pike had gone to find Harold as there was no reason to leave the island without him.

Annie still has that note, though it got soggy out on that boat and about half the words cain't be read anymore.

They found the Pikes, about a mile apart. It's hard to know how far she got on her own but she was goin' in the right direction.

A Coast Guard man who come by later to talk to us at the Red Cross motel said he figgered it was only 'cause we were on the lee side of that dune, the part that didn't get washed away, that saved us. He said the dune musta broke the power of both them waves, though we still were doggone lucky, no matter how you look at it.

Annie said the eye come upon them about the time the second wave hit—about the time me and the baby got knocked off the dune. She said she heard the wave before she saw it. She looked up and there was this smooth wall of water steamin' up behind them in the moonlight. Even though the Coast Guard man said the dune had broke that wave's back, it was still prob'ly ten foot high when it hit them. She told them kids to hang on and they rode it up and down like a roller coaster, though Annie thought for a second, on the back side, that they were gonna pitch over, it was so steep.

They washed ashore, about two miles from where I landed, and got found at first light.

After I got the baby and me up on that oak, I don't know what happened, really. I do recall, just before I blacked out, singin' to her. It was a song—a *fais dodo*—that my wife Elizabeth used to sing to Meely when he was little. At least I think I sung. I think I sung and I sung and the last I knew, the moon went dark and the wind and rain come back and the rain itself seemed like it was gonna wash us away.

But at some point, we pitched up on the far bank of that bay in a marsh near the highway and that's where the rescue people found us in the mornin'.

They said they had to pry that baby outta my hands even though I seemed to be unconscious.

They wanted to take me to the hospital but I wouldn't go. I wanted to look for Annie and them kids and Mrs. Pike. I was frantic. The rescue men told me they'd just took a woman and some kids to the shelter, so I went with them.

And there they were.

I hadn't cried since Elizabeth and my baby died. But I cried then. Every one of us cried.

They took the baby off and she was in a bad way for a week. Turns out she'd sucked in some water and they worried she would get pneumonia. Me and Annie went to see her several times. Annie told me if the baby died, I must not *ever* blame myself.

But you know what? I knew the baby wadn't gonna die. She fooled just about everybody and got better.

Them Oakley orphans all went off to live with an aunt in a town called Tallahassee.

There was one more orphan—Buster, the Pikes' dog.

Annie got Buster in the boat, too, and he turned out to be a tough li'l dog and is about the best-natured mutt you'll ever wanna meet, even though he ain't afraid of nuttin' that walks or crawls or swims. Me and Annie talked it over about Buster and we couldn't stand to just give him to the pound. So I finally decided I'd keep him, since Mr. Johns didn't mind.

He goes with me in the pens when I feed the gators and he'll go right up and grab them gators by the tail and pull on 'em and growl away. A few have tried to bite him and, lemme tell ya, gators are quick. But ole Buster is faster than an oiled snake and makes a fool of them gators every time.

Mr. Johns thinks this is so funny that he's started includin' Buster in his tourist shows that he has on Saturdays. He's even made a sign that says Buster, the Gator Wrasslin' Dog.

I cain't wait for Meely to see this. I'm kinda tickled that my dog's a star.

Billy Oakley wrote me a letter, thankin' me for savin' his baby sister. He's a good strong kid—all them Oakley kids are—and I think he'll get past this, though I know such sorrows are awful hard to manage.

I wrote back and said I was just sorry I couldn't do more for his momma and daddy and sister Barbara.

He wrote back again and said Mr. LaBauve, you did all you could do.

And that's true—though I know I'll see that poor woman's face starin' out at me for the rest of my life.

Billy wrote one other thing in his letter that I didn't know. All them Oakley kids got B names—Billy, Bobby, Bonnie, and poor Barbara who didn't make it.

Turns out they call the baby Beth.

But her proper name is Elizabeth.

Glossary of Cajun Terms

andouille (ohn-doo-EE)—a spicy Cajun pork sausage.

bec croche (beck-CROSH)—an ibis.

boude'd (boo-DAID)—pouty; upset.

boudin (boo-DEHN)—a spicy sausage, often stuffed with pork, rice, and onions; one variety is called "blood sausage."

bourree (BOO-ray)—a card game, resembling spades, played for money.

Cajuns—the modern-day descendants of eighteenth-century French-speaking exiles who were expelled to Louisiana by the British during the French and Indian War; more broadly, South Louisiana residents of various ethnic backgrounds who have adopted Cajun speech, customs, and food as their own.

carencros (CARE-en-croh)—a buzzard.

chaque'd (chah-KADE)—drunk or high.

chenier (shin-YERE)—a small, low-lying, tree-covered island rising from the marsh.

cher—in French, "dear." The Cajuns pronounce this *shah* (short *a*, as in "at") and often use it in hybrid sentences such as, "Mais, cher, how you doin'?"

choupique (SHOO-pick)—also spelled *tchoupique;* alternately a mud fish, bowfin, or grunion. Also a cypress trout.

cochon de lait (co-SHOHN duh lay)—a suckling pig; also a social gathering centered on the roasting of a suckling pig.

cocodrie (CO-co-dree)—alligator.

coup nord (coo-NOR)—a norther; a brisk north wind.

cousins (coo-ZEHNS)—mosquitoes.

craque (crock-KAY)—mad; crazy.

envie (OHN-vee)—longing; craving.

frissons (free-ZOHNS)—chills; goose bumps.

Gar ici, compagnie!—Look here, company's come.

goggle-eye—a freshwater perch.

goujon (goo-ZHON)—a flathead catfish, so named by Cajuns for its mustardlike coloration.

gros-bec (GROW-beck)—a heron.

jambalaya (jam-buh-LY-uh)—A Cajun rice dish similar to paella, often made with shrimp and/or sausage.

"Jolie Blonde"—title of a traditional Cajun ballad.

Lâche pas la patate, neg—A Cajun idiom translating to "Courage, my friend. Don't give up."

loup garou (loo-gah-ROO)—alternatively, *roo-garou;* the Cajun equivalent of the werewolf.

mirliton (MERL-ee-tohn)—a squash, sometimes known as the alligator pear or the vegetable pear.

mudboat—a small, flat-bottomed boat, powered by an inboard engine, used by hunters and fishermen to navigate extremely shallow bayous and swamps; also called the putt-putt.

nootra-rat—properly, the nutria, a South American rodent. Introduced accidentally into the wetlands of South Louisiana in the 1950s, it chased the muskrat from much of its native habitat and is now considered a nuisance.

ouaouaron (WOHN-wah-rohn)—a bullfrog.

pirogue (PEE-roh; alternatively, PEE-rog)—the Cajun equivalent of a canoe; in the old days it was typically hand-made of planked cypress.

pissenlit (pee-soh-LEE)—a wild daisy or a dandelion. Hyphenated (*pisse-en-lit*), the term describes a layer of flowers stuffed between the sheet and mattress in a child's bed to protect the mattress from bed-wetting.

podnah—partner; a Cajunism for a pal or buddy.

pop rouge—strawberry soda.

poule d'eau (POOL-doo)—a coot; literally, a water chicken.

putains (poo-TEHNZ)—prostitutes.

roseaus (ROW-zows)—a thickly clustered, canelike reed found along bayou banks.

sac-à-lait (SOCK-oh-lay)—a panfish, specifically a crappie.

sauce piquante (sauce pee-KOHNT)—a spicy Cajun tomato stew, usually made with rabbit, chicken, or turtle.

toujours fâché—always angry.

trainasse (trehn-OSS)—a boat trail through the marsh, usually man-made.

Viens donc manger—Come eat.

The author acknowledges as the primary source for these definitions *A Dictionary of the Cajun Language* by the late Reverend Jules O. Daigle, published by Edwards Brothers, Ann Arbor, Michigan, in 1984.

A Guide to Pronunciation of Cajun Names

Ancelet (OHNZ-uh-lay)

Benoit (BEN-wah)

Boudreaux (BOO-drow)

Brien (BREE-ehn)

Cenac (sin-ACK)

Daigle (deg: alternatively, DAY-gull)

Daigrepont (DEG-ruh-pohn)

Fontenot (FON-tuh-noh)

Galjour (GAL-zhoor)

Guidry (GID-dree)

Guidroz (GEE-drose)

Hebert (A-bear)

LaBauve (le-BOVE)

Lirette (LEE-rette)

Prosperie (PROS-puh-ree)

Samanie (SAH-mah-nee)

Schexnayder (SHECKS-ny-der)

Toups (toops)

Tregle (treg: alternatively, TRAY-gull)

Trosclair (TROH-sclair)

Voisin (WAH-zehn)

KEN WELLS grew up on the banks of Bayou Black, deep in South Louisiana's Cajun belt. He got his first newspaper job as a nineteen-year-old college dropout covering car wrecks and gator sightings for the Houma, Louisiana, weekly newspaper while still finding time to help out in his family's snake-collecting business. A career journalist, he was a finalist for the Pulitzer Prize in 1982 and is now on leave from his job as an editor of Page One of *The Wall Street Journal* to research and write a book about beer culture in America. He is also the editor of *Floating Off the Page,* an anthology of Page One "Middle Column" stories. Ken lives with his family on the outskirts of Manhattan and often wishes he were fishing.

Visit Ken Wells and Cajun Country at www .bayoubro.com.

ABOUT THE TYPE

This book was set in Garamond, a typeface designed by the French printer Jean Jannon. It is styled after Garamond's original models. The face is dignified, and is light but without fragile lines. The italic is modeled after a font of Granjon, which was probably cut in the middle of the sixteenth century.